Miss Martha Mary Crawford

Miss Martha Mary Crawford

CATHERINE MARCHANT

WILLIAM MORROW AND COMPANY, INC.
NEW YORK

J

Contents

PART ONE

1879 *The Habitation*

1

'Martha Mary! Martha Mary! it's beginning to snow again.' The young girl racing down the broad, shallow oak stairs almost overturned her sister who was crossing the hall, her arms full of freshly ironed linen, and Martha, steadying herself, cried harshly, 'If I had dropped Papa's shirts I would have shaken you, Nancy. I know it is snowing again; it has been for the past hour. Where've you been?'

After throwing her loose fair hair back from her shoulders, Nancy bowed her head slightly as she said, 'In the attics with Mildred; she was hoping to find a dress she could turn.'

Martha, about to walk away, stopped again and said slowly and quietly, 'Both you and Mildred know that there is only one trunk of Mama's clothing left up there and Papa will not allow those dresses to be cut up for whatever good reason you might propose. We have been through all this before, Nancy.'

'Oh—' Nancy now shrugged her shoulders—'it doesn't matter to me, I don't care what I wear, but it's Mildred. She says she'll soon be ashamed to go out, we're all like rag-bags.'

Again Martha paused from turning away and her voice, lower now, had a sad note to it as she said, 'For the kind of people we meet when we go out it doesn't matter much what we look like.'

'She's . . . she's hoping for an invitation. . . .'

'An invitation! From whom? Where?'

'The Hall. The Brockdeans. They always give a dance at Christmas and . . .'

Martha's expression now changed, as did her voice. 'And whom do they give it for?' she asked flatly. 'Their staff, their servants. Does she want to be invited as one of them?'

'She . . . she wasn't meaning the staff ball, Martha Mary.'

They now stared at each other until Martha, easing one hand from the bottom of the pile of linen, placed it on the top and gently pushed back into position a white silk shirt and without lowering her eyes to it flicked an imaginary speck of dust from the collar; then she asked a quiet question of Nancy, 'Have we ever been invited to their January ball?'

Nancy made no reply to this, but she continued to stare at her elder sister and Martha said, 'So what makes Mildred think that this year will be any different from others?'

'Lady Brockdean spoke to her when they met in Hexham last week.'

'Lady Brockdean acknowledged us when passing through the Market Place in Hexham last week.'

Instead of accepting this as the last word on the matter, Nancy stepped close to Martha and whispered, 'It wasn't only then, Martha Mary. She didn't tell you, but they met in Bell's—Bell & Riddle, the chemists—they had a conversation. Lady Brockdean asked how Father was, and she said she was going to visit our shop because there was a book she wished to order, and when they parted she expressed a wish, well, I mean she made a sort of statement, Mildred said, that they would meet again.'

'Nancy!'

'Yes, Martha.'

'You and I know that Lady Brockdean is a kindly, well-intentioned woman, and we know that Miss Rosalind is a nice girl, and Master William a very nice young man, but we also know that Sir Rupert is a hard, implacable, domineering, arrogant individual.' Her voice rose as she ended, 'So why can't Mildred realize once and for all that no one is invited to the Hall except through Sir Rupert. . . . Oh, what am I wasting time for. And where's Mildred now?'

'In her room.'

'Well, go and get her this very minute, and then both of you take wood and coal up to Papa's room and keep the fire banked, and as soon as he enters the yard help Peg carry the hot water up.'

'Yes, Martha.' Nancy's tone was resigned, and she turned away and ran back up the stairs holding her long faded serge dress almost up to her knees so as not to impede her progress. But she hadn't reached the top before she stopped and, leaning over the banister, she called down, 'Will you ask Papa if I may ride Belle tomorrow, that is if the snow doesn't lie?'

Without turning round Martha called back, 'Yes; if the snow doesn't lie.'

'Oh, good. Thanks, Martha Mary.'

As Nancy's feet pounded away up the remainder of the stairs and across the landing, Martha left the stone-flagged hall, went down a short passage, turned her back to a black oak door and with a thrust of her buttocks pushed it open and entered the room which was known in the house as Papa's study.

The room was long and narrow. It had a marble-framed fireplace, and in the open grate a fire was burning brightly. Unlike the rest of the house it was comparatively free from falderals. Apart from the antimacassars on the two leather chairs and the long couch fronting the fire, the velvet mantel-border, and the deep be-tasselled pelmet bordering the faded blue velvet curtains at the long window, it had an austere appearance. It was definitely a man's room, as was indicated by the hunting prints on the wall, the two standing pipe racks on the mantelshelf, and the littered desk to the side of the window.

Martha put the laundered washing very gently on to the round mahogany table that stood behind the couch. After dividing it into two piles in order that it shouldn't tumble, she looked down at it for a moment before turning and going slowly towards the chair at the right-hand side of the fireplace.

Once seated, she lay back, closed her eyes, and let out a long drawn breath. She was tired, she was weary, and she was irritable. She admitted to feeling all three, but at the same time she told herself that she must overcome these feelings before her papa came in, for her papa couldn't stand a long face; as he was wont to say, he lived on smiles. Unfortunately, she was finding she was smiling less and less these days.

She looked back to the time when she saw herself as a happy, laughing girl, being often chastised for giggling; but that was before her mother died giving birth to her seventh and last child. The child, a boy who was christened Harold, lived only one month; and a year later their youngest sister Jeanette died at the age of six years. This was the second sister they had lost in five years.

She was fifteen when her mother died, and from that time she had taken over the management of the household. Was it only four and a half years ago? At times it seemed that she had always managed the house, always chastised the girls, always worried over Aunt Sophie, and for ever asked questions of herself, questions that she wanted to put to her papa but couldn't, even though last year when he sold the mill she had dared to ask why. But as usual he had treated her as a young girl who wouldn't understand anything that went on outside the running of the house. And that is what he had said. Holding her chin in his hand, he had looked into her eyes and said softly, 'If I were to tell you, you wouldn't understand, little mother.'

The term, little mother, didn't, she considered, apply to her in any way and she wasn't flattered by it, for she did not see herself looking plain and homely as a little mother should. Yet she had no bust or hips to speak of, at least not now. Since she was seventeen she seemed to have lost her shape, due, she thought, to two things: she had grown taller, and she was never off her feet from morning till night running here and there.

Apart from Peg Thornycroft, who rose at five-thirty, she was the earliest about in the household. Very often before Nick Bailey, their one and only handy lad. At one time she could remember Dilly Thompson rising at five, but now Dilly was nearing seventy and was worn out with work, a life-time of work in this very house, for, like little Peg Thornycroft, she had started in service here when she was eight years old. But Martha doubted very much if Peg would be here when she was nearing seventy. Peg now, at fourteen, was a quick-tongued, high-spirited little miss who would likely make for the town before she was much older. And when that hap-pened what would she do without her, for she was an excellent worker and what was more, she helped with Aunt Sophie. . . . Poor Aunt Sophie, what was to become of her?

'And what's to become of me?'

She said the words aloud and they brought her ramrod straight in the chair. This was the third time of late she had spoken to herself, and words along these very same lines. There was something wrong with her. Her sleep was disturbed, she was having dreams that weren't quite nice. What was the matter with her?

Of a sudden she slumped back in the chair and put her hand over her eyes. Why was she hoodwinking herself? She knew what was wrong with her. She would be twenty on New Year's Day. She wanted to be married, she was ready to be married. And she could be married. Yes, she could, but would her papa countenance an alliance between his daughter and the manager of his bookshop? She doubted it. Yet Mr Ducat was in every sense a gentleman; he spoke like a gentleman; he acted like a gentleman; his manners were perfect, and he was the most intelligent person she had ever met, so well read. She had said as much to her papa, but he had laughed at her. There were gentlemen and gentlemen, he said, and how would she define the difference? Of course she had to admit she had met very few men other than tradesmen, for they had not entertained at all since her mother died. And not very much before, if she remembered rightly, part of the reason being, she supposed, they found all the enter-tainment they required within the family. And then, of course, there was the situation in which The Habitation was placed.

She did not think of her home as Morland House but always as The Habitation. Her mother was born in this house and she had loved it, and it was she who had explained the reason why those in the cottages and shacks along the river bank always referred to the house as The Habita-tion. It was because, she said, their houses being single-storied and situated on still lower ground than the house were always flooded when the river rose, and so at such times they would make for the house, and in the up-stairs rooms and the attics they would be safe until the waters subsided. It was a sound habitation they used to say. What was more, although it was built in a hollow it had the protection of a built-up river bank.

And they still said it today, although there were few people now left in the cottages, or even the hamlets, for over the past years most had made for the towns where the work and money was to be had.

The Habitation was situated seven miles from Hexham and almost twenty from Newcastle; the nearest places to it being Riding Mill to the west and Prudhoe to the east. The house itself stood at the end of the hollow with a hill rising sharply at some distance behind it, and about a hundred yards from the river. The far side of the river was banked in most places by woodland, the trees coming almost down to the edge of the water, but apart from one or two copses, the land on this side of the river merged into meadows, almost up to the tollbridge two miles away.

There were six acres of ground attached to the house, mostly rough paddock land. Years ago two acres had been given over to an ornamental garden surrounding the house and almost an acre to the growing of vegetables and fruit. Now, less than a quarter of the latter was cultivated, and the picturesque gardens were overgrown and in many places were almost impregnable with blackthorn and bramble.

The house had been originally bought in 1776 by Jacob Low-Pearson, Martha's great-grandfather. It was then not anywhere near its present size, the thirty-foot-long stone-flagged hall being the main living-room, with a room at the back and a kitchen to the side and three bedrooms on the first floor, with small attics above. But over the years the house had been added to on both sides, and because of the river's unreliability these additions had been built on higher foundations, but without the addition of more attics. Yet the extensions made the original house appear as if it were sinking in the middle. To conform with the original structure the ceilings of the new parts had been kept low, giving to the whole interior the illusion of great length.

Year could follow year when, if the river flooded, the water would reach no further than the steps leading to the main front door; but there were also times when it would swirl up the steps and flood the hall. It was said that one time it had reached the upper floor and flooded the bedrooms, and there remained the water mark around the walls as evidence to show it. Martha had her doubts about the authenticity of the mark. It was, she thought, more likely that left by the removal of a chair rail during redecoration some years ago.

To her distress she found that as she got older she doubted more and more the tales she heard about the house and those who had occupied it, and at moments like now she hoped that she wasn't turning bitter, that age wasn't going to sour her or touch her mind as it had done Aunt Sophie's. Loneliness and despair and rejected love could do terrible things to one. Aunt Sophie was a living witness.

She raised her eyes now towards the ceiling. Up there in a room above this one her Aunt Sophie spent her life in phantasy. Yet not all of it, for there could be days which lengthened into weeks, sometimes as many as three, when she would be as rational as herself, and so sweet, and so understanding of all the problems of the house. But there were other times. Oh dear, dear, yes, there were other times when it wasn't 'the turns' that worried her so much as . . . the other business. . . .

It was known that Aunt Sophie had had turns dating from a day when her father had driven her from their farm near Allendale Town into Hexham. She was dressed in bridal white, and he had hired a coach for the occasion. And there at the church she waited, but in vain, for her groom. At first it was thought that his trap had broken down; his was a long journey for his farm was miles away across the river towards Bellingham. But he could have walked the distance in three hours, and that was the time she had insisted on waiting.

Martha had been told that Aunt Sophie hadn't fainted, like some young women would have under similar circumstances, but had walked steadily from the church. The only sign of her distress had been that she didn't speak. It was said they couldn't get a word out of her for two weeks; and then the first sound she made was of laughter, gay laughter, which reached such a crescendo that it exploded in a paroxysm of weeping, which then took the place of her silence, and went on intermittently for days.

Grandfather Crawford had driven through a storm to the farm all those miles away, only to learn that the groom had the previous night run off to sea. The old farmer said his youngest son, being but twenty, found at the end he couldn't face marrying a woman three years older than himself. It was kinder than saying he couldn't face life with a woman who was subject to . . . turns.

Someone on the Crawford farm, her mother had said, must have told the young man about Aunt Sophie's turns, even though in those early days the spasms were very light.

It never occurred to Martha to question why her mother, coming from a prosperous business family with some standing in Hexham, should have married into the Crawford family. Circumstances having made her her own mistress, she had been in a position to choose for herself; and Martha could not imagine anyone resisting her father's persuasive manner for long. Equally, she could not now imagine that he himself had come from ordinary farming stock, for he had the tastes of a gentleman. True it was that he took very little interest in literature or world affairs, but such was his disposition she could see how easily he would fit into any class of society. He was very adaptable and had a keen wit and natural charm. Yet there were times when she could wish that he was less charming and more. . . .

Again she was sitting bolt upright, but now on the edge of the chair. Here she was wasting her time thinking when she should be acting. There were two buttons needed on the cuff of his shirt; there were also some loose threads to be sewn into the edge of his cravat. What was more, she should be in the kitchen supervising the meal. She must watch Peg with those potatoes; the peelings that she had been taking off of late must have been almost a quarter of an inch thick. She didn't mind her taking home the pods of the peas when in season or the turnip tops and such-like, but they themselves had hardly enough potatoes left to see them through January.

But it was fifteen minutes later when she lifted the linen into her arms yet once again, went out of the room down the passage, across the hall and up the stairs.

It was as she reached the landing that she heard Nancy's laughter min-gled with that of Peg Thornycroft, and when she entered her father's room there they were kneeling on the mat in front of the fire, one on each side of the hip bath pushing a paper boat back and forth between them.

'Nancy!'

The name, if not the tone, brought them both to their feet, and Nancy continued to laugh, but Peg, her thin wiry form seeming lost in the ill-fitting print dress and coarse apron, scurried across the room with her head bent like a goat about to ram a wall. Yet her attitude suggested neither fear nor fright, but rather impish glee.

The room to themselves now, Martha looked at Nancy with a pained expression, and Nancy, tossing her head, said, 'Aw, Martha Mary . . . aw, it was just a bit of fun.'

Martha turned away, silent now, and, going to the big mahogany ward-robe, she opened the doors and arranged her father's linen on the shelves; all except one shirt, a cravat, a pair of long linings, and a vest. These she now took to the fireplace and hung carefully over a folding rack that was standing to the side of it. When she turned again, Nancy was no longer in the room.

A bit of fun. A bit of carry-on, as Peg would have put it. There was a time when she herself had been fourteen and Peg only eight and already being harshly instructed into the ropes of a maid of all work by Dilly, when she too had enjoyed having a bit of carry-on with her.

She had been boarded at Miss Threadgill's boarding school in Hexham since she was nine, coming home only at the week-end; and although she was being versed in the ways of a young lady and Miss Threadgill had laid great stress on the divisions of class, she had always treated little Peg

Thornycroft with kindness because she felt sorry for her being so small and having to scurry here and there all over the house, carrying heavy buckets of water, and of coal; but most of all she pitied her for having to put up with Mildred's tantrums. Mildred had indulged in tantrums since she was a small baby. Then besides Mildred, there was Roland.

Roland was a year younger than herself and was a tease. When as a young girl she used to think it was fortunate that Roland was at home only for the holidays, it wasn't of Peg alone she was thinking, but of them all, for Roland loved practical joking and they all suffered from his idea of fun. Besides, the house never seemed the same when her brother was home for he demanded attention, and got it, and he had the habit of strutting about like a lord of the manor.

She stood now looking around the room. Everything was in order. She had put an extra blanket on the four-poster bed; there were fresh candles in the candelabra at the head of it; her father's slippers were by his chair, his housegown was lying across the oak chest at the foot of the bed; the towels were rolled up and lying on the safe side of the high brass open-work fender that surrounded the hearth; there were only the curtains to be drawn, and this she would do when they had brought up the hot water.

She stooped now and picked the paper boat from the cold water in the bottom of the bath, and she put it on her hand and looked at it.

> Paper boat,
> Paper boat,
> Sail me away to paradise.
> Paper boat,
> Paper boat,
> I'll pay you one penny,
> I'll pay you twice
> For a night of delight
> In paradise.

This was one of the rhymes that Aunt Sophie would quote when she was about to start . . . the other business. It wasn't quite nice, it wasn't nice at all; in fact, the implications made one hot. Where Aunt Sophie got all the sayings and rhymes from, she just didn't know. She did sometimes read books it was true, but they were those she herself selected for her, books that would be unlikely to disturb her mental state or excite her in any way. It would seem that Aunt Sophie must have made up most of the rhymes and queer sayings in her head, and they were the result of her disturbed state.

She crushed the wet piece of paper in her hand and threw it into the fire; then after one last look around the room she went out, across the landing, down two steps, round the corner, and so to the room that was situated above her father's study.

Today the door was unlocked and she went straight in and looked towards the window where her Aunt Sophie sat. Sophie did not turn towards her, not even to move her head and glance to see who had entered the room, yet she spoke to her by name. She had this uncanny habit of recognizing people by their walk. 'It's snowing, Martha Mary,' she said.

'Yes, Aunt Sophie.' Martha went and stood close to her aunt and with a tender movement slid her arm around her shoulders, asking as she did so, 'Are you warm enough? There's a chill coming from the window.'

'Oh, I'm warm enough, Martha Mary. Oh yes, I'm warm enough; I'm all warm inside.' She now turned her face up to Martha's. All her features were in repose, and because her mouth was closed she had the look of a child; yet if she were to open it a huge gap would be revealed where all her top teeth were missing, and the movement of her upper lip would push her skin into myriads of small wrinkles, which made her appear like a woman of seventy instead of thirty-eight. Her hair, that had once been corn-coloured and thick, was now streaked with grey and hung in two plaits down her back. She was fully dressed. It could be said she was more than fully dressed for she was wearing at least three top skirts over four flannel petticoats, the upper skirt bulging so far out from her hips as to shorten its length and show the other two underneath, besides which she had on a striped shirt waist with an old-fashioned silk-befringed one covering it; above this a woollen shawl, and at the back of her head, stuck between the two plaits, was a large fan-shaped bone comb studded with brilliants.

'I've been thinking, Martha Mary.'

'What have you been thinking, Aunt Sophie?'

'Well—' she now nodded her head slowly up at her niece—'I've been thinking that your father should do something about you.'

'Father do something about me!'

'Yes, yes, that's what I've been thinking, he should do something about you. You haven't got a beau and you're nearly thirty.'

'No, no, I'm not.' Martha was laughing gently now. 'I'm still only nineteen, Aunt Sophie; I won't be twenty until January the first next year . . . 1880.'

'January the first, 1880.' Sophie nodded to herself now. 'Yes, yes, of course. I was a little out; I'm sorry. You'll be nineteen . . . no, twenty. There I go again. It worries me when I get things muddled.'

Martha now took hold of the thin hands and drew her up from the wooden window seat, saying, 'Come on over to the fire, you're cold.'

'Yes, yes, I am cold; I didn't think I was but I am. I'm sometimes very cold inside, Martha Mary. And sometimes I'm very sad inside. Then at other times—' she gave a small laugh now—'at other times I feel very happy, gay. I wish we could have a dance sometimes, I mean when I feel very happy, like we had in the barn. We used to have dances in the barn. Father used to say, "Come on, John, get out your fiddle, we'll have a dance." I'm always very happy when I think about dancing.'

Yes, Martha shook her head, Aunt Sophie was always very happy when she thought about dancing. And yet these were the times she herself most dreaded, when Aunt Sophie felt very happy.

'There now,' she said as she settled her before the fire, 'you'll feel warmer.' Then she added. 'We are expecting Father at any time.'

'Has he been away?'

'Yes, yes, of course.' Martha bent down until her face was on a level with Sophie's. 'Don't you remember? He went to Newcastle to visit Great-Uncle James.'

'Did he? Oh yes, yes. But I thought that was last month.'

'Yes, he did go last month, but he goes every month, sometimes twice a month.'

'You know that's a very odd thing, Martha Mary, but I thought Uncle James was dead.'

'Uncle James dead! No, no; he's very old, but he's not dead.' She only just stopped herself from adding, 'I wish he were,' for deep within her she had longed, for the last three years, for her father to come back from Newcastle and say that Great-Uncle James had finally sunk completely away. She could remember as far back as ten years ago her father going to Newcastle because Uncle James was sinking, but he had never completely sunk.

She had only seen her Great-Uncle James once. She was quite a small child and accompanied her parents in the trap on the never-ending journey to the city. It was a very warm day, she recalled, and she had swelted inside her many petticoats, white serge dress and coat and big straw hat.

Uncle James was in bed. He had no hair on his head but he had a beard and his cheeks were red and he must have looked far from sinking because she remembered him laughing and joking with her mother. He had been very fond of her mother for she was then his only living relative. But since her death he had transferred his affections to her father.

She did not feel wicked in hoping that Great-Uncle James would finally sink, never to rise again, for although she knew very little about the business side of her father's affairs she was well aware that they had deteriorated considerably since her mother died, and there was now a great need of money which the death of Great-Uncle James would in some way alleviate.

It was frightening to realize that their livelihood now depended solely on the little bookshop and the chandler's store in Hexham, because since the mill was sold the grinding of the corn had to be paid for elsewhere, and although she was no business woman she could deduce that this must surely reduce profits. . . . But where had the money gone from the sale of the mill?

Once again she closed a particular door in her mind, and she now lifted a strand of Sophie's hair and tucked it behind her ear, saying, 'There's potato soup for supper and roast lamb; you like roast lamb, don't you?'

'I like anything when I'm hungry, Martha Mary.'

It was such a reasonable answer, such a sane answer, as Sophie was wont to come out with at times, and at such times Martha would want to put her arms around her and hold her close and say, 'Oh Aunt Sophie, Aunt Sophie,' and in a strange way derive comfort from her own compassion. But when, in the past, she had demonstrated her affection in this way it had caused her Aunt Sophie to cry, not as she sometimes did with the water gushing out of her eyes and nostrils and bubbling into the gap in her teeth while her body heaved with her anguish, but gently, a soft flowing crying which was even more heart-rending to witness than the heavy emotional paroxysms.

It was strange, but of all the fifteen rooms in the house it was in this one alone that she felt most at peace with herself. In the presence of her Aunt Sophie she felt rested, she could for the moment throw off the pressures that were attacking both her body and mind increasingly of late. Of course, she was thinking now of those intervals between Aunt Sophie's turns, for there were the times when her door had to be locked and her arms tied to the sides of the bed to prevent her tearing her hair out.

'I must go now, Aunt Sophie.' She bent down again towards her. 'I don't know what they'll be up to in the kitchen if I leave them any longer.' She shook her head and pursed her lips, and like this she looked as she had done at fifteen before she'd had to don the cloak of responsibility and become a woman before her time: a young girl, impish, joyful, with a promise in her round brown eyes of beauty.

She was going out of the door when Sophie, turning from the fire, said, 'When can I come down to supper again, Martha Mary?'

Pausing with the door in her hand, Martha said, 'Oh, soon, quite soon; it's nearly Christmas.'

'Not till Christmas?'

'Well . . . well, perhaps one day next week when you are feeling better.'

'Yes, Martha Mary; all right, one day next week. Yes, one day next week.'

Martha closed the door and drew in a long breath. Something always happened when Aunt Sophie came down to a meal. She didn't know whether it was the excitement of seeing the family all together, but definitely something disastrous would occur, if not that same night, then surely the following day. And so her father had forbidden Aunt Sophie to be allowed downstairs at all.

Her father was not unkind to his sister; hadn't he brought her from the farm to save her being put away in one of those dreadful asylums?

She hurried down the stairs now, across the hall, where the draught from beneath the heavy oak front door whirled round her ankles, then down four stone steps and into the kitchen.

The kitchen being part of the old house, like the hall, was stone flagged. It was a long room and quite wide. Even so it appeared cluttered. On the wall opposite the door leading from the hall was inset a huge black-leaded iron fireplace. It had a spit above the open grate and a bread oven at each side. The hearth was bordered by a steel fender, in the slatted top of which were inserted a pair of huge steel tongs, three different sizes of steel pokers, and two long-handled steel shovels, and all were shining as steel can shine when it's scoured with emery paper every day. A stone mantelshelf ran the length of the fireplace and on this, turned upside down, were arrayed a number of copper pans graded from one that would hold three gallons of soup down to a small porringer. To one side of the fireplace and at right angles to it was a wooden settle; at the other side a rocking chair. Between the chair and the end wall, in which there was a door leading into the yard, there stood a shallow earthenware sink and to the side of that a pump, its spout set so high that the water from it, when it hit the sink, splattered in all directions. The pipe from the outlet of the sink dropped into a tin bath. Attached to the wall to the right of the sink was a long shelf on which the crockery was stacked for washing, and, under it, another shelf that held an assortment of heavy black iron pans, their bottoms and sides permanently sooted.

On the wall opposite the fireplace, just to the side of the door to the hall, was an enormous delf rack, its shelves packed with china and crockery of all sorts, and in the middle of the room were two tables, one used for cooking, the other for eating. Three wooden chairs were tucked under the eating table.

On the flags in front of the hearth was a seven-foot-long clippie mat, its original colours obliterated by the pressure of feet; and on each side of the cooking table was a rope mat, the strands wrought into intricate patterns but leaving holes large enough to let crumbs and other dirt fall through to the floor.

At one side of the cooking table Dilly Thompson stood making pastry. Martha paused for a moment behind her; then thrusting her hand under the table, she brought out a stool and, placing it behind the old woman, she said sharply, 'Get off your feet.'

'There's plenty of time to do that when I'm finished.' Dilly did not address Martha as miss, and her tone held no subservience, just the opposite; she might have been speaking to her own kin. Deep in her heart she thought of Martha as her kin; the granddaughter she might have had, as Martha's mother before her had been the daughter she might have had. Although she showed no deference to the young mistress of the house it didn't mean that she didn't give her her place, and also saw to it that others did too.

'Sit down.' When she was jerked backwards on to the stool she gasped and exclaimed, 'You'll do that once too often, me girl, and break me back.'

'Well, better that than have your leg burst.'

Martha now walked towards the sink to where, in front of the black-pan shelf, Peg Thornycroft was sitting on an upturned butter tub peeling potatoes. As Martha approached, Peg looked up at her and their eyes held for a moment before Martha, stooping down, picked up a thick potato peeling from the dirty water, looked at it, then said, 'Your grannie's pig will be fine and fat this year if it's left to you, won't it?'

'Eeh! Miss Martha Mary, you sayin' that.'

'Yes, I'm saying that. Now you peel those potatoes properly or come January you won't get any on your plate. You understand?'

There was a slight movement of Peg's head that could have indicated a toss; then, her chin drooping, she said flatly, 'Aye, Miss Martha Mary. Aye, I understand.'

'Good!'

'There's the master.' Peg's head jerked up and she pointed to the window, and Martha hurried forward and peered out. But the yard was empty and she turned her glance down on Peg again.

Peg grinned up at her now as she said, 'He's just come in the bottom gate.'

'She's got ears like cuddy's lugs, that one.' Dilly was nodding towards the young girl, and Peg, nodding at Martha, affirmed this, saying, 'Aye, I have. I can put me ear on the grass an' tell how many horses are on the road, an' which way they're comin'.'

'One of these days when you've got your lugs to the grass they'll gallop over you, me lass, you'll see. . . . Get up out of that'—Dilly now waved her floured hand towards Peg—'an' get that hot water runnin' uphill to the master's room or I'll skite the hunger off you with the back of me hand.'

Peg's reaction to this was to dash into the bucket room, a doorless space at the end of the kitchen, grab up two large copper hot water cans, rush to the stove, step up on to the steel fender, because her height wouldn't allow her to reach over and lift the huge black bubbling kettle from the hob, turn slowly round, the handle of the kettle gripped in her small fists, step carefully down on to the mat, tip the kettle forward and fill the cans.

'An' before you make a further move you fill that kettle and put it back on.'

Dilly hadn't turned from the table and Martha, glancing at Peg, could fully understand her reaction when she clamped her teeth tightly together, compressed her lips and wagged her chin towards the old woman's back, for she was being reminded for the countless time of something she was about to do from sheer habit, if nothing else.

Martha now went to the kitchen door and called into the hall, 'Mildred! Nancy!' She waited a moment. Then, her voice louder now and in tone not unlike Dilly's, for it was almost a bawl, she cried, 'Mildred! Nancy! Do you hear me?'

The drawing-room door opened and Nancy came out followed by Mildred who was cradling a cat in her arms, and as they approached her she could really have been Dilly's daughter as she went for them now, saying, 'And the next time I call you, you answer or you'll know the reason why. Father's coming. Now go and carry one of the cans between you. And don't slop it. And test the water in the bath. . . . And put that cat down, Mildred. How do you think you can work carrying a cat around? Go on.' She pushed them none too gently through the door, and when Mildred began to protest with, 'I don't see why . . .' she checked her immediately, saying, 'Then if you don't I'll have to tell you, won't I?'

Mildred stopped and the two sisters glared at each other. Then Mildred flounced into the kitchen and Martha, shaking her head, went towards the front door.

When she opened the door the snow drifted into her face, but through it she could make out the lights of the trap below and her father raising his whip in salute. Although the trap had passed on its way to the stables she waved back and she was smiling when she closed the door.

She was about to hurry across the hall to the study, because her father always went there for a few minutes before going to his room, when Mildred came bounding down the stairs. Her manner and voice pleading now and with no touch of defiance in it, she gazed into her face as she whispered, 'Ask Papa if I may have a new gown, will you, Martha Mary? . . . Please.'

Martha looked long at this sister with whom she always seemed at loggerheads before saying, 'Now Mildred, what use will a new gown be to you at present?' Her voice was soft and had a note of understanding in it, until Mildred gabbled, 'I told you, the ball. I know I'll be asked. Lady Brockdean, she almost invited me in the shop, and I want to be ready. . . .'

They were turning the corner towards the study as Martha said, 'Don't be silly, you imagined it.' Her tone was cutting and Mildred's reply had a desperate note to it as she said, 'I didn't, I didn't. She said, "I'll be seeing you soon." She smiled at me in a special way. If it hadn't been that her maid came up at that moment with packages she would have asked me then, I know it, I know it. I want a new gown. Do you hear? I want a new gown, Martha Mary. I must have a new gown.'

Martha marched ahead to the study door, and there, swinging about, she cried harshly, 'You're always wanting, wanting; you're always thinking about yourself; your wants would fill a paddock and come up weeds.' Oh, why was she always coming out with Dilly's sayings? Yet they nearly always fitted the occasion when she did use them, because Mildred was for ever wanting and was never satisfied.

Of the four trunks of clothes belonging to their mother which had been stored in the attic she had used the contents of three and re-made the dresses and underwear, and mostly for Mildred.

She herself had only three gowns. One had to be kept for her visits to the town and she had worn it so often that she felt she'd be recognized by it if by nothing else. One other she changed into for supper when her papa was at home; and of the one she was wearing now she had re-sewn the seams so many times it was a good job, she told herself, she hadn't grown plump or she'd be going about part naked. And here was Mildred pestering, not for the last of their mother's gowns to be re-made for her, but for a new one. She had as much hope of getting that out of their father as if she were asking for her own carriage and pair.

What she herself must fight for tonight was money to pay the coal bill. Three times it had been sent in during the past month and because it hadn't yet been paid the order for coal hadn't been met. Then there was the matter of the groceries. Mr Grey had sent a depleted order this week, saying that certain commodities hadn't yet arrived, such as the best tea. He had put in an inferior quality that was only four shillings a pound, and of the three pounds of butter ordered only two had been sent. And she could barely manage on three; the girls were extravagant with butter, as was her father; and when Roland was at home they could go through as much as five pounds a week. Dilly, Peg, and Nick, of course, had pig's fat or beef dripping, which was, she felt sure, equally as nourishing. She had tried to encourage the girls to eat beef dripping on their toast of a morning, but without success.

She had for a long time wished they could keep a cow. Her mother had said that in her day they kept two cows for household use. The old churn still remained in the corner of the pail room. It would be wonderful to have fresh butter. And eggs. She had often thought, even recently, that they could keep a few hens on the scraps from the table. But then, who'd look after them? Nick had his work cut out, at least he was always saying so. He considered he was vastly overworked in having to see to the vegetable garden, the yard, and the care of the two horses. That was another thing, the fodder for the horses was a great drain on the household resources. When they had the mill they did an exchange with Farmer Croft, which had been advantageous to both parties. She had never realized until these past two years the variation that is needed for a horse's diet; besides straw there was oats, which also had to be bruised for Gip because he was too old to masticate them whole, and if she didn't keep an eye on Nick now he would often omit this chore, and Gip's stomach would become extended like a barrel and he would be disinclined to pull the trap. Then there were bruised beans and barley dust and some potatoes. But whereas Gip's food might take time to prepare, as for Belle, she'd eat twice as much, and everything whole, especially if her father had ridden her to the hunt.

At the sound of sharp footsteps in the hall they turned their angry glances from each other and looked towards John Crawford as he came into view at the end of the passage. He was dashing the snowflakes off his high hat and with a gay gesture he now threw it towards them, and Mildred, on a laugh that belied her temper of a moment ago, caught it and cried as she ran towards him, 'Oh! Papa, you're covered. Look, you're covered with snow.'

'How's my lady?' He was unbuttoning his double-breasted knee-length coat, and he bent towards her and kissed her on the brow, and as she helped him off with his coat, she said gaily, 'Your lady is very well, sir, in fact in high fettle.' And at this they both laughed.

While Martha stood by the study door watching them there came the usual pounding on the stairs as Nancy raced down them, crying, 'Papa! Papa!' and when she came into view her father had his arms wide waiting for her, and when he swung her off her feet her skirt billowed and showed the frill on her blue flannel drawers.

They both stood laughing and panting as he looked in Martha's direction, saying, 'What a welcome. You'd think I'd been away for years instead of a few days. Now, now, away with you both.' He turned them about and pushed them low down on the back with the flat of his hands as if they were small children, saying, 'Shoo! Shoo!' and they ran away laughing.

His greeting of Martha was quite different. Looking into her face, he said quietly, 'Hello there, my dear,' and she answered as quietly, 'Hello, Papa,' then added, 'Are you very cold?'

'Frozen. I'm afraid it's going to lie.' He went swiftly past her now and towards the fire, and there, standing with his back to it, he bent forward so that the heat could waft his buttocks.

'Everything all right?' He now poked his long, handsome face towards her.

'As usual, Papa.'

'No trouble?'

She turned her gaze away from his before answering, 'A few difficulties, Papa, but . . . but we'll discuss them after you've had your meal.'

'Yes, yes.' His jocular tone had changed. He turned now and faced the fire, thrusting his hands out towards it.

'How is Uncle James?'

'What?' He jerked his head to the side and glanced at her. 'Oh, Uncle James. Oh, about the same.'

'His condition doesn't worsen?'

'Not perceptibly. No—' he nodded his head now towards the fire—'not perceptibly.'

'How old is Uncle James now, Papa?'

Again he turned his head towards her, but asked of himself, 'Ah, how old is he? Now, well, let me think. Ninety-two. Yes, ninety-two. And you know something?' He pursed his lips and his pointed chin knobbled itself into a semblance of flatness. 'I'm getting the idea he's determined to live to a hundred.'

When she made no reply to this, he faced her, saying somewhat stiffly, 'What is it?'

'Nothing, Papa.'

'Something's worrying you. Come, I know my little Martha Mary.' He thrust out his arm and drew her towards him and held her close to his side for a moment.

This endearing gesture usually had the power to captivate her, but somehow tonight it had lost some of its charm. She looked up into the face close to her own. Whenever she saw him like this she could understand why her mother had married him, she could understand why people liked him, and why the girls loved him, why she herself loved him. This being so, why of late had she been questioning so many things about him, why had she forced herself to lift the façade to glimpse the man she suspected lay behind it? Yet even so, she would not admit to herself that she had discovered a weak man, a vacillating man . . . and something more, but what that more was she couldn't as yet make out.

'What is it? Something's happened?'

'No, no, nothing's happened, nothing out of the ordinary, Papa.'

'Your Aunt Sophie?'

'Oh, she's been very good, very good indeed.'

He nodded now as he released his hold on her, then said, 'Well, if you have nothing to tell me, I'll away to my bath.'

As he moved towards the door she said quietly, 'May we talk after dinner, Papa?'

He did not turn towards her but opened the door while saying, 'We'll see.'

'*I must talk to you, Papa.*'

He was not more startled by her tone than she was herself. He looked back up the room towards her, then repeated slowly, '*You must talk to me?*'

She gulped in her throat and she joined her hands together tightly at her waist before she said very quietly, 'If we are to eat, and I'm to keep Peg and Nick on, and if we are to maintain the trap and the horses, then I must speak with you, Papa.'

His eyelids shadowed the expression in his eyes. She watched his mouth, his lips tight now, draw down at the corners. She saw a vein on his neck stand out above the high stiffly starched collar; it was just below his ear and it swelled up like a little ball.

She was trembling inside and knew a moment of fear as to what form his reaction would take, but when he swung round and went out banging the door after him, her relief was so great that she slumped with it and dropped into a chair.

In some strange way she felt she had won a battle, at least the first attack. But there had been no battle, no argument as yet. But her father's very attitude had been an admission of fault. He who had demanded and been paid the homage of a king in his household for so long had, in the last moments, been toppled from his throne; and the recognition of the fall was mutual.

But at supper time it was as if nothing untoward had happened. He was gay; he praised the potato soup, he said the lamb was done to a turn, and who could roast potatoes as good as Dilly, greasily crisp on the outside and like balls of flour on the inside; and then there was the cabbage, beautifully green—he made no reference to the taste of washing soda to which it owed its colour—and the turnips mashed with butter had melted in his mouth. Then the pudding, roasted apples hidden in great balls of crisp pastry, and what pastry.

It was a great meal. Mildred and Nancy plied him with questions about the journey, about the wonders of Newcastle, about Great-Uncle James, and about Christmas. He wouldn't be going to Great-Uncle James's at Christmas, would he?

Well, he didn't know. They might not understand, but it was a case of —how should he put it—policy. When he used this word he looked towards Martha, and his look said, 'You understand what I mean?' and she did, because policy connected with Great-Uncle James spelled money. Yet all through the meal she felt sad because his charm was not affecting her.

After the meal was over he enchanted Peg by helping to carry the dishes into the kitchen. And there he complimented Dilly once more on the meal; then looking down on Peg Thornycroft he shook his head in mock seriousness as he said, 'You know, Peg, they should put you in a travelling show, you'd make their fortune, for you're the only child I've ever seen who grows downwards.'

'Aw, master, master, what you say, what you say. But I'll sprout. You'll see, master, I'll sprout one of these days.' Peg was grinning from ear to ear. She was happy; the master was joking with her.

Now he bent his long length down to her and whispered in her ear, 'Try standing in your bare feet in the stables, that should do the trick, manure's marvellous for making things sprout.'

The laugh that erupted from Peg could have come from someone four times her size, so loud was it, and she clapped her hand over her mouth before crying, 'Eeh! master, master, the things you say. But I'll try anything, anything. . . . Eeh! master.'

Now they were all in the drawing-room, a room so cluttered with furniture and knick-knacks, which ranged from an ornate sideboard, two whatnots, a davenport and a seven-piece plush suite down to a number of small tables and hand-embroidered footstools, that there was hardly a yard of floor space that wasn't covered. The walls were adorned with oil paintings depicting various members of the Low-Pearson family, all looking as if they were peering through dark gauze towards the centre of the room where the candelabra were placed at each end of a sofa table to give light to the game of chess in progress.

John Crawford had played Mildred and lost to her gracefully, following which he had repeated his failure with Nancy. It was as she cried, 'Papa! Papa! you let me win, you didn't try, we must play again,' that Martha said firmly, 'No more tonight. Papa is tired. In any case it is time for bed. Look at the clock.' She pointed. 'Quarter to nine! Come along now.'

On the last command Nancy rose from her chair; but Mildred remained seated, and now as if she were claiming the support of her father she glanced at him, then looked up at Martha and repeated, 'Quarter to nine. Really! you would think we were still babies. If we lived in a town we'd . . .'

'We don't live in a town, and if you don't wish to go to bed, then go to your room.'

'I won't!' Mildred was now on her feet, and after glaring at Martha she turned to her father, crying, 'She's always taking this high hand with us. I'm eighteen years old, and no longer a child or a little girl. I won't be ordered about so.'

'Now, now, Milly.' John Crawford put his hand out and patted her shoulder. 'Of course, you're not a little girl, and Martha Mary had no intention of implying that you were.'

'Then tell her to leave me alone and stop acting as if she were my mother or—' she now poked her head towards Martha—'my grandmother.'

Martha lowered her head now and walked down the length of the room towards the dark window, and there she stood until she heard the door close and she knew that her father had marshalled the girls into the hall.

She did not turn but waited for him to speak, and when he did his voice no longer held the jocular tone that he had used to his two younger daughters, it was as if, like Mildred, he were accusing her of being high-handed, for he said, 'She's right; she's no longer a child. You must remember that when dealing with her.'

The injustice of it! She swung round and almost glared at him where he was standing folding up the chess board; and again she was amazed at the words coming from her mouth, for she said now, not loudly but quietly and bitterly, 'I shouldn't have to speak to her as I do, but I have no support, you are away so much.'

'Martha!' It was only on rare occasions that he did not give her her full name, but now she saw, his temper, like her own, had blazed. 'You forget yourself. If you weren't running the house what do you think you'd be doing? Serving in the bookshop or perhaps in some milliner's in Hexham. I've given you a free hand, and more liberty than is allotted to most young women. . . .'

But such were her feelings that she dared break in on him now, crying, 'Liberty for what? Yes, Papa, liberty for what? I work like any servant; in fact, I'm an unpaid maid of all work. Even Peg gets her shilling a week. As for myself, I have never had a penny of my own that I can remember, or a new rag to my back for years. . . .' What was this? What was she saying? What was the matter with her? She must be quiet. She had never intended to say this. Oh, dear Lord. Oh, dear Lord. But she couldn't stop, and now she was saying what had to be said. 'A month ago you promised to clear up the grocery bill, also the three outstanding bills due to Mr White for coal; if he doesn't deliver soon we won't have enough to last us over Christmas. Altogether I'm ashamed to show my face in Hexham. Do you know I heard an assistant whisper to another last week in Robinson's? "I wouldn't rush," she said, "she's one of the Crawfords from The Habitation." I actually heard her say that.'

'You imagine things, girl.'

'I do not imagine things, Papa, I have excellent hearing. Like Peg, I too can put my ear to the ground; but there is no need to stoop so far to hear what is being said about us in the town, and I think it's only my due that I should know why there's no money to meet our debts. When Mother was alive there was money, we lived differently. Why did you sell the mill? You have never said. But even so, discounting the loss of the mill, there is the profit from the chandler's shop and the bookshop. Surely they are such that we can live decently, not from hand to mouth as we do. I've had to pinch and scrape so much of late that our meals, except when you're at home, are little better than those in the Hexham soup kitchens. . . . Oh, Papa. Papa.' She was running now towards him where he was bending over the table, one hand flat on it, the other pressed against the right-hand side of his stomach.

'Oh, Papa! What is it? I'm sorry. I'm sorry.'

He did not speak but made a sound like a groan, and she clung to his arm, saying, 'Please, please, what is it? Are you in pain?'

Slowly he straightened himself up. His face looked white and drawn and now his words cut her to the bone as he said, 'I'm sure it wouldn't concern you much if I was.'

'You're being unjust, Papa; I . . . I was only telling you . . . I was only speaking, bringing into the open things that should have been discussed a year ago, two years ago.'

He walked slowly from her and lowered himself into a chair by the fire, and now he brought her literally to her knees at his side when, leaning back, he put his hand to his head, closed his eyes, and said, 'You're right, you're right in everything you say. I haven't done my duty by you or any of you, but . . . but what you must remember is that the state of the market and things are not as they were a few years ago. Prices have risen; everything is dearer; there are Roland's fees to be set aside every quarter, and now his personal demands are double what they used to be for he's a young man and he must dress and act as other young men, and this requires money, and more if he's to go to Oxford next year.'

'I'm sorry, Papa, I'm sorry.'

'You have no need to be sorry, my dear.' He stretched out his hand and patted her cheek. 'You have done so much for me over the past years, so much, but at the present moment I'm in a tight financial corner. That is putting it mildly. But given a little time everything will be all right.'

'Have . . . have you no available money at all, Papa?'

'Hardly any. What I get from the shops I have to pay in wages and, of course, buy new stock, and whereas I have to wait for people to pay their bills, others won't wait apparently for me to pay mine.'

'Papa!'

'Yes, my dear.'

'Mother's jewellery. I . . . I know that you put it into the bank after she died, couldn't . . . I mean, I'm sure she would understand if you were to sell one or two pieces. There were the pearls and the diamond brooches and the rings, my grandmother's rings. I know that I was to have the diamond and sapphire on my twenty-first birthday, also the gold pendant with the ruby in the centre. Well, seeing that they are in a way mine, couldn't you take them out and sell them? It would help you over this bad patch and Mama would understand. I . . . I even think that this is what she has been telling me of late to say to you.'

Again his hand was pressed against his right side, and now he pushed her gently backwards until she fell on her heels and he rose from the chair, saying, 'No, no. Anyway, they would be of little help, they weren't of any great value.'

'But . . . but Mama said the ring, the ring alone was of great value.'

'Yes, sentimental value. Your mother was apt to lay too much stock on sentiment. Of course, there's nothing wrong in that.'

She watched him go towards the table and pick up a candelabrum, and it was evident that his hand was shaking because the three candles spluttered and one of them almost gutted itself.

She rose quickly to her feet and, running before him, opened the door, and as he passed her she said, 'I'm . . . I'm sorry, Papa. I'm very sorry I upset you.'

He stopped now and in the light of the glowing candles he looked at her, and it was a strange look. She couldn't put a name to it. Was there fear in it? Was there dislike in it? Was it created by pain, for he still had his hand held against his right side? But his voice was soft as he said, 'We all do things we're sorry for. Go to bed now; everything will be all right, don't worry. I shall go in tomorrow and see to as many bills as I can.'

'Thank you, Papa. Good-night.'

He had walked to the end of the passage before he answered softly, 'Good-night, Martha Mary.'

2

Martha got her coal. Mr White's cart rumbled into the yard a week before Christmas, and although the ton of coal barely covered the floor of the coal-house it was a most welcome sight. Then Mr Grey's van followed the next day with a stock of groceries that warmed Martha's heart. There were even one or two luxuries among them, things that she would never have dared order, such as a jar of preserved ginger and three one-pound boxes of jellied fruits, one for each of them. Moreover, there were currants and raisins and desiccated coconut, besides walnuts and almonds, and fresh fruit, two big bags of fresh fruit.

It was going to be a wonderful Christmas; Martha felt it in her bones. She even used that expression to Nancy, and they both laughed and hung on to each other.

Nancy was happy. Even having failed to gain permission to ride Belle because the roads were so slippery, she still appeared happy. She was happy because she saw that Martha Mary was happy, happier than she'd seen her for months past.

She loved Martha Mary, better, she told herself, than anyone else in the world. . . . Well, that wasn't quite true . . . but no matter. It was Christmas and Martha Mary had lost that worried look, and her face had softened and she looked pretty again. But then Martha Mary wasn't pretty. She herself was pretty, but Martha Mary was either plain or beautiful. . . . What an odd thing to discover! But it was true.

She pounded now up the stairs in such a way that it sounded as if she were wearing clogs, then ran across the landing and mounted the almost vertical steps that led to the attics; and there she put her head around the old nursery door, crying, 'Come on, Mildred! We're all going down to the bottom pasture. Nick is sawing up a tree; we're going to carry the logs.'

'Aw no! Look, I've only just started to embroider the front panel.' Mildred held up a length of stiff blue taffeta, and Nancy, scrambling towards her now, bent down and hissed, 'You've got all this week, and all Christmas week, and right into the middle of January to get it ready.' She did not add, 'That's if you get the opportunity to wear it,' but said firmly, 'Martha Mary had to do a lot of talking to persuade Papa to open that last trunk. And what's more, she spent hours and hours making the skirt and the bodice. All you have to do is a bit of fancy stitching on the panels.

Now it's as little as you can do to come and give a hand. Anyway, it'll be fun. And there's a frozen patch in the meadow where we can slide. It's over twenty feet, a long stretch. Aw, come on.' She held out her hand and Mildred, with a sigh, but no show of temper, laid the taffeta carefully aside; and she even laughed a quite gay young laugh as, forgetting to be dignified and proper for once, she scampered after Nancy down the attic stairs, across the landing, down the main staircase and into the hall.

There, still running, she went to an oak cupboard in a recess and pulled out two hooded cloaks, one of which she threw to Nancy. But as they donned them, Mildred exclaimed, with chilling practicality now, 'Carrying logs is heavy work; she should have waited until Roland came home.'

'Nonsense!' Nancy, hurrying towards the kitchen, called over her shoulder. 'He won't arrive till Christmas Eve, and after spending a week at his friend's grand house in Scarborough I cannot imagine him rushing to carry firewood. In any case I cannot imagine him carrying firewood at all. If I remember our lordly Roland, he's very disinclined to dirty his hands, he's much the same as . . .' Oh dear, she had almost said 'You'. She must be careful with her tongue, she mustn't say anything to spoil Mildred's good humour because Mildred could create an atmosphere that chilled you more than the frost did. Yes, she must be careful because nothing, nothing, must mar this wonderful Christmas.

As she dashed through the kitchen she slapped Dilly on the bottom, tickled Peg in the ribs, and amid loud exclamations from both ran into the yard with Mildred close behind her.

It was the sight of Mildred running like an ordinary human being that caused Peg to look at Dilly open-mouthed and exclaim, 'Eeh! did you see that? Wonders 'll never cease. What's got into her, I mean Miss Mildred? By! she'll be speakin' civil to people next.'

'That's enough, miss, that's enough of your old buck.'

Yet even as she chastised Peg, Dilly thought, she's right; something's got into her. It can't be that she's still laying stock on getting an invitation to the Hall; she wouldn't be so daft. The only day any of them'll get an invitation there will be to Sir Rupert's funeral, and then even that isn't very likely. Still—she pounded the dough in the big brown earthenware dish standing on the table—it was good to see them happy, especially Martha Mary. And she was glad too himself would be back the night, for that would mean he'd got his journey over for another couple of weeks or so. And she would pray God it would snow so hard that even ten dray horses couldn't pull that trap to Newcastle. Aye, she would.

On this last thought she took her fist and thumped it into the centre of the dough, and it was as if she were striking someone full in the face.

*　　*　　*

John Crawford always arranged his journeys, even his daily one from Hexham, so that he should arrive home before it was completely dark, for the by-roads were such that even in summer a horse, especially a tired one that had done the twenty miles from Newcastle, could stumble in a pothole and both it and the driver end up in a ditch, and they'd be fortunate if they found it dry.

But it was now turned six o'clock and he hadn't put in an appearance. He was two hours overdue for there had been no daylight since four o'clock, and he had promised faithfully he would arrive in the afternoon; anyway, not later than four o'clock.

When Martha Mary and Nancy once again came into the kitchen Dilly did not say to them this time, 'Oh, stop your worritin'. Look, I've told you, it's a dry night, sharp clear an' frosty, the only snow about is that on top of the hills. The sky's full of stars.' Nor did she say, 'Old Gip knows every inch of that road blindfold.' But what she did say now was, 'I'd go out if I was you and catch Nick afore he's away off home and get him to take a lantern along the road.'

As Martha made for the door, Nancy said, 'I'll come with you,' but Martha, thrusting her hand back, answered, 'No. Look'—she turned to Nancy—'go up on and sit with Aunt Sophie, she's restless, she's been talking a lot this last hour or so.'

'She's not going to . . . ?'

'No, I don't think so; she's never even attempted to take her comb out of her hair. She's just restless. It'll be all right. Go on.'

As Nancy turned away and Martha made for the door, Dilly bawled at her as if she were a mile away, 'Are you mad, goin' out there with nothing on! Here! put that around you if you don't want to be cut in two.' On this, she snatched a large black shawl that was draped over the back of the rocking chair and with an expert flick of her hand she threw it across the table towards Martha. In its flight it spread out into the shape of a great black wing, and as Martha caught it Nancy exclaimed, almost in horror, 'Oh, that looked awful.'

'What looked awful?' asked Dilly.

'Don't be silly.' Martha pulled the shawl over her head. 'Go and see to Aunt Sophie. Go on, now.' On this she hurried from the kitchen and into the dark yard, where the frosty air caused her to gasp and cough.

The light from the kitchen window guided her to the stables. The main stable was empty and the half-door was shut on Belle's box. Before she reached the harness room she called, 'Nick! Nick!' but there was no answer. Nick's time was from six in the morning till six at night, but it was barely six now, and apparently he had gone. Usually she never blamed him for leaving before his time in the winter for if he couldn't cross the river by the stepping-stones he had a long walk home, but tonight she felt annoyed that he had taken advantage of her leniency.

She groped her way into the harness room and to the shelf where the lanterns and tallow candles were kept, and there, still groping, she found a box of matches. She struck one and lit a candle, and from that a lantern, and then she hurried out into the yard again, past the house, down the drive that turned at right angles and away from the river until it met the by-road. Here she paused for a moment holding the lantern high, and she looked to the right and then the left.

There was no sign of any living thing on the road and there was no sound of any kind. The night was still as if the frost had frozen the wind, for not a breeze stirred the branches of the trees or wafted through the stiff grass. The night was like the shawl as it had spread in a black canopy towards her back there in the kitchen. Yet, as Dilly had said, there were stars in the sky. And she looked up at them for a moment before scurrying along the road.

The by-road leading from the drive went straight for a good half mile before it curved towards the main road, but its entire surface was pitted with potholes large and small. There came to her mind the time when this part of the road had been maintained in good condition, that was when her mother was alive and there were three men in the yard. Something would have to be done about it; you could break your neck in the dark. Yet who walked in the dark? It was the first time she could recall ever being outside the gates in the dark. She should be feeling afraid but she wasn't, just apprehensive. If she'd had any fear in her, her concern for her father would have obliterated it.

Before she reached the main road there came to her the sound of a horse's hoofs, and she made a small laughing sound as she hurried forward to round the bend. Here, lifting the lantern high, she saw in the distance coming towards her a shape that could be no other than Gip going his own gait. She again hurried forward, but stopped herself from running in case she should fall on her face, and she called out in relief, 'Papa! Papa!'

When Gip came into clear view in the light of the lantern she stopped dead on the side of the road, for, looking beyond the horse, she saw no driver sitting upright in the seat of the trap. She gave an audible gasp before running towards the slowly plodding animal. Gripping its bridle, she shouted, 'Whoa! Whoa there!', then hoisting herself onto the step of the trap, she looked down in horror at the huddled figure slumped on the floor between the side seats. Just for a moment she paused. Was he drunk? No, no; her father never drank to excess; he hated the thought of developing a paunch.

'Papa! Papa!' The lantern now resting on the seat, she was kneeling beside him in the cramped space and crying all the while, 'Papa! Papa!' After she had managed to pull him up by the shoulders he raised his lids, and she heaved a great sigh as she cried, 'What is it? What is it, Papa? Are you ill?'

When he made one small movement with his head she laid him gently back; then, thrusting herself upwards, she yelled, 'Gee up! Gee up, Gip! Gee up!' and reaching out, she wildly jerked the reins which were tied to the rail that acted as a back support for the driver.

When the horse was moving again she pulled off Dilly's black shawl and tucked it round the crouched figure. She didn't ask any more questions but kept her hands on her father until Gip turned into the drive, and when he reached the front of the house she called him to a halt, then shouted at the top of her voice, 'Dilly! Dilly! Nancy! help. Come and help, Papa's ill.'

It seemed that all the doors in the house opened at once. The first to reach them was little Peg Thornycroft. Then came Dilly; then Nancy.

As they half-dragged, half-carried the crumpled figure up the steps and through the front door, Mildred came to their aid. Across the hall they went, then up the stairs, the five of them, all with their hands on some part of the bent figure.

When finally they reached his bedroom they laid him on the bed fully dressed, and then all of them without exception stood gasping and looking down at him in silence until Martha, seeming to come out of a trance, flung her arm wide as if scattering them as she cried, 'Get hot water! A hot drink. Bring some blankets, more blankets. Go and tell Nick to ride into Hexham for Doctor Pippin. Oh—' she put her hand to her head—'he's gone. . . .'

'Let's get his clothes off first.' It was Dilly's steadying voice now taking charge. 'But you must get the doctor. One of yous must go to Nick's place and tell him to ride; an' in a hurry, an' all.'

'We can't; it's across the river, Dilly.' Nancy was speaking in an awed whisper now from the foot of the bed, while she kept her eyes riveted on the contorted body of her father. 'We'd have to go up to the tollbridge and right down on the other side, it would be four or five miles. You can't use the stepping-stones, 'cos the river's too high. I'll . . . I'll go. I could be in Hexham by the time I reached Nick's place.'

Martha now turned from the bed and looked at Nancy, and quietly she said, 'Yes, yes, you go, Nancy. But Gip's past it, he'd never make it. Put Belle in the shafts.'

'I could ride her.'

'No, no; you mustn't. And you mustn't go alone. Take Mildred with you. Go on now, go on. Tell Doctor Pippin it's most serious.'

Mildred had not moved from where she was standing in the centre of the room and it seemed for a moment she was about to protest, but when Nancy grabbed her by the arm she went silently with her. . . .

Martha had never seen her father undressed, not even in his small clothes, but as she helped Dilly to pull his linings from him she realized with a shock that she was looking upon a man for the first time, and the sight was not pleasant to her eyes. But her personal thoughts were whipped away from her when her father made a sound that was something between a groan and a scream, a muffled scream. Bending over him now, she asked, 'What is it, Papa? Where is the pain?'

With an effort his hand moved slowly to his right side and touched the bare flesh of his stomach, but when Dilly placed her hand on his and pressed it inwards, saying, 'There?' he actually did scream, and Dilly, casting a quick glance towards Martha, said, 'Pendix, that's what it is, pendix.'

'Pendix?' Martha mouthed the word but didn't say it. Appendicitis. Her papa had appendicitis. She remembered now the night when she had dared to argue with him and he had put his hand to his side and groaned, and how later that night she had gone over the scene as she lay in bed and she had accused him in her mind of play-acting to gain her sympathy.

Peg now came rushing into the room, carrying an iron oven shelf wrapped in a piece of old blanket. Dilly took it from her and placed it at the foot of the bed, but when she attempted to draw the bent legs towards it John Crawford again let out an agonizing cry; and so now Martha moved the shelf up the bed and placed it under the white feet.

After two attempts to raise him and to put on his flannel nightshirt, Dilly said, 'Leave him be; we'll just hap him up.' And that's what they did. They piled blankets on him without making any further attempt to move him.

Martha now sat by the bedside, wiping the sweat from his brow, stroking his hair back, and holding his trembling hand. At one point she looked at Dilly who was standing gripping the bedpost, and said sharply, 'Do get off your feet Dilly; it's likely to be a long night.' Then she added, 'What will doctor do?'

'Open him up I suppose, then cut it out.'

She shuddered. It was at that moment that her father spoke for the first time. 'Drink,' he said. 'Spirit.'

She cast a quick glance at Dilly, and Dilly, nodding at her, hurried from the room. And now, as if he were drawing on some reserve strength, John Crawford moved his head upwards from the swathe of clothes, brought his other hand forward and, gripping Martha's wrist, gasped, 'Martha!'

'Yes, Papa? Are you feeling better? . . .'

'No, no . . . listen. If . . . if anything should happen . . . you under-stand?' He gazed up into her eyes, but she made no movement. Then be-tween gasps he went on, 'Go . . . go to Uncle's house and tell Ang . . . Mrs Mear, that I'm . . .' At this point he closed his eyes tightly and grit-ted his teeth while the sweat ran in beads down his face. It was some mo-ments before he spoke again; then he said, 'You understand?'

She nodded gently at him, although she didn't quite understand what he meant her to do, except to go and tell Uncle James the terrible news, or at least tell this person, likely the housekeeper, who would break it to him gently.

'Martha.'

'Yes, Papa?'

'Tell no one else, no one. Promise?'

She didn't know what she was promising but she said, 'I promise.'

'Not Roland.' His voice came as a faint whisper now.

'What is that, Papa?'

'Not Roland . . . never tell Roland.'

'Very well, Papa.' She thought his mind must be wandering and soothed him, saying, 'Now . . . now don't worry, you are going to be all right. Here's Dilly. She's brought you some spirit. That will make you feel better, Papa.' She turned to where Dilly was standing pouring a measure of whisky from a bottle that was three-quarters full and when they raised his head he gulped the spirit down.

It was three hours later when Doctor Pippin arrived. The bottle of whisky was almost empty and the room reeked of spirits, but Doctor Pip-pin wasn't aware of it, for from him, too, emanated the same smell, even more strongly, and much staler.

Doctor Pippin was a very good man with the knife, even when his wits were dulled, or sharpened as he would have it, with port, but from the moment he cut into the flesh of this patient he knew he was attempting a hopeless task. After sewing him up, he sat by his side and waited for him to die.

It was just turned two o'clock in the morning when he raised his tired eyes and looked at 'young Martha Mary' as he thought of her. Then get-ting wearily to his feet, he walked around the bed and put his hand on her shoulder and said, 'I'm sorry.'

Martha did not take her eyes from her father's smooth unlined face or make any sound. She could not believe it; he could not be dead, gone, never to speak again, never to laugh or charm. Who would they now wait for to come home? What were they to do without him? He had been the joy of their lives, all of them. Oh, he had been negligent and careless about money, but what was that compared to him himself. The softness of his blue eyes, the way his mouth curved at the corners when he was happy and, yes, pulled downwards when he was annoyed. But he hadn't often been annoyed, and when he had been it would have been over such a silly thing as a crease in his shirt, even on the back where it wouldn't be seen, or a handkerchief that hadn't been ironed exactly straight so that it would fold into a complete square. Silly things but part of his charm had been this preciseness about his dress.

What was she herself to do without him? She fell forward across the bed, her arms across his body, her hands gripping the blankets. But when Doctor Pippin said, 'That's it, cry my dear, cry,' she pulled herself slowly upwards, and he saw that her eyes were dry, and he was sorry to see them so. Tears were a release afforded, he had always thought, by an inconsiderate maker of anatomy only to females, and it was always harder for them when they didn't indulge in this safety valve.

He asked her now, 'When is Roland due home? I thought he would have been here.'

She bowed her head as she whispered, 'Christmas Eve.'

The door opened and Dilly entered. She was carrying a tray with two cups on it and she looked across the room at them, then stood still and the cups rattled on the tray until she placed it on a table. Then she moved forward past the two trestles that supported the door on which the operation had been performed, across the blood-spattered carpet and towards the bed. And there she stood looking down on the waxen face. She did not cry, either, but slowly she pulled the sheet over her master, and as in her downright fashion she thought, He'll ride to Newcastle no more, she was sorry in her heart that this was so.

3

They could not bury him on Christmas Day or Boxing Day, and so he lay in state in the drawing-room for seven full days, even though on the fifth day they had to screw him down because by this time he was becoming too unpleasant to gaze upon. And when it was time for him to be taken to the cemetery they were unable to bring the hearse nearer to the house than the main carriage road, so for the journey from the house and up the by-road his coffin lay on a dray cart pulled by four sturdy horses. This, too, was only achieved by men working for two days previously to keep a way clear through the snow drifts.

Considering the type of weather and the earliness of the hour, the funeral was well attended, most of the business men from Hexham joining up with the cortège before it entered the cemetery. There were no ladies attending the funeral and the only men who made the hazardous journey back to the house were Mr Paine the solicitor, and Lawrence Ducat the manager of the bookshop, and of course Roland Crawford.

A meal had been prepared for them in the dining-room. It was not sumptuous, as such an occasion merited, consisting mainly of broth, cold chicken and pickles, and an apple tart. A very meagre affair for a funeral repast.

Neither Martha nor the girls were present at the meal. They sat dressed in their deep black in the candle-lit drawing-room, which appeared much lighter now than it had done at any time during the past seven days, for the blinds in the room and all those in the rest of the house had been fully drawn and would remain so for the next week, when they would be pulled half-way up the windows. It would be the end of January before the full light was again let into the house. But now they sat in a half circle before the fire, Martha in the middle, her hands lying idle on her lap, waiting for the entrance of Roland and Mr Paine, who was to read the will. Mr Ducat would not be present as he had no connection with the family, except as a business representative. He would wait in the dining-room until the affairs of the house had been settled, then he would accompany Mr Paine back to Hexham, and before darkness set in.

Martha allowed herself to dwell upon Mr Ducat for a moment for he had been so kind during this awful time, so very kind. Thrice during the past week he had made the journey to the house to see if he could be of any assistance to her and, of course, to Roland. He had even come out on Christmas Day, which was his holiday, and brought the takings from the shop. She had been very grateful to him for that act of kindness for she needed ready money badly. She had been unable to find any at all in the house. She had searched her father's bureau and even the pockets of his clothes, going to the length of putting her hand into the pockets of the suit he had worn on his last journey from Newcastle. This act had been very painful to her, but all she had found in his purse were two sovereigns, a number of shillings, and a few pence. Yes, she had been very grateful to Mr Ducat for bringing the takings, but she must not think any more of Mr Ducat at the present moment, not for some time ahead.

She'd had a deep dread in her for days that the findings of the will were not going to be pleasant. She had hinted as much to Roland, but he had pooh-poohed her fears, and had said he was at a loss to know why she must pinch and scrape so much.

If it hadn't been for the sorrow on the house and the sorrow in her heart she would have turned on him more than once during the past few days, for his overall manner irritated her.

She rose to her feet, and the girls with her, when the door opened and Roland entered followed by Mr Paine.

The solicitor was what could be termed an undersized man. He was no more than five foot three in height and thin with it. Every part of him was thin, his hands, his face, particularly his nose; even the high boots encasing his feet looked unusually narrow, but as though to belie what these might indicate with regard to his character, his manner was warm and kindly. After a moment, during which he nodded from one to the other, he turned to Roland and said, 'Well, shall we begin?'

'Do. Do.' The brief reply sounded pompous.

So they arranged themselves, the girls where they had been seated before, Roland in his father's chair to one side of the fireplace as befitted his present station, and Mr Paine in a smaller chair at the other side.

Placed before the chair was a small table on which Mr Paine now spread a bundle of documents, each tied with a red tape. Meticulously and slowly, he undid each bundle, and smoothed out the stiff crackling parchment; then he let his gaze rest on Roland for a moment before looking fully at Martha Mary and saying, 'I feel it is my duty, and only a kindness to warn you, that there is little in these documents that has any bearing on the present monetary circumstances appertaining to your father. His will was made some ten years ago before your mother died, and at the time when there were then six businesses in the family; now there are but two, and these. . . .' He paused, blinked his eyes, rubbed the tip of his nose with the end of his forefinger, before adding, 'But let me read the will as it stands first.'

They all sat staring at him as they listened to the legally phrased words telling them that their father was leaving all his possessions to his wife should she survive him—the irony of this, which did not escape that analytical section of Martha's mind, being that all her father's possessions had primarily belonged to her mother—but in the case of her demise his son Roland would inherit.

The reading of the will did not take long, and then Mr Paine paused, folded up the document, laid it aside, before picking up, one after the other, the remaining three parchments from the table. These he wagged gently in his hands before saying, 'I'm afraid, dear people, that these consist of the real will, for they are mortgages on the two businesses and'—his eyes encircled them all now—'this house, your home.'

They stared at him. No one spoke for a full minute; then Roland, his voice cracking on his words, said, 'There's no money?' He coughed as if he were choking and put his hand to his mouth, and Mr Paine said, 'Unfortunately not.'

'None at all?' It was Martha asking the question, and Mr Paine looked straight at her and said, 'None at all, Miss Crawford. And I am very sorry to have to tell you this, but there are a large number of debts, some of them small, some of them not so small, no, not so small at all, but all demanding attention.'

Martha now looked at her sisters. Nancy's expression hadn't changed very much except for a slight look of amazement in her eyes as she gazed back at Martha, but Mildred had turned actually pale. Her thick cream-coloured skin looked muddy, the flush that was always on her cheek-bones was no longer in evidence. She looked as affected by the news as was her brother; only Martha seemed unmoved. It might have appeared to an onlooker that she'd had previous warning of the circumstances attending her father's will, and in a way she had, yet at the same time she was shocked and not a little afraid; no money and the shops mortgaged, and, what was more, their home, this house that she loved, could now be in danger of being taken from them.

She turned her eyes on Roland. He was the one who should do the talking, ask the questions, but he looked utterly shaken; and so he might, for this would mean that he could not next year go to the university. He had, she knew, set his heart on going to Oxford University. He was clever, in a way. She always tacked on this term whenever she thought of Roland's cleverness, for his cleverness lay in only one direction and that was along the lines of history; in other ways he was, if not exactly ignorant, unlettered, for he read little beyond his subject. Moreover, he was inclined to be selfish. But she didn't blame him for this latter fault for her father had always made a great fuss of him. He being the only son, she understood this to be natural, yet she had jibbed, and more so over the past year, at the fact that he was kept in ignorance of the true state of the household, for when he was at home the table was allowed to be lavish, and he never seemed short of money.

She looked at him. He was so like their father, and in character too, for already he shied away from responsibility. But now he would have to stay at home and shoulder the responsibility that she herself had carried for so long.

With the suddenness of a shock, the picture of her brother taking charge of the house and its affairs actually appalled her. She didn't want to pass on the responsibility, however heavy, to him. Oh dear, dear! Her mind was in a turmoil. And Mr Paine was speaking again.

'Your father has spent a great deal of money during these past four years.'

'On what?' The question coming from Roland was sharp now. He seemed to be recovering from the initial shock and there was a note of aggressiveness in his tone.

'That I couldn't say, sir.' Mr Paine's reply had an official ring to it now. 'He did not take me into his confidence as to what he needed the money for. Only one thing I do know, none of it was used to lighten the mortgages. He may have paid off some debts privately, but I have no knowledge in that direction.'

'Well, what are we to do? What do you advise?'

Mr Paine now raised his eyebrows as he looked back at Roland, then said, 'That will need to be gone into, but . . . but to start with, it's a matter of priorities. If you want to save your home and remain here then I would advise that the chandler's business be sold. It is a good property, situated near the market which is in its favour; it has a number of store rooms above which could be turned into a habitable house. Yes, yes—' he nodded—'it would likely bring a reasonable price, and with the profit you might be able to clear some of the debts, and so save court proceedings, besides which you could continue the mortgage payments on the house and the bookshop. I would not advise selling the bookshop, it is placed in an excellent situation within a short distance of the Abbey, and the Abbey gets many visitors and I think, as you know—' he now addressed himself solely to Martha—'people are reading more these days, even the ordinary folk, and I can see the business of bookselling naturally advancing. No, I would keep the bookshop; but, of course, in the end it will be up to you what you decide.' He did not look straight at Roland now but moved his gaze between him and Martha.

Martha, bending slightly forward, wetted her lips before she said, 'Great-Uncle James in Newcastle, could . . . could we . . . could we not appeal to him for help? Father has been at his beck and call for years, surely he would . . .'

Mr Paine had been looking at her, in fact staring at her as she spoke, and now he sneezed twice violently, then coughed, spluttering into his handkerchief as he did so until Martha, putting her hand out towards Nancy, said, 'Bring a glass of water, quickly.'

When Mr Paine had drunk deeply of the water he wiped his eyes, then his nose, then his lips, then gathering up the papers hastily, he said, 'Well, I think this is all we can do at the moment. I would talk it over between yourselves and when you come to a decision perhaps you would care to call in and see me.'

His last remark was addressed to Roland but he didn't wait for an answer. He now rose to his feet and, picking up his papers, said, 'I'm afraid I must away if I want to reach home before dark. And then, of course, there is Mr Ducat to be considered.'

They were all on their feet and no one spoke for a moment until Martha, looking at Roland, said, 'Mr Ducat should be thanked; will . . . will I see to it, or will you?'

'You see to it.' Roland's voice and manner indicated that his thoughts at the moment were far away. So she turned swiftly and went out of the room, through the almost dark hall and into the dining-room.

On her entry Lawrence Ducat rose hastily to his feet from where he had been sitting close to the fire. He was a tall young man in his late twenties with a round pale face, light brown hair that receded from his high forehead in small waving kinks; his eyes were a clear grey and his mouth full-lipped; altogether he was a young man of very attractive appearance; added to this he had a particular charm of manner, but slightly overdone in courtesy, as his bow towards Martha showed now.

'Miss Martha.' Her name held a deep warmth, and his extended arm seemed almost to lift her towards a chair, and for a moment like one mesmerized she was about to sit down, then changed her mind and said, 'There . . . there is little time, Mr Ducat. Mr Paine is eager to get back to town before darkness sets in. But . . . but I just wanted to thank you for your sympathy and kindness in our bereavement.'

Again he said her name, 'Miss Martha,' and with it took a step towards her until there was only the distance of three feet between them before he went on, 'I have done nothing, nothing to be thanked for, nothing as yet, but I would like to tell you now, you must call upon my services at any time . . . any time at all.'

'Thank you, Mr Ducat.' She held out her hand which he took in both of his and held it as he looked deeply into her eyes, the meaning in his in no way veiled, and then he asked softly, 'May I enquire if Master Roland has any plans for the future? I mean, is he to take over the businesses or return to school . . . university? I understand from your father that he was to go to Oxford next year. Such an honour, such an honour.'

She bowed her head now, then said slowly, 'I . . . I can confide in you, Mr Ducat, because you know to a certain extent something of our financial affairs, but I'm afraid our resources at the present moment are very low. There is a possibility that one of the businesses will have to go.'

His silence brought her head up and she made haste to say, 'But Mr Paine advises that we keep the bookshop. Even if we have to leave here and . . . and take a smaller place, he advises that we keep the bookshop.'

There was a perceptible slackening of his grip on her hand. She looked into his face and saw that he was as much surprised at the financial turn of events as the rest of the family had been a few minutes earlier. His concern touched her and she waited for him to speak.

When he did his words were few but his tone conveyed his sympathy. 'I am deeply sorry for your situation, Miss Martha, and I will do all I can to further the business of the establishment.'

He had once or twice before referred to the bookshop as the establishment, as if it were on a par and even bigger than some of the finest businesses in the town, and particularly so than its only other rival, Cunningham's. Although it was an older established firm than Cunningham's and the literature it stocked was wider and touched on more scholastic subjects, the premises themselves were not half as large as Cunningham's, nor did they deal with the sidelines of Cunningham's, such as stationery and newspapers and such.

From his bowed position Mr Ducat was now extending an arm towards the door, and she inclined her head towards him and went down the room and into the hall where Mr Paine was already standing waiting, Roland beside him.

She now thanked Mr Paine, and his final words to her were, 'Call upon me at any time you need assistance.'

He might have addressed this remark to Roland but he spoke to her as if she, and she alone, carried the burden of the responsibility her father had left. . . .

The cab had gone from the drive; the front door closed; they walked side by side back to the drawing-room where Mildred and Nancy were waiting for them, and it was Mildred who voiced her thoughts first. Looking at Roland she asked pointedly, 'What are we going to do? If there's no money what are we going to do? Will we have to sell the house? It's dreadful, dreadful. How's it come about?'

'Quiet!' Roland's voice was almost a snarl. 'How do I know what we're going to do? I haven't had time to think.'

Mildred, not in the least intimidated by her brother's tone, went on, 'You'll have to remain at home now and see to the business, and improve our position.'

On this, Roland swung round on her. It was as if they were back in the nursery years ago, these two, snapping at each other, and as Martha looked at them she thought that neither of them seemed to have grown with the years; they were so alike in character they could be almost one.

As she stared at her brother she felt she was seeing her father as he might have been when a young man; yet her father would never have been surly or selfish. Wouldn't he? Her mind was questioning her last words. What had he spent the money on during these past years? Why had one business after another been sold? It was true he had kept Roland at school, but after all what was a hundred pounds or so a year?

'If we kept a cow and cleared the back garden and grew all our own vegetables and had hens . . .'

Three pairs of eyes were now looking at Nancy, Martha's in soft understanding; but Roland's and Mildred's gazes held combined scorn, and Roland cried at her, 'Don't talk such rot! And look; go on, the both of you, get out, I want to talk to Martha.'

'Why should we? It concerns us all.'

'All right, it concerns us all.' He stuck out his chin towards Mildred. 'So we'll decide first of all that to help finances you find employment; you can take Miss Streaton's place in the shop. Yes, that's a good idea, isn't it, Martha?'

Martha saw that he actually meant what he said, and she herself could see that there was something in the suggestion. She looked at Mildred whose mouth was in a wide indignant gape, but before Mildred could express her ire Nancy had grabbed hold of her hand, saying urgently, 'Come on, Mildred. Come on.' And she tugged at her sister who now appeared to be speechless, and so led her from the room—even while Mildred strained her head over her shoulder as she glared back at Roland.

Roland now nodded at Martha, and as if he were already the man of the house and in complete charge of affairs he stretched his neck out of his collar and pursed his lips for a moment before saying, 'That would bring madam down to earth. And she wants bringing down to earth.'

'We all want bringing down to earth.'

Her flat remark, combined with her expression as she looked back at him seemed to deflate him somewhat and cause his shoulders to slump and his chin to sink. He slowly sat down and, putting his elbows on his knees, his hands gripped between them, he looked up at her and said, 'This is some fix, isn't it? What are we going to do?'

'I don't know.'

His tone now one of sudden bitterness, he said, 'It's scandalous. What did he do with the money? Where's it gone?'

'Why didn't you ask him?' She noted that they were both speaking of their father without respect.

'There didn't seem any need.'

'No? But you knew as well as we did that he let the other businesses go one by one.'

'I thought it was because of trade. When he spoke of it he called it the result of the rise in wholesale prices or some such, but he always seemed to have money.'

'Yes, yes, he did.' She nodded slowly at him. 'For you he always seemed to have money.'

'What do you mean by that?'

'Exactly what I said, Roland. Even when the household bills could not be paid you never went short; he saw to that.'

'Well, how was I to know that things weren't as usual? When I came home everything appeared . . .'

'Yes, everything appeared normal. All the while you were home there was a good table.'

'You mean . . . you mean you all went short?'

'Yes, I mean just that.'

'But . . . but father liked his food.'

'Father was only here for supper, and not every night; he dined in the eating house at Hexham. And as you know he visited Great-Uncle James twice a month and for two, three, sometimes four days at a time. Even more so of late.'

'I didn't know he went so often.' His brows were gathered into a deep furrow.

'He hoped to be left his estate. He didn't actually say so but he indicated as much. That's why he's kept going there all these years.'

'Then as you said to Mr Paine, Great-Uncle James should be able to help us, shouldn't he?' He leant towards her now, his long face, the paleness of which was accentuated by his black suit, bright with the hope.

She did not answer immediately, then she said slowly, 'One would imagine so, but I've been thinking since I suggested it to Mr Paine that if Father had to sell the businesses it doesn't appear that Great-Uncle is a man one could appeal to for a helping hand in a financial crisis. It appears to me now that he has been holding out his benefits all these years as a bait so that Father would attend him to the end.'

'Yes, you may be right, but . . . but nevertheless I think we should go and see him.'

As she sat looking at him she recalled her father saying, 'Don't let Roland know, ever,' and over the past week she had pondered this and wondered what Roland shouldn't know that she herself would understand. And so she said now, 'In the ordinary way you would return to your friend's the day after tomorrow and then go on to school, and . . . and I don't see why you should alter either arrangement. Anyway, with regard to the school, your fees have been paid up to the end of the term, so it would be foolish to leave before then.'

She watched him take a deep breath, his shoulders rise, then fall again, and his voice was tentative as he asked, 'You think so? You really think I should go back to Arnold's?'

'Yes; yes, I do. Anyway, wills and such-like take time, I mean straightening the business out. And they won't sell the chandler's right away, so a few more weeks won't make very much difference no matter where you are.'

'You really think I should go? It . . . it won't look bad?' His reaction was that of a young boy being released from some obnoxious chore, and she smiled faintly at him as she said, 'No, of course not.'

'And you'll go and see him . . . Great-Uncle?'

'Yes. Yes, I'll go.'

He held out his hand to her, saying, 'Oh, thanks, thanks, Martha,' and as she took it she thought, He's a child; they're all still children.

'When will you go?' He was on his feet now straightening his cravat. He had the look of someone in a hurry to begin a journey. He's not sorrowing for Father in the slightest degree, she thought. But perhaps there was an excuse for him, he had been away to school since he was nine years old and only met his father when home for the holidays, which periods got shorter as he grew older for it had become a habit for him to spend both the beginning and the end of his holidays with his friend Arnold. It was strange that never once had he invited his friend back to the house. All they knew about this Arnold was that his father was a prosperous business man in Scarborough.

She answered him now, saying, 'As soon as the roads clear sufficiently to get the trap to the station.'

'And you'll write me?'

'Yes, yes, as soon as I have any news I'll write to you.'

He said now generously, 'I don't know what we'd do without you, Martha. It's odd, but you're not like a sister at all, you're more like a mother. . . . Yes, you are.'

He stressed the last words as if he were defending his statement against her denial, but she did not smile at his intended compliment.

In four days' time she'd be twenty. She was young and not unlovely; no, she was not unlovely; but here she was being taken for a mother, and was likely to go on being a mother in name only unless. . . . She checked her thoughts, but not quite. When she returned from Newcastle, whatever news she had, she'd stay a while in Hexham and pay a visit to the bookshop . . . and Mr Ducat.

4

She sat with the reins in her hands ready to go. Nancy held Gip's head and murmured to the animal who was fresh and eager to be off. Mildred stood by the step of the trap, her face tight as she looked up at Martha and said, 'You could have let me come with you.'

'I told you, someone must be with Aunt Sophie, Nancy couldn't manage alone.'

'Ooh!' Mildred tossed her head and her glance now took in Dilly and Peg who were standing to the side of her, and it said, 'What about these two?'

Dilly now stepped forward and tucked the rug more firmly around Martha's legs, then patted her knee as she said, 'Take care now, lass, it's a long journey. God go with you.'

'Don't worry—' Martha smiled down into the wrinkled face—'the roads are nearly all clear now.'

''Tisn't the roads I'm thinkin' of, lass, it's that train. To my mind it's like ridin' a roarin' lion. And all that way into Newcastle an' all.' She shook her head.

'I wouldn't mind meself goin' on a train.' Bright-eyed Peg voiced her secret desire only to be stamped on by Dilly, saying, 'It'll be under one you'll end up, me girl. Come to a bad end you will with your wants. Your wants 'ud fill a paddock an' come up weeds.'

Whilst Dilly was propounding her usual prophecy, Peg began to nod her head and, keeping perfect time with Dilly, mouthed the words 'an' come up weeds'; then she let out a high giggle but checked it almost immediately with her hand tight across her mouth. Eeh! it was no time to laugh, with her master hardly cold an' the blinds still drawn. But as the trap moved away she added her voice to the rest, shouting, 'Good-bye, Miss Martha Mary. Good-bye, Miss Martha Mary' as if Miss Martha Mary was going on a holiday, or at least a jaunt.

It was no unusual thing for Martha to drive the horse and trap into Hexham. She had never gone there so early in the morning, but she knew that if she hoped to return home today an early start was imperative. If the road had been icy or even snow-bound she wouldn't have been afraid of the drive into the town, but what she was afraid of, as much as Dilly appeared to be, was the journey from there into Newcastle. She had never been in a train before; the one and only time she had visited her great-uncle they had gone by trap.

Owing to Gip's freshness she made the journey to Hexham in little over an hour and a quarter, and having left him and the trap in the care of John Gilbert, who managed the chandler's, she walked briskly and with false confidence from the shop to the station. There, in the booking office, she bent down and said quietly to the man behind the glass window, 'I would like a ticket to Newcastle, please.'

'Return?'

'Pardon.'

'Return? Do you want a return, miss?'

She was nonplussed for a moment until a voice from behind her said, 'He's asking, are you coming back today?' She jerked her head towards her shoulder and looked into two round dark brown eyes.

'He's asking you if you want a return ticket, do you intend to come back today? Look—' the man glanced at his watch, then towards the door that led on to the platform, saying softly but nevertheless firmly, 'the train is almost due, do please make up your mind.'

Her indignation brought her shoulders back and her head up, at the same time she took in the number of people who were standing behind the man. Now she was bending towards the window again, saying, 'Yes, a return please.'

'First, second . . . or third class?'

Again she hesitated, until the man behind her sighed, and then she said sharply, 'Second, please.'

'Well, now we know.'

She pushed a sovereign through the arched hole in the glass, and the man pushed a ticket and her change back at her, and so great was her agitation that a shilling rolled off the narrow counter on to the dirty floor.

As she stepped to the side to retrieve the coin the man took her place and said, 'Return first class Newcastle, please,' and almost at the same time bent sideways and picked up the shilling from near his feet. When he handed it to her she kept her head bent, her bonnet shading her face, and she said stiffly, 'Thank you,' then turned away, knowing that her colour was as red as a cock's comb, and that the eyes of the other passengers were on her.

As she entered the platform the train came puffing into the station, making a great noise, and she had to force herself towards it. As she took her seat in the empty carriage she saw the rude man having a hasty conversation with another man on the platform, then make a sudden dash for a compartment further along the train.

She sat back and, opening her bead handbag, took out a folded handkerchief and wiped her mouth. That man had embarrassed her. He was a coarse individual. Yet he didn't appear a common working man. He was dressed almost as well as her father had dressed, but his square, blunt features seemed to suggest lack of breeding, as his voice, too, certainly did. It hadn't the Northumbrian burr, but it had a definite northern accent and it wasn't a refined one.

She relaxed against the wooden partition. She was thankful she had the compartment to herself, it would give her time to get used to the train, and time to think. And she needed time to think, for if no help was forthcoming from Uncle James then their plight would be sorry indeed, for she had been both amazed and frightened by the number of bills that had poured in these past few days. Some were outstanding for two years or more. Their accumulated amount seemed so colossal that she couldn't see any way of clearing them except by selling both the chandler's and the house.

She had never fully realized until these past two weeks just how much the home meant to her; even her thoughts of marriage had never carried her away from the house, for she pictured herself and her husband as living there whilst she still looked after her Aunt Sophie, and, of course, the girls until they should marry.

She had never before taken into account that Roland might marry and bring his wife to live in the house; if she had she would have dismissed it, by telling herself that Roland was an ambitious young man with three years before him at the university. Moreover, Roland definitely favoured town life; during the holidays he could never wait to get back to Scarborough. Nor did she take this into account now, for if the outcome of to-day's visit wasn't satisfactory then there was every possibility of them having to find a smaller habitation, a meaner habitation that could be run without servants.

Yet as the journey proceeded her mind was lifted temporarily from herself and her troubles for she became interested in the passing countryside. It was bleak and snow-sprinkled in many parts but there were stretches that were beautiful.

And the train journey itself, well, it wasn't so frightening after all, in fact the sensation, she could say, was pleasing, even exciting. There were times when the carriage rocked somewhat alarmingly and others when the passing scene was completely obliterated by the smoke from the engine, but altogether it was not in the least as unpleasant as she had expected.

When eventually she alighted in Newcastle she was sorry the journey was over, yet reminded herself that she'd be returning the same way.

Outside the station she stood for a moment gazing about her, and now the scene was really bewildering. Such crowds of people, and of all types, finely dressed ladies descending from carriages, some enveloped in furs and walking into the station as if travelling was an everyday occurrence, while others, and these very much in the majority, seemed most ordinary people, some in dire straits if their clothing was anything to go by.

As she stood gazing about her from under the portico a shabby-looking cab drew up towards the kerb, and the cabman, bending sidewards, shouted at her, 'Wanting a cab, miss?'

'Yes. Oh yes, thank you.' She stepped towards him, then said, 'Would . . . would you take me to this address, please?' She handed a slip of paper up to him.

The man held it at arm's length, then said, 'Me eyes're not so good, miss, read it out, will ya?'

When she took it back from his hand she realized that the poor man was unable to read. 'It's the house of Mr James Low-Pearson, Seven Court Terrace,' she said kindly.

'Court Terrace? Aye. Aye.' He now made an elongated O with his mouth, then looking down at her from under his brows he said, 'That's up Portland Road, quite a way. Now, miss, do you want to go the long way round, or the short way? The long way goes up Grainger Street an' you can see all the bonny shops, then on to Northumberland Street where I'll cut off into Sandybank Road, then you're almost there. But the shorter way, well, 'tisn't so pleasant. Interesting like, but not so pleasant, an' young ladies generally like it pleasant an' to see the shops. There's some fine shops, an' some fine buildings. Now what's it . . . ?'

She cut him off sharply, saying, 'I would prefer the shorter route, thank you.'

He stared down at her for a moment before exclaiming, 'Oh aye . . . all right then, just as you say. Well, hoy yersel in.'

He made no attempt to get down and help her into the cab and once she was seated inside, her nose wrinkled at the stale smell pervading the worn leather, and she said to herself with some indignation, 'Hoy yersel in!'

The road leading from the station had been comparatively smooth but now she was being tossed from side to side as the cab joggled its way over cobbles and through narrow thoroughfares. At one point the cab stopped and while her driver had a loud altercation with someone in front of him she put her face close to the window and was appalled at what she saw. Filthy children, some in their bare feet; women, their bodies bulbous with old clothes to keep out the cold, but all with raucous voices yelling and shouting against the hold-up in the street. They looked like creatures from another planet. There were many poor people in Hexham, and some of very low estate who worked in the factories, but never had she seen people like these, particularly the children. Even the smallest of them, who seemingly could hardly toddle, were raucous.

When at last the cab moved on there passed by her window, its wheels half on the mud pavement, a flat cart piled high with decrepit household goods. The horse pulling the cart was a sorry sight; its bones were sticking through its skin and its head was drooped in misery. Such an animal, she was sure, would never have been put in shafts in Hexham. There were lots of things to be righted in their own town. Her father had always said this, but he had also added that compared to other places it was paradise, and this was being proved to her now.

As the journey continued she felt that the cab driver was purposely taking her through the meanest streets because she had refused to go by the longer route, which, of course, meant that she would have had to pay a higher fare.

It was a full half hour later, after the cab had emerged into broader and cleaner streets, that it drew to a stop and the driver, tapping the window with the butt end of his whip, called, 'We're here. This's it!'

She opened the door and got out and stood for a moment gazing up at the house across the pavement; then swiftly turning to the cabman, and about to ask what her fare was, he forestalled her, saying abruptly, 'Half a dollar.'

'What?'

'Half-a-crown, two and six.'

Half-a-crown! It was outrageous. The shortest way indeed! He must have brought her the longest way round on purpose.

When she handed him the fare he looked at it on his outstretched palm. She hadn't increased it by even one penny. He did not ask, 'Shall I wait?' but after casting a hard glance down at her he cried, 'Gee-up there!' and she was left on the pavement alone, once again staring up at the house.

It was a very nice house; being No. 7 it was set near the beginning of a long curved line of tall houses. It had six stone steps bordered by an iron railing leading up to the front door, above which was a half-moon fanlight. Although she could recall visiting her great-uncle on that one occasion, the exterior of the house held no memory for her. Slowly she mounted the step and pulled on the brass knob to the side of the door.

Her heart was beating rapidly; the mission before her was going to be somewhat embarrassing, besides sad. She was here not only to tell her great-uncle that his constant visitor, and sympathetic supporter over the years, had gone before him, but that she desperately required his financial aid.

When the door was opened by a smartly dressed maid with streamers from her cap reaching to her waist and her uniform, not grey or brown as was usual for mornings, but blue, a light delicate shade of blue that would dirty easily, she was slightly nonplussed.

'Yes?'

Martha gave a little cough and said, 'Mr Low-Pearson's residence?'

'Who?'

'Mr Low-Pearson's residence?' Her voice had an edge to it. For all her smart attire the girl seemed stupid.

'There's no Mr Low-Pearson 'ere. You've got the wrong house. . . . Oh—' She now pointed at Martha and a smile spread over her face as she exclaimed, 'Oh, he used to live here, but that was afore my time. He's been dead and gone these four years.'

Martha gaped at the girl, she gaped at her for perhaps thirty seconds before she said falteringly, 'You must be making a . . .' She stopped, then added, 'The housekeeper, a Mrs Angela Mear?'

'Huh!' The girl's face now stretched wide in evident glee. 'House-keeper?' She leant forward, 'Eeh! You'd better not let her hear you call her that. Are you after a situation? It's only a cook she wants, an' you don't sound like a . . .'

'Who is it? Who is it, Alice?'

The girl turned aside and Martha saw the speaker coming towards her. She was a girl, no, a woman, a young woman beautifully dressed in a morning gown, the colour was violet, the material a velvet cord. She had a round pert face with an abundant mass of fair hair high on her head. Her eyes were deep blue and her lips full and her skin delicately fair.

Somewhere in Martha's bemused mind the word pretty didn't encompass all this young lady's assets.

'This person . . . the young lady's a bit mixed up. She was askin' for Mr Low-Pearson, and then she thought you . . .' She stopped as her mistress thrust her aside; and now it was the woman who was standing looking straight into Martha's eyes. She had this advantage because of the four-inch step that was dividing them. 'What's your name?'

Martha's chin went up slightly as she replied, 'I am Martha Crawford. I came to see my great-uncle, Mr James Low-Pearson.'

'You . . . you come from Hexham?'

'Yes.'

'Your . . . your father?'

'My father died over two weeks ago.'

Martha watched the young woman put her hand out and grip the stanchion of the door, then she turned away and, her voice scarcely audible, she said, 'Come in.'

As Martha followed her across the narrow hall and into a long and beautifully furnished room she saw that the young woman was much smaller than herself, and somewhat plump.

In the drawing-room Mrs Mear did not ask Martha to be seated but, facing her again, her hands now gripped at her waist, she repeated, 'He's dead? John's dead, you say?'

The mention of her father's christian name, the manner, the voice which had a high artificial ring to it as if its owner were imitating someone, the look on the face which was now screwed up in disbelief, caused Martha's whole body to stiffen. It was as if she had been suddenly frozen.

'But he can't be, he was hale and hearty. . . .' She now tossed her head to one side. Then swinging about, she walked to the end of the room, and there stood looking out of the window on to what was evidently a long back garden.

It was a full minute before she again turned, and as she walked rapidly towards Martha she said, 'Did he leave me any message . . . a letter? What did he say?'

Her heart thumping against her ribs in agitation, Martha was unable to speak, she could only stare wide-eyed at the woman before her until the woman once again demanded, 'Well! What did he say?' and then she replied flatly, 'He left you no letter. He said nothing about you except to give me your name, and—' Swallowing deeply she added now, 'Swear me to secrecy concerning you. At the time I was at a loss to know why, but now I'm no longer at a loss.'

'Oh, don't take that attitude with me, young woman.'

Perhaps it was the tone, perhaps it was the look of the woman that made Martha rear, for now she cried back at her, 'And don't you dare speak to me in that manner! It is very plain to me what you are; that girl, your maid, said my great-uncle has been dead for four years. May I ask how you came into possession of this house?'

'You may ask but I'll please myself whether I tell you or not. . . . But on second thoughts, aye, yes, I'll tell you, it'll take some of the starch out of you. Your father bought it for me. No, no, that isn't quite right, it was left to him and he passed it on to me as a deed of gift. . . . Satisfied? This house is mine and all in it. . . . Oh, don't faint.' There was a deep note of derision in the last words.

'I have no intention of fainting and I'll tell you this, you're a bad woman, an evil woman. My father has ruined himself and his family because of you.'

'Now you look here!'

It was noticeable that the person's voice was becoming coarser, almost like Peg's. 'Whatever your father gave me he got well paid for. By! he did . . . I couldn't move, mustn't have friends case he popped in, and . . .'

'Be quiet!'

'You don't tell me to be quiet. Who d'you think you are?'

The white plump hand was extended towards her, one finger wagging, and Martha's eyes concentrated on it and the ring it held. It was her mother's ring, the ring which she herself was to have on her twenty-first birthday. Her voice had an ominous quiet to it now as she said, 'That ring, that ring you're wearing.'

'Yes, what about it?' The woman turned her hand and looked at it.

'That was my mother's and should have been mine at my coming of age.'

'Huh! At your coming of age! Well now, isn't that a pity he should think better of it and give it to me! And he did give it to me, for me birthday.'

Martha felt she was about to collapse, not because her sensibilities had been shocked, but from a swift rush of anger such as she had never before experienced in her life. She actually spluttered as she cried, 'And pearls and . . . and a locket? . . .'

'Aye, yes, an' pearls and a locket.' The plump chin was up now, the head wagging and the voice had lost its refined twang altogether. 'They were all presents from your father in exchange for years of me young life. And what you seem to forget, miss, is that they were his to give. . . .'

'They weren't. . . . They were left in keeping for us, my sisters and me.'

'Well, it's just too bad on the lot of you, isn't it, that he found a better use for them?'

Now Martha was being possessed of another strange emotion. She had never hated anything or anyone, but at this moment she became so afraid of the intensity of the feeling that was causing sweat to open her pores that she dropped her gaze from the young woman and stood looking down at her own tightly clasped black-gloved hands that were gripping each other so that her knuckles showed like points through the material.

She had ceased to see the person before her, for her gaze had turned inwards and she was seeing herself. It was as if she were witnessing the birth of a new creature, someone being born out of these frightening emotions. The urge that was rising in her was horrifying, for all she wanted to do was to take her hand and strike the creature across the face, not once but again and again. She wanted to see her fall to the floor, she wanted to stamp on her, hard, hard. . . .

Oh! dear God, get me out of here. Like a child now she asked this, and as if her prayer had been heard she turned about and walked towards the door, but so blindly that she stumbled against a chair and put her hand out and gripped the handle on a tall ebony cupboard, thinking it was the door.

As the bell tinkled behind her she turned again and almost instantly the door opened as if the maid had been standing on the other side waiting for the summons, and she heard the woman's voice, with the high-faluting note to it once more, saying, 'Show this lady out, Alice.'

The maid stood aside and Martha walked stiffly into the hall, and as the door closed behind her she put her hand to her throat and a wave of blackness assailed her. The young girl, now taking hold of her arm, said kindly, 'You feelin' faint, miss?'

When she did not answer the maid looked back towards the drawing-room door, and as she did so the front door bell rang and she murmured in agitation, 'Oh dear me!' then almost pulling Martha along the hall to where a chair stood in a shallow alcove, she said, 'Sit yersel down there a minute an' get your breath.'

As Martha closed her eyes and lay back she heard the maid open the door, then exclaim, 'Oh. Eeh! Eeh! you, Mr Fuller?'

'Yes, me, Alice.'

It was the voice that roused Martha and brought her head to the side. She had heard it before, that voice, gruff, aggressive, even when it was making a simple statement like, 'He's asking you if you want a return ticket.'

She now saw the face. It was the man who had stood behind her at the booking office, and he was making for the drawing-room door as if he were familiar with the house.

Oh, that woman . . . that creature. Not satisfied with ruining her father. . . . But no, she hadn't ruined her father. She herself had some re-thinking to do here, fresh thinking, truthful thinking. But . . . but that man, he must be another of . . . of her. . . . She couldn't place on him a name such as fancy man, for then she would be putting her father in the same category. . . . Well, wasn't he? And this man, too, was from Hexham.

He had entered the room and closed the door behind him, but she could hear his voice, loud with what might be a threatening note to it. She looked to where the maid was beckoning her to the door and she rose unsteadily and walked along the passage, and it was as she passed the drawing-room door that she heard the man crying, 'You! you little bitch! Do that just once more and you know what I'll do?'

And the woman answered, 'As usual you'll just talk an' talk. Aw, shut up! I've got enough to think about the day. . . .'

Whether she had unconsciously slowed in her walk she didn't know but when the maid, hurrying from the front door, went to grab at her arm she turned on her a look that said clearly, 'Don't touch me!' then she was walking down the steps into the frosty grey stillness of the street.

Automatically, she turned in the direction from which the cab had come. She was walking like one in a dream now. When she reached the end of the street she hesitated, not knowing which way to go. She turned right and after walking through a number of side streets she came into Shields Street, then into a thoroughfare that was broader still; this was Portland Road, and in it, among the traffic, she espied a cab.

Like the cab driver at the station, this one too seemed to sense that she needed to be driven somewhere, and he drew up by the side of the kerb and when she looked up at him and said, 'Drive me to the station, please,' he merely nodded, and did not, like his counterpart, ask if she wanted to go by the shortest or longest route, for now she no longer looked, or sounded, like a country kitten come to town. . . .

It wasn't until she had almost reached Hexham that the anger in her began to subside, and like a mist clearing from before her eyes she looked through it and back on to the situation. But as she did so a sickness assailed her, for she knew that no matter how she came to view her father's liaison with that woman there would remain in her a hate of him until the day she died. And in a way she realized now it was he whom she was hating when she faced the woman. It was he whom she had wanted to strike for it was he who had duped her . . . and them all, but mostly he had duped her.

She heard his voice saying, 'I'm sorry I can't afford new gowns for you this year, but there are your mother's trunks in the attic; why don't you put the dresses to use, you are so good with your needle my dear. But leave one trunk, the one with her wedding and party gowns in it. I would like to keep them for remembrance.' And all the while he had been showering his money and her mother's jewellery on that person. And . . . the house.

The house! He had passed Great-Uncle James's house on to that woman as a deed of gift. Whatever that might mean, it must have been legal. And he had sold the mill and his shares in the other firms. And all during the past four years to keep that creature in opulence, and such opulence. For now she could see what had escaped her in those moments of stress, the house had been beautifully decorated and refurnished. It was what one would call modern, and not what an old man, like Great-Uncle James, would have lived with.

Again she heard her father's voice coming over the distance of two years saying, 'Nick will have to carry on alone. He's a lazy beggar anyway, I can't afford to keep two on any longer, and Ned will be expecting a man's wage this year.'

Nick Bailey was in some ways defective but he was not so stupid as to try to do two men's work, as the deterioration of the place showed.

Now like pus spurting from a boil, there came flooding her mind his constant jocular chastisement of her over petty misdemeanours concerning the table or his personal linen: should she omit to roll his breakfast bun in a napkin to keep it hot, should the white of his fried egg not be crisped brown while the yolks remained soft, he would bestow on her a pained glance. Even on that very morning he paid his last visit to Newcastle he had remarked on the crease in the back of his shirt just below his collar. No, he had admitted, she was right, it couldn't be seen; nevertheless he was aware of it being there. And he'd also remarked on the ironing of his handkerchiefs. 'Speak to Dilly,' he had said. 'She should after all be able to do such simple work as ironing a handkerchief straight without even thinking about it.'

She found her hands gripping the edge of the seat, and the action did not go unnoticed by the two women opposite her, and when one of them, smiling, said kindly, 'Don't worry, it's quite safe,' she merely nodded at her, loosened her fingers from the seat and joined her hands on her lap.

She was surprised that it was just turned two o'clock when she alighted at Hexham, and as she walked from the station she dwelt on the change in herself between the time she had begun the journey and when it ended. A bolt of lightning from heaven, had it struck her, could not, she considered, have done more harm to her personality than that journey. Unreasonably she thought now, she would always hate trains.

On her way to the chandler's she stopped and stood looking into a shop window, asking herself what she must do now. She could not immediately return home in this state, she must have help. Mr Paine, he must have known what her father was doing with the money. He must have known about Great-Uncle James as well. Why hadn't he told her, given her some inkling before she went to that house? She now recalled his choking attack when she had put the question to him about appealing to Great-Uncle James.

When she reached Mr Paine's office his clerk asked her to take a seat, Mr Paine had only that moment come in. He would see if he was not engaged.

Mr Paine came to the intersecting doors and looked at her for a moment before coming across the dusty office and taking her hand and saying, 'How are you, my dear?'

'I . . . I haven't made an appointment, is it possible to talk with you?'

'Yes, yes, of course. Come along in.' He led her as if she were an invalid into the inner office, which, in contrast to the outer, was very comfortable and warm, and after she was seated in a leather chair opposite his desk and he himself was seated facing her, he said, 'What can I do for you, my dear?'

'I have just returned from Newcastle, Mr Paine. I went to see Great-Uncle James and beg his assistance.'

They stared at each other and it was Mr Paine whose gaze dropped first. Taking up a pen now, he tapped the nib against the ink-well as he said, 'I'm sorry I didn't talk to you before, but it was very difficult on the day of the funeral, yet if I had spoken, what could I have said? You see—' he now looked fully at her—'I knew nothing whatever about your Great-Uncle James dying or the transfer of the house to a certain person, for almost a year after the event took place. Your father did not engage me in the transaction, and I only came to hear of it in quite a roundabout way. . . . But what could I do? It was none of my business. But it proved to be the reason for your father's lack of money, or I should say the quarter in which his money was being used, for after your mother died there was no lack of money, and although the businesses were such that they would never have made fortunes, they should nevertheless have kept you all very comfortable for the remainder of your lives.'

He now leant forward and said softly, 'I did try to speak to your father on more than one occasion but he had a disarming way, as you know only too well, of putting one off. There was always tomorrow.'

'Can . . . can nothing be done against this person?'

'I'm afraid not, my dear.'

'She . . . she has all my mother's jewellery too. You know, Mr Paine, my mother had quite a lot of nice pieces; they were her mother's and her grandmother's. They might have been old-fashioned but . . . but they were of value.'

'And this person has them too?' His eyebrows were raised high now.

'Yes. My father told me they were in the bank; he . . . he took them some time ago and said he would keep them there, until we all came of age.'

'Oh, my dear Miss Crawford.' Mr Paine was now shaking his head. 'It's a sad, sad affair. I don't know when I've dealt with a worse, and I don't know how I can help you. You see, as your affairs stand—by the way I say your affairs when it should be Master Roland who should be here now bearing the burden, not you. I understand he has gone back to school.'

'Yes, yes, we thought it wise, at least I persuaded him because my—' she could hardly make herself say the name now—'my father made me promise I would not divulge anything to Roland. I promised but I did not know what I was promising.'

'Then I think you should forget your promise; he should know the situation and why it has arisen.'

'My mind is in a most chaotic state at the moment, Mr Paine, I am sure you will understand this, so if I could think about that part of the matter for a time.'

'Yes, yes, of course. But to come back to what I was saying. There is no money whatever except the weekly returns from the two shops. Now the profits, even jointly, will barely meet the mortgage on the properties, by these I mean your home and the shops themselves. If you are asking my advice I would say, as I've said before, sell the chandler's because that after all is the biggest mortgage. Your home being so far out of town and in such an isolated spot is not worth so much in the property market; and then again, I think it is your desire to stay there.'

'Yes, yes, it is.' Her voice was merely a whisper now; her eyes were wide; she was gulping audibly in her throat, when Mr Paine rose and came round the desk and, taking her hand, said, 'There, there. There, there. Don't upset yourself, my dear.'

He was right. She mustn't distress herself. She mustn't give way to tears, at least not here; she must wait until she reached home. And not even then, not in front of the others.

What would she tell the others? . . . That would have to wait. Mr Paine had just said they could keep their home.

She looked up at him, her eyes blinking away the burning sensation under her lids as she said, 'I'll . . . I'll do anything that you suggest, Mr Paine, as long as we can keep The Habitation.'

'Yes, yes.' He patted her hand; then nodded at her, walked round the desk again, sat down, took up his pen once more and studied it before saying, 'I'm sure there's no way you can cut down on household expenses, but you could economize just the smallest bit by letting one of your sisters take up a position in the bookshop. How much do you pay the female who is already there?'

How strange he should make the same suggestion as Roland. It seemed inevitable that Mildred should work in the shop. She said on a sigh, 'Five shillings a week.'

'Well, well.' He looked to the side, arranged some loose sheets of paper on his desk and tapped the pen once more on the inkwell before he continued, 'Five shillings is five shillings. And then there's the manager. Ducat, isn't it? Yes, yes, I know the gentleman.' He nodded his head. 'Very well read man from what I gather from our conversations in the shop. Of course, there's no possibility of dispensing with his services. . . . What is his wage?'

'Fourteen shillings a week.'

'H'm! h'm! Fourteen shillings. That doesn't allow for a reduction, not when everyone is crying out to have their wages raised.' He nodded towards her now and added in a conversational tone. 'They all tell you that prices have risen over the past year as if the rise in prices didn't affect oneself. Oh, I have my own experience of this.' He glanced towards the door and the outer office, then said, 'Well now, what you have to do, my dear Miss Crawford, is to go home and talk this matter over with the family. I think Master Roland should be advised of the situation. Could he possibly come home for a time?'

'I . . . I don't think so, unless the matter was very urgent.'

'Well, as I see it, this matter is very urgent. But then it is up to you; the burden seems to have fallen on your shoulders. But you know my advice, sell the chandler's, and by doing so you will clear the mortgage, and if the sale is propitious then there might be a little over to pay a little off some of the debts and help you along for the next few months. Anyway—' he again rose to his feet—'it is for you, or Master Roland, to make the final decision. And—' once more he was holding her hand—'with regard to your father and this unfortunate business, try not to let it worry you too much. These things happen; unfortunately they happen all the time, but I can well understand what a shock the revelation has been to you.'

She wetted her lips twice before she asked, 'Do you think many people are aware of, of the matter, I mean in the town?'

He veiled his eyes for a moment, then said, 'Well I cannot but say truthfully there was some interest as to why he sold the hatter's and his share in the glove factory, but most of all why he got rid of the mill, and having done so still did not settle his debts in the town. There were, I am afraid, rumours and guesses; but I don't think anything concrete came to light.'

There was a pause before she said, 'Thank you for your help, Mr Paine, I am very grateful. I will do as you suggest and . . . and think the matter over with regard to, to explaining the situation to Roland, and I will call again if I may.'

'Anytime, anytime at all, Miss Crawford.' He opened the door and himself led her across the outer office and showed her into the corridor.

In the street once again, she stood for a moment looking towards the Abbey. She had in her mind arranged to go to the bookshop and see Lawrence, as she secretly thought of him, because she had felt in need of personal comfort and support. But that was this morning. Looking back to this morning, her troubles then compared to those of the present seemed paltry, and what she needed now was more than the comfort directed by a warm glance or a clasp of the hand; what she needed now was someone's arms about her, a voice to say, 'Don't worry, leave everything to me.' And if she went to the shop she felt, in fact she was certain, that his arms would come out to her, but that this would only be after she told him the reason for her distress, for in the telling the social barrier which had kept them apart would be broken down.

But she couldn't do that . . . not at the moment she couldn't. Later, when they knew each other better, then she would tell him as someone who was close to her, and in the telling perhaps this awful feeling of hate that had come alive in her would dissolve.

She turned about and went towards the chandler's shop, and fifteen minutes later she climbed into the trap and made for home.

It was Peg Thornycroft who greeted her as she stepped stiffly down into the yard. 'By! you look froze to the bone, Miss Martha Mary,' she said. 'Eeh! you look like death on wires. Come on in an' get your things off. Leave him—' she jerked her head towards the horse—'I'll get Nick to see to him in a minute; you get inside, miss. Eeh! you do look froze.'

As Martha entered the kitchen, Peg yelled across the yard in a voice that seemed to come from someone three times her size, 'You! You Nick there! You Nick! Come and see t'animal.' Then hurrying into the kitchen where Dilly was now helping Martha off with her coat, she said, 'Eeh! Miss looks like death, doesn't she, Dilly?'

'Less of your chatter and brew some tea, an' strong.'

Dilly did not question Martha now in any way, but, chafing her stiff white fingers between her rough palms, she made a statement, 'Them trains,' she said, 'I knew it, them trains. An' it's my bet you haven't had a bite inside you since you left this mornin'. Now get yourself into the sitting-room. There's a good fire on; take your shoes off and put your feet to the blaze. I'll be with you in a minute.'

Like someone who had lost the power of speech Martha went slowly from the kitchen and across the hall, and she had just entered the sitting-room when she heard a door close overhead and footsteps come running down the stairs. And she knew they weren't Nancy's, for they didn't pound.

She was sitting before the fire when Mildred came rushing into the room. Mildred gave her no greeting but cried at her, 'She hasn't come back yet; four hours she's been out. As soon as she finished her turn with Aunt Sophie she went out. It's four hours or more. Instead of always going for me you want to go for her when . . .' Her voice trailed away as she looked down into Martha's upturned face and, her tone softer now and holding some concern, she ended, 'What is it? Are you ill, Martha Mary?'

'I . . . m ve . . . ry col . . . ld.'

'Oh, I'll get you a hot drink.'

'Dil . . . Dilly is seeing to it.'

'You look—' Mildred didn't say how she thought her sister looked but, now kneeling by her side, she took her hand and said, 'Oh, you are cold, frozen. What is it? Was it a dreadful journey?'

'Not . . . not very pleasant.'

'Did . . . did you see Great-Uncle James?'

Martha closed her eyes. 'No, no, I didn't see him.'

'Then he's not going to help us?'

'No; we need expect no help from . . . Gr . . . eat Un . . . cle James. Now let me be quiet for a while until . . . until I get warm.' She held out her hands to the blaze; then after a moment turned and looked at Mildred who was sitting back on her heels staring at her, for once seemingly forgetting her own needs, and she said, 'You say Nancy has been out a long while?'

'Yes.' Mildred's voice was quiet now. 'I was getting worried. That's why I . . . well, it's over four hours and it'll soon be dark. I was worried.'

'Yes, yes. As soon as I get warm we'll . . . we'll go out and . . . and look for her.'

'You'll do no such thing, not while I'm here.' It was Dilly entering the room and behind her Peg, her arms stretched wide, carrying a tray on which there was a pot of tea, milk and sugar, a plate of cut cold meat and another of new bread and butter.

The tray having been put down on the side table, Dilly poured out a cup of tea and handed it to Martha, saying, 'Drink that up. No talking now, just drink it up.'

When Martha sipped at the tea she wrinkled her face and, looking up at Dilly, said, 'It's—' she paused—'it's got a strange taste.'

'I . . . I know it has a strange taste, there's a drop of whisky at the bottom. Now we won't have any talk. It's either gettin' you unthawed, an' quickly, or you'll be in bed for the next week or so. Now drink it up.'

Martha sipped at the whiskyed tea and by the time she had finished it she felt somewhat better, at least physically. She looked from Dilly to Peg, and then to Mildred, as she said quietly, 'Don't worry; I'm . . . I'm all right, I feel much better now. It turned so very cold. I . . . I think we're going to have more snow.' As she finished speaking there was the sound of running footsteps across the hall and the door burst open and Nancy bounded in, her cheeks rosy, her face bright. She made straight for Martha, saying, 'Oh, you're back then! How did the visit go?'

She paused now, taking in the scene; then looking from one to the other, she asked, 'What's the matter?'

'Everything!' Mildred was barking at her. 'Martha Mary came back almost dead with the cold and you've been gone over four hours and it coming on dark and we were worried, and you don't care. All you think of is riding, riding, and yourself.'

'I don't! I don't! It's you who always think of yourself, or your cats. I had to walk Belle back; she got a stone in her foot.'

'There. There.' Mildred was wagging her head at her. 'More trouble. You rode her too hard; you're mad when you're on a . . .'

'Be quiet! Be quiet both of you! . . . Where have you been all this time, Nancy?' Martha was looking up at Nancy now, her face straight.

'I went for a ride and . . . and I crossed the river. It was low then, but when I was coming back, well, I thought I'd better not come over that way so I went to the tollbridge. Oh, what does it matter?' She turned round and rushed from the room in a manner that caused Martha's mind to lift from the present situation and think that it did matter. Four hours. Where had she been during the four hours? From the yard to the stepping-stones where the water was usually shallow would not have taken her more than ten minutes, and even if she had to return by the tollbridge as she said, she could have covered the whole journey in an hour.

Her thoughts were brought sharply back to the present by Dilly shouting at Peg, saying, 'Well! What you standin' there for gapin'? Get about your business, miss!' And as Peg obediently scampered from the room, Dilly, looking now at Mildred, pointed towards the ceiling, and Mildred, after a moment's defiant hesitation, flounced out of the room too.

Alone now with Martha, Dilly looked down on her; then seating herself on the edge of a chair, which privilege she had accorded herself for years when with the children, as she still thought of the girls, she bent her swollen body towards Martha and asked simply, 'Well, what happened?'

Martha stared back into the face of the woman who had known her since birth, and whom she had become aware of very early in life as a sort of mother comfort, and what she answered was, 'Oh! Dilly.'

'Like that, is it?'

Martha nodded her head twice.

'You got your eyes opened then?'

'Yes, yes, indeed, I got my eyes opened, Dilly. It was horrible. . . . He was horrible . . . horrible.' She screwed her eyes up tightly against the image of her father and the young woman as Dilly, shaking her head slowly from side to side, said, 'Aw, don't take it to heart like that, lass. You would have twigged how the wind blew sooner or later; you couldn't help but.'

Martha's eyes were stretched wide now and her voice was a mere whisper, 'You knew all about it? . . . I . . . I mean before?'

'Aye, it's nothin' new. He'd been at it for years, practically since he was first married.'

'Dilly!'

'Aw, don't sound like that now, Miss Martha. It's the truth. Your mother knew of it long afore she died.'

'No, no!' She was shaking her head in emphatic protest.

'But aye. Aye, lass, aye. There was one thing he couldn't do though as long as she was about, he couldn't get his hands on the money.'

Martha was leaning back in the chair now, her hands gripping the arms. 'But they seemed so happy. They . . .'

'I suppose they were in spasms. When a woman thought as much about a man as your ma did about him she'd forgive him anything. As you yourself know, with his manner like warm butter spreadin' over you he could get you climbin' greasy poles. He's had you on one since your ma went.'

'But . . . but you seemed to like him, and . . .'

'Well, tell me who didn't. . . . An' don't go an' tell me I should have told you. What good would that have done, I ask you, eh? It's bad enough now, but if you'd had to look him in the face and know that . . . well! I ask you.'

'And he went through all the money and the businesses on . . . on . . . ?'

'Aye, he went through all the money and the businesses as soon as he got his hands on the reins. That was one thing your ma did hold fast to when she was alive, was the business. She wanted you brought up decently; she wanted Roland to go to a college an' you lasses to the private school in Hexham, right until you were young ladies. An' she planned havin' parties for you here an' people drivin' out, people with sons—' she nodded her head now—'so you could all be wed to men of standin'. But there—' she spread her work-worn hands wide—'as she used to say herself, Man proposes and God disposes. . . . What was she like, this one?'

Martha's chin was buried deep on her chest now and it was some seconds before she muttered, 'Young, not much older than me. Pretty . . . stylishly dressed but . . . but common. Did you know that Uncle James died four years ago?'

'No. No, I didn't lass. No, I didn't. But on the other hand I've had me own opinion lately as to whether he was still above ground or not, especially when your father could hardly let a week go by without riding off to Newcastle. Of course, he had visited your Uncle James afore, 'cos he had his eye on the main chance; your mother being your uncle's only living relative, there was money there. Oh, your father was a very . . .' She cut her description short and pursed her lips instead, but Martha ended it in her own mind, 'Cunning man.'

He had used her from the day her mother was buried, when, taking her face between his hands, he had said, 'Now you must be a real Martha and Mary as in the Bible,' and she had gazed up at him and answered with a full heart, 'Yes, Papa.' She had never liked her name, considering it old-fashioned, but at that moment she became proud of it when with his voice, his touch, and his smile, he had, as Dilly said, pushed her up the greasy pole.

Her eyelids were closed tight now, the scalding tears were running down her cheeks. Dilly was kneeling at her side, her arms about her, her voice soothing, saying, 'There, lass. There, lass. Cry it out. Go on, cry it out.'

But she couldn't cry it out, not yet. She drew in a long deep breath, dried her eyes, then looking at the kneeling figure she said, in something of her old manner, 'Do get off your knees, Dilly, you won't be able to move your leg tomorrow.'

Now she was standing helping Dilly to her feet and when, face to face, Dilly asked quietly, 'What do we do now, lass? Have you any plans?' she answered, 'Yes. Yes, Dilly, I have plans. I've been to see Mr Paine and he suggests that we definitely sell the chandler's. It would clear off that mortgage and pay something off the debts. He also suggests that I dismiss Miss Streaton, and put Mildred in her place.'

'Aw, well now, that's the best suggestion yet. It'll give that young madam something to think about. . . . An' what about here? The house, is it all right?' There was a deep anxious note in her voice.

'Yes, yes, I think so, Dilly.'

'Good.' Dilly turned away now and as she shambled towards the door she said, as if to herself, 'As long as we've got The Habitation, we'll get by.'

But would they? Martha asked herself this question as she went to resume her seat near the fire to snatch a few moments respite alone, but it wasn't allowed her for the door opened almost immediately again and Mildred entered the room, and coming straight to her, pointed upwards and said, 'She's asleep.' Then went on without pause, 'Now, our Martha Mary, what's happened? Something's happened today and I want to know what it is.'

'Nothing's happened. It's just business, the state of our affairs.'

'It isn't. It isn't. I'm not a child, I should know. What's happened? What happened today in Newcastle?'

They stared at each other; then Martha, her voice harsh now, cried back at her, 'Yes! Yes, you should know, and the first thing you should know is that you are going to work.'

'Work?'

'That's what I said, work. You are going to take Miss Streaton's place in the bookshop.'

If Martha had said that she was going to have her transported, Mildred could not have looked more shocked. Her lips were forming the words, but soundlessly. Work in the bookshop? She stood stock still watching Martha go towards the door. The world was tumbling about her. Lady Brockdean was falling, falling away out of her ken forever. But more so were the people she hoped to meet at the Hall after the time of mourning was over when she felt sure Lady Brockdean would approach her again. But now! *A shop assistant!* She couldn't believe it. She wouldn't have it. Her life, her whole future would be ruined. Martha Mary had never liked her. She was doing this on purpose. A governess would have been low enough, but a shop assistant!

Like someone who had received a fatal blow she sat down and cried. But her crying was not sorrowful, mere tears of vexation and frustration. She hated their Martha Mary. She did, she did, and she said so, 'I hate you our Martha Mary. And I see it all now, it was you who put Roland up to suggesting it. You've never liked me. You want to see me brought low, but you shan't, you shan't.' And she sprang up and rushed from the room.

And Martha sat staring straight ahead.

Later that night Aunt Sophie had a number of her . . . turns, and for her own safety had to be strapped down on the bed. It was well past midnight when she ceased to struggle and fell into a death-like sleep. But Martha continued to sit by her. Her dressing gown fastened well up around her neck, a rug over her knees, she sat writing a letter. It was the longest letter she had ever written to Roland, in fact it was the longest letter besides the most difficult she had ever written in her life.

After what had come to light that day, but particularly since she had talked to Dilly, she now felt in no way bound to keep her promise to her father. There was growing deep within her a mounting feeling of loathing towards him; apart from everything else she felt he must have looked upon her as a simpleton, and, of course she had been one. Here she was at the age of twenty, and up till yesterday her knowledge of the world had been garnered from novels and the slight information they imparted on life. There were, she supposed, books that could have enlightened her more fully, but she had always been most careful and conservative in her choice of authors.

But now she told herself she was ignorant no more, today her education had been furthered in such a way that she would never feel the same again. And she did not mince her words in her writing when speaking of her father's mistress and of her predecessors, and she ended her letter by relating Mr Paine's advice with regard to selling the chandler's shop. Finally, she said, 'You must think hard about the future during this last term, for as things stand now you will have to forego the university.'

She added a postscript, 'Mr Paine iterated your suggestion regarding Mildred taking the place of Miss Streaton in the bookshop, and our circumstances being such I put this to her, with what result you can imagine.'

A further postscript stated, 'I am sitting up with Aunt Sophie; she's had a very bad bout.'

5

Never before had Martha visited Hexham on two consecutive days; in the past there would have been an interval of a month between any two visits to the town.

After once again leaving the trap in the chandler's yard, she made her way now in the direction of the Abbey. She felt both nervous and excited; nervous because she had never before had the task of dismissing anyone, and because Miss Streaton was a quiet, unprepossessing individual it was going to make the business even more distasteful. Yet it had to be done; five shillings a week was five shillings a week.

With regard to her feeling of excitement, she did not need to search far for its cause; she was now her own mistress, she could pick and choose as she pleased, and that is what she was going to do. This time forty-eight hours ago she would have thrust such an idea deep down into her mind, there to stay for at least six months in respect for the dead. But the dead had killed all respect in her.

She glanced at her watch. The shop would now be closed for half an hour while Mr Ducat had his midday refreshment, which he partook of in the little room behind the shop. He had once laughingly pointed it out to her as his office-cum-dining-room-cum-second home.

As she went under an arch and up the alleyway she straightened her bonnet which the strong wind that was blowing had put awry: then turned into the narrow passage from where the back door led into a small yard. And at this point the thought came to her that perhaps she need not take on the unpleasant task of dismissing Miss Streaton, Mr Ducat would do it for her. Yes, of course. Why hadn't she thought of that before? As manager of the shop, it was really his place to engage and dismiss. He hadn't been given this privilege before, but things were going to change. . . . Oh yes, indeed they were. In this moment she felt mature, and very much a woman of the world.

The window of the office overlooked the yard and to the side of it was the back door. She had her head slightly turned towards the window as she passed it. Then she was brought up stock still; her head became rigid as she stared through the window on to the scene beyond. Mr Ducat was sitting in his shirt sleeves and well back in the old leather chair, and on his knee and cradled in one arm was Miss Streaton; his other hand was inside her open blouse and his lips were tight on hers.

It was either her shadow blocking the light from the window or some involuntary sound she now made which caused him to pull his mouth from Miss Streaton and turn his head to the side, then almost shoot Miss Streaton on to the floor.

Martha took three slow stiff steps forward, opened the back door and stood within the threshold looking from one to the other. It seemed that Mr Ducat had been struck speechless. But not so Miss Streaton. Gone was the timid, unprepossessing little creature and in her place was a pert, self-assured miss. 'Well, what of it?' she said; 'we're as good as engaged. It isn't a crime.'

Martha turned her gaze slowly on to Mr Ducat. He seemed visibly startled by Miss Streaton's announcement.

The girl now bobbed her head at him before buttoning up her blouse; then with a sharp movement of her buttocks which caused her serge skirt to make a swishing sound she turned about and went out of the office, banging the door behind her.

'Oh! Miss Crawford, I am deeply ashamed, I am. I . . . I am. It was. . . . How can I say it? It was a moment of weakness. And there is no truth in what she said.' Groping behind him now, he picked up his coat from a chair and hurriedly dragged it on, then pushed agitatedly at his shirt cuffs which were hanging almost to his finger-tips, before taking a step towards her and repeating in a soft fawning tone, 'Believe me. Please believe me, it was just as I said, a moment of . . .'

'Keep your distance, Mr Ducat. And as you are about to say once more that it was a moment of weakness, I have not the slightest doubt that it is a weakness that has attacked you every day for some long time past.'

'No, no, you're wrong, Miss Crawford.'

As he smoothed his ruffled hair back from his forehead she stared at him, or rather glared at him, seeing him as he really was, as most people saw him, a weak, shallow, upstart of a man, getting by on his good looks and his surface knowledge of literature. And she had thought she loved him! She could have sworn she had loved him. For the past two years hardly a night had passed but she had thought of him, and often with longing. Whenever there had been no opportunity to come into the town and visit the bookshop she had seemed to pine inside. And what had she been pining for? This nasty shallow, horrible individual. All men were horrible. Her father, that man in the station who had gone to visit that woman, this creature here, they were all horrible. Horrible!

She was about to turn away when he asked with no note of pleading in his voice now, 'What do you intend to do then?'

'What do you mean, what do I intend to do?'

'Are you going to give us both the sack?'

She made herself look him straight in the eyes as she said coolly, 'Not as long as your work continues to be satisfactory. What you do with your private life after all is entirely your affair. Good-day, Mr Ducat. Oh—' once more she turned to him—'you may be wondering at the reason for my calling today. It was to tell you to dismiss Miss Streaton as I have someone, a friend of mine, whom I wish to put in her place. But now I can see it would be very remiss of me to subject a young girl to the risk of being molested. Of course, I am not suggesting that you have molested Miss Streaton, I suppose that in certain classes it is not considered improper to take liberties with your future wife. Good-day, Mr Ducat.'

As she stepped into the yard he was close behind her. His voice low but rasping, he spluttered at her, 'You'll be sorry you said that; there's other places. For your information, Miss Crawford, I'll tell you this, Cunningham's have been after me. Do you know that? Do you hear that? Cunningham's have been after me.'

She continued to walk away from him, down the yard and into the alleyway. She was trembling from her head to her feet. Over the past two days she had experienced a number of emotions but this present feeling was entirely new. She felt utterly degraded, dirty, nasty, as if she had submitted her body to being handled, and by him.

She was walking by the Abbey now. She must find some quiet place where she could sit because her whole being was aching to cry. Yet she mustn't cry. Oh no, not in the open, she must control herself.

She found a seat in a quiet corner, and sat heavily down, drooped her chin on to her chest, and asked herself what more could happen. She felt she was being assailed by life all at once, and from all sides, by the horrible side of life. No longer did she feel mature, and she could even laugh at the thought of herself as a woman of the world; she saw herself again, but even more clearly now, as a gullible creature, a very young impressionable girl who, because she ran a household, had played at being a woman.

Slowly she raised her head and gazed straight before her. Well it was over, parental love and respect, romance, and any thought of marriage. She knew now how Aunt Sophie must have felt when she returned from the church unmarried. It was as if she, too, had been spurned, rejected, and not by one man alone but by two.

What had happened to Aunt Sophie had turned her brain, was it also going to happen to her? *Oh no! No!* She actually shook her head at the question. She'd become strong, independent of men and all they stood for. She would make a purpose in life, and the purpose would be The Habitation, to keep it going so that it would shelter them all for as long as they needed it. And she'd keep the businesses going, at least the bookshop. She had no doubt in her mind but that Mr Lawrence Ducat would soon present her with his notice, thinking that he was dealing her a blow and that the business would fail entirely. Well, she would show him; she would show them all.

As if the thought had spurned her to make the attempt without further delay she rose swiftly to her feet and was about to walk away when a voice from behind her said, 'Good-afternoon, Miss Crawford.'

Turning as swiftly again she gulped slightly, blinked and said, 'Oh! Good-afternoon, Mr Brockdean.'

The young man was holding his hat in his hand, his body bent slightly towards her. He had grown inches since the last time she had seen him, which was almost a year ago, and was much more handsome. His thick, fair hair seemed even fairer than usual, and he had now acquired a small moustache. She had, even up to their last meeting, thought of Lady Brockdean's only son as a young boy, but here he was, a young man. You could almost say from the looks of him a mature man, although he was not yet her own age.

He said now in a tone of voice that suited the words, 'I was very sorry to hear of your father's passing, Miss Crawford.'

'Thank you.' She veiled her eyes.

'It was so sudden.'

'Yes.' She still kept her gaze cast downwards.

He now glanced towards the seat from which she had risen and said, 'I'm sorry if I disturbed your . . .' He seemed to be searching for a word in his mind. He moved his hard high hat from one hand to the other and she relieved him of his embarrassment by saying, 'That is quite all right. I just rested for a moment; I'm on my way to collect the trap at the chandler's.'

'Oh yes.' He nodded at her. 'Well, I'm going in that direction too. I'm to meet my mother; she's visiting a friend in Gilesgate.'

They had left the precincts of the Abbey when he asked 'How is Belle? I do hope there's nothing serious wrong with her foot.' He paused as she turned her face sharply towards him, her gaze wide and enquiring, and now he appeared slightly flustered as he ended, 'I . . . I came across Nan . . . your sister just by chance when I was out riding.'

'Oh, I see. Well, Belle is slightly lame but I . . . I don't think it is anything serious.'

They walked in silence now, almost for the length of a street, and then he stopped and, raising his hat again, said, 'I must say good-bye here, Miss Crawford.'

'Good-bye, Mr Brockdean.'

They bowed to each other, then went their separate ways.

He had been about to call Nancy by her Christian name, and said he had met her while out riding. She had been out riding for almost four hours yesterday, Mildred said. And he had also referred to Belle by name. She thought back to the summer. There had been times when Nancy, returning from a ride, had appeared overflowing with high spirits, when her whole being seemed to be pulsating with joy, and she had wished that she herself could get such a feeling from horse riding. But horse riding had never really attracted her; in fact, she confessed to herself, that she was a little afraid to be mounted on a horse. She could handle an animal expertly when seated in a trap, but that was the only way she enjoyed riding.

She must speak to Nancy, and forcibly. Nancy must not harbour any ideas in the direction of William Brockdean. But then she wouldn't surely, for hadn't she seen the futility of Mildred's efforts to gain even an acquaintanceship with Lady Brockdean? Anyway, Nancy was such a child, although she was approaching eighteen.

Before she mounted the trap she told herself she had made a grave error in allowing Nancy to ride out alone, but this was one thing she would nip in the bud and instantly, the moment she reached home.

On a shuddering breath she asked herself what more could happen. . . .

However, when she did reach home she did not chastise Nancy, for Nancy herself met her at the gate and gabbled that Peg had pulled a kettle of boiling water over herself and they thought she was dead.

PART TWO

The Doctors

1

Doctor Pippin's house lay a minute's walk from Beaumont Street which fronted the Abbey and was, as everyone said, a credit to the town with its fine wide thoroughfare, a promise of more such like to come they hoped.

The doctor's house had a three-storey frontage. It looked tall and deceptively narrow for it had six rooms on the ground floor. Three of these were taken over by the waiting-room, the surgery and dispensary, and the dining-room; the rest were the kitchen and the staff quarters. On the first floor was a large comfortable sitting-room running the length of the house and overlooking the garden at the far end, a small library, a large bedroom and dressing-room, and a smaller bedroom.

The top floor was given over entirely to the use of Doctor Pippin's recently acquired assistant. This consisted of four large attics, two of which were crammed with oddments of furniture, Doctor Pippin having at one time been prone to buying anything going cheap at an auction. The third was a sparse looking bedroom, and the fourth what was called a sitting-room, only Doctor Harry Fuller had as yet no time to sit in it, even should he have wished to.

In many ways Doctor Pippin liked the new fellow, but in many ways they were deeply opposed, and not all with regard to the medical profession. One of the things he strongly disagreed with was Fuller's insistence on having that damned animal up in his room; a dog's place was in a kennel in the yard not in a bedroom, filling it with fleas. The fellow could argue as much as he liked that no one need have fleas if he kept himself clean, or was kept as clean as he kept Fred. . . .

Fred. Did you ever hear of an animal being given such a name? It was, in a way, not quite right to give a human name to an animal, and such an animal, which was neither sheepdog, whippet, nor hound. As he'd said to Fuller, its predecessors must have frolicked until they didn't know back from front.

Still, as he had continually told himself these past weeks, he could have chosen worse. Yes, yes, he could have, for he was having to admit that not only night calls but day ones too were testing him now. He had a great disinclination to rise from his bed in the mornings, and his leg at times would swell to alarming proportions. What had Fuller said? Substitute water for wine and give the leg a chance. Well, yes, he supposed he was right but he was too old in the tooth now to take advice. Anyway, he had always hated taking advice.

It was thought in the town he was nearing seventy; well, he would never see seventy-four again and he was getting tired. All he wanted to do these days was sit in his garden when the weather was clement, or by the fire at night with a pipe in one hand and a glass in the other and a book before his eyes . . . and no more medical jargon. No, he had read all that he was going to read along those lines. Reading about new ideas which filled your head with ideals was a young man's game. Let Fuller delve into it all he wanted. Anyway, that fellow had enough new theories of his own to fill a book.

That was another thing that irritated him about the fellow, his new theories. Times were changing, he knew that only too well, but you couldn't throw overboard wholesale all the work of the past, and he had told him just that last night as they sat here talking—no, arguing, almost quarrelling at one in the morning when it would have benefited them both to have been in their beds.

And where was he now? It was already black dark and freezing cold, and more than likely they were in for a great downfall of snow, and he had that journey to make to The Habitation where the maid had almost scalded herself to death, at least so said that dolt of a fellow. But then it wouldn't take much boiling water to scald poor little Peg Thornycroft to death for she wasn't the size of two pennorth of copper to begin with. . . . Where the hell had he got to!

As he made to rise to his feet he heard the trap coming into the yard, but it was almost ten minutes later when his assistant entered the dining-room.

'Where've you been all this time?'

'Where have I been?' Harry Fuller thrust his fingers through his sandy hair and his blunt-featured face crinkled in enquiry as he moved towards the fire, adding, 'Why do you ask that? You know where I've been.'

'You only had three calls to make.'

'You're forgetting that one was on Mrs Saidy and daughter Jenny.'

'Yes, well, what about it?'

'She wants her married, that's what's about it.'

Doctor Pippin now threw his head back and laughed as he said, 'Oh aye. Oh aye. She's been trying to get Jenny off her hands for years, so she's flinging her darts at you, is she?'

'More like tomahawks; if I don't watch out I'll be scalped.' He again thrust his hand through his hair and this time laughed; then shaking his head slowly he said, 'Women! I sometimes wish I'd gone in for veterinary work, I could have managed cows better.'

Again the old doctor laughed, and louder this time, before he said, 'I'm with you there; your manner with the ladies leaves a lot to be desired.' Then, his face assuming a solemn expression, he nodded towards Harry, saying, 'You must alter that, me boy. If you want to get on in this business, get on the side of the women first, particularly the bedside. I'm speaking from experience.'

As Harry turned sharply from the fire John Pippin held up his hand exclaiming, 'No arguments! Not now. Get a bite into you'—he pointed to the table—'because you've got a ride before you.'

'No! Where?'

'The Crawfords, Morland House, The Habitation, as it's known thereabouts. It's six to seven miles out. You'll have to take Peter with you; you could have found it in the light but not at night.'

'Who's that sick that I've got to make the journey at this hour?'

'The maid, a wee undersized lass. They say she's scalded herself almost to death.'

Harry now went towards the table and as he picked up a wedge of cold veal pie and began eating hastily John Pippin said, 'Seat yourself down and get something into you, a few minutes won't make much difference, I don't suppose. If she's as bad as the lad said she'll be gone afore you get there.'

'Is it a big house?'

'No, not as big houses go. And the child's their only maid besides old Dilly Thompson. The family's hit hard times. The father died a couple of weeks back. You remember, I told you, a burst appendix.'

'Oh, that case. Is the wife alive?'

'No, the house is run by the eldest daughter, has been for years. There are two other young lasses and a son. He's away at school; better if he stays there, too, I should think.'

'Why?' Harry was still eating.

'Oh, I don't rightly know, a weakling I would say. The eldest girl, Martha Mary, she should have been in his place, I mean as regards character. Well now, are you finished?' He watched Harry wiping his mouth, then said, 'Don't try any newfangled ideas on the wee lass, stick to the old ones. If the burns are very bad knock her out with a whiff and leave her plenty of laudanum.'

The younger man didn't comment on this advice but said, 'How's the road out there?'

'Oh, not too bad to within a mile of the house, then it's just a lane, a cart track. That'll be the hardest part to get through should it snow. But anyway, should it come you'll be back before it lies. And see that Bessie is well housed time you're there; the mist from the river would kill more than a horse left out in it.'

Harry reached the door before he turned and looked back up the room to where John Pippin, lost in the big leather chair, appeared like a shrivelled brown nut, and he said, 'If there's any calls leave them until the morning, unless they're all that important.'

'You go about your business and I'll see to mine.'

They stared at each other over the distance, then Harry went out, closing the door none too gently behind him.

Going into the dispensary, he now collected a small quantity of powder from a deep stoppered glass jar bearing the word, opium, then opening his black leather bag he checked its contents.

A minute later he went into the kitchen, where the cook and the two housemaids were seated round the fire, and addressing the older woman, he asked, 'Have you fed him, Sarah?' and on this the cook turned her head towards him, saying, 'Aye, doctor; he's so stuffed up he can't hardly move. Look at him.' She pointed to her feet where the large nondescript dog was stretched out on the mat in front of the fire.

The two girls were standing now and they laughed, and Annie the housemaid said, 'By! doctor, he doesn't half scoff it, he eats more than a horse.'

'Well, so he should; he works as hard as a horse.' He now gave a low whistle and the dog got instantly to its feet and came towards him as he added, 'It's hard work protecting me.'

As the girls laughed the cook said, 'You off again, doctor?'

'Yes, on a long trek. Peter'll have to come with me. He won't like that, will he?' He made a face at her and she answered, 'No, begod! he won't. He's due for home in an hour.'

'Well, he's got a surprise coming to him, hasn't he?' He now poked his face at the girls and they laughed and kept their eyes on him until he went out of the back door with the dog at his heels; then Daisy, the younger of the two girls, shook her head, her mouth still wide with laughter, as she said, 'Eeh! as I'm always sayin', he's not a bit like a doctor, is he? Not gentlemanly like I mean.'

'Gentlemen's are as gentlemen's does,' said the cook bouncing her head at the young girl. 'You remember that, miss. There's too many gentlemen in this town with too much style. An' that goes for the women an' all; all words and wind with the men, an' flounce an' delicate fart with the women. As I said, gentlemen's is as gentlemen's does.'

'Aye, cook, aye,' said Daisy in a very subdued tone now, and both girls settled round the fire again, until the bell should ring for them to clear the table, which was the pattern they followed most nights in their very comfortable position in Doctor Pippin's house.

Peter Watson had grumbled all the way from Hexham and now when it actually started to snow as he turned carefully off the main road into the rutted lane he muttered a few curses.

Harry did not reprimand him in any way for he felt he knew exactly how the fellow was feeling. He knew he himself would have reacted in the same way had he been in his position. Two nights a week the man was allowed off early and this was one of them, and old Pippin wouldn't make his time up by giving him another evening.

Funny old fellow, Pippin. Most of the time he liked him, felt quite fond of him in fact, but there were other times when he saw him as a narrow bigot, a stick-in-the-mud, who would not give an inch towards progress. That the old man himself wouldn't adopt a new idea didn't really upset him, but that he was against anyone else doing so exasperated him to the point of explosion.

He had lived in the North all his life, but mostly in the towns, Gateshead, Sunderland, Newcastle. City life was different. In the country towns like Hexham, or the smaller places like Allendale Town, or Corbridge, here it was you found the die-hards and all that went with die-hards, pig-headedness, superstitions, and the deeper you went into the country roundabout the stronger the superstitions. Yesterday he had watched a woman walk backwards up the stairs, which she said would prevent her husband's coffin from being brought down this time.

As the trap lurched he gripped the rail and exclaimed, 'Another one like that and we'll be over!'

'There's worse to come,' Peter Watson growled; 'it's a bloody death-trap this lane, he never did nowt to it for years, Mr Crawford, nor none of his property. They've got that lazy young bugger Nick Bailey there now; he could have had this flattened out time and time again. If I was over him I'd see he did it.'

'How far is it to the house?'

'Another five minutes or so, if as you say we don't land in the ditch.'

It was ten minutes later when Peter Watson drew the trap to a standstill in the yard and the kitchen door opened and two women came out. One was an old woman huddled in a shawl, the other a young sad-faced girl carrying a lantern. As she came towards him she said, 'Oh, Doctor Pippin, I'm so glad you've come.' Then the lantern moving higher, she looked puzzled for a moment until Harry said, 'I'm Doctor Fuller. Doctor Pippin's assistant.'

'Oh! Oh!' She turned about now, saying hastily, 'Through here, doctor.'

He was about to follow her, but stopped and turning towards Peter Watson said, 'You'll see to them both, won't you? and get inside yourself. I don't know how long I'll be.' Then he stood aside to allow the old woman to go before him into the house.

When he entered the kitchen he saw lying on the floor on a mattress set between a table and the fireplace, a small girl, and from the look of her it appeared to him at first glance that he had indeed arrived too late.

There were two other women in the room. One was kneeling by the side of the mattress, her face deadly pale. He glanced at her through the dim light of the lamp and his impression was that he had seen her somewhere before, but where, at the moment, he couldn't recall.

Hastily now he pulled off his overcoat and after someone had taken it from him he took off his jacket and rolled up his shirt sleeves before kneeling down and gently drawing the blanket from over the contorted limbs.

What he saw brought his teeth clamping tightly together. The hands and arms right up to the elbows were two complete blisters, and already the skin was broken in parts and oozing. The top of her breast too was blistered. Lower down her clothing had saved most of her body but as sometimes happened with maids they tucked the front of their skirts up to give their feet freer access in running to and fro, and this child's skirt must have been well tucked up.

As he stared down on the scalded limbs the girl who was kneeling opposite to him said, 'We . . . we managed to get her boots off, and most of her stockings, but . . . but some of the wool stuck. I . . . I thought I'd better leave it. . . .'

Martha had lifted her head and was looking at him and she, too, realized that she had seen this man somewhere before, but she didn't have to ask herself where.

The shock caused her to flop back on her heels and grab the nearest thing to her, which was the bottom rail of the rocking chair. The room seemed to swim about her, she saw him rising upwards to the ceiling; then she heard his voice saying sharply, 'See to her. Put her head down. Get her a drink.'

For a moment he looked at the young woman who was obviously on the point of fainting before again turning his attention to the unconscious child on the mattress. He examined her pulse. It was feeble and rapid.

He straightened up and cast a glance towards the young woman sitting in the rocking chair. She hadn't fainted. It would have been better if she had, for she, too, looked like death. He addressed the young girl who had met him at the trap, saying, 'We must get her on to a bed.' He nodded down at Peg. 'Is there a room on the ground floor?'

Nancy now turned and looked towards Martha, and Martha, pulling herself to her feet, said thickly, 'The study.'

'Could you get a bed in there?'

'There's a couch.' She didn't look at him as she spoke.

'Let me see the room.' His manner was curt, almost like that of a master speaking to a servant.

When Martha went to pick up the lantern from the delf rack Nancy took it from her and led the way out of the kitchen and across the hall, down the corridor and into the study.

Harry stood looking about him for a moment, noting the broad leather couch and the fire that had burned low, and now nodding, he said, 'This will do for the time being. Get the fire made up, keep the room warm.' Then turning about abruptly he said, 'I'll need the help of all three of you.'

In the kitchen once more he looked at Martha and said, 'Kneel at the other side opposite to me, grip my hands underneath the mattress, and you two'—he nodded towards Mildred and Nancy—'do the same at the bottom end.'

When Martha didn't move from where she was standing at the head of the narrow mattress, he, already on his knees, looked up at her and, his voice low but rasping, demanded, 'What's the matter? What are you wait-ing for?' Then his amazement showed in his face when she pushed Mildred into the position opposite to him and herself knelt down at the foot of the mattress before thrusting her hands under it and joining them with those of Nancy.

For some seconds he stared at her. What was wrong with the creature? He now looked at Mildred; then gently putting his hands underneath the straw-filled tick, he gripped those of the young girl opposite, before saying, 'Now, as easy as you can get to your feet.'

Dilly was standing at the kitchen door, the lantern held high over her head. This added to the meagre light given out by the single oil lamp in the hall, and like the rest of them, she walked crab-wise across the stone flags and down the passage into the study.

After laying the mattress gently on top of the couch they all straightened their backs, and now Harry turned and looked full at this strange young woman, who was evidently the eldest of the family and, as old Pippin had inferred, the mainstay. Well, she didn't look much like the mainstay at this present moment. She looked as if she needed some kind of attention herself. But for what, he couldn't quite make out, unless it was exhaustion.

He addressed her pointedly now as he said, 'I need help and from someone who isn't going to faint. I've got to get these stockings off her legs and her arms cleaned up. If she regains consciousness she's likely to go mad with the pain, and so I'll have to administer chloroform. Who is it to be?' He now flashed his glance around the three of them. He had not included the old woman, but it was she who said, 'I'll attend you, doctor,' and as she did so he fancied he heard a sigh of relief from the two younger girls. But the older one stood rigid; she had said neither yes nor nay, and so now he said, 'Well, let's get started. . . .'

Peg remained unconscious, which was just as well for it took him over two hours to do what he had to do, and even his strong stomach was weakened by the thought of what the child would endure when she should eventually come to, and he doubted whether her small constitution would be able to stand up to it.

It was close on midnight when he was about to take his leave. He had left strict instructions with regard to the amount of laudanum that Peg must have once she regained consciousness, and also that she must not be touched until he saw her again.

He was now standing in the kitchen donning his outer clothes. Before him stood the old woman who had been of immeasurable help to him despite her age, and much more so than ever the girl would have been.

He looked towards Martha now as she entered the kitchen carrying the last of the bowls, and it was to her he said, 'How did this happen, anyway?'

He waited for an answer as she went towards the sink, but she did not reply. What was the matter with the girl? She hadn't opened her mouth all the time he had been in that room. Back and forth she had gone between there and the kitchen doing his bidding; even when he had asked her if she could find something to form a cage-like structure over the child's legs so that the covers would not touch the wounds there was never a word out of her by way of reply.

He turned to the old woman as she spoke saying, ' "Twas the kettle, doctor.' She pointed to the enormous black kettle standing on the hob, and he went towards it and lifted it, then putting it slowly down again he looked at them and said tensely, 'That child had to lift a kettle of that weight, full of boiling water! Isn't there anyone else in the house that you could have delegated that task to?'

'Only meself, doctor; I blame meself.'

'Don't do that, old woman.' He jerked his head at her. 'There's no blame on you, you don't run the household.' And now the look he turned on Martha was as hard as her own, and perhaps because he'd had enough of her surliness he almost growled at her, 'See to it in future that you have a lighter-weight utensil, or engage a blacksmith to heave that one up.' Then directing his last remark to Dilly, he nodded at her and, his tone slightly mollified now, he said, 'I'll be back tomorrow.' And on that he went out.

For a good minute after the door had closed behind him Dilly and Martha looked at each other; then Dilly said, 'Well, he did a good job, different, but I would say good. She might have a chance. . . . What is it, lass? What was it about him you didn't like? You didn't take to him, did you?'

Martha swallowed deeply; then as if her legs were about to give way beneath her she once again reached out, but grabbed this time at the top rail of the rocking chair, then lowered herself down into it.

'You're all done up, lass. You're all done up.'

What Martha should have said now was, 'No more than you, Dilly'; but she was finding she couldn't speak. Her emotions were so confused that she felt they were choking her; words, protests, recriminations, accusations, were all tumbling about in her mind. Of all the people in the world to come into this house it had to be that man, the one who had undoubtedly shared the favours of that woman with her father.

'Go to bed, lass. I'll take a turn with Peg.'

Perhaps it was that it would be nothing short of imposition to allow Dilly to remain any longer on her feet that brought the protest, 'No, no,' from her. Putting out her hand she caught Dilly's arm, saying, 'You go to bed, I'm . . . I'm all right. Nancy will stay up with me in case I may need you. I'll . . . I'll send Mildred to bed too, if not we'll all be worn out, and . . . and we must face tomorrow.'

'Aye, lass, we must face the morrow. But it's that already.' She looked at the clock: 'I'll away then. Call me if you need me.'

'Yes, Dilly. Yes, I'll call you.'

They nodded at each other and Dilly went out of the kitchen, but Martha sat for a moment longer, repeating to herself, 'And we must face tomorrow.' Face the agony little Peg would awake to, and face that man, speak to him, be civil to him. How could she do it? She couldn't. She couldn't.

Peter Watson told Sarah, Annie and Daisy what had befallen young Peg Thornycroft and they were all shocked, especially Sarah, and she said so in front of the doctor, and boldly, that it was a crying shame them only having one maid, and her a wee thing like Peg Thornycroft, and in a rambling house like The Habitation. She knew The Habitation, and she also knew Peg's grandmother. And what was the old woman going to do now without Peg's support. Not just that shilling a week but the bits Peg took home on a Sunday had helped to keep her out of the workhouse. But by all accounts these last two years the pickings from the Crawford table had been so poor that a chicken would have turned its neb up at them.

Harry listened with interest to Sarah's talk. The more he learned about the family in that habitation the better, for then perhaps he'd be able to understand the attitude of its young mistress. He buttoned up his coat and drew on his gloves as he remarked, 'A poor table then. Wouldn't suit you, would it, Sarah?'

'No, it wouldn't, doctor. Mind, it wasn't always like that; when Mrs Crawford was alive, it was a well run house. I remember as a girl going past it many's the time when I used to go and see Nell Thornycroft; that was when her man was alive. He was a drover, frozen to death he was in a snowdrift. The do we had in '75 was nothing compared to it. Nobody could move in or out of the town for weeks. Aye—' she nodded at him— 'the gardens were well kept in those days and they had about half a dozen animals in the stables. The mistress used to ride a lot, and the children an' all. I've seen them altogether, nice sight it was. But that's some years back. Now from all accounts they're one step away from the workhouse. It'll be standing in the soup queue they'll be next, and you'll be a lucky one, doctor, if you get your money.'

'You think so?' He raised his eyebrows and poked his blunt face towards her in his characteristic way, and she answered briefly, 'Past thinkin', sure of it.'

'Ah well.' He flicked Fred's ear with his finger and thumb, saying now, 'I'll take it out of their hides if I don't. Come on.'

He had opened the door and the dog had bounded out, but before he could follow Fred, Sarah checked him with, ''Tisn't fair takin' that poor animal out in the cold; he'll freeze up in that trap.'

He looked at her over his shoulder and said flatly, 'Well, I'm not leaving him here to be ruined. I think I'll do as the doctor'—he jerked his head now back towards the hall—'said should be done, stick him in a box in the yard.'

Now she was bobbing her head at him. 'Aye, aye; I can see you doin' that, doctor; that's after you've sneaked him up to your room. Daisy said your quilt was nowt but footmarks yesterday.'

'Did she now?'

'Aye, she did now.'

They grinned at each other, and he was laughing to himself as he went into the yard. He liked Sarah and the two young ones, but particularly Sarah. She put him in mind of his mother, although his mother would certainly not have been pleased to know that she was classed on the same social standing as Doctor Pippin's cook. Yet what had her own mother before her been? Only one step removed in the servant hierarchy, you could say, a housekeeper. But of course that was never alluded to, for the housekeeper had married her widowed master, and he a solicitor. . . . Funny thing class; and strange too that there should be that in him which always tried to level it. He didn't know whether it was a genuine feeling of pity for the under-privileged, or just a perverseness that he had acquired early in order to annoy that side of his mother which he hadn't liked. Yet it was that very side, her pushing, her clinging on to the fringe of class, that had enabled him to be practising as a doctor today, for when his father had walked out leaving her with three children to fend for she could, like many another woman, have given in and let her family be scattered among relatives. But not she. She had used her one talent. Before she died nine years ago she had owned her own thriving hat shop; but he himself had not benefited from it for she had left everything to be shared between his two sisters, thinking no doubt that she had done enough for him already. Or was it in case his wife should reap the benefit from all her hard work. Women were vindictive creatures, every damned one of them.

As he mounted the small trap Peter Watson said, 'If you take my advice, doctor, you'll make your trip short and sharp.' He nodded at him from where he was holding the horse's head, and Harry, looking up at the sky, said, 'Yes, perhaps you're right, it won't keep off much longer. Up you come. . . . Come on, put a move on, man.' He now hauled the dog up on to the seat beside him, took up the reins; then bending forward, he spoke to Peter Watson as if he might be overheard, saying, 'If the doctor has to go out, you go along with him. The roads are slippery, he may need support.'

Peter Watson held his eye knowingly for a moment, then nodded once, saying on a laugh, 'Aye, aye, he'll need support.' If he had added, 'What! is he full already?' Harry wouldn't have been surprised for when Peter had been inside for his orders early this morning the old man had been sipping then. It worried him, for he could see the old fool was killing himself.

'Get up there!' The horse trotted smartly out of the yard, along the side street and into the main road. A few minutes later they were crossing the bridge over the river where the waters had risen considerably during the night. Five minutes more and they were well out of the town and bowling along a rough but passable main road. Here the air became ever colder, and the sky lower, and Harry, after peering into the distance without lifting his chin out of the deep collar of his coat, glanced down at Fred and said, 'It won't be long now,' and Fred looked back at him as if to say, 'You're right,' then swivelled his long body around in the seat until his muzzle was pressed against Harry's thigh. Again Harry looked down at him; then gathering the reins into one hand, he thrust the other through the ribs in the back of the seat and groped to where he knew the extra rug lay; after tugging it through the aperture he spread it over the dog, saying, 'Don't you dare leave a hair on it else the old fellow 'll dock your tail up to your ribs.'

Fred wriggled his body into a new position under the comfort of the rug, but kept his muzzle clear of it and pointed upwards so that his glance should be ready to catch any look his master might drop on him.

Fred was eight years old, at least as far as Harry could guess. He had first seen him on the day he buried his wife. It had been a day similar to this one, heavy with the promise of snow in the air. It was as he walked from the grave-side that he noticed the dog. It had crossed his path twice; he had almost tripped over it the second time. It was a weird looking animal, definitely a mongrel and half starved. But it was no unusual sight, for there were hundreds of such animals roaming the city streets.

He recalled that someone had guided him into the sole cab and closed the door. There had been no one to return to the lodgings with him. He was living in Manchester at the time and had been there only a matter of three weeks. It was his second appointment since qualifying eighteen months previously and he was then merely an assistant, with no hope of ever becoming an 'assistant with a view', as was his position now.

He had known perfectly well that it was madness to marry so early in his career, but when emotions run high people do mad things. But in his case he hadn't only saddled himself with a wife—saddled wasn't the correct word, for Katie, give her her due, had been no burden, not like her fifteen-year-old sister; she it was who had ruined their happiness. Yet to be quite fair, he had asked himself more than once if those first few weeks of bliss would have lasted—even without Angela's irritating presence—while moving from one temporary post to the other, and scraping and saving the while, in order to have something to fall back on when he should be lucky enough to buy himself a third, or even a half share in some practice, which could only be done by taking a depleted salary over a long number of years.

Yes, that was the question he frequently asked himself. Would her love have stood up to such trials, in addition to her having to contend with his own impatient brusque nature and uneven temper?

It was two days after the funeral when he saw the dog again. It was unmistakable, standing out from all the other mongrels in that it gave evidence, and prominently, of at least three of its forbears. It was on the step outside his lodgings and he had stopped and looked down on it, and it had looked up at him, then turned and followed him. It followed him for the rest of that day, waiting outside houses large and small, and when finally he reached home there it was still at his heels but with its legs looking as if at any moment that they might refuse to support its elongated body for one step further.

Once he had fed it he knew that he had made a mistake. It was back the next day, and the next. On the fourth night he sneaked it into his room. If he hadn't he knew that he would have found it frozen stiff on the doorstep the following morning. That was the beginning. Whatever rooms he'd had since they had shared.

Over the years he had fallen into the habit of talking to the dog and had made himself believe that it understood every word he said, and this seemed to be proved true because never did he give it an order but it obeyed implicitly. 'Stay!' he would say when he left the trap for any length of time, and when he returned he would find him sitting in the middle of the driving seat, his nose in line with the horse's tail. It was a guard position, but ruefully Harry had to admit to himself that that was all it was; it was merely a fake deterrent, for the animal in spite of his size was timid.

'Well, here we go; hold on to your tail.' He issued the warning jocularly as he turned the horse from the main road on to the rough track, then added soberly, 'I wonder how we'll find the little one this morning. . . . And what will be the mood of her ladyship when we walk in? There's the making of a dour spinster if ever I saw one.'

When he drew the horse to a halt in the yard he did not immediately alight but looked about him. This was the first time he had seen the place in daylight. It was just as Sarah said, it looked as if it were going to rack and ruin. The house was sturdy enough, being built of stone. But it was an odd shape, the middle part seeming to have sunk. It looked as if three buildings had steps leading up to long glass windows similar to the main steps leading to the front door. The gable ends were dripping with creepers and ivy. These put him in mind of huge moustaches.

Altogether it was a strange-looking place, which was probably why it had acquired the odd nickname of 'The Habitation'. To his mind the inhabitants too had acquired some of its oddness. Those three girls! He couldn't place them in any social category, their isolation had left them classless, neither fish, nor fowl, nor good red meat.

'Good morning.' He looked towards the back door where Dilly was standing, and she answered, 'Good mornin', doctor.'

He nodded towards the stables, saying now, 'Is the boy about? I don't know how long I'm likely to be and so I'd like the horse taken out of the shafts for a while; there's a bag of feed in the back.'

'I'll call him, doctor.'

He now bent slightly to the dog standing by his side and, patting its head, said, 'Go along with Bessie.' Then he turned and went into the kitchen.

Putting his bag on the table, he asked, 'How is she?'

'In deep pain, doctor. She came to for a bit around dawn and it was in me heart to wish she hadn't.'

He nodded, then picking up the bag again, he walked out of the kitchen and into the hall. Here he looked about him for a moment thinking, It's quaint inside an' all, and damn cold. He took off his outer coat and threw it over a chair, then went towards the study.

When he opened the door there was, he saw, only one of the younger sisters beside the couch. He nodded at her, saying quietly, 'Good morning.'

Nancy had risen to her feet. She did not return his greeting but said, 'She keeps waking up and crying, doctor.' There was the sound of tears in her own voice.

He walked towards the couch and sat down and looked at the small white, pain-seared face; then gently he put his hand under the sheet-covered makeshift cage and his fingers moved over the small bare breast. Her heart was still beating rapidly and feebly. If she took on a fever or pneumonia there would be no hope for her, and perhaps that would be just as well for then there'd be no weeks of agony to face, and at the end a return to lifting dead weight iron kettles. What people expected from their servants! And from a child this size.

He now drew the sheet from off the cage, and then he was staring down at the oil-soaked strips of linen covering the two thin shanks of legs.

So quick did he jerk his head that a crack sounded in his neck. 'Who did that?' He was pointing.

As Nancy stared into the face that was now flushed with anger she stammered, 'Martha Mary. She . . . she thought it . . . it might ease the pain.'

'Where is she?'

Nancy pointed her finger slowly upwards, then stammered, 'Up . . . upstairs. She . . . she went to wash. . . .'

'Go and get her.'

Damn and blast her! for an interfering young snipe. He could understand when he was up against a medical opinion as to what was the right treatment for burns, scalds or anything else, but for that stiff-necked young madam to take it upon herself to disobey his order, and his orders last night had been firm and to the effect that the child was not to be touched in any way until he saw her again. If those rags were stuck into the flesh he'd have to give her another whiff of chloroform. . . . And he'd make that one stand by and watch. More than that, he'd make her take those rags off.

When the door opened he did not turn his head towards it but he was aware that she was advancing up the room some way ahead of her sister. Not until she stopped at the bottom of the couch did he turn his head slowly and look at her. He pointed downwards, then said, 'What orders did I leave with you last night?'

'You didn't leave any orders with me.'

'I stressed emphatically that the child hadn't to be touched until I saw her today.' His voice was low but his words were like grit being pressed through his teeth.

'You did not give me any such order. You may have given it to Dill . . . the maid, but you did not speak to me about what you wanted done.'

She had been about to say Dilly, as the old one was called, but she had substituted the maid. The upstart!

'That is mere prevarication; you knew what I wished. Now you'll have the pleasure of stripping those bandages off and taking more flesh away with them. It will be a very painful experience for you but more so for the patient, for they usually scream.'

Martha's hand moved to her throat. Again she felt the choking sensation of anger that never seemed to be far from her nowadays. Her eyes dropped for a moment to the white linen strips she had put round the tortured limbs early this morning. They no longer looked white, not even olive coloured with the melted butter, but brown, a dirty brown. She felt sick. She said now, 'They won't have stuck . . . I . . . I put plenty of butter on.'

'Try one. Go on.' He flapped his hands downwards. 'Try one.' His voice was still quiet, ominously so.

She remained still and stiff, staring at him. He was a horrible man; he looked ugly, coarse, common. He had no right to be a doctor, there was no semblance of a gentleman about him, neither in looks, manner, speech, nor in any other way.

'Go on, I'm waiting to prove your theory, oiled bandages don't stick, strips of soiled linen . . .'

'They weren't soiled, they were clean.' She was up in arms now, 'Perfectly clean.'

'Clean? Lying in musty drawers. Handled by one and another of you. *Clean!* Let me tell you, miss, that no linen is clean unless it has been sterilized. What you stuck round that raw flesh was yards of germ-filled material. But, of course, you've likely never heard of germs. I can't blame you for that. Well, now is the time for you to learn about them. Go and wash your hands in carbolic if you've got any, if you haven't I can supply it.'

He now turned his head towards Nancy where she was standing staring at him as if he were the devil himself and although his voice was still low when he said to her, 'Bring me a dish of water,' she reacted as if he had barked at her.

She went scurrying from the room in a manner not unlike that which had been Peg's usual mode of walk. And it would seem that she had found the water outside the door, so soon did she return. And it could have been that time had really stood still during her absence because she saw that Martha Mary had not moved.

She watched the doctor pour some liquid into the water, swill it round, then without looking at Martha Mary motion his head towards her saying, 'Wash your hands, and be quick about it.'

There was a brief silence in the room before Martha parted her lips and in a low voice that nevertheless trembled with indignation said, 'You have no right to come into this house and speak to me in that way.'

'What!' He turned his head to the side, his nostrils widening as if he were sniffing. Then in a voice that had lost most of its aggressiveness, but which to her conveyed more insult, he said, 'Don't be silly, young woman. Come off your high horse and make yourself useful. I'm going to give her a whiff of chloroform. It won't last long. Now you take one leg and I'll take the other, and start unrolling those bandages.'

'I wo . . . I can't.'

'You put them on, didn't you?'

"I . . . I don't want to hurt her.'

He straightened his back for a moment, and again he was staring at her; then quite gently he said now, 'She won't feel anything. If you do what I tell you she won't feel a thing. Wash your hands.' He nodded towards the dish. 'Go on.'

As if she were now mesmerized she washed her hands in the carbolic water, and when she looked around for something to dry them on he said, 'Don't dry them, don't touch anything, just those bandages. . . . Now.'

A minute passed, two, three, she made the effort, some of the bandages had stuck, others hadn't. Then came the moment when she knew for certain she was on the point of collapse.

When she was pushed roughly aside, not by his elbows but by a thrust of his hip, she could not call up any feeling of indignation to her aid, but stood like a chastened child gripping the back of the couch and watching his hands moving with swift skill until the two raw pieces of flesh around the ankles and the calves were once again exposed.

When he had finished he gathered the bandages up in his hands and stared at them for a moment; then looking at her, he said, 'Why didn't you continue your good work on her arms? They're in a worse condition than her legs. Hadn't you any more linen left?'

He now thrust his hands into the bowl again, then raised his eyes to where Nancy was standing, still looking at him as if she were viewing the devil. She was a pretty girl, with a sweet face, not a bit like that of her elder sister, and he should imagine her disposition was different too. He wanted to say to her, 'It's all right. Get that look off your face, I'm not going to eat you,' but what he said was, and quietly, 'Throw these away, please, and bring me some fresh water. . . .'

Fresh. Here was another problem. The water would be all right if it was from a well, but he had seen no sign of one in the yard. If it was pumped up from the river into which the sewage flowed, well what then?

As Nancy went out Dilly entered bearing a tray on which there was a bowl and a plate of thick slices of new bread. Laying it on the side table, she said to him, 'I thought perhaps you could do with this doctor, an' there's tea if you want it.'

He was bending over the couch again, but he turned his face towards her, then looked at the tray and said, 'That's very kind of you. Soup, is it?'

'Aye, soup.'

'That will do me fine now, but I'd be glad of a cup of tea before I go; I may be here an hour or so.'

'I'll see to it, doctor.' She nodded at him, turned about and walked out of the room.

She hadn't looked towards Martha; it was as if she hadn't seen her standing with her hands still gripping the back of the couch, but she had seen her, and she thought to herself laconically, He's the last straw for her.

It must have been ten minutes later when he sat down by the head of the couch and looked to where Martha still stood as if transfixed. She had the same look on her face that he had seen on weak-stomach-students who had just witnessed a gory operation. But suddenly he found himself looking at her differently, as if at a new patient. Her face had no vestige of colour in it; even her eyes appeared colourless. He couldn't make out if they were green, grey, or hazel, only that they were lying too far back in her head for health. Her lips too looked bloodless. They were full lips; she had a large mouth. The only colour about her was her hair. It was brown, a deep brown like the back of a new chestnut shell, but without its shine. There was a lack of health in her and this was emphasized by her thinness; she was almost without shape. But there was one thing he knew for sure she didn't lack, and that was temper, and it was evident at this moment, for she was staring back at him as if she loathed him. Likely she loathed all men; when women weren't married before they were twenty their emotions took one of two roads: along one all males were put into a single category and were evaded. And it was his opinion that this was one of the main reasons the nunneries got an influx of applicants from women approaching thirty. The other, which was more usual from his experience, was to barefacedly set out to trap men. There seemed to be no happy medium with them; but then women had no power of reasoning, it was all extremes.

He spoke now, saying lightly, 'It costs the same to sit.' He even gave her a faint smile.

Whether she would have replied, he didn't know, for the door opened and Dilly came bustling in as quickly as her bulk allowed. She did not speak to him but went straight to Martha's side and said softly, 'She's goin' at it hammer and tongs. You'd better come.'

Now it was as if neither of them recognized his presence for Martha, looking at Dilly, said slowly, 'I will presently . . . in a minute.'

'Well, have it your way.' The old woman turned and went out of the room as she had come in, and Harry asked himself while dunking his bread in the soup, what all that was about. He also told himself that if this child here wasn't so ill he'd let out a bawl that would blow that stupid girl from the end of the couch to which she appeared glued.

His attention was now drawn to Peg. The chloroform was wearing off and she was beginning to moan. When she opened her eyes he stroked her brow and said, 'There now. There now.'

She blinked up at him, then closed her eyes again, screwing them up tight.

He reached out and, taking a glass from the table in which there was some liquid, he put it to her lips, saying, 'Drink this; drink it all up and go to sleep; you'll be all right.'

As Peg gulped at the liquid she looked up at him again through dazed pain-filled eyes, and he said, 'There now. There now, off you go; go to sleep, my dear, go to sleep.'

When he straightened his back, Martha had gone from the foot of the couch and was now standing by the fireplace, her back to him and her shoulders hunched as if she were crying, or in pain herself. Such was her attitude that he was forced to ask, 'Are you all right?'

She turned slowly towards him and, each word distinct and weighed down with some form of emotion, which at the moment he couldn't place except in one way, and then it would be ridiculous to think she was spewing hate at him, she said, 'Yes, I-am-quite-all-right-doctor-thank you.'

Perhaps it was her manner, the hard aggressiveness and his desire to probe why it should be turned so forcibly against himself that made him take a step towards her and say, 'I would like to talk to you, but . . . but not here, about the treatment.' He motioned his head towards the couch. 'It is so important if she is to live that my directions be followed to the letter. Is there anywhere we could talk?'

'Yes, there are fourteen other rooms in the house but I don't see why anything you have to say can't be said now, and here!'

She had spoken in a hissing whisper and he literally gaped at her. By God! she was going too far this one, and no matter for what reason she was doing it if it weren't for disturbing the slumber of that little thing behind him he'd give her the length of his tongue this minute and so loudly that it would deafen her.

He had to make an effort to collect himself before he could say, 'Very well then, I'll have my say here and now. And listen carefully. You will not disturb anything in the room such as taking the ashes out; you will raise no dust whatever, pick up no rugs. You understand me?'

'I understand you perfectly.'

'Then with regard to what she eats. Her strength must be kept up, so feed her broth, chicken broth or beef broth, in small quantities every hour or so. Administer the medicine as I will direct for the next two days. I am telling you this in case the snow lies and the roads are blocked. Moreover, if she dirties the bed, which she is likely to do, don't attempt to clean her up until she has had her medicine.'

He noticed now that with these last instructions she veiled her eyes. Dear, dear, how sensitive we were; like all her breed she refused to recognize the unpleasantries of nature. How was it, he thought, that refinement and a little education tended to blinker such as this one, while those who were denied these social blessings accepted nature naturally.

He turned abruptly from her, not to resume his seat beside the couch but to stand looking down at Peg for a moment. There was little more he could do for the poor creature; it all depended now on the strength of her constitution. If she had come from a sturdy stock, even taking into account her smallness, she might stand a chance. He went to the table and closed his bag with a snap.

He did not give her any farewell but marched out of the room and into the hall. As he pulled on his coat the younger sister came from a dim corner and, hurrying forward, opened the front door for him.

He pulled his coat collar high up around his ears and stood for a moment looking at her. She was a real pretty girl. How old was she? Sixteen perhaps. How old was that other one in there? By the sound of her she could be forty, but he guessed she was in her early twenties, perhaps twenty-three, twenty-four. He was a little surprised now when this young one spoke to him. The look of fear had gone from her face, her expression now was soft, even pleading, as she said, 'Martha Mary's very troubled. She . . . she didn't mean to be rude, she . . . she never is, but you see our . . . our father died recently and . . . and she's had to see to everything. She is really very worried, and very tired; she's never off her feet.'

He pressed his lips tightly together, then allowed himself to smile, and bending forward until their faces were not more than a few inches from each other, he whispered, 'Because she has such a good advocate I'll forgive her.'

Now she was smiling back at him, her face slowly stretching until her mouth was wide as she said, 'Thank you.'

'How old are you?' he asked abruptly.

'Seventeen.'

'Seventeen.' He shook his head. 'That's a great age.' Again they were smiling at each other.

Nancy now turned sharply from him towards the head of the steps, saying, 'I'll go and tell Nick to bring your trap. . . . It's a nice horse you've got. I . . . I love horses.' She was looking at him over her shoulder and before he could protest about her going out into the bitter wind without a coat she was gone, and he watched her running over the drive towards the courtyard, her wide skirt held up at the front with both hands, her hair flying out behind her. And as he looked at her he thought, That's youth, that's how it should be, alive, winging, its feet scarcely touching the ground, its heart soaring upwards in search of life.

He stood for a moment at the top of the steps until she disappeared from his view, then as he was about to descend them he was startled by a loud cry that swung him around.

He looked back into the hall, and there racing down the stairs was the other sister and she was yelling, 'Martha Mary! Martha Mary! Come! . . . Come!'

He saw the girl hesitate at the bottom of the steps, look towards him, then turn her gaze from one side to the other, and as she did so Dilly emerged from the kitchen, her movement swift now for all her bulk and swollen legs, saying, 'Stop your bawlin' this minute! What is it?'

There was a muttered conversation between them at the bottom of the stairs, then the girl turned about and ran up them again while the old woman followed more slowly.

It was a queer household this, a very queer household. He'd had entry into all kinds of homes already in his career but with the exception of one other this was the oddest he had come across in that there seemed to be a deep undercurrent immersing them all. He saw the girl Nancy coming towards him now leading the horse and trap with Fred at her side. Immediately he noted something different about Fred; he wasn't his bouncing self, he was walking with his tail between his legs.

'What do they call her?' Nancy was stroking the horse's neck and he said, 'Bessie,' while at the same time bending down to Fred and asking, 'What is it?' The dog looked up at him, gave a small whine, then jumped up into the trap, but when he went to sit down he yelped. It was only a slight sound but it made Harry lift him to his feet and run his hand around his hindquarters. When the dog flinched he separated the hair and said, 'Oh, this is the trouble, is it? You've caught yourself on a wire or something. That was a silly thing to do, wasn't it? Sit yourself down there for a minute.' He now went to his bag which he had put on the seat of the trap and, opening it, took out a bottle and a swab and when he applied the lotion to the puncture in the dog's hindquarters it jerked its head round, and Harry said, 'Yes, it smarts. Well, you shouldn't do such silly things.' He looked at Nancy now who was standing at the back of the trap and said, 'He's caught himself on something.'

'Oh, I'm sorry.'

'He won't die.' He smiled at her and once again she smiled back at him, saying now, 'One of our horses is called Belle, sounds almost the same as Bessie, doesn't it?' Then looking upwards she exclaimed loudly, 'I was about to say I hope you get back before it snows but you won't, look, it's starting.'

'Ah yes, it is.' He looked up at the first thinly spaced flakes and added briskly, 'And so must I. Well, good-bye. I may see you tomorrow, but by the look of it I may not.' Then bending down to her from the seat, he said, 'Help with the little one, won't you? She'll need a lot of attention for a long time.'

'Yes, yes, I will.' Her face was bright as she gazed up at him, and when he raised his whip to her in salute she lifted her hand in return, then stood watching him as he drove at a brisk pace along the drive.

He wasn't terrible, not really. There was something nice about him, well not exactly nice, but something different, although, of course, he had upset Martha Mary. And, of course, she had to admit he had frightened herself almost to death, because she had never met anyone like him before. He wasn't a bit like a doctor. Doctors to her mind were smooth, elegant gentlemen, who always spoke softly as they held your wrist. At least, that's what she had read, and that's how Doctor Pippin acted. But this doctor, he looked like . . . well, what did he look like? like a working man, although he didn't sound like one. Well, not quite. And he had strange ideas. Well, they seemed strange to them, but he wasn't a bit like a doctor.

As she made for the steps again she looked up into the sky. She didn't care if it snowed for a week, two weeks, three weeks, because William had gone yesterday. He had gone to France for further studies and he wouldn't be back until the end of the term. Oh, William, William. Her heart beat out his name with every step she took. Then she brought her ecstatic thinking to a pause, and told herself she mustn't wish it to snow for days because then the doctor wouldn't be able to get through. Poor Peg, and poor Martha Mary too.

After closing the front door she stood with her back to it and looked across the darkening hall towards the study. So many things were worrying Martha Mary and not least was the matter of money. She had cut down on the oil lamps—in the usual way there would have been one lit in the hall now—and on the fires too; and she had told Dilly they could have pastry only once a week, and that for Saturday supper. Mildred said it was mean and there couldn't possibly be the need to take such steps; but Martha Mary wasn't mean else she wouldn't have sent word to Peg's grannie who herself was bedridden that she would still pay Peg's wages whilst she was ill. No, Martha Mary wasn't mean, only very worried.

The house was very quiet at the moment. She stood quite still listening, and in the silence she heard the stair-boards creak. They creaked when you walked on them and when you didn't walk on them, it was part of the character of the house. She'd miss the house when she left. . . . If she left it? Of course, she would leave it, because at their last meeting when William had kissed her and held her so close he had whispered words to her that had made her weak, even faint with their implication and she knew it would be only a matter of time, fourteen months' time before they would be married, for when he came of age he could do what he liked, marry whom he liked. And he liked her, he loved her. And oh . . . oh, she worshipped him. She always had, she couldn't remember an hour since the day they had first met when she was but twelve years old that he hadn't been in her thoughts.

There were times she felt guilty about her secret, their secret, for he, too, had admitted he felt guilty, but had made her solemnly promise that she would never mention their association to anyone until he gave her leave because, as he said, his mother would understand, but his father would need persuading.

She knew that everyone in the house would be surprised when she eventually told them that she was affianced to William, but there was someone who would be angry, and that someone was Mildred because she knew that Mildred had the idea in the back of her mind that she had only to be invited to a ball at the Hall and there she would meet William or someone like him, and he would fall in love with her and carry her away from this house, for Mildred, strangely, didn't love the house. She didn't blame Mildred for her dreams, she only felt sorry that Mildred's dream could not come true like her own.

She had told William about Mildred's disappointment in not being, in previous years, asked to the ball, and he had laughed, he had laughed so heartily that the tears had run down his cheeks. Somehow she hadn't liked that.

A loud cry from above broke her reverie and as she bounded towards the stairs she exclaimed, 'Oh! Aunt Sophie,' but on the way up she told herself that in future she must act with more decorum, run less and walk more, and she must practise the piano, and do her embroidery, because as William's wife she must become accomplished. However, she did not at this moment take her own advice, but kept on running, because that scream from Aunt Sophie meant she was having one of her turns, and a bad one at that.

2

The snow lay for eight days blocking the roads and hampering the trains; extra men were engaged to clear the streets within the town, but work as they might they couldn't keep them clear for long. Then a thaw came and the river rose and the town was alerted against flooding.

So it was fifteen days later when Harry again set out for The Habitation. His greatcoat collar was turned up over his ears; he was wearing leather gaiters round his trousers, and gloves on his hands, and it was as he went to pick up his bag from the dispensary table that John Pippin turned from replacing a stone jar on a shelf and said flatly, 'Go kindly with young Martha Mary.'

'Go kindly you say!'—he raised his eyebrows and stretched his face at the old man—'after what I told you the other night?'

'Yes, and also because of what I told you the other night. That girl is carrying more than her share, and has done for years. Besides being buried alive in that place, she's been made to stretch everything to its limit in order that her dear papa could pay, and apparently through the teeth, for his sporting. Alfred Paine didn't mention any names, I don't think he knew himself who it was, but, as I said, Crawford's apparent visits to the uncle, who had been dead for years, was a cover up for some woman he was keeping. That girl's had one or two shocks of late, so no matter what her attitude, hold the reins tight on that temper of yours.'

'Temper!'

'Aye. That's what I said.' John Pippin looked at Harry over the top of a pair of crooked rimless glasses.

'Temper! You've never seen me in a temper.'

'No; but I've seen you having the devil of a job to control it.'

He was at the door before retorting, 'I'm making no promises, and I'm afraid it'll take more than what you've told me to stir my sympathy for Miss Martha Mary Crawford should she get on her high horse again.' And he bobbed his head twice towards the old man who was looking at him with slanted gaze, not unmixed with amusement, then went out. But he had hardly reached the front door before the voice of his superior hit him, crying, 'If the little maid is dead you won't forget to admit it was one of your newfangled ideas with regards treatment for burns, scalds, and the rest, that aided her departure, will you?'

He didn't bang the door but closed it quietly, almost softly, meaning it to convey that he was in no way upset by the remark.

Yet as his journey continued along the slush-strewn road and the wind lashed his face and caused Fred to curl close up to him, he wondered, and not a little without apprehension, what he would find when he entered that quaint dwelling. . . .

What he did find almost delighted him. If it were possible he would have taken Peg Thornycroft in his arms and run with her back to Hexham, up Beaumont Street and into Oakdean House and cried, 'There! how's that for newfangled modern treatment?'

'Well! well!' He bent down and looked into Peg's face. 'This is splendid, eh? How are you feeling?'

'Oh, not too bad, doctor.'

'Pain?'

'Aye, still a bit, mostly in me hands, though I don't feel I've got any on.'

'Well, you certainly have, and they're healing. Look at that new skin.'

'Some of it's hard, doctor, like cracklin'.'

'Pork crackling?'

'Aye.' She gave a weak laugh.

'Ah.' He put his hand on her forehead now and stroked her hair back. 'We'll soon have you up and about.'

'I'll be all right, doctor? I'll be able to walk?'

'Of course you will.'

'I'm stiff.'

'Well, you're bound to be stiff, you've been lying there how many days?' He turned now and looked at the tall figure standing in the exact place where he had seen her last. It was as if she had never moved from the bottom of that couch.

But when she didn't supply him with the number of days he looked down at Peg again and said, 'Well, let me feel that heart of yours. . . . Ah! that's better, tapping away like a good drum. Now–' he put his hands on his knees and asked of her–'what are we going to do with you?'

'I don't know, doctor, I only feel I should be up an' about an' doin'.'

'Huh! up and about and doing? It'll be some time before you're up and about and doing, me girl.'

'It's . . . it's too much for Miss Martha Mary.' She now looked towards the foot of the couch. 'She's . . . she's never off her feet.'

'Well'–he didn't turn his eyes from Peg as he said, 'good nurses are always on their feet. What I want you to do is to be a good girl and lie still, and eat because you must get strong again.' Although he felt it was hitting below the belt he could not resist adding, 'But when you are strong again there'll be no more iron kettle lifting, will there?'

As he poked his chin towards her, she said, 'Oh, it wasn't the kettle, doctor; I was used to the kettle, it wasn't the kettle.'

'It wasn't the kettle?' His brows gathered into a deep furrow. 'But you were scalded by the kettle, child, when you tried to lift it?'

'Oh, I had lifted it, I have the knack of liftin' it. It was Nick stickin' his finger . . .' She lowered her eyes now and ended, 'Nippin' me bum. I jumped an' that did it.'

Not for a long time had he had the spontaneous urge to laugh, to bellow, not at the scene as he saw it depicted in his mind with that lout outside taking a liberty with the little one, but at the look on Miss Martha Mary Crawford's face. Dear! dear! dear! we were easily shocked, weren't we? Hadn't she heard the word bum before?

He forced his expression to change when he looked at Martha and asked, 'Were you aware that this was how the accident happened?'

'No.'

'That young fellow wants seeing to, doesn't he?'

'I'll speak to him.'

'I should. I certainly should; and more than that. Well now.' He rose to his feet and still looking directly at her, he said, 'This is where you can use a little of your own remedy. You may now lay her arms on pieces of oiled sheet, also her legs.' He glanced towards the fire where the ashes were piled high on the hearth and added, 'And you can get rid of those, I don't think there's much risk of infection now. I'll look in towards the end of the week again.'

'Well now, little maid'—he was again gazing down on Peg—'you be a good girl and do as I've told you, eat and rest, and I'll see you later.'

'Aye, doctor. An' ta, thanks.'

He nodded at her, and only just stopped himself from winking.

He now went out into the hall, and Martha, after a moment's hesitation followed him, but at a distance, and she remained at a distance while he got into his coat, turned the collar up, and drew on his gloves. It was as he stooped to pick his bag up from the chair that he heard her gasp, and he turned his head quickly in her direction. But she was looking upwards towards the stairs.

In utter amazement now his gaze followed hers and settled on the apparition descending towards them. It was that of a middle-aged woman, naked, except for a pair of corsets over which her sagging breasts hung, and a pair of open drawers, their flaps showing the skin of her inner thighs with each step she took down the stairs.

This then was the Miss Sophie Crawford that Doctor Pippin had spoken of as the cross on the house, the tender cross he had called her.

Martha didn't utter a word, but as if she had been fired from a gun she shot across the hall, then bounded up the stairs. But when she reached Sophie and went to shield her and made an effort to turn her about, Sophie did an unusual thing, she slapped her beloved niece, in fact she pushed her so roughly that if Martha hadn't clutched at the banister she would have fallen backwards down the stairs. Then she exclaimed in a sweetly authoritative voice, 'You can say what you like, Martha Mary, I am going down to dinner. Yes, yes I am . . . now let me pass.'

'Aunt Sophie!'

For a moment Harry watched them struggling in such a way that both could at any moment tumble headlong into the hall. Then he took the stairs two at a time and when he put his hands on Aunt Sophie's bare shoulders she became still, turned her head and looked into his face and smiled a childish smile as she said, 'Have you come to see George? Are you staying to dinner?'

Their faces were all close, so close that he felt Martha's agitated breath on his cheek, and when he looked into her eyes he was, for a moment, touched by her distress. 'Get a rug. Let go of her, go on, let go and get a rug.' His voice was low and soft, his tone kindly.

When she hesitated, looking first upstairs and then down as if fearful of letting go of this almost naked creature he quickly unbuttoned his top coat and, pulling it off, put it around Aunt Sophie's shoulders, before turning her gently about and saying, 'This way, eh?'

'We're not going into dinner?'

'Not yet, later.'

His arm about her, he led her up the stairs and on to the landing, there to be confronted by the other two sisters, both showing their horror, Nancy with her hand tight across her mouth and Mildred with both hands cupping her face.

'The gentleman has come to see George, Nancy.' Sophie smiled from one to the other.

Nancy, staring at Aunt Sophie's bare breasts, which the coat failed to cover, uttered no word, but Mildred turned her head away as if the sight of her aunt's body was sacrilege to gaze upon.

When suddenly Sophie's steps began to falter and she slumped against him, he jerked his head towards Martha, saying quickly, 'Give a hand, put your arm around her.'

But again Martha hesitated a moment too long; perhaps it was the thought of bringing her hand into proximity with his.

'Get out of the way!' He now thrust one arm under Sophie's legs and the other under her shoulder and, lifting her bodily up, carried her to where Nancy was now holding wide the bedroom door. Going straight to the bed, he now laid the limp form on it, then turned and looked at the three faces surveying him and exclaimed angrily, 'For God's sake don't look as if you're all going to faint because you've seen bare flesh! Human beings come in two sorts, male and female.'

His attention was brought from the three even more startled faces now back to the bed where Aunt Sophie's mouth was going into one wide gap and from it was issuing an unearthly cry.

Now it was his turn to find himself thrust aside as Martha reached out and grabbed a bone letter opener from a side table and pushed it lengthwise across the gaping mouth, and as she then caught hold of one thrashing arm Harry held on to the other.

When the spasm finally subsided they both released their holds almost at the same time, and as Martha hastily drew the covers over the now sweating, heaving relaxed form, he asked, 'How long has she been having fits?'

'Fits!' The word was a denial. 'My aunt has had turns for some years.'

He turned from the bed and glared at her. 'Give them what name you like, Miss Crawford, but that was an epileptic fit. How long has she had them, precisely how many years?'

'She's had her *turns* . . . since . . .'—she hesitated. How long had her Aunt Sophie had her turns? Long before she had come here. But this man, this horrible individual calling them fits! She had come to recognize hate through her father, and she had hated his woman, but the combined feeling was nothing compared to that which she felt towards this individual.

'Well, how long?'

'I . . . I can't recall.'

'What do you give her?'

'Give her?'

'I mean in the way of medicine?'

'I give her no medicine.'

'Does Doctor Pippin not prescribe for her?'

'Doctor Pippin says what she needs is quiet and care.' She now glanced to where Mildred and Nancy were standing gazing wide-eyed at them both and she said, 'Stay with her.' Then looking directly at Harry, she added, 'I would like a word with you . . . doctor.'

He returned her hard stare for a moment before nodding while saying, 'Yes, that would suit me too.' Then stooping, he picked up his coat that had fallen to the floor by the side of the bed and followed her out of the room, down the stairs, across the hall and into what was their sitting-room.

What struck him immediately about the room was its chill. There was no fire in the grate; its clutter and knick-knacks passed unnoticed. Most of the houses he visited in this class were much the same; some people went as far as putting trousers on the table legs to prevent their being scratched.

They were standing facing each other in the middle of the room. A weak shaft of winter sun penetrated between the heavy curtains and passed over her shoulder and across her chest in front of which her hands were joined, and tightly he noted. And what he also noted in this moment was that she was greatly distressed. The business of that poor soul up there appearing almost naked must have seemed like the last straw to her.

Remembering what Doctor Pippin had advised, he took a deep breath and clamped down on the irritation she had the knack of arousing in him, and said quietly, 'Well now, what do you wish to say to me?'

He watched her gulp and her throat swell, and then he was actually startled by her answer. 'I don't wish you to attend anyone in this house again; I prefer to have Doctor Pippin, and I will write to him to that effect.'

The heat from the colour flooding his face seemed to surge downwards through his body; he was filled with an anger which he knew in his mind was far and above that which the situation warranted; she was just a narrow-minded, ignorant, stupid young female. . . . *But was she?* No, she wasn't. At least she wasn't stupid, and that statement she had just made was not, he felt sure, against himself as a doctor, but himself as a man. She hated him, he could feel it emanating from her. He had felt it from the beginning. But why? Why? In the name of God! Why? He had never seen her until he entered this house. Or had he? On first sight he thought that he had come across her somewhere, and if so, then it must have been a fleeting meeting, for she had left no impression on him.

'Miss Crawford'—he spoke her name as if there was a heavy weight attached to it—'I want a straight answer to a straight question. Why have you adopted this attitude towards me? You have shown me nothing but animosity from our first meeting?'

He now watched a faint colour seep into her pale skin and his eyes rested on her lips as they pressed hard one against the other before she replied, 'I . . . I don't like your manner.'

His face was screwed up, and he made a small movement with his head, then said slowly, 'You mean to say you've taken this attitude towards me just because you don't like my manner?'

There was a moment of complete silence, during which he stared hard into her face before adding, 'I don't believe you. A lot of people don't like my manner, especially females who have their own idea of how a doctor should look, talk and act, but I feel with you there is more in this than just dislike of my manner. . . . And let me tell you something at this point, Miss Crawford. If you refuse my services you won't be able to call on those of Doctor Pippin, for he is past travelling this journey, he's a sick man himself. And what is more, you might find it difficult to persuade another medical man to come out here because, and you force me to say this, generally they won't run up accounts with new patients, they like their fees on the spot.'

Martha could hardly believe her ears; even the grocer and the coal merchant would never have been so tactless, so coarse. He was even worse than she had imagined at first. But then, he would want money, wouldn't he? Like her father, he too would want money with which to supply his mistress.

She was experiencing that choking feeling again. There was spittle on her lips now as she almost spluttered, 'You shall have your fees, doctor. Oh yes, I shall see to it that you are paid immediately because I understand how badly you need money. Mistresses have to be well provided for, they take a lot of keeping up. . . .'

Her fingers were now over her lips, her hand looking as if it had an ague. She swayed slightly, looked from side to side for support, then felt her arms gripped and her body thrust down into a chair. And there she sat, her head back, her breath coming in deep gasps, staring up into his face now hanging above hers. She blinked twice as she watched it slowly recede; then her vision clearing, she saw that he was standing upright.

She continued to stare at him in the eerie silence that picked up the sounds in the rest of the house, a door closing, footsteps on the stairs, a cough, then from outside a dog's whimpering bark.

As Harry kept his eyes fixed on hers he came to the conclusion that she was ill. That was the girl's trouble, she was ill, mentally so. He wouldn't be surprised if, like her aunt, she had . . . turns, as they called them. She was in her twenties, unmarried, likely sitting tight on the lid of her emotions and natural desires. The forbidden pleasures denied her, every man would become a target for supposed sin, so she had tacked a mistress on to him. He felt a deep pity rising in him for her, but it was immediately checked as she spoke.

'She was my father's mistress; he ruined himself through her. For years I understood he was visiting my great-uncle in Newcastle and all the while it was her. He gave her my mother's jewellery; we are on the verge of ruin, penury. I went to see my great-uncle to ask for his help and what did I find . . . *her*, and . . . and you visiting her too.'

Her voice had gradually risen and she was shouting now, like Dilly or Peg, and what was more she couldn't stop herself. 'Well! so now you know. Now you have the reason for my dislike and . . . and why out of decency you should not visit this house again. . . .'

It was his turn to gape.

That's where he had seen her, that morning on his way to Newcastle when she didn't know how to purchase a ticket; it must have been her first train journey. He hadn't known the name of Angela's latest supporter, but it must have been Crawford. Good God! she had every right to be bitter against him. . . . But Angela his mistress? Huh! He laughed ironically inside. He would as soon think of taking a boa constrictor to his bed, at least a boa constrictor would finish you off, it wouldn't keep squeezing you till almost dry as Angela had done to three men to his knowledge, and that wasn't counting this one's father.

As if in relief he now pulled a chair towards her, and sat down in front of her, and his knees were almost touching hers when, leaning forward, he said softly, 'If your accusation had any truth in it I'd agree with you, you'd have every right to hate me, but Mrs Mear is not my mistress. In a way I wish she were, for then I could be rid of her. Unfortunately, she is my sister-in-law. I married her elder sister nine years ago. Mrs Mear . . . Angela was then barely fifteen. My wife died within a short time of our marriage and I was left with the responsibility of the girl, because the sisters were orphans. When I failed to support her in the style she expected, she took matters into her own hands and chose her own career, and one might say ironically that she has made a success of it, yet she never has enough for her wants. I happened to be there that particular morning to warn her that if she used my name to purchase goods just once more I should put a notice in the papers disclaiming any responsibility.'

He stopped talking but continued to look at her. Her body had slumped, her head hung slack against the back of the chair, her mouth was open, she made an attempt to speak, but swallowed deeply, then closed her mouth again.

Shaking her head slowly now she murmured, 'Oh, I'm . . . I'm very sorry, very sorry. Please forgive me. I . . . I don't know what to say.'

As her chin drooped towards her chest he rose to his feet, saying, 'There's nothing you need say, nor need you be sorry. As I see it now you were quite justified in your attitude. And I understand your feelings. Oh yes, yes'—he nodded at her—'If I'd been in your place I think I'd have kicked you . . . or me, out of the door.' He pursed his lips now. 'But ladies are not supposed to do that, are they?'

His lightness of tone, his little joke, did not cause her expression to alter, nor did she move from the chair, she only continued to stare at him, while she thought, Dear God! what a fool I have made of myself. He must have thought me mad. He did think me a little mad, I could see it in his eyes. And over the past half hour he must have been connecting me with Aunt Sophie. And who can blame him? Oh, I feel so . . . so. . . .

She made an effort and pulled herself upwards. She wanted to apologize again, she wanted to go on apologizing, but she felt weak, tired, and rather ill.

His voice came to her saying quietly, 'I shall leave you some pills for your aunt. Give her one every twelve hours and she will sleep on and off for the next two or three days. This will give you some respite. You must get out into the air. Look'—he pointed—'the sun is shining and although it's still very cold a brisk walk will do you good. On my next visit I shall bring a tonic.'

'Thank you.'

'Well, I must be off.'

He did not turn immediately from her but said quietly, 'Don't blame yourself, we all make mistakes. I once hated an aunt because she refused to have me for a holiday in the summer. It wasn't that I missed seeing her but there was a stream with fish in it that ran by her cottage. I hated her all that summer. She died in the autumn from a disease of the liver and she left me twenty pounds.'

He was smiling. He did not look so coarse or ugly now, the smile had softened his blunt features; in a way he looked kindly. Oh, what had she done in jumping to conclusions?

'I'll never forgive myself . . . I . . .'

'Now, now, now, forget about it. That's an order, a doctor's order.'

He turned sharply from her and went down the room, and she followed him, not only to the hall door but to the top of the steps, from where she watched him go towards the yard before turning to go back into the house, her hands gripped tightly at her waist and her head down.

As Harry approached the barn he heard Fred growling and when he entered he saw the dog standing to the side of the trap. As usual he was following a pattern and staying by Bessie, but he usually sat whilst doing his guard. The boy Bailey was at the far end of the barn, but the dog was looking towards him and growling.

'What is it?' When he stooped down and touched Fred's head the animal barked, a high angry bark that he kept for intruders, and he looked again in the direction of Nick Bailey.

Harry now called down the barn. 'What's the matter? He's not usually like this, have you been teasing him?'

'Me?' The young fellow advanced some way towards him, a rake in his hand. 'Me?' he said again. 'Why no, doctor. Me, I like dogs. One back home, but different from him; he's a mongrel, huh!' He laughed and disclosed a gap where three teeth were missing in the front of his mouth. 'Mongrel of mongrels I should say, bad tempered an' all?'

Harry stared at the lad before turning abruptly and ordering Fred up. Then mounting the trap he drove out of the barn, across the yard and into the drive. But there he stopped and, pulling Fred's hindquarters round to him, he examined his haunches. There was another puncture with blood coming from it.

He looked in the direction of the barn and his teeth ground one over the other. For two pins he'd go back there and wipe the floor with that half-wit. But there'd been enough trouble in that house for one morning. 'Well'—he nodded down at Fred—'there'll be another time, boy, another time. We can wait.' Then patting the dog's head, he took up the reins again and made for home.

3

As it had promised the river rose. Fields and roads were flooded, and outside the town low-lying cottages had to be abandoned. For eight days most of the roads were impassable; then, as if spring had forgotten what time it was supposed to arrive, there were two days of sunshine, so bright that it gave warmth, and it was on the first of these pleasant days that Harry saw Martha again, although she didn't see him.

He had called in at the bookshop to order a medical book, second-hand if it were possible, and he was browsing in front of a shelf in the corner of the shop from which led a door into what he surmised was the office when he heard her voice. As he said to himself with a wry smile, there couldn't be two people who spoke like her when she was on her high horse, and apparently she was mounted at this moment for she was saying in a tone that he recognized only too well, 'I accept your resignation, Mr Ducat. You may terminate your employment one week from today, and I shall expect you to leave everything in order.'

'As you say, Miss Crawford.' The voice replying had a deep sneer to it and he recognized it also as belonging to the smarmy fellow who ran the shop, and he cocked his ear attentively as it went on, 'And for your information, Miss Crawford, I can tell you that Mr Cunningham is offering me three shillings more and with the promise of a further raise, which will assist me to view the prospect of marriage with some certainty.'

In the moments that followed Harry kept his attention on the book in his hand while still awaiting her reply, but it didn't come. The next sound he heard was the rustle of her gown as she passed within a yard of him. However, she didn't see him for she didn't turn her head, and he only just glimpsed her profile edging her bonnet, but her walk spoke plainly for her feelings.

Now what was all that about? That man's tone had been spiteful and familiar at the same time, and he had put strong emphasis on the word marriage. Surely there hadn't been something between them. Oh no, not her and a nincompoop like him! Still, you never knew women, especially when they had turned twenty, victims of their emotions all of them.

And he said so across the dining-table half an hour later after relating the incident to John Pippin. 'Women are fools,' he said, 'and the ones who are not fools are knaves. I can never understand why that word is applied solely to men.'

John Pippin stared at the lowered head and he chewed slowly on a piece of tender steak before saying, 'You haven't a very high opinion of women, have you?'

'I give them their due.'

'Yes, no doubt you do, but it all depends upon what you consider their due. In our line of business it pays to add to their due, put up the interest on their assets as it were, it never does any harm. For instance, the person in question, what do you think Martha Mary's due is?'

'What do you mean?'

'Just what I say. You've come in contact with her a number of times, battled with her by the sound of it. Well, how would you assess her?'

How would he assess her? His chin went out, he nipped on his lower lip, then slanting his gaze at the old man, he said, 'As a perfect specimen of the tradesman class, lower middle, at least I should imagine her early upbringing could have placed her in that category. Even now when she's forced to be jack of all trades she still retains the false outlook that she and her sisters are a cut above ordinary folk.'

'Well, but apart from that what about the girl herself? She's intelligent.'

'That may be, but what has she done with her intelligence? Likely she can sew, and play the piano, and no doubt they having a bookshop, she's read a bit; and yet I wouldn't say to any depth, her outlook is too narrow for that.'

'You don't like her?'

Harry now gave a short laugh. 'I neither like her nor dislike her. No, that isn't the truth. After our first meeting it would have been nearer the mark to say I loathed the sight of her.'

'And so you set out to bring her down.'

'What do you mean?' Harry's eyebrows were straining towards his hairline now in genuine surprise. 'What! me bring her down? Miss Martha Mary Crawford!'

The old man put his head back and laughed. 'Mentally, mentally, man, you set out to show yourself to be the superior male. Oh, don't deny it.' He now lifted his hand and wagged the knife it held towards Harry. 'You hate to be bested by anyone, but to let a woman try it, never! And don't look like that as if I were accusing you of rape. Which reminds me, the Bailey girl is about due. There's a household for you. The two eldest lasses dropped within a year and not a thing done about it. There's an open case of incest if ever I saw one, and fourteen already to his credit in the family. Sometimes I think it's a pity the gibbet's out of fashion. There's only one thing to be said for him, he won't let them be born in the workhouse.'

Doctor Pippin now looked towards the window and ended, 'I'm glad the sun's shining, that's one blessing to be grateful for, for I've got to gird my loins and get over to the Hall this afternoon; that young girl isn't well at all, I doubt if she'll weather it this year.'

'How long has she had consumption?'

'Oh, since she was young. It's in the family, on both sides I should say. But I don't suppose they'll worry too much about her going. It isn't as if it were young William; they'd both go mad if anything happened to him, Sir Rupert's last link with posterity. Oh my! nothing must happen to William.' He gave a chuckle. 'I think he's arranged it with the Almighty. He seems on very good terms with Him; at least, he'd have you believe so.' He now took a deep mouthful of wine, swilled it round his decayed teeth, then swallowed before saying abruptly, 'To get back to what we were saying earlier, you feel settled?'

Harry paused before answering, 'If you mean with the practice, yes.'

'Not thinking about flitting back to the big city where the money is?'

'No, our arrangement was for two years, wasn't it?'

'Yes, yes, I know what our arrangement was all right, but you've been here seven months now and . . . and I just wondered how you're viewing the set-up since I put more and more work on to you.'

'That's as it should be, and that's what I want, more and more work.'

'Yes, yes, you would. You're a type. You know that, Fuller? You're a type. I should say you've got a constitution like a horse, and a quick judgment of you would be to say that you have more brawn than brains. But that wouldn't be right, would it?'

'No, it certainly wouldn't.' Harry's voice had now a grim note to it, and the old man laughed again and said, 'That wasn't meant as an insult but as a compliment. A good constitution is a doctor's stand-by, without it he's no good. You must have come from good stock somewhere, strong farming stock I should say. Anyway'—he turned his head towards the door—'here's Annie with the pudding. I like pudding. Put it down there, girl. Ah! that's nice.' He looked at the steaming plum-duff dripping with syrup. 'That's the style, sticks to your ribs. . . . You were saying, doctor.' He looked over his glasses as he divided the large suet pudding into two.

'I wasn't saying.' Harry took the plate from the old man's hand and they eyed each other for a moment, as if each was reading the other's mind; one amused by what he read there, the other not. Paying compliments indeed! If that was his way of paying a compliment he hoped he was never insulted by him, yet at the same time he admitted there was truth in his summing up. But one did not always view oneself through the eyes of truth. No matter how brusque his manner, no matter how ordinary his appearance, and it wasn't so ordinary as all that, he had a good sturdy body on him, a fine head of hair. All right, his face had no claim to good looks, but on the other hand it didn't scare children.

But then in the next moment it could have scared Doctor Pippin had he been a nervous man, for when changing the topic abruptly again, as was his way, he said, 'You should marry. It would be nice to have a woman about the house, an intelligent one that is; there's plenty of room upstairs that could be made into an apartment and I'd then take you on right away as an assistant with a view . . . half partnership, or a third, whichever you . . .'

'Doctor, let us get this clear.' Harry was now standing leaning slightly forward across the table and he repeated, 'Let us get this one thing clear now and for all time. I have no intention of getting married again ever. If you want a partner with a wife then you'll have to look elsewhere.'

There was a significant pause as they again eyed each other; then Harry turned from the table and walked towards the dining-room door. But before he reached it Doctor Pippin's voice stopped him as he shouted down the room, 'I'll forget about the partnership then?'

Harry was facing him now as he said grimly, 'You suggested at our first interview that after two years we would discuss that point.'

'Oh aye, aye. Well, two years is a good way off, isn't it?'

'Yes, as far off it would appear as my marriage.'

When the door closed behind Harry, the old man sat back in his chair, pulled a long face, nodded first to one side of himself, then to the other, before picking up his spoon and wagging it as he had done his knife previously and saying to an imaginary listener, 'There goes a man who thinks he knows his own mind. And who's to blame him for that?'

When a moment or so later he heard the front door close none too gently he rose from the table and, limping to the window, he knocked on it, then gesticulating to the figure crossing the yard towards the coach house he beckoned him. Thrusting up the lower part of the window, he now bent forward and said, 'On your way out of the town you could look in on Mrs Armstrong.'

'Anyone else?' There was a note of sarcasm in Harry's voice and John Pippin, ignoring it, screwed up his face as if raking his brains to find another patient to add to his assistant's list. He thought a moment, then said, 'No, I don't think there's anyone else today.'

'I'm glad of that, otherwise I've little chance of getting beyond the town.'

As Harry turned away the window was pulled down with a bang. What was he doing? Trying to nark him? He had six patients of his own to visit before he could make for the outskirts and Bailey's cottage, and he didn't relish that visit. . . .

And he was relishing it less as he stood over the girl with a distended stomach lying on a filthy bed in a corner of the small room, and as he looked down into her grinning face and saw the head lice crawling on her hair he again wondered why it was that this type always seemed to breed like rats, whereas back there in the town there were three women on his list alone who had gone into decline for the simple reason they hadn't borne children. They were nice women, decent women, and had at one time, he supposed, been sprightly, but two of them spent most of their time now lying on a couch.

'I should imagine it will be another day or two before it arrives.' He coughed now to get the fug out of his throat.

'D'ya think so, docta?'

As her grin widened he felt sick. There was no pity in him for her. Her face had never seen water for days, her hands were ingrained with dirt. The place stank. He looked about him. The mother would appear to be ignoring his presence for she was sitting huddled over the fire stirring something in a kale pot, while four children, their ages ranging from two to six, scrambled around the floor in pursuit of a hen, which left its droppings for them to crawl through as it ran. Oddly the fowl was not squawking as a hen usually would, but running silently and using all its faculties to dodge their clutching hands.

The whole place looked a shambles and smelt like a pigsty, yet strangely this wasn't a house without money for Bailey himself was not only in work but had five sons and two daughters bringing in their wages, one of the sons, that lout at The Habitation, and more strangely still he paid his debts. Doctor Pippin said he had never left the house without getting his two shilling fee, and should Bailey himself not be in at the time he would never forget what he owed.

He thought about this as he left the house and breathed deep of the fresh air, that was when he had got past the middens. There were strange quirks to human nature. Perhaps if the man had married a normal woman, because it was definitely from the wife's side that the mental abnormalities sprang, he might have acted differently. But would he? A man who would take his own daughters!

The next house he visited seemed to be at the other end of the social scale, although there was poverty here too, except in the wealth of books to be seen in the house. Samuel Armstrong was a self-educated man and perhaps his lowly state was due as much to his buying of books as to his inability to obtain work connected with them.

Samuel Armstrong was sixty-two, but he appeared seventy-two until he spoke, then you forgot his age for his voice had a vital ring to it. He had been unemployed for the past six months and they had lived, or barely subsisted, on what his wife earned from giving music lessons. It was as well she could sit through her task and didn't need to talk much for at times she was greatly troubled with bronchial asthma.

It was as Harry listened to the rumbling in her chest that an idea came to him, which he dwelt on for a moment or so while he returned the instruments to his bag. He spoke a few professional words to Mrs Armstrong, drew on his gloves, picked up his hat, then followed Samuel Armstrong to the door; and there he looked down on the small man and said, 'Has anything come up, any prospects?'

Samuel Armstrong shook his head slowly. 'No, no, nothing, doctor; I travelled the streets of the town most of last week. Even if I could do manual work I'd find it hard to come by; as for the shop assistants, in the tailor's, the haberdasher's, the hatter's, they're all clinging tight to their posts. And who's to blame them?'

'How would you like to work with books?'

'Are you teasing, doctor?'

'No, no, I'm not teasing, and I'm not promising anything positive either, only I think there's a position in the town coming vacant and it's to do with books.'

'But I was everywhere last week, doctor, in every shop in the town.'

'Well, the position wasn't vacant last week. Anyway, I don't know as yet if it's been filled, or if the owner has anyone in mind, but I'll be seeing her tomorrow and if you wish I'll put a word in for you.'

'If I wish it, doctor?'

There was a thick moisture in the eyes looking back into his, and when he felt his hand gripped, he became embarrassed by the emotion the older man was showing, and he took his departure hastily now, saying, 'Well mind, there's nothing sure, but I'll do my best,' and Samuel Armstrong's voice followed him to the trap, calling, 'Thank you. Thank you a thousand times, doctor, whichever way it goes. Thank you.'

And the next afternoon it did go well for Samuel Armstrong, that was after Harry had used a little diplomacy, lied a little, and made an effort to curb his temper . . . but only just when he found Peg dressed and in the kitchen.

He had gone in by the back door and his entry had startled them; perhaps because of the high wind that was blowing and the empty pail that had been bowling across the courtyard as he drove in they hadn't heard his arrival.

Martha was at the table. She was wearing a large apron over her faded calico dress; her sleeves were rolled up past the elbows, and like any ordinary housewife she was kneading bread. The occupation was one in which he had never imagined to see her engaged, and so it was she took his attention for a moment until he became aware that the other occupant of the kitchen was Peg, fully dressed and in the process of arraying loaf tins along the fender. She was doing this by the simple process of keeping her fingers straight and lifting the tins with the palms of her hands.

'What's this?' He turned his gaze on to Martha where she stood with her fists in the dough leaning slightly forward looking at him. 'I gave instructions that she was not to work or get her hands wet.'

But it wasn't Martha who answered him, for Peg coming swiftly forward and smiling up at him, said brightly, 'Eeh! doctor, I know, but it's me. Don't blame Miss Martha Mary, it's me. Eeh! I'd have gone clean barmy if I'd had to sit much longer. I'm not used to it, doctor, an' I'm glad to be back in the kitchen. I like the kitchen an' I'm fine, I am, I'm real fine.'

'It's too early days for you to work. You have only to get some dirt in one of those cracks and you'll have something worse than burns.'

'Oh, I'm careful, doctor, and I don't do no dirty work, ashes or nothin', Miss Martha Mary won't let me.' She glanced smilingly at Martha.

Miss Martha Mary wouldn't let her indeed! Miss Martha Mary had only to say, 'You're not to go into the kitchen, Peg,' and the girl would have remained where she was in a clean atmosphere and having her due, a well-earned rest. If Miss Martha Mary wanted help what were her other two sisters doing? . . . He remembered the aunt. Yes, he supposed somebody must keep an eye on her. He also supposed that Miss Martha Mary had her work cut out all round, but God above! she annoyed him when she stared at him as she was doing now, not uttering a word, and that superior look on her face. He doubted if her expression would change if she were cleaning a midden.

He was still looking at her when, still without saying a word, she began turning the dough again. Giving it one last flop, she picked up the heavy brown earthenware dish, carried it to the fender, then pulling a piece of sheeting from the brass rod that ran underneath the mantelpiece she placed it over the dish, dusted her hands one against the other, turned her sleeves down, then spoke. 'I wonder if you would be kind enough to have a look at Dilly's leg, doctor?'

'Dilly? Oh yes, Dilly.'

So that was why she was doing the baking. Well, it would initiate her into what real work was. Up till now he supposed her idea of it had been to give orders. God above! what was wrong with him? Why couldn't he give her credit for what she was doing? Why was he so set against her in his mind? Well, hadn't he cause? If she had been mistress of a manor or a mansion her attitude towards him couldn't have been more high-handed, now could it?

He noted as he followed her up the stairs that although her dress was full pleated at the back, and there was little doubt but that she had the usual four or five petticoats under it, her buttocks did not give a sway to the whole; she was likely as flat there as she was at the front, and she didn't seem to do anything about it by way of camouflage, as most young women of her age did.

They traversed the length of the landing, mounted a narrow flight of stairs, much steeper these, then entered the attic room where Dilly was sitting propped up in bed.

Whatever was wrong with Dilly hadn't affected her voice for she immediately cried, 'Now I told you, Miss Martha Mary, I didn't want the doctor; I'll be up out of this the morrow.'

'Hello, Dilly. Now, what's the trouble?'

''Tis nothin', doctor; me leg's swelled a bit.'

'They're both swollen.'

Dilly now turned and looked up at Martha and she nodded at her as she said, 'All right, they're both swelled, but they've both swelled afore, they've been swelled for years.'

'Let me have a look.'

He looked. He looked from the distorted legs, up the bloated body covered with a thick unbleached calico nightdress, to the deeply lined face, and he thought sadly of the number of women he had seen die thus. And Dilly wasn't far from her end, and the old girl knew it; perhaps a week or two, perhaps a month or two.'

He pulled the feather-filled coverlet up over her; then wagging his finger at her, he said, 'Miss Martha Mary'—that was a mouthful of a name, and it didn't suit her, it was too homely, too friendly—'Miss Martha Mary was quite right to make you stay in bed, but I think it would be better all round'—he now turned his gaze on Martha—'if she could be brought down to the ground floor, the study again.' He didn't smile but his face seemed to relax as he made the last statement. 'Could you manage that?'

'Yes, yes, I'll see to it.'

'Now, no, Miss Martha Mary, this's been me room since I first entered this house a wee lass and it'll be me room, I hope, till the end.'

'Now'—he was bending over her—'we're having no nonsense from you, Dilly. Your mistress says you are to come downstairs and come downstairs you will, understand?'

Dilly returned his look for a moment, then jerked her head to the side, saying, 'Lot of nonsense.'

'Well, it's all how you look at it. You've got to remain in bed for a little while and so you want everybody run off their legs up these two flights of stairs attending to you. Is that what you want?'

'I want nobody runnin' off their legs attendin' me, doctor. They never have and . . .'

'But now they will,' he ended for her. 'And I want to hear no more from you. Do as you're told, do you hear?' His face now did move into a smile and he doubled his fist and gently tapped her jaw with it, ending, 'Or else.'

He left the room, Martha following him, and they didn't speak until they reached the hall. There, he turned to her and said, 'I'm afraid she's in a bad way. She may last a few weeks, a few months at most.'

Her round eyes were stretching wide, and when he watched the stricken look cover her face he said, with an unusual feeling of sympathy, 'She's old, she's had her day. It's going to be very hard for you, she'll require nursing.'

She was shaking her head now, and there was a break in her voice as she replied, 'That doesn't matter, but . . . but Dilly, she's . . . she's been so good to us, all of us, and more, more like a friend to me.' When the tears rolled down her cheeks, she bowed her head, turned from him, saying, 'I'm sorry. I'm sorry.'

He was frankly amazed at her show of emotion. He gazed at her for a full minute before, taking her arm, he turned her about and led her into the drawing-room, and when she was seated he said, 'What is there to be sorry about in showing grief for a friend?'

He was surprised at himself now for the sudden feeling of sympathy he was experiencing towards her and he looked at her closely and without animosity for the first time. She had a pair of fine eyes. Up till now they had mostly spat fire at him, but at the moment they were soft with her tears. Her mouth was big and that didn't make for beauty in a woman, but nevertheless it didn't mar her face. All in all, given an easier life and one free from worry, she could have laid some claim to beauty; she had a splendid head of hair on her.

When she lifted her eyes to his he swallowed some spittle, then said abruptly, 'I understand you'll soon be needing a new manager for your bookshop?'

Her mouth remained open before she said in some surprise, 'How . . . I mean it was only yesterday?'

'Oh, Hexham's not a very big place, news gets around, I visit a lot of people. It was just something that I overheard. Your present manager is promoting himself to Cunningham's, isn't that so? But let me say immediately, to my mind Cunningham's is no promotion, not for a man who is interested in literature, for they deal mostly in the cheaper, popular type of books.'

'Yes, yes, they do.' She nodded at him, then blew her nose.

'Have you anyone in mind to replace him?'

'No, not as yet. I was going in today, but . . . well, Dilly was unable to come downstairs. But I was definitely going in tomorrow to the agency.'

'Well now'—he placed both his hands on his knees and tapped them—'I may be speaking out of place, I may be interfering with something that is none of my business, but I happen to know a man who is a real literary type; not young, oh no, I'm sorry to say; if you're looking for someone young and ambitious then this is not your man; but if you're looking for someone who knows books and loves books, and whose one joy is to be among books, then I think I could help you.'

'You could?'

'Yes.'

They stared at each other until she dropped her gaze, then said, 'Well, if this is possible . . . doctor'—she seemed to hesitate on his name—'I'd be very grateful. I was in quite a dilemma. I . . . I had hoped to put my sister Mildred into the shop to learn the business but . . . but. . . .' Her voice trailed away. She blinked, looked straight ahead for a moment, then said, 'There were circumstances that prevented me carrying out this intention.' She was now looking at him again as she continued, 'If as you say this is an old gentleman and I can be sure he's of good character, then it would solve two problems for me, the shop could continue to be open and my sister enter into employment.'

'Well then'—he nodded at her now—'that's settled, at least my part of it is. Now the man's name is Mr Samuel Armstrong; he lives about half a mile out from Hexham in the Dean Cottages. You know the little row of cottages on the roadside?'

'Yes, yes, I know the place.'

'He has not the means, I'm afraid, of coming out to see you but I'll be passing there on my way back; shall I tell him you will call and see him?'

'Oh, if you would, doctor, I'd be very grateful.'

They were both standing now. Her face was relaxed, her whole body was relaxed, she appeared to him like someone new, someone he had just met. He wondered why he had ever seen her in such a harsh unfeminine light. He was actually smiling at her and about to extend his hand for the first time towards her when her name being called at a high pitch from outside the house startled them both and brought them looking towards the drawing-room door.

'Martha Mary! Martha Mary!'

It was Mildred's voice coming from the hall and Martha ran to the drawing-room door, pulled it open and cried, 'What is it? What's wrong?'

Mildred came running across the hall now and almost threw herself into Martha's arms, sobbing, 'It's Nick; he's . . . he's killing the kittens, but . . . but not nicely. He's killing the kittens, Martha, it's awful, awful, against the wall. You said they were to be drowned, but he. . . .' She put her head down and shook it from side to side as she continued to sob.

Up till a moment ago Harry had forgotten about the stable lad and his intention of catching him out in his treatment of Fred, but now he was running from the house, across the courtyard towards the outbuildings.

A quick glance showed him that Nick wasn't in the barn. But Fred was sitting by Bessie. When the dog saw him it came running towards him, but with its tail between its legs as was usual when in this place. When it gave one sharp bark he said, 'Ssh! quiet!' and in the silence that followed he heard the piteous whimpering of kittens.

Running again, he went swiftly round the back of the barn and what he saw brought him to a halt for a second. There, strewn at the bottom of a low dry stone wall that bordered the yard, were the bashed bodies of four kittens and Nick Bailey was in the act of dashing the brains out of a fifth one, with two more squawking aloud while awaiting their destiny in the basket at his feet.

So totally engrossed was he in his bestial task that he was oblivious of Harry's approach until he was gripped by the collar and swung round with such force that his feet left the ground.

'Hie you! Le . . . let go o' me.'

For answer Harry dragged him struggling and punching out with his fists round the side of the barn, and as he threw him through the opening towards where Fred lay now crouched and growling, Martha came running across the yard.

On sight of her he checked her with a bawl. 'Stay where you are! Go back into the house.' He pointed, and when she stopped he turned and walked slowly now towards the trap. There he pulled the long horsewhip from its socket, and still slowly he advanced on Nick Bailey where he had retreated backwards towards the top corner of the barn.

'You don't do that, doctor; you take no horsewhip to me, or I'll fetch me da to you, an' our Fred an' Willie. They'll bash you they will. You don't take no whip to . . .'

Harry did not speak until he brought the whip across the cowering boy's shoulders, and then he cried, 'I'll give you one for each kitten, and then four more for the punctures in Fred's haunches, you cruel young bugger you!'

'Stop it! Stop it this moment! . . . *Doctor!*' When he felt his arm pulled downwards he swung round and almost thrust Martha on to her back;

then his arm dropping to his side, he stood panting deeply as he stared down at the crouching figure on the barn floor.

'Have you gone mad?'

Now his head jerked in her direction and he hissed at her, 'Yes, but not mad enough.'

'I . . . I told him to destroy the kittens, there were too many of them.'

'Did you tell him to bash their brains out one at a time against the wall? Kittens are usually drowned. That thing there took pleasure in killing each one slowly, like he took pleasure in stabbing my dog with a nail or something.'

In a blind fury of temper he stalked down the barn to where a number of implements were stacked in a corner and there, throwing them one after the other aside, he clutched at the last one, crying, 'Aye yes, this is it.'

It was a stick with a double pointed nail thrust in the bottom, like the goads used by the drovers when driving the cattle to market. He marched towards her again and thrust the implement in front of her face, saying, 'That . . . that is what he used on that animal there'—he pointed backwards towards Fred—'on every visit I've made to this house. The dog's no fighter. I wish to God he was and had worried him to death.'

Martha looked from him to where Nick Bailey was standing now rubbing his hand across his back and, her voice trembling, she asked him, 'Did . . . did you injure the dog? Tell me the truth.'

'No, never did, miss; never did nowt to the dog. An' you told me get rid of kittens. Didn't say how. 'Tis best to knock their brains out; me da knocks their brains out, easier than drownin'.'

'Easier than drowning!' It was a growl, and it looked as if Harry might spring forward and use the whip again, but what he did was throw the whip on to the seat of the trap; then stooping, he examined Fred's rump and there, quite plainly visible was a fresh hole with fresh blood running from it.

His head back, he looked at her and said, 'Would you deign to stoop and examine this?'

Slowly Martha moved forward and, bending down, she looked at the wound. Then she picked up the goad from where Harry had thrown it and she examined that too, and there, sure enough, was a thin trace of blood on its spike.

She stood still and upright, and the scene in the barn disappeared. She felt she was alone on a great plain; it could have been on one of the moors across the river and she was looking upwards and asking God why, why He was placing on her shoulders one misfortune after another: Dilly ill and dying: Peg practically useless, and would be for some time yet: Aunt

Sophie at her worst: and now she would have to get rid of the little help she had outside for Nick Bailey must go. She could not keep him on after this. Perhaps she could have overlooked the kittens. Oh, that was terrible, but to stab the dog with the goad each time he had been put into his care. No, he would have to go, there was something wrong with the boy. At the back of her mind she had always known it, but what made it worse at this moment was that it had to be pointed out to her by this doctor, by this man. Oh, how she disliked him. Yet only a short while ago she had been feeling she was glimpsing a different side to him when he had solved one pressing problem for her. But now she wished, oh she wished from the bottom of her heart that she owed her gratitude to anyone but him, for at bottom he was uncouth; he acted with no more restraint than would any common working man. She watched him thrust the dog on to the seat of the trap, then mount and drive out of the barn.

After turning the horse's head in the direction of the house he drew it to a momentary halt and called across to where she was standing in the opening of the barn, 'I'll leave you to do what you think best with that individual; only remember his pastime may not stop at animals.'

As he drove past the front of the house he cast a glance to where Mildred stood cradling a cat in her arms at the top of the end set of steps. She was still crying and was rocking the cat like one might a child.

What a household! He put Bessie into a trot down the drive, then allowed her to take her time along the rutted lane; but once they were on the main road he again trotted her briskly until they reached the rise that overlooked the curve in the river.

The hillside that sloped down to the river was bare of trees for some distance, the earth being strewn with scree and small boulders, and a number of these had been rolled into the river where the water ran shallow to form stepping-stones, and it was in the distance across these stepping-stones that he noticed the approach of two figures, a young man and a young woman.

The incline of the hill was gradual and it wasn't until he had reached the top and was descending the other side that his attention was again drawn to the couple now almost below him. The young woman had her hands on the young man's lapels, she was gazing up at him. He saw the young man now take hold of her hands and draw her towards a clump of trees, then gather her into his arms and kiss her. But it was a brief embrace; and now he was walking away back to the stepping-stones, and the girl stood watching him. But he did not turn and wave.

When the young woman turned round he saw that she had her knuckles pressed against her mouth. Her head was not bowed, but lying back on her shoulders, and he recognized her, and she him. She stared upwards for a long moment, then she was running, and before the trap had reached the flat stretch of road at the far side of the hill she had mounted the bank and was waiting for him.

He drew Bessie to a halt and looked down at Nancy, where she was now standing gripping the iron rail that edged the seat, and he said quite politely, 'Good-afternoon, Miss Crawford.' But she did not return the greeting. What she said was, 'Oh, doctor!'

'Yes, what is it?'

'Please, please, don't say anything to Martha Mary, I mean you—' she jerked her head towards the river—'you may have seen my meeting with a . . . a'—her head now wagged twice before she ended, 'gentleman.'

There was a short silence, but he said, 'Yes, I noticed you had a companion.'

'Please'—her two hands were gripping the rail now—'don't tell Martha Mary, she'd . . . she'd be so upset.'

'Then why do you do things that you know will upset her?'

'Because . . . well—' She now bowed her head, then murmured, 'She would say . . . it was all foolishness and . . . and nothing could come of it, but there will.' Her head was up. 'What I mean, something will come of it. You see, doctor.' Again she paused; then straining her face up to him she whispered, 'Could I confide in you? Please.'

'Do you think that wise?'

'Yes, yes, I do. I feel sure you would never give me away.'

They stared at each other before he said, 'Well, what do you wish to tell me?'

She swallowed deeply, blinked and cast a swift glance to where Bessie was chafing at her bit before she murmured, 'The young man you saw is William, William Brockdean, Sir Rupert's son.'

'Oh!'

His whole face stretched as he thought, more trouble in the camp. The girl was surely right in not wishing her sister to get wind of this. What did she expect of such an association for she had as much chance of marrying into the Brockdean family as he had. . . . Less, he should say. It was common knowledge that Sir Rupert needed money, and badly; in fact, in their way they were as hard up as this girl's folks.

He looked down into Nancy's pretty face, so young, so full of life and the expectation of what she thought life could offer through love. He did not imagine her to be mercenary.

His expression didn't alter when she whispered, 'We are to be married as soon as he comes of age.'

'Really!'

'Yes. We have been secretly engaged for some time but'—she put her head on one side—'it's so difficult to meet. It was different when we had the two horses but since Martha Mary got rid of Gip there's only Belle for the trap, and I can't always have her. It's difficult.'

'Yes, yes, I can see it is difficult.' He bent towards her now and asked quietly, 'Does anyone else know of your association . . . your other sister for instance?'

'Mildred? Oh, no. She would be mad at me, much more than Martha Mary, because . . . well'—she bit on her lip—'she's been angling for an invitation to their ball these last two years, and she would consider me very underhand if she knew of my association with William.'

'Do you know something, Miss Nancy?'

'What, doctor?'

'I think that you should confide in one of your sisters at least.'

'Oh no!' She stepped back from the trap. 'I couldn't, not . . . not until everything is final.'

'I think you are making a mistake.'

She bit on her lip again, then said, 'Perhaps you are right, but in any case I must wait until the Easter holidays when William returns. He . . . he's only home for a short visit; his sister is sick. . . . Then at Easter perhaps. But . . . but I'm . . . I'm really afraid of what Martha Mary might do, and . . . and if anything happened to separate us, oh, doctor, I think I should die.'

His voice had a stiffness to it now as he said, 'We don't die so easily, Miss Nancy. You're very young and should you be disappointed in this case it won't be the end of the world. There are other men on this planet you know.'

She stared at him, then asked quietly, 'You think me wicked?'

Now he laughed for the first time in days. His head went back and the sound he made was so loud that there was an echo to it. Then looking at her again, he said with mock sternness, 'Very wicked; like all youth in the world, very, very, wicked.'

She was smiling up at him now, saying, 'Oh, doctor, I feel better you knowing.'

'Well then'—he gathered up the reins—'think over what I've advised, eh?'

She nodded at him, her teeth again nipping at her lip.

'Good-bye, Miss Nancy.'

'Good-bye, doctor.'

Once again he put Bessie into a trot. That family! The things that happened to them. They all seemed touched by tragedy of some kind; they all seemed destined to suffer, even the one who loved cats, and who was the least attractive of the three. But what an explosion there would be, especially in the Brockdean household should young William dare to go against his father. Yet he couldn't see him doing that, no, not at all. He had spoken to the young man but twice, and had found him of a pleasant disposition but not one of strong will and determination, he would say. Poor child. Yet as he had told her there were other men on this planet. . . . But would they ever make their way to The Habitation?

In his mind's eye he could see the three of them growing old together; he had seen it happen so often, and whether there were two, three, or four women in a household there was always one stronger than the rest who managed the finances and in general ruled the roost, like Miss Martha Mary back there.

Why did he always sneer when thinking of her name? Because it was such a silly name he supposed; it should be either Martha or Mary. It was putting too much of a strain on any personality to expect her to live up to the two females in the parable, yet when he thought about it in some way she managed it. Yes, she managed it . . . Martha Mary. Huh!

PART THREE

Nancy

1

'I've told you, our Martha Mary, I don't want to go, I won't go! I'll be classed as a shop assistant. It's outrageous.'

'And I've told you, Mildred; you have a choice, it's either that or taking on Peg's duties of kitchen help, plus the whole of the housework and being classed as a scullery maid-cum-general factotum, or on the other hand doing Dilly's work together with Nick Bailey's as I am doing to the best of my ability, not forgetting attending on Aunt Sophie and Dilly also. But as you have already refused to attempt any of these services there is nothing for it but you must serve in the shop. . . .'

'And travel by carrier's cart each day? It's degrading.'

'Martha Mary.' Nancy was holding Martha's arm now and looking at her appealingly. 'Let me go; I'm quite willing and I'd enjoy it. As I said, I'd like serving in the shop.'

'No, Nancy. Once and for all, no. We've been over all this every day during the past week. Now I've arranged it all and so it stands.'

'I'll write to Roland and tell him, I will.'

Martha now turned on Mildred and she actually shouted at her as she said, 'Do just that! Do that! Write to Roland, and when you are busy tell him that he will have to return from college because you are not going to help support him there. Tell him that not only do you not like being classed as a shop assistant but the fact that you are not receiving a wage has annoyed you considerably. Tell him that Mr Paine is having great difficulty in selling the chandler's and that our debts are mounting, tell him all that. . . . Yes, you've got a good right to bow your head, Mildred. And there's something more that I will tell you, you've always resented our secluded life here, haven't you? Nothing ever happens, has been your favourite phrase for years. Well, now you are going out into the wide world and you can tell yourself, if only by way of consolation, that you will meet different people each day, and who knows but that a rich gentleman may one day come into the shop and whisk you off your feet and set you up as a lady in a manor house. . . .'

Mildred's head was up now. No longer abashed, she cried back at Martha, 'Well! there's one thing certain, that'll never happen to you.'

As the words pierced her like a barb with what she knew to be their truth, Martha, after returning Mildred's angry glare, turned slowly about;

and she felt no comfort when she heard Nancy defending her, crying now at Mildred, 'Oh, our Mildred! Your tongue. Fancy saying a thing like that. You should be thankful that Martha Mary has never wanted to get married. Just imagine what would have happened to us if she had. Oh, you are a cruel individual, Mildred Crawford. The only thing you think about is yourself . . . and cats.'

'And the only thing you think about is horses, horses, horses.'

'I don't; I think about other people too. You're selfish, selfish. . . .'

As their bickering became personal Martha left the landing and went into her room and after closing the door behind her stood leaning against it for a moment. As she had done so often of late she wanted to burst into tears and not just quiet crying but to open her mouth wide and scream.

She went and sat down on the dressing-table stool and, leaning forward, peered at herself in the mirror. Slowly she moved her index finger over the cheek-bones, then around her mouth. She was getting thinner, the flesh seemed to be dropping off her. She now put both hands tentatively, one under each breast. As short a time as a year ago she had a fullness there, now it had disappeared. Yesterday, when *he* called. . . . Why did she always call him *he*? Because she thought of him as he. Anyway, he had left her a tonic and told her that it would help to make her eat. His manner had been more kindly than usual, but she could not say that hers had matched his own for her mind still retained the picture of him with the horsewhip in his hand. Of course, he had been justified to some extent but nevertheless he had appeared ferocious. Altogether he was a strange man. She had never met anyone like him before. But then—she looked deep into the reflection in the mirror—how many men had she met before? She was ignorant of men and their ways. Peg had again proved it to her yesterday when she had confided, in between her scurryings about the kitchen, that she was glad Nick Bailey had gone for 'You know what, Miss Martha Mary?' she had said. 'He tried to give me a bairn. An' not once mind. He tripped me up in the barn, he did, not long ago but I was too quick for him. I took the hayfork to him and I told him what I'd do with it if he went for me again.'

Things had been happening under her nose, things appertaining to life, and she hadn't seen them, she hadn't noticed. She had been happy in playing the mother without knowing in the slightest degree the fundamental meaning of the word.

And Nancy and Mildred, did they know anything more than she did? No, no, she was certain they did not.

. . . There are two kinds of human beings, males and females. She heard his voice and saw herself standing looking down on Aunt Sophie. Her private parts exposed between the slit in the drawers looked disgusting, yet time and time again she had bathed her. But then it had been done discreetly so as not to embarrass her . . . so as not to embarrass them both.

. . . There are two kinds of human beings.

Now she was looking down at her father as Dilly pulled his linings from off his legs, and the sight was obscenely ugly.

She dropped her face on to her hands and pressed her fingers tight over her eyeballs. If she had married Lawrence Ducat. . . . She would never have married Lawrence Ducat. . . . But she might have, in desperation she just might have.

'No, no; I never would have married him.' Her head was up again and she was facing her reflection, talking to it openly. Her voice a whisper, she said, 'I would have had the sense to see through him surely. Of course, I would. Given enough of his company I would have seen the kind of man he was.'

She was nodding at herself now. 'That's it, given enough of his company. But would I have had enough of it before I was married?' She wagged her head slowly now and watched the other head moving in derision. She stopped talking to herself but her mind cried at her, 'Own up to it, you would have clutched at the chance, any chance to be married.'

And now as Mildred had truly said, there'd be no gentlemen, or otherwise, who would come riding and whisk her off to a manor house. Would any of them ever be whisked off to any house? Nancy perhaps. . . . That reminded her yet again, she must talk to Nancy. But how could she begin? Could she say, you must not speak to William Brockdean should you meet? On the occasions she used to go riding doubtless they met and exchanged harmless pleasantries, and were she to bring the matter up she would be insinuating there was a deeper meaning to their acquaintance. And after all Nancy was too sensible even to think of such a thing. Now if it had been Mildred. . . .

Her head drooped. She was tired; if she didn't feel so tired all the time, and there was a little more money, she could put up with everything. She sighed, straightened her back and rose from the chair. Tired or not, there was Aunt Sophie to see to, and Dilly. . . .

Poor Dilly. When she went the house would never be the same again, and she would take so much knowledge with her. She had instructed her how to make the bread but it hadn't turned out anything like her own. Peg would have made a better attempt at it if her hands had been all right. She must go down to her now and ask her how to prepare a rabbit pie; a hawker had called today and she had bought two rabbits from him, cheap.

She went from the room and as she crossed the landing she heard Aunt Sophie singing softly to herself, and somehow this saddened her more than if she had heard her screaming in one of her turns. . . . Fits, he had called them, and she supposed he was right, they were fits, but she would never name them such when in his presence for he was a man who had always to be right. She wished she could stop thinking about him, or if not, think about him in a pleasant way. But how could one think pleasantly about a most unpleasant man? As she reached the hall she paused for a moment. She seemed to be the only one who found him unpleasant, for Dilly liked him, and Peg and Nancy too.

In the study she stood by Dilly where she was propped up on the horsehair sofa and as she straightened the covers she said, 'The rabbits I told you about, how shall I do them?'

'Well, lass, the easiest thing for you to do would be to stew them and pop some dumplings in. Sit off your feet for a minute and I'll tell you what to do. He skinned them for you, you said?'

'Yes.'

'Well then, all you've got to do is split them down the middle and take the insides out. Peg'll point out what you throw away and what you keep. Then just chop the limbs off an' put them into the pan with an onion, a carrot an' a couple of handfuls of barley and a good sprinkling of herbs. As for dumplings, you've seen me do them. They're just flour an' water an' suet, as soft as your bread dough, you know. . . . What is it, lass, you're looking worried?'

'I'm all right, Dilly.' She took the old woman's hand.

'It's no use tellin' me you're all right, for one thing you're worked off your feet and for another I suppose it's Miss Mildred kicking up about the morrow?'

'Yes, she's not taken to the idea at all.'

'Miss Mildred'll never take to any idea unless it's a soft one.' She now put her hand over Martha's and pressed it between her palms while looking up into her face, and she said brokenly 'I don't want to leave you, lass, it's at the worst time. I'd sell me soul to the devil if he'd give me another year or so to help you along.'

Martha stared wide-eyed down into the wrinkled face as a surge of terrifying emotion filled her. It rushed upwards through her stomach, her breast, and into her throat which was too narrow to hold it and threatened to choke her. When it broke free it poured anguish from every outlet of her body. Her head on Dilly's breast and Dilly's arms about her, all restraint, all control gone, her sobs rose and the sound was like that of a woman in anguish. Dilly, her own face awash, cradled her and talked, 'There, there; there, there, me bairn, get it over, get it over. It isn't fair;

there's no fairness in this world at all, it's the case of the willin' donkey. It's always the same, the more willin' you are the more you're put on. But don't you worry, me lass, your day will come, if there's any justice your day will come.'

The noise subsided; she spluttered and coughed a number of times, and then there was silence; and after a time she pulled herself up, saying, 'Oh, Dilly. Oh . . . oh, I'm sorry.'

Her breath was still coming in gasps, her face still awash, her head wagging from side to side as if on a spring. 'I . . . I shouldn't have given way, I shouldn't, but oh, Dilly, I need you. There's no one but you I can turn to. What will I do without you? What will we all do without you? And you've never had any recompense for all the work you've done. Four shillings a week is the most you've ever had. It's scandalous, scandalous. I've thought about it a lot. . . . I . . .'

'There, there, give over now and listen to me. Now give over, an' listen I say, 'cos I want to say something serious. As you say, four shillings a week I've had, but I've had it regular for the last forty years; three shillings afore that, two afore that, and a shilling a week when I started like young Peg has now. But I've never been one to spend much. The mistress bought me me frocks, a new one every year, an' she gave me her petticoats. All I've ever bought in me life was a couple of bonnets an' me boots, an' so, as I say, listen to me, me dear.' She was gripping Martha's hands now. 'There's a tidy sum I'm leavin' an' I'm leavin' it to you; it's all arranged. I told himself, that is the doctor, I told him yesterday. An' I asked him would I have to sign anything an' he said yes, it would be better that way, an' so he wrote it down an' I put me cross to it, an' it's all yours, an' it's in me tin box under the bed up there.'

As Dilly thumbed towards the ceiling, the surge of emotion once again tore through Martha. It was too much. Her voice was a loud cry. 'Oh Dilly, Dilly. Oh Dilly.' Again she buried her head on Dilly's breast, and again she was sobbing unrestrainedly.

When the door was thrust open and Mildred and Nancy came rushing up the room, Dilly's raised hand checked them and they stood looking at the unusual sight and sound of Martha Mary crying, and crying in such an unrestrained way.

Dilly's voice now brought their eyes from Martha to herself as she said curtly, 'Go into the kitchen, both of you, an' ask Peg to show you how to cut up the rabbits. Tell her it's for a stew. Go on now.'

They both hesitated, Mildred evidently about to bristle, but on this occasion thinking better of it she turned abruptly and went out of the room and Nancy, after staring at Martha who was showing such unusual distress, bowed her head, bit tight on her lip and, turning, followed Mildred.

In the hall they looked at each other, and the tears now raining down Nancy's own face, she bent forward and whispered fiercely, 'You see . . . you see what you've done.'

'Me? Now don't you dare blame me . . .'

'Yes, I will blame you. You were the last straw, and . . . and you're a fool. You . . . you don't appreciate what a chance you're getting. Oh . . . !'

Mildred now watched Nancy running towards the kitchen and she stood for a moment, her lips pressed tightly together as she considered her last words. . . . Perhaps it was a chance, she would be going out into the world, she'd meet people; and Martha Mary's gibe might not be so far out either. If only she hadn't to suffer the indignity of riding on the carrier's cart. That was too much, most undignified. She now cast her glance back towards the drawing-room door as she thought, And that scene in there too was undignified, Martha Mary giving way like that, howling her eyes out in the arms of Dilly as Peg or any of her like might have done. She recalled Miss Simpson's words when teaching deportment in the private school, 'A lady never shows her emotions in public, we leave that to the common people.'

She walked slowly towards the kitchen now. In a way there were lots of things about Martha Mary that were common; she raised her voice, she showed her temper, and she had no idea of keeping servants in their rightful place. Now if she had been the eldest. . . .

2

It was the end of March and the wind was still sheathed in ice; it raged round the house and penetrated the warped window frames, the doors and the chimneys; particularly the chimneys, for it whirled down the drawing-room one and blew the smoke all over Mr Paine and made him cough. And Harry, too, coughed for he was sitting straight opposite the fireplace. Roland who was sitting to the left of him did not cough but turned his head away while the three girls to the right of him bowed their heads and made small noises in their throats.

Mr Paine's bout of coughing over, he now cast his glance about them all as he said, 'It would appear that I never visit you except on sad occasions, yet I am very pleased to say there's a little brightness attached to this particular one. The deceased, Miss Lilian Thompson, who worked as a servant in this house from when she was a young girl did not forget the kindnesses shown to her, particularly by you Miss Martha.'

Martha looked straight back through the pale grey atmosphere at Mr. Paine. She knew what was coming and she felt a deep embarrassment, but it was not untouched with excitement. Dear Dilly had left her her savings, and no matter how small they might be they would be the means of alleviating the financial stress which at present was more than ever weighing on the house.

'Miss Thompson confided her wishes on this matter to Doctor Fuller'—Mr Paine inclined his head towards Harry—'and the doctor, after writing down her wishes, brought the document to me, because he was not sure of its legality as she was unfortunately only able to make her mark with a cross. I was able to point out that this being so a witness would be needed and as, you may remember, I happened to be passing this way when the doctor was calling, together we made the document legal.' He now exchanged a penetrating look with Harry before saying, 'Isn't that so, doctor?'

'Yes, Mr Paine.'

'Well, now, there are no complications in this will, so I shall read what it says.' He now lifted up the sheet of ordinary paper and read:

I, Lily Thompson, who am in my right mind and, having no relatives of my own left upon this earth, leave my life savings, which are in a tin box under my bed, to Martha Mary Crawford, who I helped bring into the world, and who has been like my own since, and who is now lovingly seeing me out of it.

Two wishes I will make: first, that she spend most of the money on herself, and second, that she give to Peg Thornycroft ten pounds.

Signed this fourth day of February, 1880.

Martha's chin was now on her chest and all she could think was, Oh Dilly, Dilly. And there returned to her the feeling she'd experienced as she washed and dressed Dilly for the last time that she had lost the only friend she had on earth. No one had understood her as Dilly had. She had never been demonstrative, her tongue had been sharp at times but always Martha knew that Dilly had liked her . . . loved her, were the words she should use. And she had loved Dilly. But she hadn't shown it, not until that night when she had cried her heart out in her arms.

Tears were choking her again. There was a silence all about her and in it her sensitivity picked up a feeling of hostility. She raised her head and looked from one to the other. Oh, she wished Dilly had spread her savings and had left the others something, particularly Roland and Mildred. But they would get the benefit of it in the long run because she would spend it on the house. . . . Yet it wasn't the same and their expressions endorsed this.

'Well, we'd better open the trunk.' Mr Paine was now inserting a key into the padlock of the red tin trunk that the doctor had lifted on to the table at his side. The key made a grating sound. He lifted the lid, stared downwards for a moment, then looked about him before putting his hand into the trunk and lifting out one small calico bag after another.

When the last bag was on the table he passed his hands around the inside of the trunk, saying, 'I think that is all. What is left in here now appears to be a few personal garments.' Then looking at Harry, he asked, 'Would you help me, doctor?'

Harry, getting to his feet, went to the table and together they undid the strings that tied the small hand-sewn bags. One after the other they turned out their contents until there was lying on the table a goodly pile of sovereigns and half-sovereigns, and such was its size that it amazed all those present, even Harry, but mostly it amazed Martha.

When she finally heard Mr Paine saying, 'Two hundred and twenty-three pounds. Would you check again, doctor' all her mind seemed capable of saying was, Oh, Dilly, Dilly.

'Yes, two hundred and twenty-three pounds, Mr Paine.'

They both now turned and looked at Martha, but she couldn't see them; it was quite impossible to prevent her tears from flowing. She heard

Mr Paine's voice saying, 'A tidy sum . . . indeed a tidy sum. I'm happy for you, Miss Martha Mary.'

She should have said, 'Thank you,' but she couldn't speak. She heard the door opening and Peg's voice saying, 'Tea's all ready, Miss Martha Ma . . .'

Peg's voice trailed away as she realized she had come in at the wrong time, but the doctor was speaking to her, 'Come here a minute, Peg,' he said.

Martha hastily wiped her eyes and saw Peg tentatively approaching the company. She saw the doctor stooping down to her and then pointing to herself, saying, 'I think your mistress has something to tell you.'

She watched him press Peg towards her, and when the slight form was standing in front of her she put out her hands and took hold of the two scarred ones and, her voice breaking, she said, 'Dilly . . . Dilly left you some money, Peg, ten pounds.'

'What!' The single word crescendoed at the end, then she glanced round at those present before looking back at Martha and saying, 'Me? She left me ten pounds? Dilly! Why, 'tis a fortune. Eeh! I never thought to see the day. An' she always went for me.' She had turned her head and was nodding up at Harry now. 'But I never took no notice, 'cos I knew how she meant it, her bark was worse'n her bite. But ten pounds.'

Her mouth was in a gape when Mr Paine said, 'Would you like to give it to her now, Miss Crawford?'

'Yes, oh yes.' She rose to her feet and went to the table and counted out, not ten sovereigns, but fifteen, and she placed them in one of the linen bags that Dilly had so carefully sewn and, smiling softly, she handed it to the small girl.

'Eeh! Miss Martha Mary, eeh! that I'd live to see the day. Thanks, ta, to think that Dilly would remember me. An' you to stick another five in. You had no call to do that, you give me enough, an' the way things look you want every pen . . . ny.' Her voice trailed away under the sea of eyes looking at her.

Martha closed her eyes for a moment. There was too much emotion filling the room, she would break down completely if she didn't curb it. Putting her hand on Peg's shoulder now, she pressed her in the direction of the door, while at the same time saying, 'Would you please come into the dining-room?'

As she walked ahead they filed out of the room after her, Mildred, Nancy, Roland, Mr Paine, and lastly Harry, and as he passed the table strewn with the shining sovereigns he thought that it certainly was one of the quirks of life that a servant could leave the daughter of the house what was equivalent, as Peg had said, to a small fortune, while its master

had left her nothing but debts. She would, he supposed, use it to help ease
the burden on the house, and in so doing it might help to take the strain
from her shoulders . . . and her face.

It was two hours later. The guests had gone, and the family was back in
the drawing-room.

The money had been removed from the table but not from their minds,
and Roland spoke briefly of what was in his, and not without bitterness.

Standing with his back to the fire and taking up most of the heat, he
said, 'She mustn't have had much use for the rest of us.'

Martha turned her head slowly and looked up at his averted face. 'She
knew I would use it for all our good,' she said.

'That isn't the point.' He was now glaring down on her, 'She could
leave Peg ten pounds, why couldn't she leave us a similar sum just to
show she had no animosity towards us?'

'Dilly held no animosity towards anyone.'

'On the face of it I don't agree with you, but what she certainly had
was favourites.'

'I spent more time with Dilly than any of you.'

He did not take up her remark but said, 'She indicated you were special
because she brought you into the world; she brought us all into the world
for that matter.'

'Roland's right, I think it was spiteful. It wouldn't have mattered so
much if she had left you the bulk as long as she had remembered us in
some small way. What do you say, Nancy?' Mildred now turned to Nancy
who, seeming at this moment to have to collect her thoughts, replied, 'Oh,
well, it doesn't matter; as Martha Mary says, she'll use it for all our good.'

'What will you use it for?'

Roland held Martha's gaze as she paused for a moment before answering, 'I haven't quite decided yet.' She turned her eyes away and looked
down the long room towards the window and the grey day merging into
fast approaching twilight. That wasn't true, she knew what she was going
to do with the money, yet at the same time she asked herself why. Why
had she thought straightaway of using it to send Roland to the university?
Why not use it in an effort to alleviate the pressure of the debts? Or on
herself as Dilly had wished? Why was it she didn't want Roland at home?
Was it that she was afraid he would take her status from her, and he
would have the first say in everything? Didn't she want to get rid of the
burden of responsibility? Or was it because he was so akin to Mildred
that, at bottom, she didn't really like him? *Oh no, no.* What was the matter with her that she could think this way? The reason she was doing it

was in order that with a university education he would have the qualifications to take up a profession.

She left the matter here and said quietly, 'I do know how I'm going to use it. If you're still so inclined Roland, it will help to keep you at the university, at least for a year or so.'

They all remained still until Roland spoke. 'Martha Mary!' His body was slowly bending towards her, his hands were extended, and as she looked up into his face she saw it as an exact replica of her father's when he was pleased; and he was pleased, delighted.

'Oh, that is kind of you, generous. But . . . but I can't really accept it.'

It was her father speaking, all his charm evident. 'The money was left to you . . . no, no . . . but I'll always remember the gesture. Yes, yes, always. No matter what happens, Martha Mary, I'll always remember you made this generous offer to me.'

A surprising irritation not unmingled with regret for her generous action brought her to her feet and for a moment she was tempted to say, 'All right, I'll pay off some of the debts, and I'll buy a new gown, and I'll do a thousand and one other things I've always wanted to do.'

She went hastily from the room and left them all silent. No word followed her. But as she mounted the stairs she heard his voice, the doctor's, saying to her, as she thanked him and bade him good-bye, 'I don't know on whom or on what you're going to squander your fortune, but if you were to ask my advice, which I am sure you wouldn't, I'd say make a big effort to start with yourself.'

And why hadn't she? Why hadn't she? She had been mad to make that offer to Roland. Here she was, maid of all work, even reduced to mucking out the stables. She could have an outside boy; she could have a new gown and bonnet. . . . No, a hat with a feather on it, a brightly coloured feather lying around the brim, a hat that would make people notice her as she walked through Hexham, and when she ran into him, he would be startled by her changed appearance. . . .

Shut up! Shut up! You are going mad. You are.

3

The sun had been shining all morning, but the wind was very high and the air still bitingly cold. Nancy hugged her cloak about her as she walked from the house towards the meadow that bordered the river. It was a great effort not to run, but she had just said to Martha Mary if she couldn't ride Belle then she must take walks.

She had answered Martha Mary with unusual sharpness today and she was sorry, but she couldn't help it, and she would apologize to her when she returned because then she'd be feeling better. Oh, she hoped she'd be feeling better because today he'd surely be there; if not, she would surely find a note in the hiding place.

He had been home for a week now, a full week and they hadn't met. It had never happened before, and he wasn't indisposed because he had been riding in the town. Mildred had been so full of her news yesterday, telling how he had accompanied his mother and sister and a guest into the shop, and how she helped them to choose books. She had talked of nothing else the whole evening, not so much about William, or his sister or their guest, but about Lady Brockdean herself, because her ladyship, she said, had spoken to her for quite a while and asked her opinion on current literature, and had thanked her so warmly for her services.

Mildred had been in high fettle all evening, she had even been gay and had made Roland laugh as she imitated some of the customers who came into the shop. Over night she seemed to have been turned into a different being, all because Lady Brockdean had paid her a little attention. Well, hadn't she herself been turned into a different creature because William had paid her a little attention? More than a little attention. . . . Oh, William. William.

Her step quickened as she walked along the river bank, but she still did not run until she had crossed the stepping-stones and mounted the far bank. It was hateful of her, she knew, but she suspected that Martha Mary might have taken it upon herself to go up into the attic from where she would have a view of the river bank almost to the stepping-stones. Martha Mary had been acting oddly of late.

Once into the wood, however, she picked up her skirts and ran along the well-known path. She ran until the trees thinned out where the ground became steeper. She was panting hard when she reached the top of the rise, and when the wind caught her cloak and billowed it out she turned her back on it and looked about her for a moment. She nearly always stopped at this spot, not only to regain her breath but because the view all around was so beautiful.

She looked back over the way she had come and she could see over the tops of most of the trees. The river was hidden from her, but there, away to the left of her and looking as if it had sunk into the ground, was the house. It was only when viewing it from this point that she realized how low down it lay in the valley.

She now faced the wind again. In the far distance the hills rose. There was no snow on top of them now. They appeared to her to be floating in the clear air; as did the homesteads dotted here and there. She couldn't see Corbridge or Hexham, nor if she turned to her right any part of Prudhoe. All she could see was a clear sky, the racing clouds, and what she would find in ten minutes' time . . . who she would find in ten minutes' time.

She scampered now over the open land, her skirts held well above her ankles, her hood lying back from her head and the tendrils of her hair flying loose from the ribbon that bound it.

She thought on a laugh, as she had done often before, that she wished she could join in the hill races for she would beat them all. It was only the wind that could beat her when she was running at her best.

And she was running at her best today, leaping over small boulders, skirting large ones, bounding over rutted holes until she came to the point where her running always stopped. It was a small copse of trees, but unlike the other groups of trees hereabouts it stood within what appeared at first sight to be a circular crumbling wall, closer inspection of which showed that it was not man-made but made up of outcrops of rock. Inside, the trees were so sparse she could see through them to where, beyond the farther side of the circle of rocks stood a dying oak, its bark scaling away, its lower branches so bleached of life that it looked naked.

She stopped dead for a moment, her mouth open to call as she looked through the freckled light at the outline of the man sitting with his back to the far side of the trunk. She had never before known William to sit like that; he would always be on the watch, and would come hurrying to meet her.

She forced herself to walk slowly through the trees, but even so her footsteps were audible as they crunched the dried leaves and undergrowth. When the figure on the ground made no move she screwed up her eyes against the light. Then her hand came up sharply and pressed against her mouth; she was staring at the man's boots. They weren't William's boots, highly polished and reaching almost to his knees, they were big ugly working men's boots.

She couldn't see the upper body or the face of their owner. She stood perfectly still now wondering if she could make her escape without disturbing him, but apparently not, for the figure sitting on the ground moved, and when the head was turned towards her she made to run, but in turning stumbled and only saved herself from falling.

The man was on his feet now, but with the light in her eyes she couldn't define whether he was really man or boy; then he moved away from the tree and came slowly towards her, but stopped within two yards distance of her.

'Hello,' he said.

Some seconds passed, during which the fear in her subsided and she managed to answer in the same vein. 'Hello,' she answered. 'It's very windy today.'

'Aye, yes it is. You taking a walk . . . ?'

'Yes.'

'Aye, I thought you were.'

What a strange young man, and he was a young man, and so odd looking. Well, not really odd; but his hair was unusually fair, and thick; and stranger still, he wore neither hat nor cap on it. And he should have worn a cap, being an ordinary working man by the sound of him. She noticed too that he had freckles right across the upper part of his face, and she was relieved to note that his mouth looked kindly.

As her fear of him subsided her impatience grew. Why didn't he go about his business? William was likely somewhere in the vicinity waiting for him to take his departure.

He now turned from her and went back towards the oak tree, and her face stretched in surprise when, his head to one side, he said over his shoulder, 'You're one of the lasses from The Habitation, aren't you?'

When she thought about it later it shouldn't have surprised her that anybody knew that she was 'one of the lasses from The Habitation', except that she had never seen the young man before.

'How do you know that?'

'Oh, I go past your place pretty often, me da and me. We're drovers, we cut across that way when bringing the sheep from the hills over yonder.' His head moved slowly back on his shoulders. 'I was past there yesterda'. 'Twas late on, mind, being market day in Hexham. You've never seen me afore, have you?'

'No, no, I haven't.' As she spoke she walked forward into the open and glanced about her. William would never show himself as long as this young man remained here. Oh, she wished he would go about his business.

'I've seen you many's the times.'

'You have?' She looked at him again. He was quite pleasant to look at, not very tall but thin and straight, and rather arresting because of his hair.

'It's funny you know, folks can live cheek by jowl most of their lives and never clap eyes one on t'other. Our place is not four miles as the crow flies from your house yet you've never caught sight of me.'

He was a strange young man, a very strange young man. 'No, no, I haven't.' Again she looked about her.

'Look, come on along o' me for a minute up to the rise an' I'll show you how near our place is to yours.'

'I'm . . . I'm sorry.' She half turned from him, about to go back through the copse, but his voice stopped her, not so much by what it said, but by its tone. It was soft, very quiet, it was as if he were talking to a sick or frightened person in an effort to soothe them. 'Now don't be afraid of me, I mean you no harm. No, never that. But you're out for a walk, so come on, walk along o' me up the rise. Come on—' he made a small motion with his hand—'you can keep your distance, only walk up the rise with me.'

Her head turned towards him, her eyes fixed on his, she found herself walking across the open land, then up the hill. It was a steep hill and she slipped once or twice, but he didn't put his hand out to save her falling. Then they were standing on the top. He didn't look at her now as he spoke but swept one arm wide as he exclaimed 'Did you ever see anything like it? A finer view? It's a bonny place this, wild at times, creepy like at others, but always bonny. Look, follow me finger. You see over there, like a thread of light? Well, that's the river scurrying itsel' towards Newcastle. Now take your eye to the side a bit, to the left side, you see that bump? Well, it's more than a bump, it's a goodly hill, and it's got some white specks on top of it. You see them? Well, that's our house, an' the shippens an' outbuildings.'

She looked at the white specks; then she looked at him, and he was saying now, 'It seems a long way off but it's only four miles as the crow flies from door to door, I should say. But our doors are different, 'cos the river'll never reach our door. Me great-granda was wise to the river an' all it can do so he built high on a hill-top.'

Her face was straight. For the moment she thought of Martha Mary and what her answer would be to that, for he was implying that their forbears had been stupid in building low down in the valley. But now he was compensating apparently for his tactlessness for he was going on.

'But mind, you've got one advantage and it's a big one, you're sheltered down there. Of course you've got to risk floodin', but that doesn't happen but now an' again, where us! Oh, Windy Nook isn't in it. We wonder many times how the house holds to the ground, but it does. Stone it's made of, stones from the Roman Wall; oh aye, as me da says, we live plumb in the middle of history.'

He was a strange young man, very strange.

'Well then, now you've seen our place, you'd better be gettin' back then, hadn't you?' He turned from her abruptly and began to descend the hill, and she followed at some distance.

He made no further comment until they were approaching the tree, when, looking at her, he said flatly, 'My name's Robson, Robert Robson, but I'm mostly known as Robbie. An' your name's Miss Nancy Crawford.' He nodded his head sideways at her. 'You see, I know what you're called. An' you've got one sister Martha an' another Mildred, an' you buried old Dilly Thompson not long ago. You see'—he was bending towards her, laughing now—'I know all about you.'

For a moment she now experienced an acute fear of him. Why was he talking like this? What was his intention? She had heard of young ladies being attacked on the highway, and not so long ago either; but then, of course, they had been in coaches, and it was mostly one or two desperate pitmen, on strike, who had been driven to robbery.

They were standing one each side of the tree now facing each other. She had the feeling that William was somewhere close at hand watching them, waiting impatiently for the intruder to take his departure. But now the young man dispelled this feeling for he was saying something that again brought her fingers to her lips. His eyes were turned from hers, his head slightly bent while he spoke, saying, 'There was a young gentleman here an hour or so ago, he left you something in the tree trunk.'

She could not close her mouth. This man, this person, had been spying on her, on them. She knew instinctively that this was not the first time he himself had viewed their meeting at this particular place, and likely he knew all about the previous letters that had been left in the hollow between the branches and which she had to stretch hard to reach into. And did he also know where she buried her letters? No. No. Oh no. She was burning with humiliation; her face was afire.

He was looking at her again, saying stiffly now, 'It's all right, 'tisn't what you're thinkin'. I wasn't spying, I've come to the rowan ring ever since I could walk this far. Me da brought me first 'cos the outcrops had power to heal warts. You spit on the wart, rub it on the outcrop three times, then walk away and don't look back and the wart goes, and it does. So, so you see you're not the only one who uses the place. That's what I'm tryin' to say. An' I just happened to see you and him, but I didn't spy. I'm no spyer; I've got enough in me head to keep me occupied without doin' a peepin' Tom, but I can say this, an' in truth, that I come here more often than either of you do.'

Her fingers were going through her hair now, and it seemed to bring home to her that she was without a head covering. Almost snatching at her hood, she pulled it forward; then taking her eyes from him she looked towards the tree.

He, too, turned and looked at the tree; then moving towards it he reached up, put his hand into the hollow and, turning towards her, held out the letter.

She looked at it. She wanted to snatch it away from the broken-nailed fingers, from the rough-looking hard-skin hand; but she made no move towards it.

'Here, take it.'

She took it, but did not look down at it but straight into his face, asking herself should she beg him not to mention what he knew of her meetings with William, for if he knew all about her and her family, then he certainly knew the name of the man she was meeting, for the Hall lay not two miles from where he said his home was.

As if reading her thoughts, he broke into them saying gruffly, 'You needn't be afeared of me an' what I might say; I mind me own business, and let others get on with theirs. We're like that, we Robsons; we're not scum. We never have been. Drovers aye; but that's only now; me granda was a farmer with his own acreage until they started the enclosure business, an' like many another he was wiped out. The big pots, they never have enough, they must grab. An' why do they grab? 'Cos they're afeared, that's why. An' why are they more afeared than we are? Why? 'Cos they've got more to lose. That's why. Anyway, that's another subject altogether; I just want you to know you can go back with an easy mind.'

The wind seemed to have fallen, died away altogether, so quiet was the space between them, and all around, and she broke into it, saying haltingly, 'Thank you. Thank you very much. You're . . . you're very understanding. Now I must say good day.' She swallowed, made a motion with her head, then again said, 'Good day,' and turned from him.

She had gone about half a dozen steps when he spoke again, not wishing her good day but saying, 'If ever you want any help, a service done, I'd be pleased to give it, very willin'.'

She half turned towards him, and as she looked at him she couldn't believe he was real. The whole scene appeared now as if she were dreaming it, his great mass of fair hair, his thin freckled face, his voice that of the common man yet the substance of his talk not common at all.

'Thank you.'

'You're welcome.'

She was walking away again, and when she had passed beyond the far boulders she did not run, nor did she open the letter that she still held in her hand. She didn't open it until she was nearing the wood that led down to the river.

Leaning, as if exhausted, against a tree trunk, she hastily split open the envelope and read:

'My dear Nancy,

I am so sorry I shall be unable to see you during my present visit home; circumstances are such that I must pay a visit abroad. Nor do I expect to be home for the summer term. Nevertheless, I shall be thinking of you. I must say that I shall always think of you no matter what happens, and I thank you from my heart for all the pleasure you have afforded me in the past. Please think of me kindly.

Ever your true friend,
William.'

Her mouth was agape again, the back of her head touching the trunk, her eyes gazing upwards into the branches, while her hands hung by her sides, the letter dripping from the fingers of one hand.

No! No! She couldn't believe it. She wouldn't believe it. She was no fool, she wasn't such a silly young girl that she didn't know that this was a dismissal, a polite good-bye. No, he couldn't do this. He mustn't do this. She must see him.

'Lady Brockdean's visitor is a young French lady.' She could hear Mildred's voice as she chattered away last night. 'She's not beautiful, but very smart. Oh, really elegant. Her suit was edged with fur, and she wore a fur hat, and she spoke English very well, but quaintly. They were all very merry, Miss Rosalind, William, and her.'

They were all very merry. They were all very merry. *They were all very merry.*

No! No! William, you mustn't do this. You promised. You promised, since you first kissed me when I was but fourteen. You always said one day we should marry.

She swung round and pressed her face tight against the bark of the tree while her arms encircled it, and she prayed, 'Oh, Lord, Lord, don't let it happen. I won't be able to live, I won't be able to bear it. Please Lord, there'll only ever be William. If I don't marry William I'll marry no one. . . . I'll be like Aunt Sophie. . . .'

As if the tree had spoken the last words she sprang back from it, then beat her fists against it, crying at it, 'No! no! I won't, I can't, I can't be like Aunt Sophie.' And she continued to batter her fists against the trunk until suddenly, all strength leaving her body, she slumped and slid down to the foot of the tree and, her face buried in her hands, she rocked herself while the tears flowed through her fingers. . . .

It was some time later, the spasm over, she was leaning sidewards against the trunk gasping when of a sudden she turned about and looked back over the way she had come. For a moment she had the idea that that young man was somewhere in the trees watching her. Although she could see no one, she dragged herself hastily to her feet and began to walk homewards.

She did not run but all along the way she cried, a slow quiet painful crying, the while telling herself that this wasn't the end, it couldn't be the end. She would write to him, write to him openly the minute she reached home, and she would catch the carrier cart on its return to Hexham, and the driver would post the letter for her; she would ask him to do it immediately he reached the town, and it would be delivered at the Hall tomorrow. In it she would ask him, beg him, to come and see her before he took his leave. And he must come. She must look on him again, touch his face, feel his arms about her, and when they were close he could not but help continue their association.

It was when she came in sight of the house that she stopped. If Martha Mary saw her in such distress she'd want an explanation. What could she tell her? The truth? Oh no. Yet she couldn't bear to suffer this alone. Yet she would be alone, she'd always be alone if William went out of her life, and she would pine, pine away and die. . . . Martha Mary would have to know.

But first she must write that letter and to do so she must get into the house without anyone seeing her. She would let herself in by the drawing-room window; she knew how to lift the latch from the outside. Martha Mary would be in the kitchen at this time of day; if not, she would be attending to Aunt Sophie. There were writing materials in the drawing-room; she would write the letter there, then slip out again. . . .

Nancy had been right about one thing. Martha had been watching her. She had watched both her departure and her return. She had seen her go round to the side of the house, and she had heard the window creak below.

She now held her head to the side listening for the drawing-room door to open and for the soft padding of footsteps on the stairs, because it was evident Nancy wanted to get to her room without being seen; but when she heard no such sounds she looked down towards the floor puzzled.

She went quickly out of the bedroom, across the landing and down the stairs, then walked softly towards the drawing-room door and paused a moment before opening it.

Nancy was seated at the escritoire. She didn't swing round in a startled fashion but she put both hands over the paper on the desk before turning her head slowly and looking down the room.

'What is it, dear?' Martha Mary was standing at her side bending over her, looking down on her bowed head. 'Tell me, come.' And she took her by the shoulders and turned her about. 'You can tell me. Anyway, I think I know.'

Nancy raised her face upwards. The tears were raining down her cheeks again and she stammered 'Ab . . . about William?'

'Yes, about William.'

'Oh! Martha Mary.' Her head was buried against Martha's waist now, and Martha's arms were about her holding her tight.

As Martha stroked the tousled brown hair she looked towards the window. How simple they all were, how trusting, even Mildred, for from her chatter last night she was still of the opinion that Lady Brockdean had an interest in her. When she realized that it was condescension, at best mere politeness on a lady's part, would her hurt be comparable with Nancy's? Well, it all depended on what value you put on your desires.

She pressed Nancy gently from her now, and taking a handkerchief she wiped her face, saying, 'There now, there now; no more, or else you'll be ill.'

'I feel ill now, Martha Mary.'

'I know you do, dear. I know you do.'

'I love him.'

To this Martha wanted to say, 'You imagine you do, you're so young'; but what she said was, 'This will pass, dear. I promise you this will pass. And you've only known him for a short duration. . . .'

'No, no—' Nancy was shaking her head vigorously now—'that isn't true. I've known him for years.'

'Well yes, of course, I know that, dear, but not on—' she had to force herself to end, 'familiar terms.'

'But yes, Martha Mary.' Nancy's tear-stained face was upturned and her expression pathetic. 'Yes, on familiar terms. We . . . we were going to be married; he promised as soon as he came of age. We were secretly engaged, we were. We have been for over a year now.'

Martha drew back and stared open-mouthed at this young and beloved sister before she exclaimed in a tone that held deep reprimand, 'Oh, Nancy!'

'Well, I knew how you'd look upon it, but. . . . And I wanted to tell you, I did, I did, but I promised him to keep it secret. And he promised me faithfully. He did, he did.' Her head was now wagging from side to side. 'Only a few weeks ago when we met and he—' Her head now dropped deep onto her chest, but almost instantly it was jerked upwards by Martha gripping her shoulders and hissing, 'You didn't, Nancy! You never allowed him to . . . ?'

'No, no, Martha Mary, not that, but'—the face crumpled like a child's—'but nearly, because he promised. . . . Please, please don't look so shocked, don't, please.'

But Martha was shocked, profoundly so. She had thought a moment ago that they were all simple, but Nancy was no longer simple in that way. And she was forced to wonder, too, now if Mildred was, for sometimes her conversation inferred that there was nothing she didn't know. It would appear that she herself was the only simpleton among them.

She stared down into Nancy's distressed face, seeing her now in a new light as if she were much older than herself; and she was older, in that she had studied duplicity and carried it through, not for just a few weeks or months, but, as she admitted, for years. What had she said? 'No, no, Martha Mary, not that, but nearly.' What liberties had she allowed William Brockdean to take with her that she could say but nearly? Yet did she really realize the seriousness of her conduct, for she had said those words, but nearly, as a child might confess to some small misdemeanour?

Nancy had picked up her letter from the table, and was now saying, 'I'm going to write to him and ask him . . .' But Martha cut her words off, demanding now, 'What happened today when you met?'

'He . . . he didn't come. He left a letter.'

'A letter? Then let me see it.'

'No, Martha.'

'*Let me see it.*'

Nancy now put her hand inside the bodice of her dress and slowly withdrew the envelope, and she watched Martha's face as she read the letter, but when Martha looked at her and said slowly, 'This is a breaking off, a dismissal in fact,' she cried back at her, 'No! No!'

'But it is, Nancy.' Again she was gripping Nancy's shoulders. 'It's as plain as a pikestaff. He is telling you that the association is ended.'

'But Martha Mary—' Nancy's voice was almost a whimper now—'you don't know what he said, what happened, what . . .'

Martha drew in a long breath before she spoke again. 'I have a very good idea, Nancy.' Her words coming from deep within her throat, she went on, 'I know that he has deceived you. To my mind he's a young scoundrel and this letter proves it; it is a polite and heartless dismissal. . . . And remember what Mildred said last night about the French visitor. Doesn't he say here . . . ?' She brought her hand from Nancy's shoulder and held out the crumpled letter, shaking it almost in her face now as she repeated, 'Doesn't he say here that he is going abroad? Nothing could be more evident. And . . . and you mustn't write that letter.' She was now pointing down to the desk, 'You mustn't demean yourself any further. Have a little dignity.'

'Dignity!' Again Nancy's head was shaking from side to side. 'What does it matter about dignity when you are going to lose someone you love? You don't know anything about it, Martha Mary, you don't know. . . .'

'I do know.'

The tone brought Nancy's head to a stop and they stared into each other's eyes, and Nancy whispered, 'You do?'

'Yes, I do.'

'But you haven't known any men, except Mr Ducat. . . . Was . . . was it Mr Ducat?'

'Yes, it was Mr Ducat. Now this is between you and me. I am telling you this in order that you will recognize you are not alone in being humiliated. Mr Ducat gave me the impression that he was only waiting for my permission in order to speak. And you know something, Nancy? I would have given it willingly last year if it hadn't been for Father and fear of his displeasure. Thank God I was afraid of that displeasure. It saved me from taking an action that I know now I should have regretted for the rest of my life.'

Again they were staring at each other; and now Nancy slumped in the chair and, her hands joined tightly between her knees, she began to rock herself as she murmured, 'But how am I to live, Martha Mary? I love him so. And'—her head drooped lower now—'I was looking forward to being married. I keep thinking about being married because . . . because I don't want to end up like Aunt Sophie. I love her but . . .'

'Don't be silly. Don't talk stupid. You won't end up like Aunt Sophie. Aunt Sophie was rejected because of her ailment, because of her fits.' There, she had called them fits. He said they were fits and they were fits.

She shut off her thinking and went on, 'The man did not want to be hampered with a wife with an ailment that she'd likely pass on to her children. It's understandable. But you, you are so young and beautiful and healthy . . .'

'And I'll die an old maid right here in this house, in this isolated house.'

'Oh, Nancy! Nancy!'

'You can say, Nancy, Nancy, like that, Martha Mary, but I know that will be my lot in life. Anyway you know that no one visits us except the coalman, the grocer and of course the doctor . . . and Mr Paine when someone dies. Does Roland ever bring his friends here? No, he goes out riding and visits houses but he never asks any of his gentlemen friends back.'

'He has no gentlemen friends about here, you know that, his friends are in Scarborough. He has lived most of his life in Scarborough. Anyway, you know we are in no position to entertain; and haven't been since Mother died.'

'That is what I mean, we are in no position to entertain.'

Nancy rose to her feet. There was now a strange sort of resignation in her manner. She looked down at the letter lying on the desk before picking it up and slowly tearing it into shreds.

As Martha watched her she became enveloped in sadness. It was as if her dear sister had, in the last ten minutes, added ten years to her life. Gone was the young impulsive girl; the person who walked past her was a woman, and she sounded as such when she said, 'I can't take my turn with Aunt Sophie today, will you see to her?'

'That's all right, dear. Go and lie down for a while and I'll bring you up a cup of tea.'

When the door had closed, Martha sat down in the chair near the escritoire, and she looked at the fragments of the letter lying there. Men were cruel. All men were cruel. Poor Nancy. Poor dear Nancy. What could she do to lighten her present burden? If she'd had money. Oh yes, if she'd had money she could have sent her away for a holiday; if she hadn't been so reckless in her gift to Roland then she could have done something about it in that way. Oh, if only she had someone to discuss things with, someone to turn to for help and guidance. She missed Dilly. Dilly's homespun philosophy had usually been able to clarify most troubles, now there was no one.

Yet there was someone she could talk to if only she could bring herself to do it. He had shown that he had her, no their, interest at heart by sending the boy. She saw herself opening the back door in answer to a knock to see standing there a fifteen-year-old boy. He said his name was Dan Holland and he had heard she was looking for a lad to work out of doors and to do heavy chores around the house. . . . She had never had the courage to ask the outside man to do any chores around the house.

'How do you know I need outside help?' she had asked the boy, and he had answered, 'Doctor Fuller, he 'tends me ma. There's no field work now and we're hard put to it. It's a five-mile tramp but I don't mind that, an' I'll work hard for me wage.'

She had said, 'It's a small wage,' and at this he had answered, 'Well, four shillings a week is better than nowt, an' I'd be grateful for it. As I said I'll give you good value; I'm strong. As long as I get me grub, I'm strong.'

Four shillings! She had paid Nick Bailey only three shillings a week, but now she needed someone badly because she was feeling physically worn out, and so she had said, 'I'll give you a trial, one month. When can you start?'

'Right now, miss,' he had answered. And he had started there and then, and since, the whole of the outside had taken on a cleaner, brighter look. What was more, he was clearing the land.

So there was someone she could turn to if only she would allow herself to do it, for hadn't he solved the management of the shop as well? In fact business was better than ever it had been in Lawrence Ducat's time.

But, of course, she couldn't speak to *him* about this latest trouble for this was a private family matter, and there was nothing he could possibly do with regard to it. So she had best put him out of her mind as a possible source of help and deal with the matter herself. And what that meant, after all, was simply trying to console Nancy. . . .

And so she put him out of her mind while she took a tray of tea up to Nancy, while she attended to Aunt Sophie, while she made the evening meal; but then he was recalled sharply to her attention again when Mildred came in almost half an hour before her usual time, and in such a good mood that her sharp features had taken on a look of prettiness. And what had caused the change? Doctor Fuller had driven her right from the town to the end of the lane.

Mildred took off her bonnet and swung it around by the strings and she laughed with her thin-lipped mouth wide as she said, 'I find I like him more and more every time I see him. He isn't the dragon you make him out to be. Well, anyway, he doesn't act like that with me.'

She went down the length of the kitchen now towards the door leading into the hall, her step was almost a prance, and she held her bonnet in both hands, her arms fully extended in front of her, as if it were an offering. At the door she stopped and, turning around, she put her head on one side and seemed to muse for a moment before saying, 'Do you know, he can be very amusing; he says the most outrageous things in the quaintest way. He came into the shop three times last week.' Again she paused and mused, her chin tilted upwards, but with her eyes directed now towards Martha, their slanted gaze cold and without merriment as she ended, 'You may not have been so far wrong after all about a gentleman coming into the shop and whisking me off my feet. It's odd how things come about, isn't it?'

Their gaze held through the dim light of the room, each reading the other's expression, when finally Mildred's attention was diverted by the mewing of the cat rubbing against her shoe. She stooped slowly down, picked it up and cradled it in her arms before opening the door and leaving the kitchen.

Martha lowered her head, laid her hands flat on the table and looked down on them. In this moment she was hating Mildred almost as much as she had done their father . . . and him. But she no longer hated him. Dear God! Oh, dear God! . . . And Mildred was cruel. What was more, she was cunning and perceptive. She always saw more than was good for her.

She raised her head, gulped deep in her throat, then reaching out, she grabbed up the knife she had been slicing the meat with, and so quickly did she bring it through the joint that she cut deep into the top of her thumb.

4

The spring had passed, the year was well into summer; for eight days in succession there had been bright hot sunshine. The roads were baked hard and here and there showed wide cracks. The air was heavy and thundery, and when the clouds did burst it would be a deluge, everyone said so.

Nancy walked slowly up the drive towards the house. She had been to the main road to meet the post van and collect the letters. Less and less she made the journey now with hope, yet her resignation was in no way strengthened.

As she approached the house she stopped abruptly and looked at it. The centre block looked more sunken than ever; like everything else it seemed to be wilting in the heat. The front door was wide open and all the windows too. This time last year she would have thought how homely, how comforting the whole place looked, but not any more. She hated it; every time she entered it now she had the desire to turn and run as if out of a trap. She felt so unhappy; in comparison everybody about her seemed to be enjoying some form of happiness. Martha Mary seemed a little more content now she had the outside boy, and Peg was very content and also possibly because of the outside boy. And there was Mildred. Mildred was just beaming. She dreaded the evening conversation which would alternate between Lady Brockdean and the doctor. She wouldn't be a bit surprised if she married the doctor. And Aunt Sophie, Aunt Sophie was singing all day long. At one time she had loved Aunt Sophie, but now she got on her nerves. Yet she no longer saw herself ending her days like Aunt Sophie. Oh no! No! not if she could do anything about it. She would suffer anything but that.

She went up the steps and into the dim and cool hall, then turned towards the kitchen where she expected to find Martha.

Martha was at the table preparing some fruit for a pie. At the far end of the kitchen below the shelf that held the iron pans Peg sat in her usual place peeling potatoes, her scarred fingers moving with their former dexterity now. She raised her bright face and looked towards Nancy, saying, 'Eeh! you look stewed, Miss Nancy.'

Nancy did not, as at one time she would have, come back with some laughing quip such as, 'Well, I'd be nice served up with custard,' instead, putting the letters on the table, she looked at Martha and said dully, 'There's one from Roland.'

'Oh, open it, my hands are stained. Read it out.'

Nancy opened the letter and began to read:

Dear Martha Mary,

I am sorry I've been unable to write before but I've been so busy. As you know, a fortnight sees the end of term and the end of my time here, and I'm not sorry, in fact I'm delighted, and for more reasons than one.

I shall not be returning home directly, but when I come I shall be bringing a guest with me. Would you mind having Papa's room freshened up? I may tell you now I have some surprising news for you. I hope it will delight you as it has done me. I cannot say more at the moment.

My love to Mildred and Nancy and, of course, to your dear self.

Your affectionate brother,
Roland.

'He's bringing a guest!' Nancy looked straight into Martha's face and, her tone slightly caustic, she said, 'He's starting late, isn't he? It's the first time he's ever brought anyone home. We should feel honoured.'

Martha nodded slowly. 'It's likely this friend he calls Arnold.' She did not say 'Oh dear me, I wish he wasn't', but her mind stressed the words. And he wanted his friend to have their father's room, and only three weeks at the most to see to everything. What could she do with that room to freshen it up. It needed all stripping and redecorating. And what about food. The young man would be used to all kinds of special dishes. Oh dear, dear, he shouldn't have done this knowing the circumstances, it was thoughtless of him. Still. She turned and looked at Nancy. This man's visit might be a blessing in disguise, it could be an answer to her prayer with regard to Nancy's happiness. And so she must see what she could do with that room; besides which, she must look up her cookery book.

Forcing a note of pleasure into her voice she said, 'Well, that'll be nice, won't it, to have a guest in the house again. We'll have to start scurrying round, all of us.' She glanced back at Peg who was grinning at her, but when she looked towards Nancy again it was to see her walking out of the kitchen, her body limp, her shoulders stooped. She no longer ran everywhere.

She returned to her pie making and she prayed directly to God asking Him to make the coming guest so nice that Nancy would forget William Brockdean. And when she finished the thought entered her mind as to what Roland's surprising news might be.

By three o'clock in the afternoon the air was so heavy that it seemed to scorch the throat. Martha, seeing Nancy crossing the drive, went to the window and called, 'You're not going walking in this heat, surely Nancy, it's bad for you!'

Nancy slowed her step but did not stop and she spoke to Martha over her shoulder, her manner off-hand, detached. 'It's cooler down by the river,' she said, then she walked on.

The river was low, there was merely a trickle flowing between the stepping-stones. She crossed them but instead of mounting the wooded bank she walked for almost half a mile further along the river bed which now looked like a boulder strewn beach; then she went up the incline, which was actually the river bank, crossed a field and began to climb upwards, until she paused panting and sweating on a rise that overlooked a winding road and a valley with low hills beyond.

She stared at the hills. She had seen him driving the sheep down them on Monday in the direction of Hexham, but he hadn't been alone, there had been another man with him, likely his father, most assuredly his father because he often spoke of him and how they worked together. He seemed to be fond of his father, he seemed to be fond of both his parents, yet he laughed at his mother and said she didn't know Sunday from whistle cock Monday, whatever that was supposed to mean, but that she could count silver quicker than a money-lender.

She had seen him at least once a week since their first meeting on that dreadful day, that seemed but yesterday, yet when she tried to recall the events in it they fused into the past like old history, and she could get nothing clear in her mind concerning it.

She liked the drover . . . Robbie. He was twenty years old and could neither read nor write, he had told her so, but without any shame. There was something about him that attracted her with an irresistible force. He was so alive, his litheness, his movements, his voice, they all spoke of vibrant youth. Then his eyes, and the way they looked at her, sparkling from their depths with that precious thing she had lost when William spurned her. She knew that something was going to happen between her and the drover, she didn't know when or exactly what, but she knew that he would make it happen, and soon.

She saw him when he was afar off. He was alone, hatless as usual, his hair even in the distance making his head appear as if it were three times its size.

She knew he had caught sight of her when he stopped; then she watched him, like one of his sheep, or more like a ram, bounding over the ground, coming ever nearer until he was at the foot of the hill, where he paused for a moment and looked upwards, then came scrambling towards her, and when he straightened up she saw that his face was running in rivulets of sweat.

'It's singeing, isn't it?'

'Yes, it's very hot.'

'You been waitin' long?'

'Waiting? I wasn't waiting.'

'Oh.' He smiled at her but without derision, then added, 'You've never been this far afore. Why, you're not more than a mile away from our house.'

'Really!' She turned and looked in the direction in which he was pointing.

'That clump of trees on the top of the hill just to the right there. . . . Oh my, listen to that.' He cocked his head to one side. 'We're going to get it.'

She looked up into the low sky. Of a sudden it appeared to be falling on to the hills. The light was going like a guttering candle and the rumbling thunder came nearer.

'You'll get wet afore you get home. You must have walked all of three miles. . . . You look baked.'

She rubbed her finger round her sweating cheeks and she smiled as she said, 'I feel baked.'

'Wouldn't like to come back and shelter in our house?'

'No, thank you.'

'Aw well, you'll have to shelter some place. . . . Look, here it comes.' As he spoke large drops of rain spattered on them. 'Come on. Come on this way.' He grabbed her hand now and pulled her into a run as he said, 'There's a shippen over beyond that ridge; it's clean, not used any more. The house was burned down years ago. Coo! Lord, but it is comin' down.'

She was running in step beside him now, her body bent against the deluge, and not until he pulled her through the doorless aperture into the derelict shippen did she look up; then gasping, she stood with her back against the wall, while he stood in front of her panting.

'By! you can run. I used to watch you runnin'. I used to think you looked like a young deer; but it's different altogether to feel you running, like being on a horse.'

She made no comment, she was still gasping. The water was actually running down her body to her waist, where the bands of her petticoats sopped it up.

'You're soakin'.' His hands were on her shoulders. 'You should've had the sense to bring a cloak with you. . . . Stop shivering, you can't be cold, it's like hot water.'

Still she made no reply, and he took his hands from her shoulders and, turning from her, went and stood in the opening. He stood there saying nothing while the slanting rain beat on to his head and face.

When she turned her head and looked at him, he did not move but very quietly he said, 'You like to marry me?'

The sound of her indrawing breath turned him towards her again, but he did not go to her but went on, 'You're ripe for marrying.' He paused now, then demanded, 'Well, aren't you?'

'I . . . I don't know what you mean.' She was moving slowly along the wall towards the corner where the light was dimmer.

'Aw, you know what I mean all right, an' you know you do. And I know what I mean. You know something? I've wanted you since I first clapped eyes on you, but as things stood I thought then, she's not for me. But now I think you are.' His tone was light as if he were talking about everyday things, like the sheep.

He went towards her now, and when his hands came forward she gasped and shrank back against a protruding wooden partition; but he didn't touch her with them, he placed them on the rotten wood at each side of her head. And now his voice coming from deep in his throat and all lightness gone from it, he said, 'I could take you down and you wouldn't put up a fight 'cos you're ready for it, but I won't have you that way, I want to marry you. Do you understand what I'm sayin', I want to marry you.'

As his face moved slowly closer to hers, her eyes stretched wide and she stared as if hypnotized into the depths of greyness that now were shadowed into black. When his mouth touched hers, his hands slid over her shoulder blades and drew her towards him. With a soft pressure she was held tightly against him and he kept her there for a full minute and she did not resist in any way.

Their bodies were apart again, but he still had his hands on her when he said, 'Well, what is it to be?'

She could not answer; it was impossible to say 'Yes', but she bent her head and slowly she fell forward against him again, and it was the answer. It was done.

5

'You are mad, girl, stark-staring mad, you can't do this.'

'I'm going to do it, Martha Mary; it's all settled.'

'Oh no, it's not.' Martha's voice was loud and strident. 'I shall go across to that place and . . .'

'There's no need, he's calling to see you today on his way back from the market.'

Martha now held her face tightly between her hands and screwed up her eyes as she repeated, 'Nancy! Nancy! you don't know what you're doing. This is a form of panic, a rebound from William.'

'Yes perhaps, but I'm doing it.'

'I can stop you, you're not of age.'

'Well, if you do, then I shall take matters into my own hands and go and live with him in sin.'

'Nancy!'

'Don't look like that, Martha Mary, please.' There was a semblance of the old Nancy in the tone and expression now. 'I like him, and more than like him, I could say. And, more to the point, he asked me to marry him, and—' All lightness leaving her tone, she ended, 'I intend to be married, Martha Mary.'

'But you will, my dear, you will. I know you'll be eighteen shortly, but remember Roland's letter and the guest he's bringing, it could mean something.'

'Yes, it could mean something, or it could turn out to mean nothing. Remember what Dilly used to say when she used to tell us the tales of the starving people in the strikes, when they had no hope of money or food and wanted to return to work but the agitators used to make them promises. She always ended with "Live, horse, and you'll get grass". Well, I cannot wait to see if I will get grass, Martha Mary. I might, like Dilly's people, starve to death . . . for want of love. . . . What is more I want to get away, away from this house, everything.'

'Oh, don't say that you will never be without love, and don't say you want to get away from everything.'

Nancy's head drooped; then she said, 'Not from you, Martha Mary, not from you, but you know what I mean.'

'Yes, I know what you mean, Nancy, and who you mean. But Aunt Sophie cannot help her condition, and you used to love her.'

'Yes, I know, but . . . but now I fear her, I fear I'll become like her. I do. I do.'

'That's utterly ridiculous. I've told you time and again her illness is not hereditary.'

'You could keep on telling me but I still wouldn't believe it. She became worse after she was jilted and I can see myself just like her, withering away, shut in that room day after day, year after year just like her until I died.'

Slowly Martha bowed her head. What could she say? There was nothing she could either say or do that could convince Nancy that she was wrong, that she was working through the turmoil of a broken heart and that some day soon she'd come up out of her misery.

What would happen to her when she did emerge and found herself married to this drover boy? A drover. She couldn't believe it. She had seen these men in Hexham on market days. They all gathered together in the evening and frequented the inns, and she understood they fought like madmen. What was more, they were merciless to the beasts they drove, prodding them unnecessarily with goads. And Nancy, her dear, dear Nancy, was determined to marry one of them. What could she do to prevent it? This was something requiring immediate attention. If only Roland were at home. She could send a letter to him but it might not reach him before he left the school to join his friend. She had been expecting word from him any day to say when he should arrive. What was she to do?—She was expecting *him* today. Could she tell him? Could she ask for his advice? Would anything he had to say have any effect on Nancy? But she must do something, get help from somewhere. Failing the doctor, she would go into town and see Mr Paine; but first she must face this man, this sly, low individual whom Nancy had openly admitted to meeting frequently over the past weeks.

Robbie Robson arrived at the house at three o'clock. He did not go to the back door but came up the steps and pulled the bell.

It was Peg who opened the door to him. She knew Robbie and she knew his father because his father had at odd times left a shive of mutton at the cottage for her grannie; she also knew why Robbie was here now. She had heard all that had gone on between Miss Martha Mary and Miss Nancy and, as she told herself, she just couldn't believe her ears, and if she had anything to do with it she'd lock Miss Nancy up. Not that she had anything against Robbie Robson, he was a decent enough fellow, and a good looking one at that, and his people weren't scum, but still, for him to cast sheep's-eyes on Miss Nancy, why it was. . . . She couldn't think of a word that indicated sacrilege but her thoughts told her that's what she meant.

She strained her neck up out of the collar of her frock and looked up at him as she said in no polite tone, 'You've got to go across there to that door.' She pointed. 'You're expected.'

He stepped into the hall, bent down to her, smiled and said, 'Hello there, you little 'un, I haven't seen you for a long time. You all right now?'

'It's no matter to you Robbie Robson if I am or not, an' it'd be better if you weren't seeing me now an' all.'

She marched before him now, her small buttocks wagging their disdain, knocked on the drawing-room door, opened it, and said in a tone that expressed plainly how she felt about this matter, 'Robbie Robson, Miss Martha Mary.'

Martha turned swiftly from the window and watched the figure of the young man walking slowly up the room towards her. She hadn't known what to expect as regards his appearance except that he would certainly have the stamp of the common working man on him, but what she saw surprised her. He had a thin clear cut face, freckled heavily across the nose and cheek-bones, large grey eyes, and an enormous mass of fair hair, and his dress was respectable, very much so, being that his suit wasn't made of either thick grey homespun or corduroy. The first impression she was forced to admit was good, but it was wiped away when he opened his mouth.

'After-noon, miss.'

'Good-afternoon.'

They surveyed each other for a moment before he said, 'No need for any preamble is there, you know why I'm here?'

'Yes, I know why you're here and I must tell you at once that my answer is no, a definite no. Your suggestion of a union with my sister is out of the question.'

'I expected you to say that, but 'tisn't for you to say, miss, whether it is out of the question or not; that lies between her and me. She wants me, I want her. Oh, I know she would never have looked the side I was on if young Brockdean had played the game by her, but then he didn't, did he? An' to my mind she's well rid of him 'cos he's nowt but a weakling, always was an' always will be. He doesn't take after his father 'cos his father's no weaklin'. No, he's no weaklin', but he's a swine of a man. I can say here and now, miss, she'll stand a better chance of happiness along of me an' mine than she ever would up in the Hall. And when we're on about suitability, miss, I know your sister's a cut above me, but then the Brockdeans consider themselves more than a cut above her, an' hers. . . . So, well, to my mind it sort of evens things out.'

Martha stared at him amazed. She could see now what attracted Nancy, how in fact she had come under the spell of this strange individual, for he wasn't without personality or spirit. In fact, she would say, for his class he had too much of both for his own good, but as he had dared to point out to her his aspirations towards Nancy were, she had to admit, on a par with Nancy's towards William Brockdean. Yet there were insurmountable flaws in his logic, for whereas Nancy had been educated he showed not the slightest semblance of any learning.

As she stared at him and found his eyes holding hers in an embarrassing fearlessness, she knew that she must not take a high hand with him for it would get her nowhere, she must try persuasion, even pleading. She attempted the latter device first.

Her hand extended, she pointed to a chair, saying, 'Will you take a seat?'

'No, miss, thanks all the same, I'd rather stand during this business. An' there's a time factor, I'm due to collect some animals from Pearce's farm within the next hour, an' as you know it's a good five miles away.'

How could she deal with this person? He was putting her at a disadvantage. Her face, she knew, was suffused with colour. But she must make an effort.

'Mr Robson.' She now joined her hands in front of her waist and bent slightly towards him and, her voice low, she went on, 'I beg of you not to take this matter any further, it would only end in unhappiness for you both, for you must see that you . . . you are not suitable for her as a husband, and she would be equally unsuitable for you as a wife.'

'Oh no, no, miss.' His head gave a little jerk to the side which dismissed her statement even before he went any further. 'As I see it we're well suited in the fact that we both want to marry, for different reasons like, I grant you. With me I want to marry her because I want her, with her, well, she's marryin' for marryin's sake 'cos she was let down. She sees it as a way of saving her face. . . . You needn't look so surprised, miss, because it's the truth.'

Yes, it was the truth, and this young man was bringing it into the open, which was all the more astounding. She said so.

'You astound me. You would marry her knowing that she is just taking this way out as a means of escape? Do you realize that presently, when she comes to her senses, she will regret it? Oh, how she will regret it!'

'I don't see it like that, miss. The way I see it is that by the time she comes to her senses, as you say, she'll be thinkin' along different lines, I'll see to that.'

What could she say? She had no words with which to combat him. Her mouth had opened and closed twice when there came a knock on the drawing-room door, then a head appeared around it, and a voice said, 'There was nobody about, the place seemed deserted. May I come in?'

She stepped to the side and looked down the room, saying, 'Oh yes, yes, doctor, please come in.'

As Harry entered the room and closed the door behind him, he smiled to himself as he thought, She sounds pleased to see me, that's a change. Then he looked into the sunlight in which her visitor was standing. He hadn't recognized him at first, never imagining finding Robbie Robson in Miss Crawford's drawing-room. But it was Robbie Robson. There weren't two heads of hair like that around here. He smiled widely as he advanced towards the young man, saying, 'Well, well! Hello, Robbie. I didn't expect to see you here.'

'Good-day to you, doctor. I never expected to find meself here, but we never know where God an' the weather will land us.'

'We don't that.'

Martha stared from one to the other. They were exchanging greetings almost as friends. She had looked upon *his* entry as an answer to an unspoken prayer, but now she wasn't at all sure if God had understood what she was asking.

She looked directly at Harry now and said with a certain primness, 'You're acquainted?'

'Yes.' He nodded back at Robbie. 'You could say we are acquainted. I was able to do a little service for his father a short while ago. Give him a hand, so to speak.'

She watched them now exchange a soft laugh together and then the young man, looking towards her, said, 'Give him a hand is right. He broke his knuckles an' his forearm in two places; he missed a man's jaw an' hit a wall. But the doctor here did a fine job on it.' He turned his head towards Harry now, ending, 'It was a night an' a half I'd say, doctor, wasn't it?'

'Yes, it was a night and a half, Robbie.'

Really! She knew they were referring to a brawl that this young man's father had undoubtedly been in, and they were laughing about it as if they both had enjoyed it. She had been foolish to think that she could turn to him for help on this matter for from his present attitude he was almost sure to condone it.

But there she was wrong, for Robbie Robson, looking at the doctor straight in the face now, said, 'You'll no doubt get a bit of a gliff, doctor, when you learn why I'm here the day. I've come to tell the miss'—he motioned his head towards Martha—'that her sister Nancy an' me, well, we're aiming to be married.'

A tense silence followed this statement before Harry said quietly, 'You're what?'

'Just what I said, doctor. I said it would give you a gliff. Nancy an' me are aiming to be married. You heard aright, we're aimin' to be married.'

'Since when?' The question was sharp, there was no friendliness in Harry's manner now.

'Oh, we've been acquainted this while back, since the early part of the year, but things came to a head a week agone, an' so I came to put it to the miss here.'

'Do you know what you're saying, Robbie?'

'Aye! Very well, doctor, very well. I'm sayin' that young Nancy and me are wanting to be wed.'

'It's impossible.'

'No, nothing's impossible, doctor. Them were your very words when you pushed the splintered bone back in me da's arm an' he said, "I'll never use that again", you said to him, "Nothing's impossible". I remember those were your very words.'

'This business has nothing to do with broken bones, you're dealing with lives now, Robbie, a precious life, a delicate life, a life of a young girl, an untried, innocent young girl.'

'No, no, doctor; there you're wrong.' Robbie's voice was stiff, as was his face as he went on, 'She's not as innocent as all that. Anyone meetin' as often as she did with William Brockdean would not remain all that innocent, at least not to the extent that you're implying. Up to a point she knew what loving was so I'm not snatchin' up a baby from the cradle.'

Harry did not take his attention from Robbie as he heard Martha's sharp intake of breath, but bending towards him, he cautioned, 'Be careful, Robbie; you've gone too far already.'

'Plain speakin's best, doctor. I want you to know there's things on my side an' all. An' when I'm on with plain speakin' I'll say that I care for her, I always have done since I first clapped eyes on her, and although I never thought to have her, yet I never stooped to second-best. It's me way; I'm odd they tell me, but anything I own I like it to be good. I have two fine bred dogs, but they don't always drive good cattle. Few or many, when I get cattle, an' I'm gona get cattle, they'll be good.'

Harry now swung about, bent his head, doubled his fist and beat it softly against his mouth; then turning as quickly, again he looked at Martha and asked quietly, 'Will you leave us for a moment, Miss Crawford?'

Martha said nothing, she did not even make an assent with her head, but she walked quickly from the room, leaving them facing each other again. And now Harry, his tone changing to one that he might have used to a familiar friend, said, 'We're not talking of cattle, Robbie, we're talking of a refined young girl. You can't do this, Robbie. Look at this house. Look—' he waved his hand about the room—'look about you. She's been brought up in this and rooms like it, and she's spent years at a private school in Hexham. Imagine taking her from this to your place.'

'There's nothing wrong with our place, doctor; it's better than most; in fact it's twice the size of most. You've never seen it.'

'Yes, I have; I've passed it. It's two cottages knocked into one, but what's that after this.'

'It's not just two cottages; there's a room been built at the back that runs the length of them both with the finest views in the county. An' our furniture is hand-made, most of it by me great-granda, an' there's outhouses better than you find on any farm. We haven't always been drovers; as ma da told you, we were farmers one time.'

'Yes, yes, I know all that, Robbie, but you're from different worlds.'

'The needs of the body all stem from the same place whether you're up in the world or down, doctor.' Robbie's voice was harsh now, almost a growl as he went on, 'She needs me, she's ripe for marriage. If she doesn't ease herself with me then she'll do something that will make that sister of hers bow her head in shame. An' I tell you something else, doctor, and it's just this. It would have been as easy as blinkin' for me to be the man that could have brought that shame on her, but I held back. But should I let her go she'll jump the hurdles like any penned sheep an' make for the ram; shamelessly she'll make for the ram, any ram. She was hurt, doctor, humiliated bad, brought low inside herself by that snot of a so-called gentleman, an' if I ever come face to face with him I'll spit in his eye, then black it, even if it means going along the line for it. But I doubt if I'll get that chance for he's off to France, isn't he? His parents proudly announced his engagement a few days gone, in fact I heard it in the market the very day I told her it was time we wed.'

Harry turned slowly away. Like Martha, he felt utterly defeated. This fellow, this young drover, was worth twenty William Brockdeans, yet such was life and early environment that he could not see young Nancy having the faintest chance of happiness with him, whereas with Brockdean she could, at least in the eyes of society, live a full life. What went on behind closed doors was another matter altogether; but in the eyes of that same society a union with this young man would be looked upon askance, not only among her own class but among his. Yet let him face it, what after all was her class? They were merely on the fringe of the upper middle class, and like many another family they had clawed their way there through commerce. But as they stood now it was likely they were no better off financially than Robbie Robson and his family.

As if Harry had spoken his thoughts aloud Robbie now said, 'And she won't have to go beggin', I can promise you that, doctor, for we're not without a shilling or so, and we owe nobody a penny. And that can't be said for everybody, now can it, doctor, for this establishment, fine and refined as you pointed out, is on the black list in Hexham, an' has been for many a year, but more so than ever now. So taking all in all, I can't see what all the fuss is about. Apart from the fact that I can neither read nor write, I consider meself as good as the next one.'

Harry turned about again and was now nodding slowly at Robbie and saying, 'And if anybody asked me that question I should endorse what you have just said, you're as good as the next one, and better than a few, but I must be honest with you: I can't see any good coming out of this affair, and I wish I could persuade you along those lines. I must warn you that her brother will certainly attempt to stop the union. He, in a way, is her guardian until she comes of age, and should you go ahead with it he could take it to law.'

'Aye, I'd thought of that; but then it needs money to go to law an' I think at the present moment I'd be more able to meet the costs than him. An' you know somethin'; it would be the worst service he could do her if he took it to law, because she's got a spirit in her that hasn't quite risen yet, and she'll go her own way in the end, and happen it could be the wrong way if she was frustrated at this point, 'cos she's got so much love in her she's got to give it vent.'

They stood silent for a moment staring at each other, and it was Robbie who spoke again, 'Well, doctor,' he said quietly, 'I've got animals waiting for me an' I must be off.' He now pulled from his pocket a heavy lever watch and, tapping its face, said, 'An' it'll take me all me time even if I run. I hate to be late. A set time is a set time. So will you tell'—he now motioned his head towards the door—'the miss, that things stand as I go out the same way as when I come in. Good-day to you, doctor.' He did not touch his forelock but gave Harry a kind of salute by placing his fingers to the middle of his brow.

Harry mumbled a farewell, waited until the sound of the front door closing came to him, then slowly he walked out of the room and into the hall and, glancing upwards, he saw Martha standing at the top of the stairs.

He stood waiting while she walked slowly down towards him. When she reached the last step she stopped, and he shook his head as he looked at her and said, 'I'm afraid it's no use.'

She stepped down into the hall, her arms now folded across her chest, each hand gripping a forearm. 'He can be stopped. When Roland comes home he'll take it to law.'

'I'm afraid he's thought of that, in fact he's thought of everything. He's a very intelligent fellow, uneducated, granted, according to social standards, but he's got much more in his head than most, educated or otherwise. You'll have a hard job to stop him, and, from what I can gather, an equal task with your sister. It would seem to me, and believe me I am very reluctant to say this at this moment, but he appears to be the least of many evils confronting her due to the state of her mind at the present time.'

'She's been disappointed, she'll get over it.'

She turned fully to him now and, her voice deep with pleading, she asked, 'Couldn't you explain that to her, that these things pass, and in a few months' time she will be thinking differently altogether?'

Harry found it almost impossible to meet her gaze as he replied, 'If you haven't been able to make her see sense I don't think I have much chance in that direction. She appears very fond of you, and I feel sure if she could please you by changing her mind she would do so.'

'Doctor—' She had taken a step closer to him now—she could have touched the lapel of his coat with her bent arm—and he saw that she was finding it difficult to speak; then swallowing deeply and as if admitting to something shameful, she said softly, 'Her whole trouble is that she's afraid of ending her days like Aunt Sophie. She sees spinsterhood as something to be ashamed of. If you could only convince her that it isn't, and that Aunt Sophie's trouble is . . . is as you once said—' she paused and the look in her eyes was soft on him now as she ended 'epilepsy . . . it might have an effect.'

He wished the occasion warranted him saying, 'Ah, so now we recognize Aunt Sophie's turns as epilepsy; as for convincing your sister that spinsterhood is nothing to be ashamed of, as I've never been a spinster I can't be expected to know how one would feel, now can I?' But that would be turning this matter into a joke, and it was no joke. And spinsterhood was no joke; it was the cause, he knew only too well, of much of the malaise of the women under his care. Those who weren't married pined for the experience, while many of those who were pined because of it, and these, too, took to their couches and developed a neurosis as a way of preventing further access to their bodies.

He looked hard at Martha. It would be a great pity if she ever had to take to her couch because under that assumed exterior of primness he had detected a fire blazing; sometimes of late he had caught a glimpse of it and it had given him hope for her future. Yet he knew that she would allow the fire to burn her clean out until her life was left in ashes rather than take the step that Nancy was proposing. Such were the differences in their characters. All the strength in this family seemed to have been allotted to the first-born. She was a difficult girl to understand. He had thought at one time that they were approaching a friendly footing, then quite suddenly a few weeks ago her manner towards him had reverted almost to that of their first acquaintance. He couldn't begin to understand her. Yet today she had approached him like an ordinary young person needing advice, needing help. This only went to show how much she was taking this situation to heart; it was the case of any port in a storm.

He was about to speak when a loud cry from above turned them both to face the stairs, and glad to escape from this discussion for a moment he said, 'We'll continue this later. How has she been?'

At the foot of the stairs he stood back to allow Martha to proceed, and as she hurried up them, she said, 'Very uneasy for the past week. Yet she doesn't want to get out of bed, and her mind is wandering a great deal.'

When they entered the room Sophie was lying with her arms stretched back above her head, her hands gripping the brass bed rails, and when Harry stood over her she did not release her grip on them but smiled up at him, saying, 'Oh, I'm so glad to see you, doctor, now you'll be able to help George; he's pushed them all out of the room. They were going to take me away.' She turned now and looked at Martha. 'Did you know that, Martha Mary? They were going to take me away. Did you tell them to take me away?'

'No, of course not, Aunt Sophie.' Martha now went to the head of the bed and gently unloosened the fingers from around the rails, then said gently, 'There, lie quiet now. That's a good girl.'

'Good girl. I like it when you call me a good girl, Martha Mary and I'm always quiet, and I'm always listening. I listen to them all talking, talking, talking; everybody talks, doctor.' She was looking at Harry again, and he nodded at her and said, 'Yes, Miss Sophie, everybody talks. There's much too much talking goes on in the world.'

'Oh, I don't really mind people talking. Ever since I married I've listened to people talking. I used to be very shy before, doctor, but not since I married. George taught me not to be shy.'

'That's good.' He felt her pulse, then put his hand on her brow. It was heavy with perspiration and he asked gently, 'Have you a headache?'

'Yes. Yes, I've a headache, doctor, but I think it's the wedding. Weddings always cause worry, don't you think so, doctor? And this new one coming along . . . well.'

They both exchanged quick glances which asked how on earth she found out about the proposed wedding. In a whispered aside he asked, 'Does she know?' and Martha shook her head vigorously. Then his head jerked sharply to the side as Sophie said, 'It'll be nice to have a doctor in the family, won't it?'

Again he and Martha were exchanging glances, now showing their bewilderment; then Martha, pulling the covers further up around Sophie's shoulders, said gently, 'You've been dreaming, Aunt Sophie, Nancy's not . . . I mean no one's going to marry a doctor.'

'Oh yes, yes there is.' Sophie chuckled now. 'Yes, there is, Mildred told me last night when she was sitting with me; she was very gay and she made me laugh and she's so happy because when she's a doctor's wife she'll then get into society and she'll be able to meet with Lady Brocker. No, no, that isn't the name. What is the name, Martha Mary?'

'Brockdean, Lady Brockdean.' Martha's voice was very low now. It was as Aunt Sophie said, Mildred had been very gay of late, and there was one name constantly on her lips. At times she had wanted to scream at her, but she had contained herself; she would not afford Mildred any further satisfaction.

She did not raise her eyes, afraid at this moment to what she would read in his face. Yet whatever she read there would not be entirely unexpected. Mildred had certainly prepared her, and for it at this moment she was grateful.

'She said it was a secret. We all have secrets, haven't we, Martha Mary?'

Martha made no reply, and she kept her head bowed until Harry said, 'Well, this is news. So Miss Mildred is going to marry a doctor. Well, well! I wonder who that can be. There's only one eligible young man in Hexham practising at the moment, that is Doctor Norman. Is the gentleman's name Doctor Norman, Miss Sophie?'

He was bending over Sophie now, a smile on his face, and she shook her head and smiled back at him and said, 'No, no, she just said it was a secret.'

He made no reply but raised his head and found Martha staring at him with a look in her eyes that brought his body stiffly upright and caused a number of impressions to race through his mind at once. The expression on her face had stretched it; her mouth was open and her eyes wide. It was as if she were slightly shocked by surprise and was making an effort to hide it.

He glanced down again at Sophie, then hastily back to Martha, and he thought, No! She couldn't be under that impression. But why not? That Miss Mildred was a minx; just what kind of a minx he hadn't realized until he had become better acquainted with her when he drove her home that one and only time.

During a conversation in the shop she had told him she was reluctantly getting used to being a shop assistant, but that she'd never get used to travelling by carrier cart, and so he had laughingly said, 'Well today is one time I can relieve you of that obnoxious journey. I shall be going out to

Nolan's farm around four o'clock, would you care to take the ride with me?'

He recalled how he had been surprised at her pertness and her spiteful mimicking of customers; also he had found her rather pathetic in her adoration of the upper class, namely the Brockdeans. He recalled too that he had made a number of visits to the bookshop of late. True, he had wanted books, but his visits had primarily been to see how old Armstrong was faring. He remembered now, with a slight heat to the face, that last week he had accepted Mildred's offer of a cup of coffee in the office.

Lordy! Lordy! how careful one had to be. But on the other hand he couldn't blame himself; he had done nothing, nothing whatever to give to that little madam the impression he was interested in her. Good God! no. Yet, apparently she had got that impression, or she was determined she was going to make the impression on him. More apparently still, from the look on Martha Mary's face at this moment, the secret had been no secret from her. Damn the little bitch! because that's all she was.

He coughed hard, cleared his throat, patted Sophie's hand, saying, 'Now you be a good girl; I'll be seeing you again soon,' then walked abruptly out on to the landing.

When Martha joined him he turned fully to her and said, 'I must congratulate Doctor Norman, that's if . . .'

'I wouldn't, doctor, not . . . not at present.'

'No? Why?'

'Well'—she was blinking rapidly now—'as Aunt Sophie said it was supposed to be a secret.'

'Oh yes.' He wagged his head. 'Well you tell your sister that I'm in the secret, will you, and that I cannot wait until I congratulate the doctor on his good fortune. Tell her that.'

She stared at him for a moment, then her head moved slightly downwards and her lids covered the expression in her eyes when she answered softly, 'I'll do that, doctor. Yes, I'll do that.'

'Well now—' he was making for the stairs—'weddings seem to be in the air, don't they?'

She made no comment on this but when she reached the hall she walked straight to the door and opened it for him, then stood watching him pick up his hat from a chair, and when he stood before her she said, 'Thank you, doctor, for . . . for all you have done.'

'For all I have done?' He raised his eyebrows. 'I can't see that I have done very much, in fact nothing as regards Miss Nancy; as for your aunt, well, we both know that little can be done in that quarter. The only thing is to keep her as happy as possible.'

'Yes, doctor.'

'Good-day then.'

'Good-day, doctor.'

He had reached the top step when he turned again and, his head slightly back on his shoulders, he moved his chin from side to side before he asked, 'Would you like me to call in if I'm passing during the week to see how things are faring with young Robson?'

'I'd be very grateful, doctor.'

'I'll do that then, I'll do that.' He turned abruptly from her now and ran down the steps to where Dan Holland was standing ruffling Fred's ears. He mounted the trap, nodded at Dan, saying, 'Thanks Dan,' then, turning, he looked to where Martha was still standing at the top of the steps and he touched his hat with his whip by way of salute, then drove smartly down the drive.

Martha went slowly back into the house. She crossed the hall, went down the passage and entered the study; then she stood with her back to the door, and now she did something she hadn't done since she was a child, she pushed three of her fingers into her mouth and bit hard on them.

6

Martha met Roland at the station and his first words to her were, 'What's all this about? Couldn't it have waited another two days, you knew I was coming?'

Her reply to this, and tartly, was, 'It couldn't have waited another day, it's waited a fortnight too long already. It may be too late now, you might have been able to stop it if you had come home earlier, or if you had left me an address to write to, but I had to telegraph to the school and ask them to forward it.'

'Stop what? What are you talking about?'

She turned from him. 'Let us get away from here; the trap is outside.'

As she mounted the trap and went to take the reins, he said, 'Move over; give them to me.'

Silently she did as she was bid, thinking it would never do for the son of her father to be seen to be driven through the town by a woman, it might lessen his maleness in the eyes of the ladies. She did not chastise herself for this way of thinking, but sat looking straight ahead as Roland applied his attention to getting the horse through the streets.

It wasn't until they were leaving the town that he slackened the reins and said, 'Well now, what is the great tragedy that requires my presence at home? That's what the message said, "Urgently request your presence at home".'

She still kept her gaze ahead as she replied slowly, 'Nancy is going to be married.'

He drew the trap to a standstill, crying, 'Whoa there!' then screwed round on the seat and stared at her and, his tone voicing his incredulity, said, 'And you brought me post-haste to tell me that Nancy is going to be married?'

'Yes.'

'God above! have you taken leave of your senses?'

'Not quite.' She still looked ahead as she added now, 'She's marrying a drover.'

Almost thirty seconds elapsed before he repeated, 'A drover?'

'Yes, a cattle drover, one Robbie Robson. You may know of him, you have ridden about the country much more than I have. He lives in Hill Cottage. It lies, I understand, back from the Prudhoe Road. He can neither read nor write but he has in his favour a presentable appearance and an intelligence above the average—for his class.'

'A drover! Has she gone out of her mind? She cannot do it—*she cannot do it, not at this time.*'

She was looking hard at him now. 'Why not at this time? I should have thought you would have said at any time.'

'There is a strong reason why I say not at this time. My God! what were you up to to let her get to know this fellow?'

'I am not a gaoler. I cannot control her actions. Apparently I never have, for I may tell you now that she has taken this step because of a disappointment, a love disappointment. She has, which may seem incredible to you as it did to me, been meeting William Brockdean for some years past, and she imagined—no, she was led to believe, I am sure of this—she was led to believe that his intentions were otherwise than what they turned out to be. When you were last at home you remarked on the change in her, but you were not interested enough to ask the reason for it.'

'Well—' he grabbed up the reins again and swung the whip across the horse's flanks as he cried, 'I'll put a stop to it.'

'I hope you succeed. But you may find it difficult; he is no ordinary individual, and she is in a state of defiance. The doctor thinks that if she is frustrated in this present madness she'll take a more dangerous course still.'

'By damn! She won't, not if I know it.'

Martha glanced at him. He was playing the man. But he was still a youth, a pimply-faced youth; yet there was the appeal of her father all about him, but it didn't touch her, not in any way, for she saw through it right to what lay beneath, and as Dilly would have said it was mush.

Her father had been mush. Inside he had been all mush.

'Where is she now?' He lashed at the horse again.

'She went into Newcastle this morning early. He was driving her there. She said she was going for a new gown. She didn't ask me for any money, and I know she had none of her own.'

Again he was about to check the horse but jerked his head in anger towards her, saying, 'In the name of God! why didn't you stop her?'

'I have never yet attempted to take up fisticuffs against a man. He called for her with a horse and trap, and the turnout was much smarter than this one. It may have been hired, I don't know. If you had been there perhaps you would have come to grips with him . . . perhaps.'

'Why do you say it like that?'

'Because you've never met him. He is, I imagine, a man one would be very wary of before directing a blow towards him.'

'Blow? I'd knock him down.'

'I wouldn't promise yourself so much success; it's diplomacy that is needed in this matter, and perhaps law.'

'Law? *Law* . . . that's it. Talk about law, create a scandal. Look, I told you I was bringing a guest. It's very important to me. Oh my God!' He jerked the reins in his hand. 'I came home with news, in fact my idea was to bring the news with me but Eva couldn't get away until Friday.'

She was looking at his profile now, squinting at it, her mouth was agape and her eyes screwed up to pin points. She put her hand up suddenly to her bonnet as a gust of wind lifted the front brim upwards and she pulled it back on to her head before she repeated, 'Eva? Your companion, your guest is . . . is a woman?'

'No, not a woman, she's a girl, a very dear girl.'

'It's the same thing.' It was as if she were listening to someone else's voice because most of her, she felt sure, had become frozen; yet the wind itself was warm.

She asked now, very quietly, 'She's your friend's sister?'

'What do you say?' He leant his head towards her.

'I said is she your friend's sister?' Her bawling startled him.

He turned his head to the front again and made a number of small motions with it before he replied, 'No, no, she isn't.'

'Who is she then?'

'I'll tell you when we get home.'

He almost toppled over the side of the trap as she grabbed the reins from his hands and pulled the horse to a standstill, and she was leaning partly across him as she demanded, 'You'll tell me now . . . now!'

'Now look here Martha Mary.'

'Never mind, look here Martha Mary. What is it you've got to tell me about . . . this Eva, whoever she may be?'

He now thrust her from him, straightened his cravat, stretched his neck upwards first one way, then the other, and said, 'She's the girl I'm going to marry, we're engaged. I . . . I was bringing her home to meet you.'

She flopped back against the wooden bar that acted as a back to the seat. She didn't believe it, no, she didn't believe it, this couldn't be happening. She wasn't sitting in the trap on the highway and being told that her brother was going to marry, that her nineteen-year-old brother was going to bring a woman into the house. Strange, but she had never really thought about him ever getting married; that was stupid of her, but he has always seemed so young, even at nineteen he didn't appear his age, more like a youth of sixteen or seventeen. Yet here he was telling her he was a man and going to be married.

That same feared rage she had experienced for the first time on the morning she met her father's mistress was rising in her again, but with more strength and power than it had possessed at its birth. She turned her head slowly and looked at him. Her face dark with passion and in a voice like no other she had ever used, she said two words, 'Drive on!' and after looking at her for a long moment he drew in a breath, bit tightly on his lower lip, took up the reins and drove on. . . .

Immediately the trap stopped on the drive she jumped down from it, missing the bottom step, and actually ran at a pace up the steps and into the house. Once in the hall, she dragged off her bonnet and flung it towards a chair, throwing her grey faded dustcoat after it, and when it missed the chair and fell to the floor she left it lying there.

Peg, having come from the kitchen to give Master Roland a word of welcome, had stopped dead just beyond the kitchen door and gazed in amazement at Miss Martha Mary who, as she expressed it to herself, looked as mad as any March hare, and when she saw Master Roland enter the hall and follow Miss Martha Mary across to the drawing-room she uttered no word of greeting. There was something up.

She snatched a duster from the pocket of her apron and busied herself in the hall in order to find out what it was. But she could have stayed in the kitchen and heard equally as well because Miss Martha Mary was now shouting, 'You have the effrontery to come back from school—school I say—and tell me that you are going to be married! May I ask how you propose to support your wife?'

They stood facing each other before the empty fireplace, their faces blotched with their anger, and Roland's voice was now as loud as hers. 'Yes, I'll tell you how I'll manage to support a wife. There's the shop. Much more could be made out of it. And what is more we have ideas, plans for turning this place—' he now jerked his forearm in an arc in front of his face—'into a school.'

She wanted to sit down, she wanted to grip something for support. No, no, not for support, she had the most terrifying feeling of stretching out her hands and gripping his neck and choking him. Her little brother, as she had thought of him until recently, had with his announcement blown her world into pieces. It lay about her in fragments. She, who had toiled and slaved, yes, slaved after them all for years, but more so of late when she had been called upon to do the most menial of household tasks, and all without payment, or thought of payment, was now to be relegated . . . to what? To what position would she be relegated in this household under Roland's wife? Still a maid of all work but without the dignity of being recognized as the mistress.

That was the rod that was flaying her at this moment. The one compensation she asked, indeed the only compensation she asked in exchange for all her labour and love was to be recognized as the mistress of The Habitation.

She had told herself often of late that she was stupid about many things, ignorant through prudery, and bigoted about matters she didn't understand, but now she also saw that she had been purposely blind. Hadn't she realized that Roland was the son of his father and that women would be a necessity to him from early in life? But she had never imagined so early. He was but a boy. . . . No! No! Why did she keep harping on about him being a boy. Why should William Brockdean be considered a man and entitled to marry, or Robbie Robson for that matter, and not Roland Crawford? It was she who had been at fault, at least as regards her blindness, for this was self-inflicted.

Yet she saw it now as a blindness that had shafts of light penetrating it, selfish shafts of light. Why had she been so keen for Roland to maintain his scholastic studies? Why had she offered him the small fortune that Dilly had left her? Why? As a means of keeping him out of the way for another two or three years so that she could continue to act as mistress of this house, that's why.

Well, that being so it would seem that she was being paid out for her duplicity, wouldn't it?

But no! Her whole being reared in denial against the accusation. Whatever her ulterior motive had been she didn't deserve to be treated thus. Turn the house into a school indeed! And who would be the schoolmistress? *Mrs Eva Crawford* of course. And who would be the school matron? And the housekeeper? And the doer of all the mean chores? Poor Miss Martha Mary Crawford, the spinster sister of the owner.

No. No. Never.

When she banged her fist on the occasional table and the knick-knacks skidded here and there she brought a startled look of fear to Roland's face and he cried at her, 'Stop it, Martha Mary! Take hold of yourself. Don't go mad.'

'Don't go mad, you say. Huh! Don't go mad. You come home and barefacedly tell me you are going to be married and you expect me to accept it calmly after all that's been done for you.'

'What d'you mean, all that's been done for me? Father kept me at school. . . .'

'Father didn't keep you at school, I kept you at school,' she cried, digging her fingers into her chest, 'through scraping and saving over the household, and on clothes for us all, and denying myself and the others the small comforts of life; if I hadn't, Father wouldn't have had enough money to spend on his mistresses and his whoring. . . .' My God! what was she saying, using a word like that aloud? But she had said it, she had brought this foul thing into the open, this thing that in her distress she had written to him about the night she had sat by Aunt Sophie's bed. But never once in his letters had he referred to it, and she could see now the reason for his silence on the matter; he had thought little of it, and it was more than likely he was at the same game himself.

Oh dear, dear! why were her thoughts so raw? She was thinking as Dilly might, and she had been talking as Dilly might.

And why not! It was a pity there weren't more people in the world like Dilly. She now thrust her face towards his red flaming countenance and cried, 'Whoring I said, and whoring I mean. You ignored the implication of this in the letter I sent you after he died. But now I'm giving it a name, its right name, and because of it there were times when we almost starved here. Yes, starved, and that's no exaggeration, in order that you and he should live your lives as prescribed for a gentleman, so called, and his son. . . .'

They were glaring at each other in open hate, yet his hatred was but a weak shadow of the emotion that was tearing her to pieces; and this was proved when, his head suddenly drooping, he turned from her and sank into a chair. But she wasn't finished with him, for now she cried, 'There's one thing I accomplished which pleases me mightily at this moment; I don't know how I had the sense to do it, I must in some way have been forewarned, but I opened a banking account of my own, and put Dilly's money into it. I remember thinking it would be nice if only for a short time to imagine it was mine. But it is *mine*, two hundred and eight pounds, and now it will stand me in good stead while I am choosing a career for myself.'

He turned his head and looked at her. The flush of anger had gone from his face leaving it almost deathly white except where the spots stood out. He was gaping at her open-mouthed and his voice had a tremor to it now as he said, 'Martha Mary, you wouldn't, you couldn't, you couldn't leave me in the lurch.'

'What did you say?' Now her voice was low, but weighed with disdain. 'Leave *you* in the lurch? Leave you in the lurch, you say? What exactly do you mean? Tell me. Tell me.'

'Well, there's the house . . . I . . . I told Eva that you were so good at managing everything, and you are, you're wonderful, Martha Mary, I've always said it, and . . . and Eva would be quite willing to let you run things just as they are now. She wouldn't interfere. She would just see to the educational side. She's . . . she's rather brilliant that way; she speaks three foreign languages fluently. And she . . . well, she wouldn't—' he hung his head for a moment before ending, 'She wouldn't be cut out for . . . for . . .'

'Well, go on. Tell me what she wouldn't be cut out for. I suppose you mean she wouldn't be cut out for household chores.'

When he raised his eyes to hers but remained quiet, she said on a bitter laugh, 'Well, that's a great pity, Roland, because she'll have to learn, won't she? As you know, Peg cannot do half the work that she used to, and the hall floor is so very large, and it always seems larger when you're on your knees scrubbing it; it's much worse than the kitchen, but I'll be quite pleased to show your future wife the best way to prevent calloused knees. I made special pads for myself; of course, Peg has always had her own . . .'

'Shut up! I forbid you to go on. Shut up!'

His face now looked ugly and she stared back into it, her own expression grim and her voice equally so as she said, 'You cannot forbid me to do anything, I am not in your employ, Roland.' She paused; then again came the bitter laugh as she went on, 'I'm just trying to be helpful. If I don't meet your future wife to give her some practical advice as regards how this particular household is run then I must give it to you to pass on to her. . . . And, oh, we mustn't forget there's Aunt Sophie; she'll have to be told how to deal with Aunt Sophie.'

As if he had suddenly remembered there was an Aunt Sophie he gripped his chin in his hand and murmured something under his breath, and Martha repeated it aloud. 'Yes,' she said, 'it is a case of Oh my God! But I shouldn't worry unduly, she may find Aunt Sophie amusing, and no doubt her fits will be an experience. Of course, some people are afraid of those who have fits, but you must tell her that Aunt Sophie is utterly harmless.'

'You won't do this, Martha Mary. You can't do this.' His voice sounded like that of a pleading child until he ended, 'I forbid it.'

'Huh! Don't make me laugh, Roland. You forbidding me! You forbidding anybody! In fact you, Roland, are a weakling. Do you know that? You are a weakling. You are like our father, you are a good-looking weakling. But take a word of warning, don't let your fiancée see you as such or she'll despise you. . . . Now, dear brother, if you will excuse me I shall go to my room and get my things together because I don't intend to be here when your future wife arrives.'

But when she went to pass him, he gripped her arm and, his face now white with passion, he ground out between his teeth, 'You mean to ruin me out of spite, don't you? You're a bitch. Do you hear? A bitch! It's as Mildred said, you're like a frustrated spinster.'

'Leave go of my arm!'

When he didn't release his hold but even tightened it she took her other hand and brought it with a resounding blow across his face. As much from surprise as from the force of the blow he staggered back against the mantelpiece and only stopped himself from falling backwards into the fireplace by spreadeagling his arms. From this position he glared at her and she at him, then in a voice that sounded eerily calm, she said, 'And don't forget, brother, you still have the business of Nancy to straighten out.'

On this she left the room, went through the hall and up the stairs and into her own room, where she did not sit down and cry, for the fury in her was still keeping her upright, but she stood rigid staring out of the window. The wind had gone down and it had started to rain. It was a straight, steady rain, blocking out the river and the woods beyond, blocking out all concern for everyone but herself, and what faced her at this moment.

She had told him she would take up a career. What career? She couldn't even be a governess. No, the most she could hope for was that of a housekeeper. Well, if she took up such a position she would get paid for it, wouldn't she? And that would be something.

She turned and looked about the room which had been hers alone since she had taken over the management of the house after her mother died. She recalled her delight at having a room to herself, and the honour of being on the main floor and what was more, her bedroom door being right opposite that of her father's room. And he himself had supervised the moving of special pieces of furniture into it, such as the Sheraton dressing table, and the mahogany tallboy chest and the carpet from the guest room, and when the time of mourning was over he had taken her into Hexham and let her choose some chintz for the curtains and to cover her easy chair. The room was still the same, except that the chintz was faded a little. And now she was going to leave it. The enormity of the change appalled her for a moment, but only for a moment, for she told herself in deep bitterness that she was leaving this house tomorrow and no one would stop her.

As she pulled out a dressing case from a cupboard to the side of the window the question came at her, 'What will happen to Aunt Sophie?' and she answered without a pause, 'That's his responsibility.'

But he might put her in a home! This thought did bring her to a halt. No, no, he wouldn't, because he would have to pay for her and he was in no position to do that. No, Aunt Sophie would remain here, but without the love and care she herself had lavished on her for years.

She stood stock still now in the middle of the room looking back down those years, the years in which she had played the mother, the housekeeper, the mistress of the house. It was only six years in time but it was six lifetimes of youth. She had given her youth, her girlish days, to this house and them all. She'd never had any fun, any joy except that of service; and after all, what joy did that bring in the years between fourteen and twenty? Those years were never meant for service, they were meant for growing, for searching, for experiencing, for enjoying that particular period of life that would never come again because this should be a time of wonder, of phantasy, of dreaming, but when it was over, they were over, the wonder, the phantasy and the dreaming. Life never offered you that period of experience again. Life from twenty was reality, looked at with eyes wide open; the dream period when with lids half closed the mind outdid the fables in imagining the wonders that life could hold was over.

She had once read a very cynical remark by one of the modern writers who said that the teen years held days of disillusionment, weeks of heartbreak, months of bodily torture, and years of false values. Perhaps he was right, but she wouldn't mind at this stage looking back from the saneness of twenty into the magic madness of youth if she had been allowed to experience it.

She went now to the bed and, slumping onto it, she buried her head into the pillow and filled her mouth with it in order to prevent herself crying out aloud.

7

The rain was coming down heavy and steady as Harry neared the turning that led to The Habitation. Since setting out from Hexham he had been in two minds whether or not to call in. His last visit had been but three days ago; to call so soon might look a little marked as if he were nosing into the doings of the house, yet she had asked him to interfere in the matter of Miss Nancy, hadn't she? And more than once. But being of the temperament she was, she would doubtless look upon today's visit as yet another fee to be added to the bill. And he could hardly say he was visiting unprofessionally. Good Lord no, not that. But the rain decided him against breaking his journey to Nolan's Farm, and so he went straight on past the turning.

But still he could not help wondering how the odd affair was progressing between young Robbie Robson and Miss Nancy. Twice on his travels during the past fortnight he had espied her in the distance; and she had seen him too, but she had made no move to speak to him. The first time she actually turned and ran. She had been on the open hillside then. The second time, she was walking along the main road that led to the Robson's cottage, but again on catching sight of him she had climbed the bank and disappeared.

Then, as if his mind had conjured her up, he saw her, he saw them both. They were seated side by side in a trap which Robbie was driving into the main road from a side lane that led back over the hills.

Harry drew Bessie to a standstill as he came abreast of them, and Robbie, too, pulled up his horse. It was Harry who spoke first. 'Summer seems to have left us,' he said.

'It does, doctor.' Robbie nodded back at him. His face although running with rain had a bright look about it, and if the same expression had been on a woman's features it could have been termed starry, and he went on, 'But winter's a long way off yet. Still, I like winter, long nights by the fire, a good roof over your head, something warm inside an' the door closed tight an' a wife by your side. What more could a fella want?'

The smile slid from Harry's face. He was looking at Nancy, her head was bent. His gaze now lifted to Robbie, and Robbie nodded back at him, saying, 'Aye, doctor, yes, we did it the day in Newcastle, right and proper with a licence.'

'No!'

'Oh, but aye, doctor, aye.'

'But she's not of age. They can . . .'

'She's old enough to wed. Anyway, she's an orphan, doctor, she has nei-ther mother nor father. Now who would she get her consent from, I ask you? Don't let it worry you, doctor, she'll be happy, I'll see to it.' The ex-pression on his face had changed now, it was serious, stiff. 'By the way, you can do me a service. Are you callin' in at The Habitation on your way back?'

'I didn't intend to.' His voice was cold.

'Well, as I said, doctor, it would do me a service, both of us, if you'd tell her, Miss Martha that is, that Nancy here has gone home, she's married an' gone home. An' if she's got a mind to let her have her things well an' good, if not, 'tis no matter, I can buy her things. I bought her this dress the day.'

When he touched her cloak Nancy tugged it from his hand and drew it closer about her, at the same time bowing her head deeper onto her chest.

Robbie stared at her for a moment, his face stiff; then glancing in Harry's direction, he said, 'It's soaked we're all gettin'. I'll bid you good-day, doctor. An' if you can't do me that service 'tis no matter.' And with this he cried, 'Get up there!' and his horse trotted off smartly.

Harry continued on his journey towards the farm. As the saying went, possession was nine points of law, and after tonight who would want to break that law as regards those two? Yes, he would call in at The Habita-tion on his way home.

Martha had been in her room for almost three hours. Twice Roland had knocked on the door and she had told him to go away. She had been up to the attic and brought down a trunk, a hat box, and a small valise. Now, together with her dressing case, all her belongings were arrayed around her, and as she looked down into the half-filled trunk she realized how lit-tle she possessed of anything.

Her plans were made. Tomorrow morning she would go by carrier cart into Hexham and there find accommodation. She thought she might call on Mr and Mrs Armstrong; they were kindly folk and she would need to be with kindly folk for a little time until she got her bearings. They had, she knew, a spare room, for it had been arranged that Mildred should stay there overnight if the weather towards the end of the year were to become too inclement for her to travel by the carrier cart.

Once she was settled she'd send a cab to collect her belongings and that would be the end of it. Or the beginning. But of what? The question had the power to create fear of the future, but she challenged it with: whatever the future held, whatever subservient position she was forced to take in order to make a livelihood it could not be more humiliating than would be her existence in this house under a new mistress . . . a school mistress. That was the worst part of it. The house to be turned into a boarding school, the rooms turned into dormitories, and classrooms. And they'd want all the rooms, wouldn't they? This, her own room, would be considered an unnecessary luxury, and she would be relegated to the attic again —the picture was so vivid that she banged down the lid of the trunk to shut it out.

There came another knock on the door and she turned her head sharply towards it and cried, 'Go away!'

''Tis me, Miss Martha Mary.'

She drew in a long breath, then went to the door and withdrew the bolt, and she looked down on Peg, and Peg looked up at her, and she knew from the sadness expressed on the small girl's face that there was nothing that had transpired between herself and Roland that Peg wasn't aware of. 'What is it, Peg?'

''Tis the doctor, he's called.' She strained her neck upwards as she whispered, 'What'll I say to him?'

'The doctor?' She wasn't expecting him. His last visit was only three days ago. But perhaps he had come with some news concerning Nancy. . . . Well, whatever he had to say about Nancy it didn't interest her any more. Nancy was Roland's concern. She was finished, finished with everything, all of them.

'Where is he?'

'I . . . I put him in the study. I . . . I said you had a splittin' head and had gone to lie down but I'd tell you. What'll I say to him?'

Martha, looking over Peg's head, thought for a moment, then said, 'Tell him I'll be down directly.'

'Aye, yes, I will, I will, Miss Martha Mary.'

Peg watched the bedroom door being closed before she turned and scampered across the landing and down the stairs and straight to the study again, and there without ceremony she opened the door and, still scurrying, went up the room and stood close to Harry, and looking up into his face, she hissed, 'I'd better tell you, doctor, afore she comes down. There's been trouble, in fact the divil's fagarties here the day. She's leavin'. She's been up in the attic and got her trunk, an' she's leavin', Miss Martha Mary's leavin'.'

'Leaving? What do you mean, leaving?'

She now stood on her tiptoes, strained her neck upwards and whispered, ''Tis Master Roland. He came home the day. She sent for him 'cos of Miss Nancy, but he hit her with a bombshell, he told her he was gona be married an' his lass is coming in two days' time. She's a school marm or some-thin' like that. They're going to turn the house into a school. . . . Did you ever hear owt like it?'

Harry, his eyes narrowed, his face puckered, bent down now towards her and asked softly, 'You're sure of this, Peg?'

'Sure as I'm lookin' at you, doctor. I was beyond the door an' I've got ears like cuddy's lugs, an' I heard every word. There was hell to pay in there. Never heard Miss Martha Mary go on like it afore. An' I won't stay if she goes, I won't. I'm tellin' you, I won't. She's been me mistress all this time and a good 'un at that, not like others. I'll go along of 'er, I will. I'll go along of 'er.'

'Ssh! someone's coming. Go on.' He pushed her.

Peg reached the study door as Martha entered, and Martha looking onto the lowered head guessed immediately that Peg had been talking, and her suspicions were confirmed when she looked at Harry, for never had she seen his face as she was seeing it now.

When he put his hand on her arm and said, 'Sit down,' she gulped be-fore answering, 'I'm . . . I'm all right.'

'You're not all right. You don't look all right. Sit down.' He pressed her on to the couch, then seated himself, not close to her, yet not at any great distance.

'Peg's just given me the gist of something that I can't believe,' he said quietly. 'She . . . she says you're leaving the house.'

'Yes. Yes, I'm leaving.' She was staring towards the empty fireplace that was hidden by a hand-worked screen. 'And Peg will likely have told you why.'

'She says your brother is going to be married.'

'Yes, he's going to be married.'

He paused for a moment before saying, 'It must have come as a shock to you. After all you were providing for him to go to university.'

'Yes, yes.' She nodded slowly, still staring straight ahead.

'Did . . . did you never consider that he would some day marry?'

When she turned her head slowly now and looked at him there was a look in her eyes that hurt him, and he glimpsed how deeply she had been humiliated in her own sight.

'No, doctor, no, I didn't. But I see now I have been blind, selfishly blind, perhaps because I did not wish it to happen. This was my home; I . . . I have been in charge of it for such a long time, at least it has seemed a long time to me, that I imagined—' She drooped her head now as she ended—'At least I must have hoped that I would always be in charge of it.'

'You wouldn't consider staying on and seeing what she's . . . ? No, no.' He shook his head. 'I can see that would be too much to ask of you.'

'Yes, yes it would.' She raised her eyes to his now as she said, 'I'm glad that you agree with me in this at least, doctor.'

'You may not believe it, but I have agreed with you on many things, though my manner unfortunately may not have conveyed this to you. I am, as you will have gathered, of a very quick temper—' he smiled tentatively now—'but . . . yes, yes, I do agree with you wholeheartedly that under the circumstances your position would be quite untenable. But may I ask what you intend to do when you leave?'

'Find lodgings first. I may go to Mr Armstrong's, then . . . then seek a position.'

'As what?'

She did not answer him immediately but stared back into his eyes while her lower jaw wobbled slightly from side to side. 'As a housekeeper.'

'A housekeeper?' He made a small obeisance with his head.

'Yes, a housekeeper.'

'Oh.'

Again they were looking at each other in silence, and he had the most frightening and overwhelming desire to thrust out his hands, grab hers and say, 'Come and be my housekeeper.'

During the still seconds that followed the madness subsided, but did not entirely fade away for now he hitched himself nearer to her on the couch and was actually calling her by her name.

'Martha Mary,' he said, 'I'm going to call you by your name because everybody else seems to do that, and it will smooth the ground between us, for this is a time I think when you should look upon me as a friend and not as an . . . an opponent.'

Her eyes seemed to be getting wider, her face seemed to be stretching at all points. She knew that in a moment she would break down. He had called her by her name, and it didn't sound silly, or matronish, or biblical. He had, in some way, made it sound a pleasant name. He was being kind to her; she had never imagined he could be so kind, at least not to her. She was going to cry.

He had taken her hands; in spite of himself he had taken hold of her hands. 'Don't upset yourself, try not to cry.' Yet even as he gave her this advice he knew he should be saying, 'Let go, cry your fill, howl out your anguish,' for he knew she was actually suffering anguish.

Years ago when he first came into practice one of his patients was a refined gentlewoman dying in utter poverty, and in this moment he recalled the substance of her words, as he had done on many other occasions: 'Nearly everyone has sympathy for the pain they can see,' she had said; 'the children in the mines, the factory workers, those on the land, they all elicit sympathy from thinking people. I have always worked to help the poor, and when I say to them I understand their plight they always answer, "You'll never know what misery is like, miss." But there is a misery of the mind, doctor, a misery of the spirit that the poor fortunately know nothing about, because you have to have a certain amount of education before you are introduced to the torture chambers of the mind, wherein the membranes, sensitized by your early environment, sharpen the agony of living.'

The misery of the spirit that the poor know nothing of. It was quite true. The poor were inured to misery from their birth, and they seemed to withstand misfortune with a stoicism because it was untouched by the torture of the mind.

He looked down on to the hands held within his and felt the movement of her thumb unconsciously scratching at his knuckle, which was a sure sign of the tension within her, the tension that would eventually, and not so very far ahead, snap her nerves into a mental illness. And so he shook the hands up and down vigorously, saying, 'It may all be for the best. One never knows at the time why these things happen, but looking back you see they are for the best. And don't ever feel you're alone, do you hear me?'

She nodded slowly but was unable to answer him.

'Oh!' He now nipped at his lower lip. 'Miss Sophie. What's going to happen to her?'

She swallowed deeply. 'I don't know. It . . . it is his responsibility.'

'He may put her in a home.'

'No, no,' she shook her head, 'that would cost money.'

He gave a small laugh, saying, 'Yes, you're right, it would cost money.' He rose to his feet and walked up and down the hearthrug twice before saying abruptly, 'Your sister?'

Her voice sounded calm now as she answered, 'That, too, is his responsibility, and . . . and I know only too well, in fact I think I have known all along that in the end she will do what she wants to do.'

'She has already done it.'

She looked startled for a moment, her own misery forgotten. 'How . . . how do you know?'

'I met them just a short while back returning from Newcastle. They had been married by licence. They must have left very early this morning.'

She looked now towards the window and the falling rain, and after a moment said, 'Yes, she left very early this morning. So 'tis done then?'

'Yes, 'tis done, and . . . and I don't think anything can undo it. No effort that your brother can make. . . .'

'I don't think he'll make any effort in that direction, he is not one for making efforts. No.' She sighed now a deep slow sigh, and looked up at him. 'He will say he has cut her off, he will use that term.' Her head nodded as if in agreement with her statement. 'And if he meets her in the town he'll pass her as if he doesn't know her, as my father would have done. Roland is a hypocrite, as my father was too.'

He could say nothing to this, only continue to look at her and think that it was a damn shame, in fact it was a bloody shame, and that was swearing to it, that a girl like this should have lost her youth slaving after such a worthless family. And they were all worthless, from the father down to the pretty one who had married the drover today. They were worthless and selfish. It was always the one who did the most in a family, worked the hardest, shouldered the responsibility who in the end was handed the dirty end of the stick. And there was no doubt that she had got the dirty end of the stick today. Only one thing surprised him, that she should be leaving the old aunt without apparently showing any qualms as to what might happen to her, for he had noticed that there was a bond between them. Still, who could blame her? Not he, definitely not he. In a way, let him face it, he was glad it was happening. Oh yes, it was like watching her being released from prison, seeing her coming up out of a dungeon, a dungeon of petty class values and prejudices; seeing her going out into the world would be like watching someone having their fetters hacked off them and released into clear open air for the first time since birth.

He watched her now rise to her feet and walk to the window and, standing with her back to him, say, 'I . . . I don't wish you to be sorry for me, doctor.'

'Oh!' He, too, was at the window now. 'Oh, I'm not at all sorry for you, at least not because you have been forced to make a stand and are going out into the world. No. But at the same time I am sorry that you have been treated in such a fashion, for as I see it you have given your young life to the family, and almost . . .' He only checked himself in time from saying 'lost your entire youth'. But that wouldn't have been true. She was still young, so very young, in fact, he had never seen her looking so young. It was as if in throwing off the responsibility of the house she had thrown off surplus years with it. When he first saw her he had imagined her to be anything up to twenty-six. Now she looked a vulnerable girl of seventeen or eighteen.

'When are you leaving?'

'First thing in the morning.' She turned from the window.

'You say you're going to the Armstrongs'?'

'Yes, if, if they'll have me, for a short time.'

'Oh, they'll have you all right; be only too pleased; he's very grateful to you, very grateful.'

'He has repaid that many times over. As you said, he knows books.'

'Well.' He looked about him now for his bag and hat, then said in a slightly embarrassed tone, 'Oh, I left them in the hall, I . . . I must be off.' He went towards her again, but he did not take her hand, he merely looked straight into her face and said, 'Consider me your friend, will you?'

Again her eyes were stretching and the muscles of her face twitching. 'Thank you. Thank you, doctor . . . I will.'

He stared at her for a moment; then poking his face within inches of hers, he whispered, 'My name's Harry.' There was another pause before he added, 'Good-bye, Martha Mary. I'll see you tomorrow either here or at Armstrong's,' and with this he turned from her and went out. . . .

In the yard, young Dan said, 'By! you're gona be sodden afore you get to the town, doctor.'

'I'm pretty sodden already, Dan; but my skin's like leather, it never goes through.'

Dan laughed up at him as he answered, 'Shouldn't wonder, doctor. Shouldn't wonder, all the weathers you go out in. But he knows when he's on a good thing.' He pointed to where Fred was snuggling under a sheet of oilcloth, then called, 'That's what you should have, doctor, a suit of oilskins like the sailors.'

'I'll have to see about it, Dan. Get up there.' He jerked the reins, nodded to Dan, then put the horse into a trot out of the yard and down the drive, but as always, and more so today, he saw the caution of bringing the animal to a walk when they went onto the rutted road.

As the rain beat into his face and dripped from his collar down the back of his neck, he thought, Leather skin indeed! He'd have to have some real cover come the winter; he'd have to try to get the old man to indulge in a cab of sorts. He gave an inward chuckle at the improbability of this, for a cab would mean a driver if one of them were to remain dry.

When he reached the main road he again cried, 'Get up there! Bessie. Get up.' He felt strangely happy, in fact he knew a feeling of slight elation. One man's meat was another man's poison; her sorrow would lead to his joy. . . . What! What was he thinking? Aye, what? Was that what he really wanted? *Her?* Come on, face up to it; did he want her so badly? Aye. Aye, that was it, that was just it, he wanted her badly. It was no good hoodwinking himself any more. But what was it about her that attracted him, and had done from the first, so much so that he had deliberately fought her off with his bawling and rudeness? To this he couldn't give himself an answer, except to say, well she's my kind of woman, no . . . girl; because she was still a girl.

When he was married first he'd had really little experience of women apart from their anatomy, but by God he had made up for it since. There was now no facet of their minds that he hadn't explored, and had been amazed at how many would have been accessible had he proposed to explore their bodies.

It was a tricky business doctoring. It forbade you to pick where you might fancy. Yet had he fancied any patient over the last eight years or so? No, not one until he had met her, Martha Mary Crawford. And come tomorrow, what would he say to her? Well, he'd say, 'I've got you a post, Martha Mary.' But what if she refused it?

Aye, that was a point, what if she refused it? It would knock the stuffing out of him, to say the least.

As the trap mounted the hill he rubbed the rain from his eyes and looked to the right, but he couldn't see the river. Nevertheless, the position recalled the day he had seen Nancy and young Brockdean embracing down there. But now she was married, and to a drover lad. Life was strange.

As he rounded the bend to go down the hill he looked sharply upwards and to the left. Here the land rose steeply, and only last week a number of boulders had rolled down on to the road, missing him only by yards, but causing Bessie to rear and go off into a gallop. When he had managed to stop her he had turned her about and gone back, to find two good-sized lumps of rock lying on the edge of the roadway; a third had tumbled down towards the river. As he had looked at the size of them he could not but help feel what a narrow escape they'd had. The small landslide, he had surmised, was brought about by dry weather.

Recalling it now, he peered through the rain but couldn't see the top of the hill, nor yet, he realized, would he be able to hear any rumble because of the noise of the rain and the wind that was carrying it straight into his face.

The trap was down on the level now and he screwed up his eyes to slits as he thought he saw three hooded figures standing in the middle of the road ahead of him. On his journey out he had seen three men with sacks over their heads running across the fell. He had noticed them particularly because he'd thought they were trying to hail him, but they stopped when some way off. Now the figures on the road in front of the horse were, he felt sure, the same three men.

Then, before he knew what was happening, he saw Bessie rear up, then be pulled down to a quivering standstill by one of the men, and when two figures mounted the trap at either side and hands grabbed him he lashed out with both the whip and his fist as he yelled, 'What's this, you ruffians! What . . . d'you think you're up to?'

As his fist crashed into the side of the hessian hood and one of the men tumbled backwards on to the road, the other got his arm around his throat and he felt himself being dragged downwards, at the same time being aware that Fred was fighting and tearing furiously at the assailant.

He was on the ground now. The man still had his arm tight around his neck and he realized, if dimly, that in another minute it would be all over with him and he would choke to death. As he heard a sharp cry he was only just aware that Fred's teeth had entered some part of the man who was holding him. With a twist of his body and kicking out with one leg after the other he managed to free himself. As he swung round to rise to his knees he saw that the man who had held him by the throat was now fighting Fred who had a grip on his leg. The sack had fallen back on to his shoulders, his mouth was wide open as he yelled in agony, and Harry recognized the toothless gap. Then the breath seemed to be shot from his body as a foot caught him in the ribs under the armpit. He rolled over, took one agonizing deep breath before the foot came at him again. In one last desperate effort he grabbed at the leg, and as the man toppled on to him he was completely winded for the moment, but also had the satisfaction of knowing that this particular assailant was also out of action for, rolling off him, he lay prone on the road now. Somewhere in his mind he was telling himself that only one was left, for Fred was still dealing with the ringleader; and he had recognized the ringleader.

He was heaving himself upwards when he heard Fred give an agonizing yelp; the next moment a blow on the back of the head carried him into blackness.

Dan Holland usually left the yard at six o'clock and by taking short cuts and running most of the way he could reach home in under the hour, but his short cuts meant crossing low lying fields that were soggy at any time, but were almost impassable during a heavy rainfall such as now, and so under these circumstances he kept to the main road for the first two miles.

He walked with a steady untiring swing; he had a sack round his shoulders, and his cap was resting on his ears. He had reached the bottom of the hill and was hugging the dry-stone wall for partial shelter when he tripped over something. It became entangled in his feet, and when he looked down he recognized the yellow piece of oilcloth that had covered the doctor's dog. Stooping, he picked it up, thinking to himself, By! it must have been a wind to lift that off him 'cos he was lying on half of it.

He stood for a moment and peered about him; then he noticed something else, and he thought it strange it should be lying at the other side of the road right opposite the dog's cover. When he picked up the butt end of a whip his face crinkled in perplexity. Then his eyes travelling downwards into the ditch, he saw two more pieces of splintered wood. It looked as if somebody had broken a whip into smithereens.

He lifted his hand now and wiped the rain from his eyes. This was funny, odd. It could be anybody's whip, but that over there was the piece of oilcloth that had covered the doctor's dog.

The bank beyond the ditch was clear of scrub and rolled down straight to the river. He screened his eyes and peered through the rain, but he couldn't see very far. Should he go down? No, no, nowt could have happened the doctor. He looked down at the pieces of wood again, then along the ditch to his left where the scrub began to border the road and form a hedge.

Dropping down from the road into the ditch, he reached the hedge, then pulled himself up and walked behind it. Again he shaded his eyes and peered into the distance. There was nothing there. Anyway, he asked himself, what did he expect to find? The doctor had been driving a horse and trap and if there was a horse and trap lying about he would see it, wouldn't he? A blind man couldn't miss that.

It was as he turned to retrace his steps towards the road that he heard the faint whine, more like the wheezing of a puppy. He hurried forward now towards the sound. The shrub hedge curved at this point and when he rounded it, his step was checked and he became stock still. There, not five yards distant, lay the doctor and across him lay the dog.

Eeh! God Almighty!

He was bending over the two forms now. They were both covered with blood, but it was the condition of the dog that brought his thumb into his mouth. It had been cut in several places. It looked as if its legs were hanging off, yet it was still alive for it looked up at him and made that weak little sound again.

My God! what was he going to do? The doctor was bleeding from a wound somewhere under his hair. The rain had washed the blood over his face and it appeared like a pink mask. One knee was pulled up almost to his chest. Tentatively, he touched his shoulder then shook it gently, saying, 'Doctor! Doctor!'

When there was no response he stood up and looked about him in trembling agitation. He could do nothing on his own, he'd have to get help. He'd have to get a door or something. Which was the nearest house? Back where he had come from, of course. Aye. Aye.

But wait, what about Fulman's cottage? That was just across on the further bank. Don't be daft, he told himself; if the river hadn't risen and covered the steppy stones he would have used them as a short cut, wouldn't he? There was nothing for it but to hare back to the house.

One last look downwards, and then he was running with almost the swiftness of a hare along the bank, over the ditch and on to the main road, and he didn't stop to gasp for fresh breath until he turned into the lane, and then his pause was only a matter of seconds before he was off again.

When he burst into the kitchen Peg let out a thin scream and she hung on to the end of the table as he yelled at her, ''Tis the doctor! The doctor an' the dog. They've been murdered on the road. Tell miss and the young master. Go on, fetch them, quick!'

'The doctor? My God! No, no. Where?'

'Just beyond the rise. Go on; don't stand there.'

Peg went. She scrambled out of the kitchen, across the hall and up the stairs, crying as she did so, 'Miss Martha Mary! Master Roland! Miss Martha Mary!'

Martha was in her bedroom; Roland was in the drawing-room; but so desperate was Peg's cry that they both appeared at once.

'What is it, Peg?'

''Tis the doctor, miss. Dan has just come back; he's found them on the road; murdered he said.'

Martha's two hands went up and cupped her face as she whispered, 'Murdered?'

''Tis what he says.'

When she reached the bottom of the stairs Roland was there, and he followed her towards the kitchen, saying, 'What is it? What's the matter? What's this about a murder? What is it?'

Martha was now standing over Dan. 'The doctor; he's hurt you say?'

'Looks dead to me, miss.' He shook his head slowly, then bit on his lip. 'An' the dog's done for, cut up to bits. He . . . he was still breathing but'— he screwed up his eyes now—'he's an awful sight.'

'Where?'

'Yon side of the rise. I could do nothing; you'll have to have a door.' He now looked towards Roland, then repeated, 'You'll have to have a door, Master Roland, or . . . or the trap. Aye, the trap. Will I get the trap ready?'

'Yes, yes, do that. Quick!' It was Martha who answered; then almost pushing aside Roland who seemed slightly bewildered, she ran into the hall, grabbed her cape from out of the cupboard, dragged on a pair of old shoes she used for the garden; then, encountering Roland as he entered the hall, she said, 'Don't stand there, get into something. You heard what the lad said.'

A few minutes later when they reached the stable, Dan was bringing out the horse and trap, and they mounted in silence; and the silence continued until they entered the main road when Martha cried at Roland who was driving, 'Don't just trot her, hurry!'

'And have us all in the ditch? The road's like glar.'

'Belle is surefooted.'

'Nothing is surefooted in weather like this. . . . And stop it!' He hissed the last words at her and she knew that they weren't meant only in answer to her present urgency, but were in protest at her overall attitude towards him.

A few minutes later Dan said, 'He's just there, miss, beyond those bushes, to the right of you.' Then he added, 'I'd stop here, Master Roland. You'll have to bring him along the back of them until the way's clear to get him up the bank.'

Even before the trap had actually stopped Martha was on the road and she was side by side with Dan as he scrambled over the ditch. Then she was running behind him until, as he had done, she stopped dead.

She made no sound at all as she gazed down in horror on the mutilated animal now lying with his head at a strange angle, which spoke of death. Its mouth was open and its tongue was lying against the edge of Harry's chin.

The soft 'Oh my God!' from Roland behind her seemed to bring her out of a horrified daze, and then she was kneeling on the boggy ground, repeating between gasps, 'Doctor! Doctor! . . . Doctor! Doctor!'

As the dog was drawn slowly away, she put her arm under Harry's head and raised it, and now, her face close to his and her fingers wiping the blood from his cheeks, she bent hers close to his and again she said his name, which now had the sound of a plea, a forceful plea, a plea for him to be alive. 'Doctor! Doctor!'

Call me Harry, he had said. Oh Harry, Harry, don't die. Please, please, don't die.

'Is he alive?'

She watched Roland's head drop sideways on to Harry's chest and when he looked up at her his eyes told her that he could hear nothing.

She swallowed deeply. 'We must get him home,' she said. 'We'll have to carry him to the trap. You . . . you and Dan take his upper part, I'll take his legs.'

'Do you think you can?'

Some loud voice inside her cried, 'Of course I can! I . . . I would carry him myself if necessary,' but her reply came as a whisper, saying, 'Yes, yes, I can.' And she did.

While Roland and Dan supported his trunk she, her arms under both his legs and walking sideways, slipping and sliding on the sodden sloping grass bank, she helped carry him to the trap, and the term dead weight struck her as they laid him partly on the floor of the trap with his shoulders supported by the back of the seat.

As Roland quickly mounted the trap to drive away she called to him,

'Stop a moment!' Then looking at Dan, who was still in the roadway, she said, 'Fetch the dog.'

'Don't be silly.' Roland screwed round in the seat, wiping the rain from his face as he did so, and, his voice holding anger now, he cried at her, 'I thought the main concern was to get the doctor back home, the dog's done for.'

'I know that but he was fond of the animal, more than fond. If we leave it there it will be worried by foxes in the night. Dan, fetch the animal.'

'Aye, miss. Yes, miss.' But Dan hesitated.

'What is it?'

'I've got nothing to carry him in, miss. . . . Oh . . . oh, I know, the oilcloth.' He now darted from her and ran down the road for a few yards, and as she saw him jump the ditch with a piece of yellow material in his hands Roland growled down at her, 'I'll never understand you, never!' and again she knew that he wasn't altogether referring to the present situation.

She made no reply but she bent down and supported Harry's head against her knees; there was not enough room for her to get down on to the floor. The bleeding had stopped; the wound, she surmised, must be on his scalp and covered by his hair. She could only guess as to what his other injuries were for both his outer and underclothes were torn and covered with mud.

And where was his horse and trap?

She raised her head as she heard Dan say, 'I'll have to put him to the side here, miss, at your feet.'

To this she merely nodded and watched him gently lay the yellow misshapen bundle near her feet and alongside Harry's thigh.

The journey back to the house seemed interminable; and then once again they were carrying him, from the trap now, up the steps, across the hall and into the study.

It struck her as they entered that death gravitated towards this room. Her mother had died giving birth here; Dilly had died here. . . . But then Peg had got better. Oh, pray God he would too. She hadn't known, not really known, until this last hour just how she considered him, but now she knew, and dead or alive the awareness would stay with her for life.

Tearing off her soaking wet outer things, she said to Peg who was standing to the side of her wringing her hands, 'Get blankets and a hot shelf quickly. Quickly now.' Then turning to Roland, she added, 'And you must ride in for Doctor Pippin.'

When he half glanced towards Dan she put in harshly, 'You must go yourself,' and she watched his teeth champ together before he replied, 'All right. All right, I'll go. Give me a chance. But first let's see if the journey needs all that haste, let's see if he's alive.'

Yes. Yes, she was forced to concede he was right, and she quelled a wave of sickness that was about to envelop her and said, 'Help me off with his coat.'

Between the three of them they raised him up and took off his coat and waistcoat and when they laid him back, it was she who pressed her ear to his chest. Her head still on the side she looked slantwise up at her brother, and she almost laughed her relief as she whispered, 'He's alive. I . . . I can hear his heart beating. It's very feeble and fast, but it's beating.' Now she was kneeling looking up at Roland, saying beseechingly, 'Hurry, Roland, please.'

He looked down into her face, staring at her hard for a moment; then he looked at Harry and back to her before swinging round and leaving the room.

A moment later Peg rushed in laden down with blankets and dropped them and set off for the door again whispering hoarsely, 'I'll get the oven shelf now, miss,' and Martha called to her, 'No; stay. Dan will get it.' She looked at Dan. 'Dan, take one of those blankets and wrap it round the oven shelf. I . . . I want Peg to assist me.'

'Right, miss.'

Immediately Dan left the room, she said, 'We must get him undressed, Peg; you must help me.'

'Aye, miss. He's sodden, sodden to the skin, he looks like death.'

'We . . . we must take his trousers off, Peg.'

Peg looked at Martha with a knowing glance before she replied, 'Aye, miss, we must.'

Together they unbuttoned the side flaps of his trousers, then pulled them down over his legs. His small clothes, Martha noted, were not long as her father's had been, they only reached to his knees, but before divesting him of them she placed a blanket over him.

It took much longer to get his shirt and vest over his head, even with the help of Dan, who had returned with the oven shelf. But when it was done and he was wrapped in the blankets she looked at Dan and said, 'Dan, we'll need a fire; it will get cold in the night. Would you be kind enough to bring us some wood and coal in before you leave?'

'Aye, miss, I'll do that an' willin'. An' if you like I'll dash off home and come back to give you a hand 'cos by the look of him you're going to need all the help you can get.'

Martha smiled gently as she looked down on the young lad and said, 'It's very kind of you, Dan, but you'll have a full day tomorrow and I'll likely need you more then. Just get me a fire going and then Peg will give you something to eat. Won't you, Peg?'

'Aye, miss, aye, I'll do that.' She now looked at Dan, saying, 'I'll give you some broth; it'll warm you up 'cos you're sodden an' all.' She put out her hand and felt Dan's coat, and he smiled down on her and grinned. 'Oh, that's nowt; I've been wringin' since I could first remember. Wet to the skin I've been day after day an' I never catch cold.'

As Martha turned from the couch and glanced at them, she thought for the moment that they had forgotten where they were and she knew a certain envy of them. She said briskly, 'Soup . . . you said soup, Peg? That's a good idea; keep the broth pan going. The doctor will have to have some nutriment as soon as he recovers.'

'Aye, miss, I'll do that.'

'And bring me another oven shelf, Peg, and the two hearth bricks. Clean them well before you wrap them up.'

'I'll do that, Miss Martha Mary. Aye, I'll do it right away.'

Left alone with Harry, she now knelt by the couch and gently put her hand down under the blanket and laid it on the bare flesh of his chest, but when her fingers felt no heart beat now she almost tore the blankets down from him and again laid her ear against his ribs. After a moment the sigh she gave obliterated the faint beating.

She did not immediately put the blankets into place but looked at his right shoulder. There was a great bruise forming on it, and she saw the edge of a dark patch where his arm lay, and when she lifted it gently aside she saw another spreading bruise.

Covering him again, she stared down into his face, the face that at one time she had thought ugly, coarse, common; now she knew it could be all three, and she would ask for nothing more but that she could look on it every day of her life.

She had gone mad; she knew she had gone mad; the madness had exploded in her heart and burst open the sealed room when he had said, 'My name is Harry.' She had the strongest desire now to lay her cheek against his.

She thought for a moment it was the desire that had startled her, but no, it was the slightest movement he had made. It was so small that it was almost imperceptible, but she could have sworn his hand had moved beneath the blankets.

Yes, there it was again; and now it was accompanied by the faintest of groans.

'Doctor! Doctor! Can you hear me?'

There was no response to her plea, and she continued to call his name for some little while but he lay as he had done before, utterly immobile as if he were already dead. But he wasn't dead, he had moved, and he had made a sound. She put her hand under the blankets again and caught at his hand and pressed it as she murmured, 'Oh, get well. Get well. Please, please, Harry, get well.'

It was nearly eleven o'clock when Doctor Pippin limped into the study. He looked wet, weary, and anxious. Martha took his caped coat from him, then she peered into his face in the dim lamplight as she said, 'You're very tired, doctor. I'm so sorry to bring you out at this time of night but I didn't know what to do, and . . . and I thought he wouldn't recover.'

John Pippin was bending over the couch now, and he said to her, 'You did quite right, what else could you do? Has he spoken?'

'No, just made one small sound.'

'Not moved?'

'A slight movement of his hand.'

'Bring the lamp nearer.'

He now pulled down the blankets, and he made a sucking sound through his lips; and Martha made a sound too, but it was an inward groan. When she had last looked at his body there had been dark patches here and there but now the colour had deepened, and the patches seemed to have spread until there seemed very little ordinary flesh to be seen.

'Damned scoundrels whoever did this. Why? Why?' He flashed a look at her. 'Who would want to beat him up like this? Who?'

She made no answer but watched him as he examined Harry's head.

After a while he straightened his back and, looking at her, said, 'He's lucky he's got a thick skull; a less tough individual wouldn't have survived that blow.'

'Will he . . . will he be all right, doctor?'

'I hope so, I sincerely hope so. He's concussed, and badly. . . . By the way'—he coughed now—'I could do with a hot drink, soup, anything.'

'Oh yes, yes, doctor.'

She actually ran out of the room. He'd be all right. He'd be all right. And yes, the poor old doctor would need something hot. But he was used to something more than soup, and there were no spirits in the house. But Harry would be all right. He would be all right.

When she burst into the kitchen Peg jumped round from the table where she had been cutting cold meat and setting a tray to meet Roland's demands, and she said, 'Aw, Miss Martha Mary, he's not?'

'No, no.' Martha shook her head. 'He's . . . he's going to be all right. I'm . . . I'm sure he is. Doctor Pippin would like a hot drink, broth.'

'This minute, miss, this minute.' As Peg hurried to the stove she turned her chin onto her shoulder, saying, 'Eeh! you gave me a gliff when I saw you runnin'.'

Yes, she had run. Like Nancy, she had run. . . . Nancy! She had forgotten all about Nancy. Hours had passed since she had given her a thought. She looked at the clock. It was turned eleven. . . . Nancy would now be in bed. She bowed her head for a moment, then lifted it on the thought that it was strange that neither Nancy nor Mildred were here with her and yet she felt no miss of them. Likely because tomorrow she'd be gone too and she had already severed herself from them. . . . But would she be gone tomorrow? Would he be able to travel? Would they send a conveyance for him? Because if they didn't then she couldn't leave him, for who would there be to look after him? Mildred? Mildred had planned in her own mind to marry him. She had even gone as far as to make herself believe it was as good as settled. She would be sorry she wasn't here tonight to minister to him.

Since it had been arranged with the Armstrongs that if the weather was very inclement, she would lodge with them, Mildred had said this morning that she would not be returning home tonight; and she had added that she thought it scandalous for them to charge sixpence a night, and another sixpence if she had a meal, for they were doing him a favour, at his age, to employ him and they should, therefore, at such times treat her as a guest.

Of course under ordinary circumstances the cost would have been nothing. But if Mildred had to stay two nights it would amount to two shillings. The week before last she had stayed two nights and the weather hadn't been all that inclement, just showery. But what did it matter? It wasn't her worry any more. What was her worry was now lying in the study.

'There, miss; look, I've made a tray.'

'Oh, thank you, Peg. By! you were quick.'

'It was already half set for Master Roland.'

She looked down at Peg. It was odd but of all those in the house, apart from Aunt Sophie, she was going to miss Peg most of all.

Even more than Nancy?

When the question came at her she nodded to herself, Yes, if the truth were to be told, even more than Nancy. She couldn't understand why this should be, but she knew it to be the truth.

Since she had nursed Peg back to health there had grown between them a close affinity; perhaps because she was so small, so childlike, she had in an odd way clutched at her and put her in the place of a daughter, a waif daughter, because she needed a daughter. . . . She needed a child . . . and a husband. Oh yes, she needed a. . . .

What was the matter with her? Her mind was wandering again as it had done a lot of late. She was tired; in all ways she was tired. There had been for a long time now a weariness growing on her. Nancy had forced her to fight it off for a time; then it seemed to be overwhelming her again; until today when, first, Roland dropped his bombshell and caused an explosion of anger in her that brought her back into the stream of life again; and then, the anxiety and concern of the last few hours had upheld her. But now with relief flooding her she had the desire to drop where she stood, and she felt sure that if she were to lie down on the mat on the stone floor in front of the fire she would fall asleep immediately and sleep for days and days . . . for ever, and never wake up. . . . Oh no, that desire had gone; she wanted to wake up now, she wanted to live.

It was as the hour clock chimed three on the mantelpiece that she awoke startled from a deep doze to see Doctor Pippin bending over the couch. When she had last looked at him he was asleep in the big leather chair by the side of the fire; now he was holding Harry's arms, saying, 'It's all right, man, it's all right. Lie still, don't struggle. Go to sleep. It's me, you're all right. It's me, Doctor Pippin. You know me, don't you? You should.'

She was standing by John Pippin's side now and staring down at Harry. His eyes were open but he still seemed too dazed to recognize them. She listened to the old man's voice saying soothingly, 'There now, there now. Quiet. Go to sleep. Do as you're told for once.'

As she watched Harry's lids slowly droop she said softly, 'He . . . he wasn't really conscious?'

'No, he's still in shock. But that'll pass. He'll sleep naturally now, and so can we.' He turned her about and led her towards the chair opposite his own, saying, 'Get what rest you can for you're going to have a few busy days ahead of you. Listen to that.' He cocked his head on one side. 'It's still coming down whole water. Never ceased for the past twenty-four hours. The roads will be like quagmires. He'll have to stay put I'm afraid. Will it be too much for you?'

'Oh no, no, not at all.'

When he was seated and had pulled the rug over his knees she rose from the chair, stirred the fire into a blaze and put more logs on it, and as she did so he said softly, 'I heard a strange tale in the town today. It concerned Miss Nancy. Is there any truth in it?'

'Yes, there is truth in it.'

'So she's married young Robbie Robson?'

'Yes, so I understand. The doctor brought me the news just before he was attacked.'

'Well, well. I knew it was in the air, but I didn't think either of them could go through with it. . . . Are you very distressed?'

'No, doctor, not any more. A thing like that happens and you think it's the end of the world until something of more import hits you.' She turned from the fire now as she said, 'My brother came home today, or'—she gave a jerk of the head—'yesterday, and informed me that he also is going to be married. His future wife should be arriving . . . tomorrow . . . no, today.'

He bent so far forward that the rug slipped from his knees. 'But he was going to the university. I was under the impression that . . . well, you were seeing to it.'

'Yes, yes, I was, doctor, but now he has decided to marry and'—her voice dropped to a mere whisper—'his future wife is already planning to run this house as a school.'

He said nothing, he just peered at her through the flickering firelight, then grabbing the rug up around his knees and leaning back in the chair again, he sat for a moment longer in silence before asking, 'And what about you?'

'I'm leaving. I should have been gone later this morning had it not been'—she turned her head now towards the couch—'for the doctor's accident. But . . . but I am more than willing to stay and look after him until he can be conveyed back to his home.'

'And what then? What do you intend doing once you leave here?'

'I'm going to look for a situation.'

'As what? Governess?'

'Oh no, I . . . I am not qualified enough to be a governess. A nursery maid yes, but that doesn't attract me. But I hope the experience I have had in running this house for the past six years will enable me to take up the post of housekeeper.'

He mumbled something that sounded like, 'God Almighty!' then he said aloud, 'Does he know about this?' The jerk of his head indicated the sleeping form, and she answered after a moment, 'Yes. When he called to give me the news about Nancy I . . . I was greatly distressed and I told him the reason for my going.'

She watched the old man now twist his body about and look straight at the couch; after which he turned back again, nodded his head, closed his eyes, and said, 'Well, there's no doubt he'll be very grateful that you've decided to stay on and attend to him until such time as he can make the journey back to the house. Of course, how he will show his gratitude is another matter because he's a very unpredictable fellow. Oh yes, very unpredictable. I could venture to say he might buy you a diamond ring, or I could say he might just bawl your head off; or he might do neither. But what I really feel he could do is to be the means of securing you a post after your own heart. Yes. Yes, he could do that, if he'd let himself.'

His voice had trailed away into silence and now he was apparently asleep. Wide-eyed she lay and watched him.

A diamond ring, bawl my head off, or secure me a post after my own heart. That would be as a housekeeper.

Judging from the tone in which he had said this, she didn't know whether or not Doctor Pippin liked his assistant; that he should be sitting up all night with him was no proof, doctors did that for all sorts of people.

She did not know what time it was or whether she was half asleep or awake when she started upwards at the sound of Nancy calling her name from the hall. It was so loud that she could still hear the echo of it when she was standing on her feet.

Doctor Pippin hadn't stirred. She looked swiftly from him to Harry. He was still lying in the same position, apparently in a deep sleep.

Swiftly now she tiptoed down the room and up the passage and into the hall. The lamp had been turned down, but she could see that the hall was quite empty; the door was closed, bolted. She looked towards the stairs. Roland and Aunt Sophie were up there but there was no sound. Peg was in her room beyond the kitchen.

She drooped her head. She must have been dreaming, yet the voice had been so clear, with an appeal in it. It was the way Nancy used to call her name after she'd had words with Mildred. 'Martha Mary! Martha Mary!' She'd come running down the stairs and cry, 'Do something!' It was that kind of an appeal that the call had held.

She walked slowly down the passage and into the room again. All sleep had gone from her and for a moment the dead feeling of weariness, for once again she had been alerted to life and the needs of those dear to her.

Had Nancy actually called to her from that house? From that room wherein she would now have to spend a lifetime of nights with a man to whom she was in no way suited?

Her mind gave her no answer. Quietly she placed more wood on the fire, then sat down, pulled the blanket around her and waited for the dawn.

8

It was still raining the following morning at eleven o'clock when Doctor Pippin, ready to take his departure, stood by the side of the couch and, looking down at Harry, said, 'Well now, I must be off. You know your own treatment, doctor, don't you; and if you follow it you will be well enough to rise in a few days. But I'll be back long before then, that's if I can make it through the mud, you understand? This hired horse is not a patch on Bessie. Poor Bessie. How she made it home with that stab in her rump I'll never know.'

Harry didn't speak but he made a slow painful movement with his head.

Doctor Pippin now lifted the cape of his coat upwards around his chin, pulled on his gloves, looked towards the door where Roland was waiting, definitely chafing with impatience, turned his gaze on Martha, who was standing to his side, and said, 'I'll leave him in your hands, Martha Mary! When he starts bawling you'll know he's better and ready for the road.' He turned a twisted smile on Harry; then his voice becoming serious, he said slowly, 'There's one thing I'd like to know before I go, if you're not up to answering we can leave it, but I want the constabulary after those would-be murderers as soon as possible. Have you any idea who they were?'

Harry gazed up into the doctor's face. His mind was in a fog; he couldn't recall anything about the attack except a faint recollection of looking into an open mouth that had the front teeth missing. He screwed up his eyes against the pain of thinking, then his hand moving slowly up to his mouth, he muttered, 'Nick Bailey, no teeth.'

'Nick Bailey!' It was Martha who repeated the name; and then she murmured, 'Oh no!'

'He was your outside boy?' Doctor Pippin was looking at her now, and she said, 'Yes, doctor."

'Doctor Fuller had some trouble with him over some animals, cats I gather?'

'Yes, yes, he had.'

'And so this was by way of retaliation.'

The old man's face was grim as he looked down on Harry. 'All right, leave it to me, I'll see to it.' He was about to turn away when Harry, his voice now more like his own, said, 'Fred.'

Doctor Pippin opened his mouth, closed it, glanced at Martha, then said tersely, 'Don't worry about Fred, he's . . . he's all right, just do what you're told, rest and get yourself out of that as soon as possible because I need you. Do you hear?'

Harry made no sign, he just lay and watched the doctor and Martha leave the room.

In the hall Doctor Pippin looked at Martha and said quietly, 'He mustn't know about the animal yet; he thought a great deal of that dog. . . . Is he buried?'

'Yes, I got Dan to do it early this morning.'

'Good, good.' The doctor, now glancing towards the stairs and nipping at his lower lip, said, 'I should have a look at your Aunt Sophie while I'm here but . . .'

'Doctor—' Roland's voice brought his head sharply round—'the journey back is going to be difficult, it may take much longer than anticipated, and I have to meet a train. We shouldn't waste any more time.'

The tone and the words were a command and the doctor cast a look on Roland that caused him to turn away towards the door; then speaking to Martha again and his words unhurried, and his tone subdued but loud enough to carry to Roland who was now descending the steps, he said, 'Well, my dear, expect me in a day or two; although as I said, it all depends on the weather. But should it prevent me from coming out I'm sure it won't prevent Doctor Fuller from returning as soon as he's steady on his legs, nor you from coming into town to take up your new position.'

Martha did not reply to this; she imagined the doctor was taking it for granted that she would get a position in Hexham. What she did notice was that his words checked Roland on the third step and brought him round to look up at her, but she avoided his eye, bid the doctor good-bye, closed the door on the driving rain and stood for a moment breathing deeply as she looked around the dim hall.

Never before had the hall and stairway appeared to her as shabby. She had the odd sensation she was seeing it, really seeing it for the first time. The worn turkey carpet lying in the middle of the flagged floor, the grey uneven flag stones surrounding it, the green embossed wallpaper faded to a dirty grey, the blanket chest looking like a coffin; and the china cabinet in the recess full of her mother's collection of china appeared from this distance nothing but a jumble of odd pieces of crockery. Her eyes lifted to the bare oak stairs leading to the landing. Up there was the same shabbiness in all the rooms, except that which had been her father's and which Peg had hastily prepared for the coming guest. . . .

. . . Coming guest. Was that the reason why she was seeing the house as it really was, because this is how a stranger would see it? And what would Roland's future wife think of the dining-room and its meagre fare? She herself would have to prepare some food for them all. Under ordinary circumstances she would have gone out of her way to lay on a good meal, but tonight the honoured guest would, like the rest of them, have to savour the remains of yesterday's meal, which was stewed mutton, with an apple and blackberry pie to follow.

As she was about to cross the hall, Peg appeared at the top of the stairs carrying a tray and she spoke to her as she descended, saying, 'She hasn't eaten half her breakfast, Miss Martha Mary, she's gone right off her food. As I've said afore, she's still got plenty of fat on her to keep her goin', but at one time she was always ready for her food, wasn't she?'

'Yes, Peg.'

Resting the tray on the corner of the side table at the foot of the stairs, Peg now looked up at Martha Mary and asked quietly, 'What's gona happen her when you go?'

'That's Roland's responsibility.' She had since yesterday omitted the 'master' when speaking of him.

'I'm not stayin' you . . . you know, not when you're not here, Miss Martha Mary, I'm not, no.'

'You must think about your grandmother, Peg.'

'I've thought about her; an' I've talked it over with Dan early on this mornin'.'

'With Dan? Why?'

''Cos . . . well'—she lowered her head and wagged it from side to side—'Well, I'm fifteen on Wednesda'; another year or more an' I could get sort of engaged like. He's for me . . . was right from the start, an' me for him an' all. An' he thinks the same as me; he doesn't want to work for nobody but you, but as I said to him, we both can't go stark starin' mad, so he'll stay on an' I'll go along of you.'

Martha now bent down and gently touched Peg's cheek. 'Do you want to please me, Peg?'

'Aye, miss, more than anybody in the world.'

'Then . . . then stay on here for a while and look after Aunt Sophie. I . . . I don't think she'll need you all that long, but . . . but if you do this just for me I won't forget it. And later . . . well, we'll see, we'll work together. If I get a housekeeper's position I could always make room for you and. . . . Oh, don't, don't cry, Peg, please.'

Peg now wiped her face roughly with her apron; then picking up the tray, she looked up as if in defiance at Martha, and said, 'It's a bloody shame, that's what Dan says, an' I say it an' all an' that's swearin' to it, that you should be so treated like this. There isn't no justice, there can't be no God; Dan says there can't be no God.' She was walking sideways now, nodding back at Martha. 'He says there can't be no God except for those who earn more than two pounds a week; then they make him up just to thank somebody for their luck.'

She was still mumbling as she put her buttocks to the kitchen door, thrust them backwards, then edged herself in with the tray.

Martha hadn't moved from the bottom of the stairs. There was no justice, there could be no God except for people who earned over two pounds a week and then they made him up in order to have someone to thank. It was odd, strange, the things that Peg and Dilly had come out with from time to time . . . and boys like Dan. It was as if they worked out a philosophy all their own.

Her throat was full; she turned about, went down the passage and into the study, and as she entered the room and looked at the prone figure on the couch she wished in the back of her heart that she was as simple as Peg and the man lying there as uncomplicated as Dan.

It was almost at the moment when she heard the trap drive into the yard that Harry opened his eyes for the third time that day and looked at her, but it was the first time he had spoken to her. 'Hello there,' he said, and as she looked down on him she had difficulty in answering in the same vein. 'Hello to you, too.'

'What time is it?'

'Just on four o'clock.'

When he made to raise himself on his elbow he groaned and she put her hands gently on his shoulders and said, 'Now please, don't move, lie still, and . . . and don't talk.'

He blinked up at her as he gasped, 'Know something?' Then his eyes closed before he ended, 'I don't want to talk.'

'Well, that's very good.' She turned her head slightly away from him now as she heard voices in the hall. But when her name was called, and in quite a loud cheerful way, her chin jerked slightly upwards.

By the sound of his voice her brother intended to pass everything off as normal.

The door opened, but Roland didn't enter, he merely put his head round it, saying, 'Martha Mary, can you spare a minute?'

She looked back at him, her gaze straight; then turning once more to Harry, she said gently, 'I won't be long.'

When he murmured something she bent right down to him, her face close to his, and said, 'What is it?' Again she watched him close his eyes, swallow deeply, then say slowly, 'I said . . . it's arrived.' His lids lifted;

they were looking at each other and there was the faintest exchange of amusement in their glance.

It's arrived, he had said. He had called the invader it, not she, madam, or her ladyship, but it. She wanted to laugh not only at his effort to put a jocular side to the situation, but with relief at the fact that his brain was clear. He was remembering all the incidents of yesterday. He remembered who was expected. Doctor Pippin had said the concussion might block from his memory a number of events that occurred yesterday, and there was one in particular that she wished him to remember: 'Call me Harry,' he had said.

When his hand came up slowly from under the blanket and touched hers and he said, 'Go on and do battle, but . . . but don't give in an inch,' she could say nothing.

Slowly she withdrew her hand from his, straightened her back, stared at him for a moment longer, then turned about and went from the room. . . .

In every way the visitor was a surprise.

When Martha opened the drawing-room door from where she heard the voices coming and the visitor swung sharply about and faced her, all her preconceived idea of Roland's choice was whipped away. She had imagined someone tall, even as tall as Roland, with a scholastic bearing, seeing that she wanted to turn this house into a school, and educated to the extent of speaking three foreign languages. But what she saw was a person who hardly came up to Roland's shoulder. Moreover, she was plump. Martha was reminded instantly of her father's mistress, but as she advanced and took a closer look of the visitor she saw that there the similarity ended, for this young woman's hair was not in ringlets but taken straight back from her forehead, and she had no claim whatever to prettiness. When they came face to face what struck Martha more forcibly than anything else and with something of a shock, was that Roland's future wife was already a woman, and of . . . an age. She could be all of twenty-five years of age or twenty-seven. What she was certain of was that she was much, much older than herself.

'My . . . my sister Martha Mary. And this is Eva . . . Miss Harkness, Martha Mary.' Roland's introduction was brief, and hesitant.

'How do you do? I am so pleased to meet you. I have heard so much about you from Roland. He's for ever singing your praises to the sky. In fact at times it has given me a feeling of inadequacy.'

Martha hesitated before taking the hand extended to her. When she did, she merely offered her finger-tips, while the voice went on non-stop: 'What a charming house! I love it already. And the setting, so wild and beautiful. How fortunate you both are.' She flashed a look towards

Roland, who stood to the side smiling at her as if captivated by her charm, her ease of manner, her cleverness, the whole of her.

And yes, Martha detected at once that this person should be admired for her cleverness if for nothing else, for she certainly had mesmerized Roland.

'I've been wanting to make your acquaintance for so long. Although Roland told me what you would be like I couldn't help, well, but be a little afraid of you.' She now joined her hands together under her chin as if in prayer, and the childish attitude she posed was so ill-suited to her self-assured manner that it was almost embarrassing, so much so that it penetrated Roland's trance as she finished, 'I have so much to learn from you. But I can assure you you'll never have a more willing pupil,' for now he brought his sheepish gaze to rest on Martha.

The smile had left his face; he now looked like a young boy caught out in some misdemeanour, and when he lowered his head Martha, speaking for the first time, said, 'I'm afraid, Miss . . . Harkness, isn't it? I'm afraid my brother has misled you, I shall not be able to instruct you in any way as I am leaving the house in the very near future. In fact had our doctor not suffered an accident last night I should already be gone. But I'm staying only as long as he requires my aid, which I should imagine will be another two to three days at the most.'

Miss Eva Harkness seemed to be taken off her guard for a moment, her expression looked blank; but then with the same swift twist of her body with which she had turned to view Martha as she entered the room, she now confronted Roland, saying, and as if to a naughty child, 'Roland, you didn't inform me of this, why?'

'There wasn't time, Eva, and . . . and I wanted you to see the house and explain in full. . . .'

'Your other sisters, are they staying at home?'

The glance Roland now flashed towards Martha was no longer boyish but held a look of venom, and she stared back at him as she said quietly, 'Miss Harkness asked you a question, Roland.'

'You are out to make it difficult, Martha.'

'I don't agree with you, Roland, but . . . but as I said, Miss Harkness is waiting for an answer.'

'Perhaps you would give me the answer.' The small figure was confronting her now, any touch of girlishness in her manner having utterly disappeared.

'Very well, since you insist. My sister Mildred, who is next to me in age, works in Hexham in our bookshop; she returns each evening except when, as now, the weather makes the roads almost impassable. My youngest sister Nancy'—she paused now and glanced at Roland—'was married yesterday and has taken up her abode some four miles away. And now to save time and further misunderstanding, Miss Harkness, I think you should be informed that there is no staff here to speak of, except a young girl of fifteen called Peg Thornycroft and an outside boy. Moreover, there is an invalid in the house, but I suppose Roland has informed you of our aunt and her condition.'

Apparently Roland hadn't told his fiancée about his aunt, for now he had walked to the window, his hands joined behind his back, which again reminded Martha forcibly of her father when vastly displeased.

Miss Harkness appeared slightly shaken. She looked towards Roland, then back to Martha, whom she had recognized immediately not only as an obstacle to her future, but as an enemy, one who was determined to frighten her away. Roland had given her the impression that he had three sisters who would fall upon her neck, especially the eldest one. He had spoken of the house and its situation as idyllic. Well, on first sight she had found it far from that. And the journey out here had been torturous. Nevertheless, she had told herself that beggars couldn't be choosers, and having already suffered four rejections she was determined this was not going to be a fifth. All right, let this madam go; she would have been a thorn in her flesh anyway. But the sick aunt, that was something that would have to be dealt with; as also would one solitary maid. Yet give her time to get a ring on her finger and call herself mistress of this house, then they would see changes. . . . And what about the bookshop? Was that a kind of myth too? Why had he not taken her there today? He had said they mustn't linger because of the weather and the conditions of the roads. Had that been merely an excuse? Well, the house wasn't a myth, although it was old and frightfully shabby both inside and out. But these were things that time and management, her management, could and would change.

Seeing the best form of attack at the moment to be submission, she looked up at Martha and said softly, 'You seem determined to frighten me, Miss Crawford.'

'I'm merely placing the facts before you, which would not have been necessary if my brother had given you the true picture before you arrived.'

'You can't rule my life, Martha.' Roland had swung round from the window.

'I have no desire to rule your life, and never had, Roland.'

'That's not true, you've ruled this house and everybody in it since Mother died. You planned my career.'

'Only because up till recently you wished it planned for you. And I may add, by going to the university you saw yourself as being freed from responsibility for some years ahead.'

'I did nothing of the kind. Anyway, this house and the business is now my responsibility, and for the future I would have you remember that. Come Eva, I will show you to your room as no one else seems to have the courtesy.' With this he marched up to his fiancée, took her masterfully by the arm and led her out of the drawing-room.

Martha stood exactly where they had left her. She looked about her, bit on her lip, then lowered her head; she didn't know whether to laugh or cry. The last scene had put her in mind of one of the only two plays she had seen in her life. It was in the chapel hall in Hexham. The hero had so overacted his part it had been embarrassing, and Roland acting the master of the house for the first time had been equally so.

But strangely now, she felt a wave of pity for him filling her because he had become ensnared by that cunning little woman, and she was a woman fully grown and long past the period when the term young lady could be applied to her. Moreover, she had detected in her manner and voice the essence of a refined termagant, and there was one thing sure, should there . . . no, *when* was the word needed here, when the time came that Roland needed to look for solace elsewhere, as his father had done, he would not dare make such a move.

He had treated her abominably, thinking only of himself, yet in this moment she could forgive him because of what lay ahead of him.

9

It had rained for forty-eight hours without ceasing, then early on the Thursday morning the leaden sky lifted and the sun came through.

Harry, turning his head slowly towards the window, looked at the rays streaming into the room and thought, Thank God, then added, And may it last, because as soon as the roads were passable the sooner he'd get away from this house.

He had never been out of the room, he had never left the couch in fact; yet the whole atmosphere of the place seemed to seep in through the very walls. How she had stood it all these years he didn't know, yet the truth of it was she would have gone on standing it and been glad to do so if it hadn't been for her dear brother and his burning love for that little vixen. If he had ever observed teeth and claws sheathed in a human being he had observed them in Miss Eva Harkness. And that young silly idiot was utterly bemused by her. God help him when he wakened up.

He had met her last evening when the lord of the manor, which pose Roland was now adopting, had brought her in to show her off. After a prolonged gushing of greeting and sympathy she had become quiet, perhaps because he had stared, unblinking, at her while she talked, but it was in the look with which she returned his stare that he recognized she was wise to the fact that her charms were being wasted on him.

He now pulled his pain-racked body further up on the couch, and as he lay breathing deeply his thoughts turned to the vile young devil and his friends who had done their work thoroughly, almost too thoroughly. What if Dan hadn't found him when he did? Well, Dan had and he was here and alive, but he was as weak as a kitten and so damned sore. And his head was still muzzy. But he must shake this off and get on his feet and get home for once he was on his way she'd be on her way too. He'd see to it that she accompanied him, and the sooner the better, because underneath that practised calm of hers she was near breaking point. She was cooking for the damn lot of them; she was running up and downstairs to Aunt Sophie; she was attending him; and all the time she was carrying the feeling of rejection because that little upstart of a woman was in the house and already rearranging the whole set-up to her own liking.

The whole situation must be galling in the extreme. He imagined what he himself would have felt had he been in a similar position. There was one thing he was sure of, he would never have been able to control himself as she was doing, and it was himself in this instance who was the cause of her having to endure it. . . .

He paused in his thinking, closed his eyes and a warmness crept over his body. He hadn't thought about it that way before. Yes, he was the cause of her still being here. She was staying on only because he needed looking after. Well, well. His chin went to jerk upwards but was halted by the pain in his neck.

What would old Pippin say when he told him what was in his mind? Get the shock of his life, he supposed, and he wouldn't take to the idea of him leaving the house and setting up an establishment on his own, would he? Oh no, not if he knew the old boy. . . . But wait, wait. He'd better not count his chickens before they were hatched. He'd have to make sure first that there was need to set up an establishment on his own. . . .

When should he ask her? Before they left the house? Yes, oh yes. Because that would determine where she was going to stay when they reached Hexham. If he was to have any say in her life he would see that she was housed in a comfortable hotel; and if he wasn't. . . . Well then. . . .

The door opened and she entered carrying a tray with a steaming bowl of soup on it and a plate of bread. As he watched her putting the tray on the side table near to him he thought, She's too thin, skinny. I'll have to alter that, first go off.

'You shouldn't be sitting right up like that.'

'I am going to get up today, so it's wise that I should sit up.'

'You're not. You mustn't.' She was bending over him. 'Doctor Pippin said you must stay there until he sees you again.'

'That could be a week.'

'No matter. Now do please lie back a little and have this soup.' As she went to put her hand on his shoulder he caught it, stared up at her for a moment, then said, 'Will you marry me?'

She started as if she were stung. She did not immediately withdraw her hand from his, but when she did she covered it with the other one and pressed them both against her waistline and her lips trembled as she replied, 'I . . . I don't know whether you meant that as a joke, doctor, but . . .'

'Don't be silly. And I am in no condition to argue with you; I want an answer, and before you leave this house and hit the world head on in your position as housekeeper.'

Her chin rose slowly and she continued to stare down at him as she said quietly, 'I thank you for your offer, doctor, but I don't need pity; nor do I need to be rescued from becoming a housekeeper, because I'm sure I shall make a very competent one.'

'Yes, yes, I know you will; and I want a housekeeper. I . . . I . . . Aw, my God!' He put his hand to his head and made no apology for the blasphemy; then leaning back, he closed his eyes and murmured slowly, 'Martha Mary, as I said I'm in no condition to argue with you. I made that proposal in all sincerity, and don't talk about pity, or compassion, or any other tommy rot because I'm not the kind of fellow to take up the stresses and strains of matrimony through any of those virtues. I'm selfish, domineering, and exacting. I think you already have some knowledge of the latter two characteristics. . . . Now don't say any more.' He lifted his hand and flapped it weakly at her. 'Just think on it, and ask yourself would it be harder to be my wife than say, be a housekeeper and bow the knee and "Yes, ma'am", and "Yes, sir", and perhaps'—he now opened his eyes wide at her—'find yourself in a position of having to say, "No, sir".'

As he watched the flush come up over her face he closed his eyes again, turned his head to the side, and said, 'I'm even too weak to control my tongue. Forget it. No'—he was staring at her once more—'don't forget it, I mean except the last bit, but think over the main issue. Please. Please, Martha Mary.'

Her hands were pressing into her waist, her whole body was hot; if she could only have dropped down by the side of the couch and said, 'Oh, Harry, Harry, thank you.' But no, she could not on the present terms. 'Will you marry me?' he had said. He wanted a housekeeper, he had said; she'd find a situation with him in his home easier than being a paid servant in someone else's, he had said; but he had not said, 'I . . . I care for you, Martha Mary, I have a deep affection for you . . . I love you.'

As if he had suddenly said what she longed to hear she again gave a start, but now for the same reason that she had woken in the middle of last night and the night before that when she had imagined she heard Nancy calling her name, for now she was hearing Nancy's voice again calling, 'Martha Mary! Martha Mary! . . .' She must be dreaming, or had she suddenly become ill with the kind of illness that possessed Aunt Sophie?

She swung round now as the door burst open and her hands flew to her face because there stood Nancy, a strange wild looking Nancy dishevelled from head to foot, all her clothing mud-bespattered, and her face as white as a piece of bleached linen.

'Nancy!'

They were approaching each other now; the next minute Nancy was in her arms and she was holding her tightly, and as she stroked her hair and tried to soothe her she looked back over her shoulder to where Harry was once more sitting upright on the couch.

'Oh! Martha Mary, Martha Mary, what have I done?'

'There, there, quiet now. Quiet. Come and sit down.'

It was only as Nancy stumbled forward that she became aware of Harry, and she stopped and gaped at him, and Martha said, 'It's the doctor; he met with an accident two days ago. Come . . . come and sit down.'

'No, no.' She now shook her head and turned round in a bewildered fashion; then grabbing at Martha's arm, she gabbled, 'I must talk to you, I must. I must explain. There are things . . .'

'All right, all right, dear.'

Before leading Nancy away, Martha glanced towards Harry, and he returned her bewildered look and shook his head slowly.

Nancy was holding tightly on to her as they went up the passage towards the drawing-room door, but before they reached it it opened and there, preceding Roland from the room, came Miss Eva Harkness, and she and Nancy stopped and stared at each other.

Then Roland was by his fiancée's side and he too was staring at his sister. No, glaring at her. 'What is this?' It was the master's voice speaking as he looked her up and down.

When Nancy made no reply he jerked his chin upwards and wagged his head as he said, 'So you've come home, have you, found your mistake out? Well, we'll have to see into it, won't we? We must now consider if you are acceptable. This'—he now turned to his fiancée as he shot out his hand towards Nancy—'this is my erring sister, and she'll have to be dealt with.'

'Get out of the way.'

The thrust that Martha made at him with her forearm toppled him backwards against the door stanchion, and he took Miss Harkness with him.

'How dare you! Now look here, Martha Mary, you have gone too far.'

Martha had pushed Nancy into the drawing-room and she now turned on her brother, hissing, 'Gone too far, have I? Well, I'm going a bit further and tell you I've had enough of your high-handedness and your empty chit-chat over the last two days. I shall deal with Nancy if she has to be dealt with. And furthermore, if you want your guest's remaining stay to be even partially comfortable, keep your tongue quiet, because I could now order a cab and take the doctor into Hexham, and, for your information'—she now poked her face towards him—'Peg would go with us, and Dan too, and if this should happen it would give you the opportunity to initiate your fiancée into household chores, such as I've done for years. Start her on the cooking.' She now turned her furious glance on the red-faced Miss Harkness. 'Then show her how to lift the kettle off. That's an art in itself. And as I told you she can have my knee pads for scrubbing the kitchen floor. In any case she'll have to come to it sometime if she remains here. Now put that in your pipe and smoke it.'

With this last shaft she went into the drawing-room and banged the door on them but she did not immediately go towards Nancy, who was standing now wide-eyed looking at her, but she closed her eyes and told herself she shouldn't have turned on him like that. And to end up with one of Dilly's sayings too. That alone would stamp her as one of the peasantry in madam's eyes. But what did she care about her? Still she shouldn't have said all that to Roland. Her heart was beating as if it were going to burst out of her breast. With one of them and another she was near the end of her tether. He had said, 'Will you marry me?' Why hadn't she accepted him on any conditions? No. No. Her mind was in a whirl. And now here was Nancy flying from her mistake, and if she knew anything the mistake would not be long in presenting himself at the door, and then there would be more scenes. She was tired of scenes. . . . She was really tired of everything. . . .

'Martha Mary—' it was Nancy who had her by the arm now—'who is she?'

Martha walked slowly down the drawing-room, her hand clasped in Nancy's as she said, 'That, my dear, is your future sister-in-law.'

'What!'

'Yes. Don't look so surprised. I sent for Roland to try to stop you from doing what you were determined to do, and what you did do. When he arrived he was rather peeved at my hasty summons. The reason? Well, you've just met her, his future wife, Miss Eva Harkness.'

'But he can't; he was going to the university and . . .'

'Why can't he, dear?' Martha looked straight into Nancy's eyes. 'You shouldn't be so surprised, he's just proposing to do what you did.'

Now Nancy bowed her head deeply on her chest and she groaned, 'Oh Martha Mary! Martha Mary!'

The sound was so full of pain that Martha put her arms around Nancy's shoulders and, pressing her tightly to her, asked, 'Was it so terrible? Is the place awful?'

Her face showed some surprise when Nancy moved her head against her, saying, 'No, no; it . . . it wasn't the place, in fact it's very . . . very comfortable, much larger inside than it looks from out.'

'What then? His people?'

Again there was a slow shake of the head and her voice was a mutter now. 'His . . . his father's hardly spoken to me, but his mother is kind; she's . . . she's very like Dilly, and she, too, has a swollen leg.' Nancy now lifted her head and looked deep into Martha's face, and it was with evident effort that she forced herself to say, 'I . . . I really didn't know

about marriage, Martha Mary. I thought I did, but I didn't. It's awful.'
Now her head was turned to the side, her face twisted as she added the
last word, 'Nauseating.'

It was some moments before Martha asked quietly, 'Would you have
found it so with William?' and to her surprise Nancy's answer was, 'Perhaps.'

'Well then, if that is the case you would have been . . . nauseated as
you say, by marriage with any man. Is he'—she did not say 'cruel?' but
'very unkind?'

'No. I . . . I suppose according to his lights he . . . he saw himself acting kindly, considerate.'

'Then what is your complaint?' Martha was holding Nancy by the
shoulders now and Nancy, her head wagging, swallowed deeply, sniffed;
then closing her eyes tightly, muttered, 'It's. . . . Oh, you wouldn't understand, Martha Mary, but it's just . . . just marriage.'

'I . . . I understand more than you think.' Now there was a harshness
in Martha's voice. 'You broke your neck to get married, you were terrified
of not being married, you were terrified of ending up like Aunt Sophie;
well now, let me tell you this. Since you have come back, should you be
allowed to stay by either your husband or Roland, you are going to find
yourself in the position of an unpaid servant. Under the new order you
will be in constant attendance on Aunt Sophie for there will be no one to
share the load, and in time doubtless your fears will be realized and you
will become like her, and you will have no one to fall back upon but yourself, because I won't be here. . . .'

'You . . . you won't? Where? . . . what?' Nancy's mouth was agape.

'I'm leaving. I would have been gone two days ago, the very day you decided to get married, if the doctor hadn't been attacked by Nick Bailey
and two others and left for dead. And he would have died if Dan hadn't
come across him. So'—she nodded vigorously at Nancy now—'the way I see
it is, you have a choice, either you go back to your husband, or you remain
here. But if I were in your place, and speaking from only a short acquaintance with our prospective sister-in-law, I know which road I would
take, and quickly. And I may tell you this, Nancy. It is my opinion from
what I've seen of Robbie Robson that if he had been born into an environment which provided him with some form of education he would certainly
not have been a drover, he would have been a man you would have been
proud to marry. But as things are he is what he is, and I told you from the
first that you were making a mistake, but such is the position now that I
will say to you, don't make a bigger one and remain here. . . . Anyway, I
doubt, knowing your husband as I do, even slightly, but that he will be

here before long, and if he doesn't drag you out and over the hills I'll be surprised. . . . Where is he now?'

It was some seconds before Nancy answered, and then it was on a gasp, as if she had come to the end of a long run. 'He . . . he went out early this morning with his father. They are herding cattle.'

'Do you dislike him . . . I mean apart . . . apart from marriage?'

There was another long pause before Nancy said, 'No, I . . . I don't dislike him.'

'Then take that as a start and build on it.'

'Oh, Martha Mary.' Now Nancy fell against Martha's breast. 'I'm so unhappy.'

'That will pass. Anyway, as I said, you have your choice.'

A moment later, when Nancy lifted her head, Martha saw by the look in her eyes that she had made it, and she bent forward and kissed her, saying softly, 'Come up to my room and wash your face and hands, and we'll see about getting some of this mud off you. Then after you've had something to eat, go out of this house for the last time, and without regret, for it'll never be again as you knew it; and take the road to your home, because from now onwards his house is your home. Make the best of it, and make yourself into something that he will be proud of. Yes, that's what I said, because this much I have gathered, he doesn't consider any of us anything to look up to at the moment. Moreover, he himself has a fierce pride and you'll never break it, but you could foster it and channel it into something good.'

They stood now looking deeply and sadly into each other's eyes; then without further words they joined hands and went quietly out of the drawing-room.

It was about fifteen minutes later when Martha came downstairs to set a tray of food for Nancy that Roland came hurrying from the passage and, catching up with her as she neared the kitchen door, grabbed her, saying, 'Come back here a minute, I want to talk to you.'

'Leave go of me!' She slapped not only at his hand but at his chest, saying angrily, 'If you lay hands on me again like that I shall strike you in the face.'

He actually gaped at her as he said thickly, 'What's come over you? You're acting like a common hussy. It's him, isn't it, that fellow back there. There's something between you and him. He's putting you up to this. . . . Well, anyway, you're not going to persuade Nancy to go back there. . . .'

'Nancy is going back there. I'm sorry to dash your revived hopes of an unpaid servant for your future wife, but Nancy has already chosen. I think she would rather go into the workhouse than stay here with that person and you.'

'You are a hussy . . . a mean, spiteful hussy.'

'Don't you dare call me such names.'

'I can and I will; you're as far from a lady as . . . as Peg back there. And what you forget is I have the power to keep Nancy here. I can make her stay; I can take it to law.'

'Do that. Try it on. You do just that, and you'll find yourself the laughing-stock of the county because by that time she herself will fight you. And another thing I'll tell you, you'd put up a poor show in any court, private or public, against such a man as Robbie Robson. To use one of Dilly's expressions, he'd wipe the floor with you. His grammar may not equal yours but his intelligence far outweighs any you possess.'

As she turned from him with a look of disdain and thrust open the kitchen door, he yelled after her, 'You've turned into a fiend, a common loud-mouthed fiend,' and she answered as loudly and without pausing or turning her head, 'And it's not before time.'

It was three o'clock in the afternoon when Nancy, her clothes as clean as it had been possible to get them, her face washed, her hair combed, her bonnet strings tied neatly under her chin, said her farewell to Martha at the end of the drive leading into the lane.

After they had embraced tightly and kissed each other, Martha stood holding Nancy's hands as she said, 'Take heart, my dear; there are new lives opening for all of us, and whatever happens we'll see each other quite a lot in the future. Ask . . . ask your . . . ask Robbie if I may call. And do as I said, tell him that you just felt you wanted to take a stroll. And about your clothes—' she looked down at the stained cape and dress—'explain that you were foolish enough to take a short cut across the fields. Now, go on, and . . . and keep to the main road all the way. Good-bye, my love.' Again they embraced, but now they couldn't see each other because of their tears.

With a gentle push Martha now sent Nancy on her way, and she watched her until she reached the bend in the lane, where she turned and waved; then slowly she walked back up the drive and into the house, and to the study.

She had not returned to the room since she had left it with Nancy earlier and it was as if he had been waiting for her since that time.

Slowly, she walked towards the couch and at the foot of it she stopped and said simply, 'It's done; she's gone back.'

'Good. Sit down and tell me.'

'I . . . I can't, not at present. I heard Aunt Sophie singing as I came in; it's always a bad sign. I'll . . . I'll come back later. Will you excuse me?'

'No. No, I won't.' He hitched himself further up on the couch. 'Anyway, tomorrow or the next day Aunt Sophie will cease to be your responsibility. . . . Look. Don't go. I want to talk to you. . . . Please.'

Martha was half-turned from him, her head was bowed and she remained still; then after a moment she walked down the room and he did not now try to detain her.

As she crossed the hall she said to herself, 'Will you marry me? I want a housekeeper.'

She was upstairs attending to Aunt Sophie when Peg came scurrying into the room, whispering loudly, 'He's come, miss, Robbie Robson; he's downstairs with a face like thunder. I . . . I didn't tell him Miss Nancy's gone, he nearly knocked me on my back.'

Martha looked towards Sophie who was sitting propped up in bed and she said hastily, 'I'll be back in a moment, Aunt Sophie.'

'Who's Robbie Robson, Martha Mary?'

'Just . . . just a young man.'

'There's different people in the house now, isn't there, Martha Mary, different footsteps?'

Martha stroked the thin hair back from Sophie's forehead, saying, 'It's . . . it's a guest.'

'Roland's not a guest and Roland hasn't been to see me.'

'He will, he will shortly.'

'There's only you who's constant, Martha Mary, only you.'

Oh dear God! She had felt riddled with guilt every time she had come into this room during the past two days, but now this was awful. Only she who was constant. And she was going to leave her to the tender mercies of that madam. But . . . but she was going. Yes, she was going. Nothing would stop her, nothing must stop her. . . .

Robbie Robson was in the hall. He watched her descend the stairs, and as she approached him she thought that Peg's description of his face being like thunder was far from accurate, for it wasn't dark but white with passion.

She raised her hand in a warning sign for him not to begin there and then but said hastily, 'Come this way, please.'

Going quickly before him, she led the way into the dining-room, and when he closed the door behind them he didn't start by saying, 'Where is she?' but 'You knew this would happen, didn't you? You were prepared for it.'

'Please listen to me for a moment. . . .'

'I'm not listenin' to anything I don't want to hear. She's me wife, legally an' afore God though we weren't joined in any church, and so it'll be until the end. Now no more talk, just tell her I'm here and we're goin' home.'

'She's not here.'

'Miss Crawford.' He moved a threatening step nearer to her. 'I'll go through this house like a small toothcomb in a dog's coat if you don't fetch her here an' now.'

'I'm telling you'—her voice was almost as harsh as his—'she is not here. She came, but she went again.'

'Went where?'

'The only place she could go, back home to you.' She watched him blink and she noted that he had extremely long eyelashes for a man.

'Then she's gone because you sent her.' His voice was quieter now, and hers too as she said, 'Sit down.' She motioned to a chair and took one opposite him, and she looked at him for some time before she said, 'Would you do something for me, and incidentally for yourself? It might mean the difference between happiness and unhappiness for you both. I would ask you to go back home now, and should you find her already there act as if nothing had happened. If you should notice her mud-bespattered clothes, and she tells you that she fell into some mire when she was taking a short cut across the fields when out for a stroll, accept her explanation. Anyway, it would be understandable that she should want to take a walk because the day is now so fine and we've had such a lot of rain lately. . . .' She now bowed her head and ended, 'It all sounds very lame, but what I'm asking you to do is to ignore her running away.'

When he made no answer she raised her head and looked at him and now said softly, 'Be gentle with her; she's . . . she's a very fragile thing. . . .'

'She's not.' The statement was definite, flat and knowledgeable. 'She's as tough as they come. And she's not above using her cl . . . aws.' His voice trailed away on the word, and now he bit hard on his lip and turned his head to the side.

An embarrassed silence enveloped them both for a few moments, and they avoided each other's eyes until he, getting to his feet, said, 'I can see why she likes you, an' why she misses you so.'

She was standing facing him now and she asked, 'May I come and visit her?'

'Anytime. Oh aye, anytime. You'd be very welcome. An' after all, we're practically next-door neighbours, aren't we?' For the first time a faint smile touched his lips.

'Not for much longer, I'm . . . I'm leaving here.'

'You're leavin' here?' He screwed up his face at her.

'Yes; marriages seem to be in the air, my brother is getting married.'

'The young one?'

'The only one. . . . And I wish to make a life of my own now.'

He nodded at her, a slow understanding nod; and then he said, with a new note of bitterness to his voice, 'Is that what persuaded her to come back to me?'

'Partly I suppose, but . . . but not altogether. She likes you. Liking can blossom into love, and that will be up to you.'

He looked past her towards the window now as he asked, 'How long ago is it since she left?'

'Just on half an hour I should say.'

'Half an hour.' She watched him thinking; then he said, 'Who knows, I might meet up with her on the road if I go now.'

She smiled faintly in return. 'You might. Yes, you might if you hurry.'

He turned from her, reached the door, then turned again and said, 'You'll do as you said and come an' see us?'

'As often as I may, or can.'

'Good enough. Good-bye.'

'Good-bye.'

When the door closed she walked up the dining-room to the window and stood looking out. When he came into view he was running, and there was something about his running that reminded her of Nancy. There was the same swift grace about it, although she doubted if Nancy could ever run as fast as he was running now. When he disappeared from her view down the drive she had the strange thought that Nancy was after all a lucky girl. . . .

In the hall again, she hesitated at the top of the passage. Should she go and tell him what had transpired? She'd have to talk to him sometime, so it might as well be now. But what if he should bring up the marriage business again? Well, what if he should? He had been honest. I want a housekeeper. . . . Oh, dear Lord, if only. . . .

She went hurriedly along the passage and into the study.

He was lying back now with his eyes closed and he didn't open them until she said, 'Robbie's been.' She did not now say Robbie Robson.

'Oh! And what happened? Did he blow up?'

'Yes, at first; but he went away much calmer. I . . . I think he will try and understand her, and be patient with her.'

'Oh well, if he left you with that impression I should imagine it'll work out and you'll have no more worry from that quarter. . . . But'—he now pursed his lips—'from what seeps in here from outside I imagine you're having trouble from other quarters.' He put out his hand towards her and said, with deep earnestness, 'When can we leave? I'm fit enough, at least I will be tomorrow. If this weather keeps up the roads will have dried somewhat and the doctor will get through and we could go back with him. What do you say?'

'I . . . I think it would be wise for you to wait another day or so longer. You haven't done any walking yet, and . . . and you're very bruised, and bound to be stiff.'

'Well, it won't help the stiffness if I go on lying here, will it?'

She looked at him for a moment in silence before she said, 'After supper then, get up for a little while and see how you feel.'

When he lay back and stared at her unblinking, her colour rose hot about her face and, somewhat flustered, she turned away, saying, 'The sun has disappeared, it is overcast again. I do hope it isn't a sign of more rain because Mildred will be on her way.'

'Oh yes, Mildred. I'd forgotten about Mildred, I've forgotten so many things over the past two days. She's another one who's going to get a shock; but then, I think Mildred is the kind of girl who can withstand shocks. . . . Martha!' He had said her name sharply following a short silence. 'How is Fred? You've never mentioned him for some time. And I'd forgotten to ask. Fancy me forgetting Fred.'

She had turned towards him now and she jerked her head to the side as she mumbled, 'Oh . . . oh, he's all right.'

'. . . Martha?'

'Yes?' She glanced at him over her shoulder.

'Look . . . come here.' He had pulled himself upwards again and was now leaning over the side of the couch. 'What's happened to him? Look, I'll know tomorrow or whenever I get outside, what is it?' His voice was rising.

'Please. Please.' She was standing by his side now. 'Don't excite yourself. All right . . . all right I'll tell you. He . . . he died before we got him home.'

She watched him slump back on to the pillows, turn his head aside and gnaw at his lower lip with his teeth until she thought the blood would spurt from it. A full three minutes passed in silence before he asked thickly, 'How . . . how did he die?'

It was an impossibility for her to describe the animal's injuries; even now when she thought of them it made her stomach heave. The horse had been lucky to get off with one jab of a knife. She murmured, 'A blow, on the head I think, such as was aimed at you. I'm . . . I'm sure he died quickly.'

He was looking straight up at her now.

'Where did you find him?'

'He . . . he was lying across your chest.'

Again his head went to the side, and she turned quietly away and went out of the room in order that he could give way to his distress without embarrassment. But as she went she admitted to surprise in herself at his almost feminine reaction to the death of his dog. Such emotion did not match up with his rough, brusque exterior. His whipping of Nick Bailey was, she thought, in character, but not the tears he had almost shed in front of her. Yet this very facet of tenderness would, she knew, have delighted her if it had been shown to a . . . a human being. But no, he reserved it for his dog, whilst to her he had said, 'I want a housekeeper.'

Mildred arrived home at half-past five. She talked non-stop from the moment she entered the door. She was very hungry. The Armstrongs' food was appalling; and what was all the fuss about the doctor being attacked? Was he still here? And anyway there wasn't much sympathy for him in the town because he wasn't well liked, he was without style or manners. She herself could never understand how he became a doctor; she was sure he would never get into the Brockdean household, they aways sent for Doctor Pippin.

Martha was cutting a shive out of a bacon and egg pie on the kitchen table and she didn't raise her eyes as she said, 'I thought you rather liked him.'

'You thought wrong. I'm civil to him. And anyway, who could like him? Just think of the way he treated you when he first came to the house. He's churlish. By the way, what's for supper? Not just that!' She pointed to the pie.

'I'm afraid so; I haven't done much cooking these last two days.' She stopped now, rested her hands on the kitchen table and looked across at Mildred, saying, 'I've got some news for you, in fact two kinds of news. One leads to the other. First, Roland is going to be married. . . .'

'Our Roland!' Mildred had sprung to her feet from the kitchen chair. 'You're joking.'

'I'm not joking. His future wife and he are at this moment parading the grounds with a view to what purpose they can be put. I should imagine she is measuring out the squares for a playground or playing fields.'

'What are you talking about?'

'Just what I said, Mildred. I sent for Roland in haste to come home in order to prevent Nancy marrying.'

'Our Nancy?'

'Don't keep saying our Nancy and our Roland in that fashion.' She could not help herself from adding now, 'You yourself would be the first to check anyone for using such colloquial terms. You knew that she was contemplating marrying Mr Robson.'

'But you were going to stop it.'

'It wasn't in my power to stop it. If anyone's it was Roland's, so I tele-graphed him. When he arrived he gave me his news and I responded with mine, I told him that under the circumstances I wouldn't stay here.'

'Why not?'

'Why not!' Martha put her hand up to her mouth, realizing that she had yelled; then leaning across the table, she said grimly, 'Because I don't intend to be a non-paid servant to a school marm, because she intends to turn this house into a private school. And I'm sure she had been given to understand that I would do all the dirty work, assisted no doubt by your-self and Nancy.'

'Roland would never have said that about me! I've got my position in the bookshop now.'

'Yes, yes, of course, you have.' She nodded slowly at her sister, then ended, 'Well, he would have had Nancy and me in mind for the unpleas-ant dirty work, but I'm afraid he's made a mistake about us both.'

'But you can't leave, what about Aunt Sophie?'

'Aunt Sophie is not my responsibility, she is Roland's.'

'You would leave Aunt Sophie?' Mildred's tone was full of indignation.

'Yes, yes, I would leave Aunt Sophie, but with less worry now because I can see that you'd be quite willing to stay on and no doubt you will help with the night nursing which, as you know, Aunt Sophie has been requir-ing more and more of late.'

'You are being nasty now.'

'Yes, yes, I'm being nasty now, Mildred; and, as I see it, it's not before time. Oh—' she cocked her ear to one side—'if I'm not mistaken, they have just come into the hall. You'd better go and meet them and offer your con-gratulations.'

Mildred, her mouth grim, stood wagging her head for a moment at Martha before swinging about and going out of the kitchen.

As the door banged after her, Peg came out of the pan room and her presence startled Martha; she had thought her to be in the yard, and when Peg grinned at her and said, 'That was telling her, miss. By! you've given them all shocks one after another, an' not afore time,' she looked down at the table where her hands were splayed tight against its white-wood surface, and she thought, Yes, one after the other, and she couldn't believe that it was herself that was doing it.

She had changed, everything about her had changed, since the day she had met her father's mistress there had come alive in her a new being, which had grown rapidly, and during the last few days it had thrust itself out through her skin, her innocent skin, her gullible girlish skin, and it was the kind of being she should take pride in, but she didn't, for in this moment she mourned for the girl she had once been, the girl who had loved her father, and this house, and whose only need was a husband. She now closed her eyes on the thought that even the girl she once had been had needed a husband.

PART FOUR

The River Decides

1

It had rained heavily all night, and now in the early morning it was still raining heavily.

Mildred was in a very bad temper. She had informed Martha late last night that she didn't like her prospective sister-in-law; in fact, she went as far as to say if she could hate anyone it would be Miss Eva Harkness. And she had asked what she herself was going to do. Where would she live if she couldn't live here? Everybody had gone mad, marriage mad.

Martha had refrained from making any comment even when Mildred had ended, 'I'm not putting up with it; I'll do something about it.'

And now dressed against the storm, she stood in the hall dragging on her gloves and looking towards the window against which the rain was beating and said, 'And if this keeps on I won't be able to get back tonight; and I hate staying at the Armstrongs'.'

'They're nice people; he is a very intelligent man.'

'You know nothing about him. I'm with him all day, he's an old dotard.'

'Really! Well, I don't see him like that. And I shall shortly be very pleased to accept the hospitality of the old dotard and his wife.'

'You wouldn't . . . you wouldn't go and stay there!'

'Why not? You lodge there.'

'That's different; I merely take advantage of them when the weather is bad.'

'Take advantage of them? If that is how you view their kindness I would, if I were you, look out for more suitable lodgings. But for myself, I shall be pleased to stay with them.'

'Oh!' Mildred tossed her head with annoyance. 'You're so . . . so'—she stopped, lost for words.

'Go on, say it.'

'I can't . . . I can't find words to fit you at this moment, but one thing I will say, and I agree with Roland about it, you'll never have a clear conscience as long as you live if you leave Aunt Sophie with no one to look after her. I think you should be ashamed of yourself.'

They were glaring at each other now through the dim light of the hall, then Martha said thickly, 'I think you'd better go, Mildred, before I say something I will regret. But this I will say, if you're so concerned about Aunt Sophie you stay at home and look after her. As I see it now, it's your turn to take on some of the odious duties of this household, duties that I've shouldered for years, so don't imagine that either you or Roland will work on my conscience to make me stay. You and Roland between you, and, of course, his lady wife, should be able to manage Aunt Sophie.'

Mildred now pulled open the door but before she stepped over the threshold she turned once again and, thrusting her face out towards Martha, she hissed through tight lips, 'And him in there!' She actually jerked her thumb in the direction of the study. 'You want to mind what you're about; he's dangerous, he's a philanderer; I know.' She now gave one definite bounce of her head before turning and running down the steps

Martha did not stay to watch her progress but closed the door quickly against the driving rain; then she went hastily towards the stairs. She didn't ascend them right away, but stood gripping the knob of the balustrade as she wished, for a moment, that she was Dilly or Peg and could cry out aloud, 'Damn them!' for they were both using one telling weapon against her: her conscience with regard to Aunt Sophie.

And there was no doubt about it, no matter how she protested that she wouldn't be troubled about leaving Aunt Sophie, she knew she was merely putting up a thin defence, and that once away from the house, her conscience would beat that defence down, so much so that when Aunt Sophie finally died her sorrow would be nothing compared to her feeling of guilt. Heavily now, she walked up the stairs and made her way towards Sophie's room.

It was strange but it seemed at times that Aunt Sophie had second sight for only last night she had said, 'The house is uneasy, Martha Mary; everybody is at sixes and sevens, all except you. You'll never be at sixes and sevens.' And first thing this morning when she had taken her her early cup of tea she had found her sitting on the side of the bed half dressed in her shift, corsets, and drawers, and no amount of persuading would make her take them off, and like that she had got back into bed again.

When she had left the room she had thought this was one of the occasions when it would be prudent to lock the door on the outside, yet at the same time she imagined the scene should Aunt Sophie appear in the dining-room as she had done recently on the stairs. How would Miss Eva Harkness view the apparition?

Apparently Roland had taken her for a brief visit to Aunt Sophie last night. She did not see Miss Harkness after the visit but she had seen Roland, and he had looked at her as if he would take pleasure in killing her.

Aunt Sophie was lying very much as she had left her an hour earlier.

She appeared very quiet and in one of her near rational periods. 'It's raining again, Martha Mary,' she said.

'Yes, and it looks set in for the day.'

'I think it will be set in for a long time, Martha Mary. The river's rising rapidly.'

'Is it?' She went to the window. The river always rose with heavy rains, but now she could see the dull leaden grey of its waters were covering the bank, and it was running fast. Here and there dark objects were whirling on its surface, likely branches of trees washed down from the hills, but the very fact that they were still flowing straight down meant that there was no blockage up at the bridge.

The footbridge further up the river wasn't very high and when the river was really in flood the debris mounted there until the water spread it out over the fields. She turned to the bed, saying, 'It hasn't risen very much; it's nothing to worry about.'

'Oh, I'm not worrying, Martha Mary; the river never worries me; I like the river. Do you know something? I've always imagined myself floating down on it, floating away, away, down on it. I sometimes long to get up and walk down to the river and do just that, float away and away. . . .'

Martha went quickly to the wash-hand stand in order to shut out the pathetic face with the faded blue eyes that held that strange depth of appeal; always they had held that look of appeal. She stood pouring some water from a jug into the wash-basin. Her throat was tight, and her heart was crying, 'Oh Aunt Sophie! Aunt Sophie! What am I doing?' while at the same time her head was saying, 'Don't weaken; it's your life, or hers.'

When she took the bowl and towels to the bed and placed them on a side table Sophie raised herself on the pillows and said, 'I can wash myself this morning, Martha Mary; I feel very well this morning, as if—' she looked about the room, then towards the window—'as if it were a beautiful day, and it isn't, is it? But that's how I feel, as if it were a beautiful day and I was going on an excursion. Father used to take me on excursions when I was a girl. I wish I had remained a girl, Martha Mary.'

'Wash your hands, Aunt Sophie.'

'Yes, Martha Mary. You know something, Martha Mary?'

'What, Aunt Sophie?'

'It's a dreadful thing for a man to leave a girl, a young girl in a church, in front of all those people, waiting, waiting. If he had been kind he would have done it before, even the day before would have done, and then there might have been some hope for her. Don't you think so, Martha Mary?'

Martha stared down into the upturned face. Her Aunt Sophie was sane; she was talking sanely. She'd had her bright periods before, but never,

never had she admitted in them that she was anything but a married woman. Now the eyes that looked back into hers were showing an intelligence, an awareness of herself that she hadn't seen there before. Perhaps it had been there all the time and none of them had realized it. But she should have known, she who had spent so much of her time in this room, she should have realized that the poor creature had to have a shield, and the shield had been the phantasy she presented to them. Yet she also knew that there were times when Sophie had been far from normal; these were the periods following her bouts of fits when she was so bad that afterwards when she had seemed normal no one had accepted that this could be so.

'Oh! Aunt Sophie.' She leant over and drew the trembling wasted frame into her arms and her tears flowed as she said, 'Yes, it was a terrible cruel thing to do to you. Oh, my dear, my dear.'

'There, there.' It was Aunt Sophie actually comforting her now. 'Don't cry. Aw, Martha Mary don't cry. That I should make you cry, you above anyone. You've been my daughter Martha Mary; even in my bad spells you gave me the love of a daughter, and I've had very bad spells, haven't I? . . . Martha Mary.'

'Yes, Aunt Sophie.' Martha turned her head away as she wiped her eyes.

'Don't let such a thing happen to you.'

She blinked now and looked down into the upturned face, but she made no answer, she only shook her head as Sophie went on, 'You have such a lovely face, my dear, and one day some man will take it in his hands. But make sure they're honest hands, won't you, Martha Mary?'

'Yes, yes, Aunt Sophie.' Her throat was so tight she felt she would choke. She looked towards the floor. The hands were downstairs, the hands that she wanted to touch her face, even if he saw it only as the face of his housekeeper. And she had known all along that should he repeat his proposal she would accept it on his terms for she needed to be near him. She needed comfort; but now even comfort would have to wait, wouldn't it, for she could not leave this poor creature. Roland had won.

'You're a fool. Do you know that? A fool.' Harry was sitting on the side of the couch with a blanket around him, and he pushed it roughly under one buttock, then gave a small groan before continuing, 'But you're a nice fool, a compassionate one. I knew from the beginning you wouldn't leave her. You know, with good nursing she could last a year, perhaps two. But as I've told you, her heart is pretty weak and if she were to have a bad bout of fits it could give out.'

'Long or short, I can't leave her. I'm very sorry.'

'So am I, for your sake, for you need to get away from her. And let me be honest, for my own too; I'm a very impatient individual. I like things cut and dried. Anyway, I've never had your answer from the other day, but now it would seem there's plenty of time. . . . Your brother will be delighted.'

His tone was flat, his words clipped. His attitude to the situation was defeating; it appeared to her that he wasn't much troubled by her decision, and so she answered dully, 'Yes, he will.'

'You'll stand up to his lady wife, won't you? And don't let her make a drudge of you.'

'Yes, I'll stand up to her.'

'He was in here a minute ago looking for you. Have you seen him?'

'No.'

'From the glimpse I got of him he looked in a bit of a tear; I don't think things are running as smoothly as he expected, perhaps it's the servant shortage.' He now smiled wryly up at her.

'That and other things. She was introduced to Aunt Sophie last night.'

'Oh. Oh, Aunt Sophie seems to be the root of the matter.'

When the door jerked open they both looked towards it to see Roland standing there.

'I'd like to speak to you for a moment, if you can spare the time.'

Martha, looking down at Harry, now said, 'I won't be a moment, I must see to your dressing,' then she turned and went slowly towards the door where Roland still stood holding it wide.

When she had passed him she walked towards the entrance of the hall, and there she turned and asked, 'Where would you like me to go?'

He gave her no answer except a look of utter impatience, then marched into the drawing-room, and she followed him.

After she had closed the door she did not move from it because he was standing only a few paces from her.

His voice now little more than a growl, he said, 'You'll be pleased to know that Eva is cutting her visit short and is returning home today. Your attitude and the treatment she has had since she arrived has become unbearable to her.'

'Really!'

'Don't use that sarcastic tone to me, I won't stand it.'

'Then there are two of us who don't intend to stand it.' Her voice had risen.

He now glared at her for a while before saying, 'I'm taking her home, it's as little as I can do. I shan't be able to return until tomorrow, or the next day. Is it too much to ask that you stay on until I get back?'

She could have said to him at this point, 'I'm not leaving, not as long as

Aunt Sophie is alive,' but she could not at the moment bring herself to give him this satisfaction, so what she said was, 'I can do that.'

'Even if your friend goes?' There was a deep sneer in his tone.

She felt a warmth spreading over her face, but she made herself remain calm as she replied, 'Yes, even if my friend should go, which is very likely, because as soon as the rain eases Doctor Pippin will be calling for him.'

For a moment longer they stared at each other, then he flounced past her and out of the room. She remained standing for a moment before she returned to the study and there, with her hands gripping the horsehair head of the couch, she made a small sound that could have been the forerunner of laughter or tears as she said, 'It's funny, it's really funny, but . . . but she's going, he's taking her home today, now. She . . . she cannot abide my presence any longer.'

'Really!'

'So it seems.'

'Do you think she will change her mind?'

'Oh, I doubt it.'

'I do, too'—he nodded at her now—'because she's a desperate woman.'

'Desperate? In what way?'

He did not answer her immediately but when he did the warmth again returned to her face for he said, 'For marriage. Some women become desperate about marriage when they reach their late twenties.'

She busied herself now at a side table and her tone was prim as she said, 'If that is the case, then I would feel inclined to be sorry for her.'

'Oh, I shouldn't waste your sympathy; the only thing you should be sorry for is that she's set her sights on your brother because, and I'm not going to say pardon me for saying it, but he's a very immature young man and, to my mind, not yet ready for the responsibilities of marriage. . . . You didn't tell him that you were staying?'

'No.'

'I thought not, or he'd have induced her to stay in spite of your annoying ways.'

If he had meant this to cause her to smile he was disappointed for she remained silent, and she did not speak until after she had renewed the dressing on his forehead and he had remarked on an impatient note, 'Listen to that rain, it seems to be getting heavier.'

'The river's rising.'

'The river? Is it? . . . Does it flood here, you're lying very low?'

'Yes, but very rarely. It must be all of eight years since it got as far as the door. There was a tale that it once reached halfway up the landing wall; there's a mark on the wainscoting; but my opinion is that the landing being wide was once used as a room, and the mark is where a chair rail ran round it.'

'Well, there's one thing, if this keeps up we shan't see the doctor today.'

'Perhaps that will be just as well, for I don't think you are fit to travel yet.'

He lay back and looked at her as she busied herself at the table and he said, 'Perhaps you're right. Anyway, the urgency to leave has gone. And if I did return home the old fellow wouldn't let me get down to work, so it doesn't matter really where I recuperate, does it?'

She gathered up the soiled linen from the table and, without looking at him, she answered, 'No, not really,' then walked down the room; and he watched her. There was still no sway to her gown, he imagined she was even thinner than when he had that first time walked behind her up the stairs, and he wondered if there would come a day when he'd see her hips so round that her skirt would dance with each step. Strange, but he wanted to see her plump, even fat, and happy, which in a way proved something to him. He wasn't just in love with her . . . he loved her.

2

The rain did not stop, it poured incessantly all day and all night and all the following day.

Mildred had not returned home last night, nor would Roland return today because the main road beyond the hill was under water from the river.

Peg, running into the kitchen, shouted to Martha, who was putting a pan on the fire, 'Miss Martha Mary! It's at the bottom of the front steps; another couple of feet and it'll be into the kitchen.'

'Don't worry, Peg, it'll be all right. If the worst comes to the worst and it does come in we'll only have to make for upstairs and stay there until it goes down.'

''Twas said that once it reached halfway up the landin' wall.'

'That was nonsense.'

'Eeh!' Peg now bit on her thumb. 'We're in a right fix, aren't we, stuck out here in the wilds you might say, and no one to give a hand should anythin' happen, 'cos the doctor's still as weak as a new-born kitten, an' Dan not come. He couldn't get across the river, 'cos he would have been here if he could, he would, Miss Martha Mary, he would. . . . An' he would have gone an' seen to me grannie. . . .'

'Peg.' Martha now went to the table where Peg was standing, her scarred hands idle for once, and she said quietly, 'Now I've told you, don't worry about your grannie. Your grannie's a sensible woman; she would have left her cottage long before now.'

'Aye, Miss Martha Mary. Aye, aye, she's a sensible woman, an' it isn't the first time she's been flooded, is it?'

'No, it isn't. Where does she usually go?'

'Oh, to me cousin Alice's. She's up on the hill, not a stone's throw from Robbie Robson's place; not as high as them but still high enough to keep out of the river's way.'

'Well then, don't worry. Now here, carry that tray into the study and I'll take this one, and when you come back take Aunt Sophie's tea up, then get your own, by which time we'll be able to see if it's necessary to take foodstuff and some hot drinks upstairs. Now go on, take the tray. . . .'

By six o'clock in the evening Martha was as concerned as Peg about the situation, for the water had reached the top step and was seeping into the hall. Looking out through the hall window she could see nothing but water, with the outhouses and stables seeming to be afloat in it. Yesterday she had taken the precaution of putting Belle in the back field, for the ground there rose quite a bit towards the boundary, and should the animal become afraid of the water she could jump the dry stone wall, or kick it down in parts. She was glad there was no other livestock to worry about.

She turned hastily from the window now, thinking, I must tell him, he must sleep upstairs tonight.

Half an hour later when Harry limped into the hall and saw the water now easing its way towards the bottom of the stairs he cast a sharp look at her as he said, 'Have you got the necessary things up above, food, drinks, etcetera?'

'I've . . . I've got it all ready to take up, but let me show you your room first.'

'Where are my clothes?'

'They're upstairs. They have been sponged and pressed but I'm afraid your coat and trousers are torn in parts.'

'That doesn't matter, let me have them.' The words carried his old tone; it was as if he had just come into the house on a visit and was finding that his orders had been disobeyed. 'Where's Peg?'

'In the kitchen. Don't worry I'll get her, just come along, please.'

He now made an impatient movement but when he went to mount the stairs he had to grip hold of the balustrade and take one stair at a time.

'Is it very painful?' As he paused she looked down at his leg.

'Just stiff, that's all; it'll wear off with use.'

When they reached the top of the stairs she went before him to her father's room, in which Miss Harkness had left a strong odour of perfume, and when he lowered himself into a chair she said, 'If you'll make yourself comfortable I'll go and bring up the food and . . . and the necessary things for the night.'

He nodded at her, then watched her hurrying from the room. What a situation to be in, the house flooding with water, and at the rate it was going across that hall floor it could be up to this landing in no time, and here he was almost helpless, with an ill woman on his hands, a small maid, and a very tired Martha Mary. And she was tired; the strain was showing more and more on her face every day. If she was allowed to decline at the present rate he had no doubt but that the aunt would survive her.

What a sequence of events he had experienced in this house during the last few days. And now to end up in a flood. Well, it was a good job there were attics up above, although from what he remembered of them when he attended on Dilly they were of no height, and the small windows were set on the floor. Still, let's hope they wouldn't be their last resort. It seemed an oversight that they hadn't built attics over each of the wings they had stuck on this old structure.

The door opened, and Martha and Peg entered both carrying laden trays, and when they set them down on the table Peg turned towards the doctor and on a shaky laugh said, 'Well, that lot should see us through the flood, doctor, eh? Eeh! it's like Noah's Ark.'

'You're right, Peg, we'll likely find ourselves afloat shortly.' He smiled at her but she didn't smile back.

'D'you think it'll get this far up then, doctor?'

'No, no; I was merely joking. But mind, you're going to have some mess to clear up once the water goes down.'

'Oh no, I won't, doctor. Oh no, I won't, 'cos I've told Miss Martha Mary here I'm not stayin'. No, thank you. I'm gona' long of her, I am.'

'Light the lamp, Peg, it's getting quite dark.' Martha turned to Harry and said, 'I'll get your clothes.'

When Martha had again left the room Harry asked, 'Do you mean to go, Peg?'

'Aye, I do, doctor; course, I do . . . I'm not stayin' on here without her.'

'Good for you, Peg.'

They smiled at each other.

A few minutes later when Martha brought his suit and small clothes all neatly pressed she laid them on the blanket box at the foot of the bed, saying, 'I don't really think there is any necessity for you to dress tonight, why not wait until the morning?'

'I'd rather. . . .'

'As you wish. . . . Come along, Peg.'

He waited until the door had closed on them, then he limped to the window and peered downwards through the slanting rain. He stared for a full minute at the first sight that looked like a great expanse of sea, then muttered, 'Good God!' for now he could just see the top of the door of the first outhouse that bordered the yard; by a rough calculation that would mean that the water was about up to the second stair already.

Turning, he limped down the room and in fumbling haste got into his clothes, but by the time he had donned his coat he found it necessary to lean back against the bedpost and rest while he took stock of himself. He was as weak as a kitten; he had never felt like this in his life before. Blast young Bailey! By God, he'd make him pay for this if it was the last thing he did. Well, not so much this but for Fred. Oh yes, he'd make him pay for Fred. He had tried not to think of Fred and how he had died, for knowing Nick Bailey he couldn't imagine that the swine would let the animal off with a mere blow on the head. . . . But about this water. He pulled himself upright again, pressed his finger and thumb tightly against each eyeball; then rising, he went slowly towards the door and on to the landing. With one hand supporting himself against the wall, he hobbled towards the stairs and looked down almost in horror. There was water everywhere, but unlike the turbulence outside its rising was quiet, soft, sinister. As he watched a tread disappear under the grey flow he rapidly counted the rest of the stairs. There were only eight to the landing, and they were shallow steps.

He turned hastily now and shouted, 'Martha! Martha!'

A door opened at the far end of the landing and she came running. 'What is it? What's the matter?'

When she reached his side he pointed down the stairs, saying, 'It's rising too quickly to be healthy; I think it would be wise to get up above.'

'Into the attics?'

'Well, look at it.'

She looked, and she gave a slight shudder but made no comment.

He took her arm as much for support as anything and turned her about, saying, 'We'll be safe enough up above.'

'But . . . but if it reaches here it'll mean the whole valley is flooded. They said it had been flooded once before but I didn't believe them.' She turned her head over her shoulder and looked towards the stairs again.

'Come on, there's no time to waste.' Again his tone was abrupt, no friendliness in it. 'You'd better get Miss Sophie up and dress her. And get Peg to take some blankets and covers upstairs, we may need them.'

She made no comment now, but hurried from him, and his voice followed her, saying, 'And candles. Is there a lamp up there?'

She turned at Sophie's door, saying, 'Yes.'

'And oil? You'd better see if it's full . . . in any case we can take them from here.'

She drew in a short sharp breath as she went into Sophie's room. She wished he wouldn't talk like that, so domineering; he seemed to be two distinct people. It always seemed that his manner changed for the worse when he was worried or annoyed, and now he was likely very worried, as she was, and she was tired. Oh, she was so tired. She couldn't remember the last time she'd had a full night's sleep; while her body ached for sleep her mind wouldn't allow it.

And when the waters went down, what then? The place would be a shambles and she would not only have to see to its cleaning, but help clean it. She didn't want to do any more work, not of any kind, she wanted to lay her body down and let it rest . . . together with her mind. Oh, she wanted to put her mind to rest.

'Why are you dressing me, Martha Mary?'

'We have to go up to the attics, dear; the river has overflowed its banks.'

'I know; I saw the water flooding the meadow this morning.'

'But it . . . it has reached the ground floor, dear. Come along now, put your arms into your blouse.'

'But why need I be dressed, Martha Mary, to go up in the attics? I have never been dressed for a long time. Now if I intended to make a journey of course then I'd be dressed. . . . Are we going on a journey, Martha Mary?'

'No, Aunt Sophie, no, we're not going on a journey, just up into the attics.'

'It is very strange to be dressed to go into the attics.'

'There now, you look very nice. I'll get your coat, it may be a little chilly up there.'

She went to the wardrobe and took down a coat that had hung there for years undisturbed, except every spring when the wardrobes were washed down inside and hung with camphor; and as she took it across the room she noticed that it was even more moth-eaten than when she had handled it last. No one had thought of throwing the coat away although Sophie had never worn it since she had taken it off when she first came into the house.

As Martha helped her into the voluptuous old-fashioned garment, Sophie persisted, 'But why must I wear my coat if I'm not going on a journey, Martha Mary?'

'I've told you, we are going up into the attics, Aunt Sophie, just in case the water rises and . . . and there's no heat up there, and you know you never keep your shawl about your shoulders, so you'll be warm in your coat.'

'Strange. Strange.'

'What is strange, Aunt Sophie?'

'Many things these past few days, many things, Martha Mary. Are you afraid of the water rising?'

'No, no, of course not.' She lied glibly. 'Now, there, we're ready, come along. You take my arm as if we're going for a walk.'

Sophie did as she was bid, but she had taken only two steps when she stopped and laughed.

'What is it, Aunt Sophie?'

'It's just that you are very funny, Martha Mary, you keep reassuring me yet you are more afraid of the water than I am. I'm not afraid, do you know that? I'm not a bit afraid of the water rising. I wouldn't be afraid because I've often wanted it to come right up the stairs. Do you know that? Right up the stairs, and flood my room and take me sailing away on a great wave.'

'Don't talk like that, Aunt Sophie. Come along now, come along.' Martha's voice and manner were brisk and she pressed Sophie forward along the landing and towards the attic stairs to where Harry was standing, as if waiting for them.

'Why, hello, doctor.' Sophie greeted him as if they were meeting on the street. 'It's such a long time since I saw you. Are you going on a journey too?'

'Yes, just a short one, up into the attics. That's it, up you go.' And she went up and laughed quite gaily as Martha steadied her from behind.

When they all reached the top of the stairs it was to see Peg standing surrounded by blankets and kitchen utensils and trays.

'Which room will I put them in, Miss Martha Mary?' she asked.

'Into the schoolroom. Aunt Sophie will go into Dilly's room.'

'No, I think it's better that we all stay together.'

'But Aunt Sophie may—' Martha hesitated on her whispered protest, and Harry, nodding at her quickly, said, 'Yes, yes, I know what attention Aunt Sophie may need, none better, but no one of us is likely to collapse because of it. Now do as I say, choose a room that will take us all. Where's the schoolroom?' He turned to Peg, and she pointed towards a door, and he lifted a lamp from a narrow shelf attached to the wall and, opening the door, went in. There were two windows set some distance apart on one wall and both began at floor level and reached no higher than his waist. He bent his aching back low and peered out of the nearer window, then turning to where Martha was now placing Sophie on to a chair, he said, 'Where do they face, the windows?'

'The front of the house.'

'Where are you going?'

Martha stopped on her way to the door. 'To bring the mattress from Dilly's bed.' She now glanced back towards Sophie, and he nodded at her and said, 'Yes, yes, that's an idea. I'll come and help you.'

'No, no, stay there, Peg will help. It's only a single feather tick and not heavy.'

He made no protest for at the moment he was feeling in no condition, he told himself, to lift a single feather, let alone help with a tick full of them. . . .

It was an hour later and Sophie was lying down on the mattress. They'd all had a cup of tea, lukewarm, but nevertheless welcomed, but not one of them had eaten anything. Martha and Peg were sitting side by side at the rickety and stained nursery table, but Harry was sitting on blankets which were placed on the floor between the two windows, his back supported by the wall. He said he felt more comfortable this way, and he did, for his whole body was aching, particularly his hip bone where a boot had apparently found its target a number of times.

Because of the fear he could see in Peg's pinched face he started a jocular conversation with her, saying, 'You know something, Peg? In years to come when you have a family round you I can hear you spinning them the yarn, saying, "Up in that attic for three weeks we were, three solid weeks without a bite".'

Peg gave a shaky hoot of a laugh, saying, 'Eeh! doctor, that would be stretchin' it, wouldn't it? Three weeks! Three days'd be enough.'

'Can you swim, Peg?'

'What! me swim, doctor? me? Why no, I'm not a duck. No!'

'You can't swim, and you living near the river all your life? I'm surprised at you.'

'The river's not for swimmin' in, doctor, you've got to go to the sea to swim. Dan an' me are goin' to the sea one day . . . Whitley Bay. It's a long way off but we'll land there one day. He says we will; we made up our minds.'

'He's right. I'm sure you will, Peg.'

He now looked from Peg to Martha, but she had her head bent as if she were dozing, yet he knew she wasn't, and he addressed her, saying, 'I think we'd all better settle down, and the floor's the best place.'

When she raised her head and looked at him, he asked, 'How much oil is left?'

'It'll do the night if turned low.'

'Good.'

He now pulled himself to his feet and, turning to the window, he tried to raise the bottom sash.

'What is it? Why are you opening the window?' She was bending down by his side.

'Apparently I am not opening it.' He tugged at it, then gasped for breath. 'It does open, doesn't it?'

'I . . . I can't remember it being opened for years. But why?'

He cut off her question by putting his face close to hers and whispering, 'Just because I think it's necessary. . . . Can *you* swim?'

She drew her head and shoulders back from him and glanced towards the window again before saying, 'No, no, I can't. Why . . . why do you ask? It can't surely get up this far.'

Now his voice was scarcely audible as he said, 'The way it has risen in the past hour it could swamp the two end wings, never mind this part of the house.' Then shaking his head, he added, 'Why didn't they put attics on them too when they were at it, or better still use some forethought and build the place further back on the rise?'

She had often thought this herself. It seemed madness when you came to think of it to build a habitation where the foundations were below river level.

'Listen to that.' He was still whispering, 'The wind's rising into a gale.' He now raised his eyes towards the apex of the sloping ceiling and said, 'There's an ornamental parapet, partly covered with ivy, isn't there, running across the front?'

'Yes. . . . Yes, there is.'

'It'll be just above these windows, not right on the top?'

She too looked upwards and nodded, then lowered her gaze towards the window again, and when he saw the stark fear in her face he caught hold of her hand and said softly, 'We may not have to do it, but we should be prepared. If the water reaches the top of these windows and we are trapped in here. . . . Well!' He made a small movement with his head. 'But once outside on the roof there's always the ridge to cling on to.' He now brought her hand and pressed it tight against his ribs for a moment before whispering hoarsely, 'We'll make out, never fear.'

Her voice seemed frozen in her and it was seconds later before she could murmur, 'Aunt Sophie . . . we could never get her up there.'

'It's amazing what can be done when you've got to do it. I think that if this window was open and you stood on the sill you could almost pull yourself up, at least we could, and if we can do that we can hoist her between us. But . . . but it won't come to that; I'm just preparing for the worst. It's a habit of mine.' He smiled widely at her, then said, 'What you must do now is to rest. There's room for you on the mattress.'

'No, no, I couldn't. . . .'

'You'll do what you're told. Peg and I will keep watch; we'll talk to each other.' He now looked towards Peg's small white strained face and ended, 'I like talking to Peg, I always learn something. . . .'

She was glad to lie down on the mattress. Aunt Sophie was sleeping peacefully, and in this moment she envied her, for that's what she wanted to do, sleep peacefully for a night and a day and another night and a day. . . . Would they have to climb on to the roof? But they'd never get Aunt Sophie up on to the roof, never. And what if she wouldn't attempt to leave the room? The question was left unanswered in her mind when sleep overtook her and her head fell to the side on the pillow.

Harry watched her for some time before beckoning Peg towards him, where once again he was seated on the floor his back against the wall, and when she was kneeling beside him he whispered to her, 'She's well away, we'll let her sleep, eh?'

'Aye, doctor. She's worn out; with one thing an' another she's worn out. Will the water come in, doctor?'

'I don't think so, Peg. It's got to stop some place, and I think it's almost reached its bent. Bring your blankets and sit down here beside me.'

When she was settled by his side he leant over her and whispered, 'Now you go to sleep, everything's going to be all right!'

'I don't feel tired, doctor.'

'Well, you will shortly when I say, "Come on, now's your turn to keep your eyes open and do your watch", so go on with you, lie down.'

She peered up at him. 'Everythin'll be all right?'

'Everything will be all right. Don't you worry.'

Slowly she eased herself onto her side and rested her head on her crooked arm, but it must have been a full hour later when her lids drooped and she gave in to the drowsiness, and she, too, fell asleep.

He waited another fifteen minutes before he moved; then quickly he took off his boots and laid them aside and, rising slowly, he picked up a candle and held it over the glass shade of the lamp until it ignited.

When he reached the door it creaked as he turned the handle, and he looked back towards the sleeping figures, but none of them had moved. A moment later he was looking down the well of the attic stairs where the candle's pale gleam showed the water lying seemingly still, halfway up them.

He turned and now moved cautiously towards the door opposite the schoolroom, and when he opened it and held the candle aloft he saw it was a storeroom. There were pieces of old furniture and trunks scattered around, and here were the same type of windows. And these were repeated in the other rooms he entered.

What a situation. He was even beginning to feel panicky himself. It would have been different had he felt fit; in that condition he could see himself hoisting them all on to the roof one after the other. But what did one do in a situation like this? Pray?

What for? Noah's Ark? A boat?

He must use his wits, but how? There was nothing to grapple with. If that water touched this floor they would have to get out, or when the river finally went down the rescuers would find four corpses, for once the water passed the top of those low windows they'd be trapped completely.

At this side of the house the wind sounded more menacing. There were constant bumps and thuds against the structure, and he guessed that this was the debris caught up for the moment against the walls. The wind had an eerie sound similar to that which you got on a high mountain, wild, unfettered, menacing in its freedom. He imagined it levelling everything it touched before whirling into endless space.

He shook his head against his fancies, and went softly back to the schoolroom.

They were all lying as he had left them and once more he settled on the floor with his back against the wall. . . .

He hadn't intended to fall asleep; in fact he couldn't imagine himself falling asleep for his mind was too active with worry, but he knew he had been asleep when he started bolt upright from the wall and gazed about him for a moment trying to recollect where he was.

Something seemed to have hit him in the back. He turned round and peered at the wall before he decided that he must have been dreaming.

It was as he settled back that it came again, a dull thud like a blow aimed at his buttocks.

He was on his feet now and peering out of the window, and once again for a moment he imagined he was dreaming. The moon was shining, the sky was adrift with scudding clouds, and everywhere his eyes flicked in amazement was water, seemingly at his feet, and not just water for on its surface, forming grotesque shapes and angles was debris, all kinds of debris, and all flowing fast as if in a mad race against the clouds.

A few yards away he made out a roof. He didn't know if the house was beneath it, it passed so quickly. Then came a horse caught up in a wall of timber; likely its stable. But just below the window, a little more than a foot below it, was what looked like part of a floor, an old floor; the joists sticking out were big and rough-hewn, and one of them, somewhat longer than the rest, had got jammed in the wooden scrollwork that formed the eaves above the windows on the first floor.

'Oh dear Lord!'

He jerked his head to the side to see Martha standing, her hand tightly pressed across her mouth. Instinctively his arms went out and, pulling her to him, he held her close for a moment, and she in turn clung to him. Then gently pressing her from him, he whispered, 'There's only one thing for it, we've got to get out of here.'

'Oh no! no!' She shook her head in a despairing fashion.

'Yes! But yes. Listen. Now listen, Martha.' He was gripping her hands tightly. 'Once the water comes in and reaches halfway up the window there'll be no chance at all of getting out; the upper frame is fixed, the panes are too small for even a dog to get through, let alone us. Look.' He pointed. 'That down there seems an answer to an unspoken prayer; it's a wooden floor of sorts, it'll float. We must all get on it, and push it off from the house and cling to it for dear life.'

'You . . . you said we'd get out on to the . . . the roof.'

'Yes, yes, I know. But we'd never manage it in this wind. I can see now it was out of the question. I doubt if I could have got up there myself the way I'm feeling, never mind Miss Sophie. Now look.' He paused; then his voice lower still, he said, 'Be brave, Martha dear, because we must survive.

Do you hear? We must survive. Now do as I tell you. Wake them up. I'm going to force open the window now, and I'll hang on to the platform or whatever it is until you're all through. . . .'

'No! no! I'll . . .'

'*Martha!*' It was the doctor speaking now, the overbearing individual. 'Do what you're told! And do it now because by the look of things in a very short while it'll be too late.'

'Peg! Peg! get up. Aunt Sophie! Aunt Sophie!' She sounded hysterical, even to herself. 'Come on! Come on, Aunt Sophie! Sit up.'

'What is it, dear? It isn't morning.'

'Aunt Sophie, please.'

'All right, dear, but . . . but I'm very sleepy. Where are we going?'

She had Sophie by the shoulders now, shaking her into full awareness as she cried, 'We are leaving here. The water's still rising, it'll soon be in the room and we must get out. Do you understand?'

'Yes, yes, I understand, my dear. And don't shout at me.'

Martha straightened her back and tried to steady her trembling hands. It was ridiculous, but of the four of them her Aunt Sophie was the most calm, but that, she thought, was because she didn't realize the danger.

A minute later when Sophie stood by the open window and the wind tore at her hair and lifted it from her brow upwards, she laughed, and looking down on Harry, where he was now leaning well out and hanging on the structure below, she cried excitedly, 'I always knew I'd go down the river in a boat one day, I said so to Martha Mary not so very long ago, didn't . . . ?'

The thrust of Harry's right arm as he twisted round and made a grab at Peg pushed Sophie aside while at the same time Peg retreated from him, crying, 'Eeh! no, doctor. Eeh! no, I'm frightened. I am, I am.'

'Martha!' He looked up desperately at her. 'You go first. If the beam slips out I doubt if I'll be able to hold it.'

Martha stared at him for a second. Her mouth opened, then shut; she gulped twice in her throat, then, kneeling down, she put the upper part of her trembling body through the window and grabbed at the black beam below her. But having done that she made no further move towards the tossing platform below. The wind screaming in her ears, the moon showing up the great mass of whirling debris, was so awesome that she became frozen with her fear. Even her scream was lost to herself when she felt her legs hoisted upwards and she tumbled in a heap down on to the heaving wooden floor.

Her hands now madly gripping the jagged edge of a floor board, her eyes gazed down in terror at the bursting bubbles and dirty scum just below her face; then she cried out again, this time as Peg's whole body landed on her back.

She was lying flat on the platform now, the wind knocked clean out of her, and there she would have stayed petrified, and motionless in her terror, had not Peg's arms, which were around her neck now, tightened with such force that she was on the point of choking.

With an effort she turned on to her side, and now she was screaming at Peg, 'Lie down! Hang on to this.' She thrust the thin arms into the water and around a beam.

What happened next indeed seemed like a dream for in the present situation it was as out of place as the events in any dream, because now she was kneeling on the platform, one hand gripping a thick stem of ivy attached to the wall, while with the other she was steadying Sophie as she let herself down from the window.

It was the older woman's calmness that created the sense of unreality, for once her feet touched the heaving floor, Sophie let herself down on to it as gracefully as if lowering herself into a drawing-room chair. And she did not attempt to lie on her face and clutch the timbers for support, until Martha, thrusting her hands downwards, cried, 'Keep a hold, Aunt Sophie! Keep a hold!'

Harry was now climbing out of the window and Martha saw that he more than any of them needed support, and she held on to him until they were both kneeling facing the wall and clutching at the ivy. Gesticulating to her, he now indicated she should lie down, and when she didn't his bawl, whipped away on the wind, came to her like a thin scream. 'Get down! woman. Get down!' With one hand he pushed her roughly and blindly backwards, and she landed sprawling over Sophie's feet and only a foot or two from the far edge of the platform.

He let go of the ivy and crawled towards her, and, his arm about her, he tugged her towards the middle of the floor, the while mouthing something at her that she couldn't hear.

The next thing he did was to try to push Sophie flat on to the floor, but she resented this, and for the first time her manner changed, and she struck out at him. Turning now on to her hands and knees, she attempted to get to her feet, and had almost succeeded when both he and Martha, grabbing at the skirt of her coat, tugged her sharply downwards, and so sharply did she fall that the whole platform was submerged for a moment, and within seconds they were mostly wet through. At the same time the jerk had released the trapped beam from the eaves and the next second they were swept away to join the great stream of madly whirling debris.

Harry, clinging for dear life at the extreme edge of the platform, raised his head and glanced towards the huddle of bodies in the middle of the floor. Then he thought it had all been too much for him on top of the blows he had sustained, for now he was having hallucinations, because the bodies seemed to be piled high on top of one another. When the wind swung them round once again he realized that it had been filling Sophie's voluptuous coat. Now, having subsided somewhat, it looked like a curled sail, a silvery grey sail, an unearthly sail.

Hand over hand now he painfully pulled himself towards them. Peg was nearest to him. He put his arms about her. Her wet body was as stiff as the plank she was clutching. She made no movement, nor sign, there could have been no life left in her. He now put his arm across her and gripped Martha's shoulder, and when her head turned stiffly towards him, he shouted, 'It's all right. It's going to be all right. Just hang on,' and he was surprised that he could hear his own voice. Still shouting, he ended, 'The wind's going down. It'll be all right.'

When she made a small motion with her head he smiled at her and again called, 'We'll land up on the river bank somewhere.'

'I . . . I want to sit up, Martha.'

Now he bawled, 'Stay where you are! Miss Sophie. Do you hear me? Stay where you are! If you don't, I'll have to tie you down.'

What he would have tied her down with he didn't know, but the threat seemed to have its effect for she lay still. Yet her head was back on her shoulders and she gazed about her as the raft swirled and dipped first one way then another among the debris. . . .

. . . How far they travelled before the platform rocked itself to a stop, none of them could even guess, but to Martha the time had seemed like a long life spent in terror. The moon had disappeared, buried behind a maze of white cloud that turned grey, then black.

'We've stopped.' She whispered the words first to herself then louder. 'We've . . . we've stopped!'

'Yes.' Harry was a moment or so in answering. 'But stay still until we find out where we are. There's bound to be a lot of stuff piled up, so don't move until the moon comes out again.' Yet before he had finished speaking he himself was moving. Cautiously, he now reached out towards the end of the platform and immediately his groping fingers became buried in the sodden wool of a sheep. Then, when his hand, passing beyond the sheep's body, came in contact with something soft yet stiff he gave a slight start. Then after his fingers had examined it blindly, he drew himself back from the edge and towards the middle of the platform again.

'Are you there?'

He answered her trembling voice, saying, 'Yes, I'm here. It's all right.'

'Where do you think we are?'

'I haven't any idea except that we are jammed in a pile of debris. . . .

Ah!' He glanced upwards, 'Here's the moon coming out again, we'll soon see now.'

It was but a weak glow at first; then the clouds passing, the moon revealed their position to them. A dark shape away to the right of them looked like the top of a hill, but between it and them and for a great space all around there was piled debris of every shape and size.

Martha drew herself slowly up into a kneeling position and gazed in amazement over the upper part of a chair that had been blocking her view, and she couldn't believe what her eyes were seeing. Everywhere she looked were dead animals: horses, cows, chickens, and in some places they seemed to be merely resting for amid boxes and tree trunks and odd pieces of furniture they were piled upwards on top of one another. The wind had gone down but the noise about them was more eerie than any wild wind, for it was made up of creaks and groans and deep sucking sounds.

She imagined that she heard a duck quack and at the same moment she had almost to pounce on Sophie to stop her crawling towards the edge of the floor.

'Don't, Martha Mary. Don't, Martha Mary. Leave go of me, do. I just wanted to get the duck; it's under the chair.'

She was right. There was a duck floating under the chair, and it was alive.

It was Harry who stretched forward and lifted the animal on to the questionable safety of the floor. Then on a shaky laugh, he looked back at Martha, saying, 'Would you believe it! It's incredible.' He glanced now from the squatting animal to Sophie's bright countenance, and putting his hand out, he gently touched her wet hair, saying, 'And you're incredible too, Miss Sophie.'

'Well, I knew it was a duck, doctor. Anybody should be able to recognize a duck.'

'Yes, yes, of course. Anyone should be able to recognize a duck. But it took you to recognize this one. . . . Look, Peg, we've got another companion, a duck.'

He had forcibly to loosen Peg's fingers from off the floor boards, and, turning her over, he held her shivering body close to his for a moment as he said, 'It'll be all right. Once it is light they'll have the boats out searching and we'll be picked up.'

When a few minutes later he felt the floor tilt sharply, he said hastily, 'I think it'll be better if we all lie flat again and take a firm grip on the boards.'

'But the duck!'

'It's all right, Aunt Sophie, the duck will be all right. Look, it's wanting to come near you. Lie flat, that's it, like that. Now put your arms out. There, you see, it's lying in between them.'

'Martha!' He pointed downward, and Martha laid her shivering body alongside that of Sophie's. She had never felt so cold in her life before. Try as she might she couldn't stop her teeth from chattering, and it was as if Harry had heard their rattling for he said now, 'If we lie close together we'll keep warmer. Move close to Miss Sophie, Peg. That's it. That's it.'

When the moon disappeared again he began to talk. He talked about everything: about his boyhood, about his youth, about his hospital training, even about Doctor Pippin. The only thing he didn't talk about was his marriage. At what stage in his talking his arms went around Martha, he didn't know, but they were lying clasped tightly together when the dawn broke, and so stiff were they that their untwining took some embarrassing time.

It was as the light got stronger that the floor began to tilt at a sharper angle. It was as if the pressure of the daylight was forcing more debris beneath it.

'It's . . . it's tilting. It's tilting more and . . .'

He took hold of her arm as he muttered, 'It's all right. It's all right. . . .'

The last word had hardly left his lips when there was a roar as if dam gates had burst open. The next minute the whole floor was upended and they were all being tossed and swirled in a maelstrom of debris.

As Martha screamed she had a fleeting glimpse of Peg, her mouth wide open as if she were calling someone. She saw her enfolded in Aunt Sophie's arms like a child; then her own head was forced below the mad swirling waters and she was lost in what she knew to be death for a moment before she was wrenched from it by the most excruciating pain. It was as if her hair was being torn from her scalp.

Her head above water now, she was clinging to something, an animal, hanging on to its legs while it in turn was borne down the river on something else.

She was still clinging to the animal when its progress was checked. She wasn't aware of the branch overhead, or the hand that was clutching it, nor the painful slow struggle that Harry had in easing the dead sheep and the hen cree it was lying on around the branch and towards where the land sloped upwards.

He himself didn't know from where he drew the strength to unclasp her hands from the sheep's wool and drag himself and her up the slope, and not until they were well above the water-line did he let her go. And then, his hands dropping from her shoulders, he collapsed by her side. . . .

When he awoke it was to the sound of voices calling over a distance and a light so strong he couldn't look into it. He didn't seem to have any feeling in his body, only a surprised feeling in his mind that he was alive —Or was he? He opened his eyes again and realized he was looking up into bright sunlight. So that was all right. But he couldn't seem to move. What had happened? Where was he?

The voices came to him again, but nearer now, and he cast his glance downwards and now saw two men in a boat rowing towards the bank below him, and on the sight of them, memory flooded back, and as he gasped out, 'Martha! Martha!' he heaved himself on to his side and saw her lying like one dead.

He was on his knees bending over her when the men reached him, and one exclaimed, 'Why, doctor! Aye, I'm glad to see you. They'd given you up, along with t'others. But who have we here?'

Now the men were on their knees, and the second man said, 'Poor beggar! Who is she? Well, whoever she is she's done for by the look of her.'

'No! No!' Harry sat back on his heels. 'She's . . . she's still breathing.' He looked about him now as he asked, 'How far are we from the road?'

'Oh, some way, doctor. There's a vehicle, but the boat's the best bet. Just leave it to us, we'll get her down, 'cos you look as if you could do with a bit of help yourself.'

As the men settled Martha in the bottom of the boat and then helped Harry in, he asked, 'Have you seen any sign of an oldish woman, and a small girl?'

The taller of the two men who was now pushing off from the bank with an oar, nodded quickly saying, 'Aye, they picked two up like you say from near the bridge down below earlier on this mornin'. They were clinging together, like a mother and child sort of.'

'Are they all right?'

'Aw, I wouldn't know that, doctor; there was a number of bodies all mixed up with cattle and such, but they looked dead to me. Still, you never can tell. The poor body there looks a gonner, but you say she's still breathing. It's a case of where there's life there's hope. But I should say there's little hope for many who came down the river last night. I've seen a few floods in me time but never one like this—Guess it'll alter a lot of lives, this flood.'

Yes, he too guessed it would alter a lot of lives, and none more than his own if she didn't survive this ordeal.

He put his hand down and placed it on her sodden breast and prayed as he had never ever done before.

3

She didn't know how long she had lain here, whether it was hours, days or weeks, and at times she didn't know whether she was alive or dead. She had been sure she had died and was resting in one of the many mansions of heaven when she had opened her eyes on to a window, through which she saw the sun shining on to the limb of a tree, and when nearer still her eyes had come to rest on a bowl of white and yellow roses, from which she imagined there came a perfume. But when a human voice said, 'There now. There now. Off you go to sleep,' and she had looked up into the face of Doctor Pippin, she knew she wasn't dead, but just dreaming.

Following this, the dream took on a strange pattern. It always took her to the same room. Sometimes it was filled with light, sometimes it was lit by a lamp, but each time the dream occurred she was allowed to see a little more of the room, pieces of furniture, all shining. In one dream she actually saw someone polishing a chest of drawers. She had a round, merry face and a mass of auburn hair on which was perched a starched cap.

In another such dream she saw the doctor . . . Harry sitting by her side, and she imagined he put his lips to hers. That had been a very sweet dream. Another time Aunt Sophie and Peg were sitting by the side of the bed. She had cried during that dream. Oh, she had cried long and bitter. Then someone had given her a drink and the dream had faded, as all her dreams did.

There was one dream that disturbed her greatly. It was when the sun shone through the window and on to Roland's stiff, white, angry face, in sharp contrast to the expression on Mildred's who was standing by his side, because her expression was bright with a hauteur that suited her yet made her seem like a stranger.

Roland was not looking at her, he was talking to someone behind her. He was saying, 'It's in a dreadful state; everything inside is ruined, but it hasn't daunted my fiancée. As she said, perhaps after all it was better to make a clean sweep.'

'Or a thorough wash-out.'

'I can't see anything amusing about the situation, doctor.'

'No, no, perhaps you can't, young man. Perhaps you can't.'

She recognized Doctor Pippin's voice and the laughter in it and she thought, That was very good, a wash-out. And now he was talking to

Mildred. 'I've heard that you are going up to the Hall as Lady Brockdean's companion. Is that right, Mildred?'

'Yes, quite right, doctor. Lady Brockdean came to the shop and made the suggestion herself. As Master William is to be married shortly and will then leave for France and Miss Rosalind is in Switzerland taking the cure, she said she would be rather lonely, and so she approached me.'

'And you like the prospect?'

'Oh yes, I feel I'm amply suited to such a situation and I mean to give her ladyship every satisfaction.'

'Yes, yes, I'm sure you will. The bookshop will miss you. I heard that you were very good as a saleswoman.'

'Whatever I take on I aim to do thoroughly, doctor, but I never liked my position in the shop; in fact, I disapproved of it from the beginning. I made this quite plain to Martha Mary.'

'Yes, yes, I'm sure you did. Lots of things were made plain to Martha Mary, too many things in fact; that's why she's in the state she's in now.'

'You are blaming us?' Roland's voice was sharp, and the doctor's was equally sharp as he replied, 'Yes; if you want plain speaking, yes, I'm blaming you, I'm blaming all of you. She's been nothing but an unpaid servant for years.'

'You have no right. . . .'

'Don't raise your voice in this room, sir, and for that matter don't raise your voice in my house either. Now will you both please go along, for Martha isn't really aware of your presence.'

That was a strange dream, very strange. Mildred. Fancy dreaming that Mildred was going to get her heart's desire and live in the Hall in close proximity to Lady Brockdean. It was a fantastic dream.

Some time later there followed a sweet dream. She blinked in the strong light and looked up at Nancy with young Robbie Robson by her side. Nancy was full of concern for her but she was a different Nancy; perhaps it was the dress she was wearing; she had never seen her look so pretty, it was blue with three velvet bows at the neck. But Nancy didn't speak, she just cried.

And now here was the recurring dream of looking through the window at the tree, then letting her eyes rest on the bowl of roses. But today they had changed colour for they were pink and red, and Doctor Pippin had come into this dream again. She couldn't see him but she could hear his voice like a deep whisper saying, 'It's time now; you must let her come to gradually, and as I said last night, she'll need care for a long time.'

'I know that; I'm prepared for it.'

'And have you considered my proposition?'

'Yes, I have.'

'Well, come on, what is it? You're not usually so reticent.'

Martha found that she, too, was waiting for Harry's answer and she hoped it came before the dream faded, as it was apt to do.

'Well, it's as I have already said. If I were to accept it your home would be a very crowded house. You've been used to your own way of life for so long; comings and goings would likely irritate you . . . and you'd have to take into account that when I, too, am irritated, I'll be an unpleasant customer to live with.'

'Yes, I know all that, and your last remark I certainly have taken into account, but after weighing it all up I decided I'd choose the irritation rather than live the rest of my years, few or many, with only the port bottle for company, or comfort. And from that you'll gather that when I put the proposition to you it wasn't really out of kindness but selfishness on my part. . . .'

'But if I took the property up the street we'd only be six doors away. Have you thought of that?'

'Yes, but six doors are six doors and I want people round me.' The last words were muttered, then they rose to a smothered laugh as he ended, 'Even Aunt Sophie. And you know something? It's my belief she's not half as muddled in the head as she makes out at times. Anyway, she had the sense to survive and is in fitter shape than any of you and it's thanks to her the little maid was saved too, for without her she wouldn't have stood a chance.'

'Don't forget the duck.'

The softly joined laughter floated round Martha as the dream faded; then like an echo she heard Harry's voice, saying, 'Well, thank you. Thank you doctor, and for my part I'll see you never regret it.'

Regret it . . . regret it . . . regret it . . . regret it.

'Wake up. Wake up. That's a girl. Come on.'

'The water . . . Harry . . . the water.'

'It's all gone. It's all over.'

'Where am I?'

'In my home, Doctor Pippin's house.' He paused a long moment before he said, 'Our house.'

She stared back at him, then asked quietly, 'Am I ill?'

'You have been.'

'How long?'

'Oh, a fortnight or more.'

'Aunt Sophie and Peg . . . I . . . I dreamed. . . .'

He was bending down, his face close to hers now as he said softly, 'You won't believe this but Aunt Sophie's alive and well.' He raised his eyes towards the ceiling. 'She's upstairs in her room at this moment with Peg waiting on her.'

'They're alive?'

'That's what I said, they're both alive.'

'And . . . and we're in Doctor Pippin's home?'

He paused for a long moment before he said softly, 'Our home from now on. Your home when you're well enough to be mistress of it. . . . Now! Now! you mustn't. Don't cry, my dear. Don't cry. You must save all your energy and strength to get well because you know a doctor can't have a wife who's abed all day. . . . Aw, please, please, don't cry like that. I never want to see you cry again. If it lays with me you've done all the crying you'll ever do, because from now on I'm steering your life, do you hear? Look at me, Martha.' He put his hand gently under her chin. 'Did you hear what I said? I'm steering your life, and that's whether you like it or not.'

'But . . . but we can't all live here.'

'We can. The doctor wants it that way, and particularly he wants you. And something more I'll tell you now, I've got the strong feeling he's planned that you should come here and be mistress of this house from the moment I came back after my first visit to The Habitation. He's a wily old beggar is our Doctor Pippin. He always says he never does anything without putting himself first. It's meant to be a joke, but since you're here, and I've tied myself for life to him as a partner, I've got me doubts about the joke.'

'Oh, doctor. . . .'

'*Harry.*'

'Harry, what . . . what am I expected to say?'

'Well, you could say you liked me a little bit. . . . Well, don't you just . . . just a little?'

She was looking straight up into his eyes as she murmured, 'More than a little. . . .' There came a quirk to her lips as she ended, 'Well, at least at times.'

He put his head back now and laughed, saying, 'That's my Miss Martha Mary Crawford. Oh, what a mouthful of a name that is. And I'm afraid it won't sound any better when it's Mrs Martha Mary Fuller.'

'It's an awful name . . . Martha Mary.'

'No, it isn't, my dear.' His voice was gentle, his eyes held a soft depth. 'I was only teasing. It's a very special name, to be kept for special occasions. Ordinary times I'll merely address you as Martha, but on special occasions when I'm flaming mad at you, then I'll bawl, Martha Mary! or as, like now, when I want to say to you, I love you, I'll say Martha Mary, do you hear me, I love you, Martha Mary.' His face moved down to hers.

'Oh, Harry, Harry.'

'Martha Mary. Martha Mary.'